LADY ON THE COIN

The historical novels of
MARGARET CAMPBELL BARNES

THE PASSIONATE BROOD
(first published as *Like Us, They Lived*)
MY LADY OF CLEVES
WITHIN THE HOLLOW CROWN
BRIEF GAUDY HOUR
WITH ALL MY HEART
MARY OF CARISBROOKE
THE TUDOR ROSE
ISABEL THE FAIR
KING'S FOOL
THE KING'S BED

Lady on the Coin

MARGARET CAMPBELL BARNES
and
HEBE ELSNA

MACDONALD AND JANE'S · LONDON

First published 1963
Second impression 1972
Third impression 1974

ISBN 0 356 01829 6

Published by
Macdonald & Jane's (Macdonald & Co. (Publishers) Ltd),
St Giles House, 49 Poland Street,
London, W.1.

Printed in Great Britain by
REDWOOD BURN LIMITED
Trowbridge & Esher

"I am related to the King of England," boasted the fair girl Frances, who was practising her dance steps before a tall, tarnished mirror.

"The one who had his head chopped off?" enquired her small sister Sophie, glancing up from her dolls.

"Well, yes, Charles the First too, of course. But I meant his son."

"Then much good may it do you!" scoffed Lord Culpeper's niece, pushing a needle rather viciously into her embroidery frame. "The last time I saw Charles Stuart he hadn't the money to buy new shoes either for himself or for his horse."

As Dorothy Culpeper was older than the other girls in the room and had been in Paris when the unfortunate young Prince first came from Jersey to join his mother, twelve-year-old Frances Stuart was not in a position to deny it.

"My mother says that royal blood is more important than money," she retorted, holding out the sides of a shabby gown and sweeping a truly royal curtsey to her own reflection. Being even poorer than any of her exiled companions at the Château de Colombes, and pretty enough to evoke their snubs, Frances occasionally felt the need to find *something* to boast about.

"Not these days," said Dorothy, who was growing tired of a loyalist's life of exile. "We all know that even Queen Henrietta-Maria was hard put to it to find nourishing food for her own daughter last time Princess Henrietta-Anne was ill."

In spite of her frivolity, real sickness or sorrow could always catch at Frances Stuart's heart. She instantly stopped her pretty posturing and darted across the room to perch on a stool at the elder girl's side.

"It must be terrible for her after being Queen of England and having everyone jump to obey her lightest wish. Far worse for her than for any of us. I have often wondered," she added, picking up various coloured silks to try their effect against her faded gown, "why young King Louis doesn't let her live at Court. After all, she is his aunt. Does he dislike her?"

"Not that I know of. But I have heard milord Clarendon say that it would be very embarrassing for the French royal family to do so. You see, Cardinal Mazarin—who really rules France—still feels it necessary to keep on good terms with our country, even while this Cromwell monster is in power." Dorothy firmly took back her disordered silks, but found it impossible to be angry for long with the Stuart girl. "But I do assure you, my dear, that any privations the Dowager Queen Henrietta-Maria suffers now are as nothing to what she has been through in the past. My mother and her other ladies were hunted across England, helping her to escape, and she carrying an unborn babe, which was delivered on the journey at Exeter. Imagine, the rest of her family imprisoned by the Roundheads or in exile, and then hearing that her beloved husband had been beheaded. . . ."

"No wonder she is . . . difficult . . . sometimes, and seems to quarrel with people," put in plump fourteen-year-old Janton Lovelace, frowning down at a broken stringed lute which she was trying to mend.

"It must be bad enough having a baby even with one's own bed to have it on," sympathized Frances, who was still rather hazy as to how such things happened. "Perhaps that is why poor Princess Henrietta is so delicate. Being jolted about mile after mile on a horse litter, I mean, before she was actually born." After contemplating this interesting matter for a moment or two, she added inconsequently: "And so you have really seen him?"

"Seen whom?" asked Dorothy Culpeper, with pardonable irritation.

6

"Henrietta's eldest brother. Charles. The one she is always talking about, who should be King. The one I said I was related to."

Giving up the intricate pattern she had been working on, Dorothy laid aside her silks.

"How your mind does skitter from one subject to another, Frances! I cannot imagine what sort of future you can expect unless you try to concentrate more. Yes, I was there when he first arrived from Jersey."

"And what was he like?"

Frances settled herself comfortably on the stool, elbows on knees and chin cupped in palms. She had a devastating way of delaying more sober people who wanted to work.

Dorothy had not been very old herself, and cast her memory back with an effort.

"Tall and lean as an undernourished maypole. But I don't suppose you can even remember a merry English maypole."

"My family lived in Scotland, anyway."

"Where, I suppose, you are too strict to have maypoles. Though he was only sixteen, he tried to be *sympathique* with his mother, but he seemed to be most at home with his cousin Louis' horses and dogs. His French was terrible."

"What did he look like—apart from this maypole thing?"

"Dark and French-looking like his mother. The rest of the family are all Scots—fair like you, I believe."

"Was he handsome?" persisted Frances, thoroughly enjoying her gossip.

Dorothy had to laugh. "*Oh, mon dieu, non!*" she answered decisively.

Janton took the end of a lute string from between her excellent teeth, the better to join in the conversation.

"Yet some of the girls seemed to go crazy about him," she recalled. "I wasn't much older than little Sophie there, but I do remember how annoyed they were because his mother kept prodding him on to pay court to that fat Mademoiselle de Montpensier, his heiress cousin. So there must have been something about him . . ."

7

"What?" asked Frances.

"Well, charm. . . ."

"Like his sister Henrietta?"

"I suppose so."

Dorothy Culpeper rose with a sigh and crossed to a window. She stood for a moment or two looking out at the typically French landscape of grey-green vineyards and tall poplars bordering a bend of the Seine; and when she turned back it was to survey with a kind of compassionate anger the half-dozen English girls grouped listlessly about the room.

"They all have it, haven't they, these Stuarts?" she demanded. "Else why should our fathers have given their lives for them? And our brothers be fighting as mercenaries all over Europe sooner than live on French charity? Why are we all stuck here in dreary exile when we might have been enjoying life in our parents' pleasant English manors or Scottish castles? Now, during the best years of our lives, when we ought to be wearing pretty clothes—waking up to womanhood—marrying our fellow countrymen?"

They all looked up at her in rather shocked surprise, the older ones roused to a momentary longing for their own country by her impassioned words. But they had been refugees for so long, and some of them—like Frances—had been mere babes when they were hustled to safety in their nurses' arms across the Channel. Frances, whose father had died only recently in France and who had somehow been born incapable of listlessness even in polite captivity, might have answered, but at that moment the door opened quietly, and the girl who had most to lose by Oliver Cromwell's Commonwealth came in.

Fourteen-year-old Henrietta-Anne Stuart, whose royal father had seen her only once in infancy after her mother had escaped, and who had soon afterwards walked with dignity to the scaffold, could not have made a less regal appearance. She was painfully thin, dark and sallow-skinned. Because she had spent the morning painting she wore a black *tablier*, French fashion, over a simple woollen

8

dress; and because there was no *coiffeur* to curl her chestnut-brown hair into fashionable ringlets, it hung wispily straight to her shoulders.

Frances ran to her in her impulsive way. "Henrietta! *Ma chère!*"

"*Maman va descendre,*" warned the youngest Princess of Britain, who often saved them from her mother's displeasure. And then more generally to the rest of them: "Her Majesty would have you accompany her to Mass. Better, for all of you, to have your heads ready covered and missals in hand."

Like the rest of them, she spoke in a mixture of two languages, but to her French came by far the easier.

"More prayers!" pouted Frances irreverently.

"My mother will soon be taking us all to the Convent at Chaillot for another—how do you say?—retreat. And that means chapel thrice daily, with no good-looking acolytes for your distraction." And when Henrietta smiled teasingly at her young friend it transformed her plain delicacy to a promise of irresistible attractiveness.

Because it was difficult for Frances to sit still, she brought a pile of missals from their shelf and distributed them among her companions, who were hastily putting away their various occupations.

"Let's talk of something more gay while we still have time," she entreated, carelessly pinning a black lace veil over her golden head. "It is true, is it not, Henrietta, that I am related to you?"

"*Mais bien entendu*—of course," agreed the daughter of the late King of England, whose mother was a daughter of the renowned Henry of Navarre.

"But there are many Stuarts. Her family live quite ordinarily, like some of the rest of us. Frances' father was a doctor," objected Janton. She picked up Frances' worn but treasured missal and read aloud the inscription: "To the Hon. Walter Stuart, M.D., from his grateful patients."

"And a very clever one," corroborated Henrietta with quiet finality. "He was enthralled when my father's

9

physician, William Harvey, discovered about the circulation of the blood, and his family risked everything for ours at Naseby. Frances and I are cousins."

"Distant cousins," Frances had the grace to admit. "Through Lord Blantyre."

"Oh well, of course, with you Scots . . ." murmured Kentish-born Dorothy.

"Blood *is* thicker than money."

It was inexcusable in anyone with royal pretensions, of course, but the pink tip of pretty Frances Stuart's tongue shot out in the direction of milord's daughter, and small Sophie, seeing it, giggled delightedly.

"We are of the same clan," explained Princess Henrietta as if explaining something elementary to a foreigner. But she spoke gently, pouring oil on the troubled waters of their mewed-up discontent, as she so often did.

And then the door was thrown open with some poor attempt at ceremony and the sad, widowed Queen Dowager of England came in, followed by her friend, Madame de Motteville, and Lady Dalkeith, who had cared for the baby Princess in Exeter and so courageously smuggled her out of England, and Mistress Stuart, the mother of Frances and Sophie. Queen Henrietta had endured months of civil war and anxiety for a husband she adored. She had been stunned by the news of his execution, and not long afterwards learned that her daughter Elizabeth had died alone in Carisbrooke Castle. Tragic grief and subsequent ill-health had made her look far older than her age. She was kind to these young exiles who shared her fortunes, but all unaware that her deep mourning and religious devotion were an oppression to their pleasure-starved youth.

But today there was a firmer purpose to her tread, and a gleam of triumph in her dark eyes. The illuminated missal in her left hand seemed to give momentary place to the importance of a letter which she waved triumphantly with her right.

"I have news from England," she told the girls dramatically. "Oliver Cromwell is dead."

"At last!" The involuntary whisper went up from all of them, as they formed a respectful circle about her.

Henrietta-Anne ran to her. "Does that mean that Charles——?"

The Queen's arms went round her tenderly, missal, letter and all.

"I fear, *ma mie*, that Charles will still have to wait a little while longer. It is too soon to risk another landing. Only *le bon Dieu* and his own resourceful courage brought him back safely to us after the Battle of Worcester."

"The good news was brought to him while he was playing tennis, by a trumpeter from Dunkirk," Lady Dalkeith told them. "At Hoogstraeton, in Holland. The whole town seems to have gone delirious with relief."

"But will it make so much difference?" asked Madame de Motteville. "*Ce brut* Cromwell—has he not a son? Will he not become Protector in his place?"

"Richard Cromwell is a weak waster, by all accounts," explained Lady Dalkeith. "He would have little power over the army."

The Queen folded the momentous letter between thin fingers.

"No. Regicide though he was, Cromwell was a strong figure-head. There is no one to replace him," she agreed. "If only Charles will restrain his impatience and have the subtlety to let these Roundheads weaken their cause by a few months' scuffling for power among themselves!"

The chapel bell had ceased ringing. For the first time in memory they would be late, although of course Father Cyprien would dutifully await the Dowager Queen's party. She rallied them round her with an almost happy smile.

"Let us go and pray for Charles the Second," said Mistress Stuart, guessing how much as a man he needed their prayers.

"And for the restoration of his kingdom," added his royal mother firmly.

Before turning to follow, Princess Henrietta-Anne stretched back a hand to give Frances' fingers a joyful squeeze. And

Frances, keeping close behind the Dowager Queen's ladies, hurried along the cloister to chapel more eagerly than usual. Perhaps her worldly little mind needed something more concrete than virtue to pray for. Or her heart was stirred to pity by the thought of a tall, plain prince who had lost his father as she had, and who had, like herself, endured years of boring exile, waiting for some new shoes and a good meal and the chance to enjoy a merry life.

2

Queen Henrietta-Maria was right. Charles—and all his supporters—had still to wait the best part of two years. But they no longer waited without hope.

The exiles at Colombes, hanging on every scrap of news from London, heard how that sincere man Oliver Cromwell had been taken for burial in Westminster Abbey with the crown of England laid upon his richly-clad effigy. But they hugged each other in relief when the indefatigable diarist John Evelyn wrote: "It was the joyfullest funeral that ever I saw." Apparently the sombre procession had provided an opportunity for a people long oppressed by puritanical restrictions to give vent to an opposite extreme of feeling. Apprentices danced and shouted outside Whitehall, soldiers forgot all discipline and reeled drunkenly along the streets. These were crude reactions by the rowdiest elements, but in sober fact the temper of the whole nation was changing. It was not long before the town rabble tore down their Protector's new monument in the Abbey, and serious plots and risings were afoot all over the country. The penniless King of England and his brother James tramped the dunes in Holland waiting for a propitious time to attempt a landing, or for the moment of their unanimous recall.

It was wise old Lord John Culpeper who insisted that General Monk was the man to approach. George Monk had been a royalist before he joined the Parliamentarians, the army respected him and he was tolerant enough to realize that there might be worse things for his country than a good-natured, modern-minded monarch who must by now have learned a long, hard lesson about the result of insistence upon the divine right of kings.

Serious negotiations began between Monk, who was in Scotland, and the royalists across the water. Soon everyone was prophesying that August would be the month when all their fortunes would change. But summer dragged on into winter, local uprisings were quelled, and nothing definite was done. As usual, Edward Hyde, Earl of Clarendon, counselled caution. To make a landing now with a small army of supporters *might* be successful, he admitted, but to wait for official invitation, which was so nearly in sight, would be more dignified and decisive, and spare many lives.

At the Château de Colombes no one talked of anything but the hoped-for Restoration, and, to cheer a bleak November, word actually came from Charles that he had definite hopes of landing at Dover in the spring, and would be riding to Paris to bid goodbye to his mother and sister.

"Charles is coming!" cried young Henrietta, over-joyed. "He will be with us for Christmas."

Frances clapped her hands and broke into a twirling dance with flying skirts.

"It will be our first real Christmas! We must arrange games and masks like King Louis has in Paris. Your brother has suffered so much, we must give him a right merry time."

In her generous innocence she had no idea what the hardened young king's idea of a right merry time might be. Nor did it occur to her that a riverside village a few miles out from Paris would seem to him exceedingly dull. Far less did she stop to think that perhaps a visit to a sad, deeply religious mother who still tried to order him about might be no more than a kindly eldest son's conception of duty.

"But what in heaven's name shall we be able to give him and his hungry gentlemen to eat?" wondered Mistress Stuart, preparing to bustle away to the ill-staffed kitchens.

"Everything that we have. No matter about afterwards," recommended her elder daughter characteristically.

"We could go and fish in the Seine as the monks do," suggested good-natured Janton Lovelace.

"In mid-November?" jibed practical Dorothy Culpeper, shivering in the ill-heated room.

"Far better spend your time seeing if you can find something decent to wear," advised Mistress Stuart, regarding her small Sophie's much-mended garments with a new dismay and wondering if she could borrow suitable clothes for her baby son up in the nursery.

"Charles doesn't have any fine clothes for himself," his sister reminded them sadly.

"But His Majesty will be going from here to his state entry into London," said the Dowager Queen, appearing in the open doorway with quiet stateliness. "I pray you, do as Mistress Stuart says."

So the young girls in her household spent the next few days furbishing their scanty wardrobes. They pressed lace collars and used their small stock of ribbons for making fresh bows. All grievances born of boredom were forgotten as, with excited laughter, they tried on each other's garments, all anxious to look their best. And so it happened that Frances was wrapping the young Princess in her own fur-lined cloak when King Charles arrived.

There were no gentlemen in attendance, hungry or otherwise. Only his valet, Toby Rustat. And Charles had ridden in such a blinding hurry that he arrived hours before he was expected, with the consequence that the Dowager Queen had retired early, and he found himself shown by a flurried young man-servant into a room full of giggling girls.

"You must wear it in case you are asked to go out riding. It is beginning to snow, and you do feel the cold so," Frances was insisting, although the cloak had been her beloved father's last gift to her.

"*Mais pour moi ton manteau est beaucoup trop long*. It hangs on the ground like the train of a bride," Henrietta was protesting, wrapped to the eyes in the proffered garment.

And so it was that Charles did not immediately see her. Puzzled by the sudden cessation of chatter, Frances turned. She saw the tall King looking uncertainly from one of them to the other. And when she smiled at his obvious embarrassment, to her horror he suddenly leapt into decisive action, crossed the room in a few long paces and swept her up into his arms.

"Henrietta! *Ma chère petite soeur!*" he exclaimed in a deep, attractive voice, and kissed her soundly.

Frances struggled to free herself, to move aside.

"No, no, sir! Here is your sister," she tried to explain, dragging her concealing cloak from the amazed Princess.

The painful moment or two of silence which followed showed him that he had embraced the wrong girl. They all realized that he might easily not have recognised Henrietta, but only Frances guessed how much the perfectly understandable mistake would hurt the sensitive young sister who had been talking about him so adoringly for months. Instinctively, she stepped backwards, trying to hide herself among her companions.

If Charles made any momentarily disappointing comparison between the tall budding beauty whom he had thought to be his relative and the delicate-looking girl who really was, he concealed it very cleverly. He had the wit to rely on frankness and sincere affection.

"My dear, forgive me! It is so long since I saw you." He looked at Henrietta-Anne more closely, obviously liking what he saw. "But God send it may never be so long again!" And then he kissed her very tenderly and drew her down on a bench beside him. "So that you do not get a crick in your neck by having to look up so far," he explained.

"I know I am small for my age," she apologized, setting her disarranged hair to rights. "And although she is nearly two years younger, Frances here is more the height you had expected."

But Frances had tactfully faded from her side; and, in any case, the King seemed to have forgotten her existence, for Henrietta reached up impulsively and put her arms round his neck. She was part of the family life from which his affectionate nature had been so abruptly torn. And when her eyes shone with such loving happiness, Charles knew that he had found something infinitely precious. Hardened and cynical as the last half of his thirty years had made him, nothing would ever impair his liking for children and young people. And here was one who had suffered grievously through their common misfortunes.

"You came alone?" she asked, almost dazed by happiness.

"Except for good old Toby. It was quicker—and cheaper."

"Oh, Charles! Have you had enough to eat? You, too, are very thin." Exploring the tough leanness of his arms, she discovered that his coat was almost threadbare. "And you must let Madame de Bordes mend that tear in your sleeve. She is my *femme-de-chambre* and so clever with her needle that it will not show." Suddenly, in the midst of her concern, she burst out laughing. "How odd to be talking about meals and mending like this when you are King of England!"

"But still without a crown, my sweet. It will be good, I warrant you, to have the spending of some of our father's gold coins again. Best of all, perhaps, to be able to repay some of the loyal folk who have helped me. But do not worry your pretty head about me. A French tailor is taking me on trust and is going to make me some summer clothes in the hope that I may impress my Londoners with your Paris fashions. And I will try to coerce him into sending you some of his best silks for a few new gowns."

"But, *mon cher*, I do not really need clothes as you will. We live so quietly here."

"Then it is high time you enjoyed yourself as our sister Mary does in Holland. And now that our fortunes are mending," he added cynically, "Cousin Louis will be probably inviting you to Court."

"If you really think that, then I pray you, dear Charles, send some for my friends here, whom I will present to you." In her eager loyalty she was about to do so when she remembered a far more pressing duty. "But first you must go to our mother, the Queen," she reminded him regretfully. "If she has already heard of your arrival . . . "

He stood up immediately. "Yes, I must wait upon Mam," he agreed. And if their glances met in an amused, resigned smile, it helped to draw their hearts all the closer.

"I had so much wanted you to tell me about this man Monk," she said hurriedly. "I shall always pray for him."

Impulsively he bent to kiss her again before leaving.

"Had it been a century instead of six years since we met, how could I have mistaken you for any other girl?" he exclaimed.

He spoke softly, with intimate contrition, but Frances overheard him, and later in the evening, when all the girls of the Queen Dowager's household were presented to him, she realized that, for all his charming courtesy, she was just "any other girl" to him.

"Our cousin on the Blantyre side," he recalled, and picked up a very sleepy Sophie in his arms, and spoke to Mistress Stuart of her recent grief and with understanding appreciation of the long years or privation which all present had suffered for their loyalty.

With his coming a new kind of zest seemed to bring the quiet suburban château to life. He radiated the easy good humour which had once made a rough old Irish peer swear that he would sooner live with his exiled prince on six sous a day than be tasting all the pleasures of the world without him. Even the elder ladies of the household ceased worrying unduly because the fare was plain and the faggots few. Charles listened dutifully to all his mother's advice, even if he had no intention of taking it. He pleased her immeasurably by creating Master Jermyn, the over-trusted master of her household, Earl of St. Albans. And never once did he refer to his anger when she had tried almost forcibly to convert his youngest brother to her religion after the Parliamentarians had allowed "young Henry Stuart" to come to her from Carisbrooke. The moment of his rarely provoked authority was finished, and never again alluded to, even though at the time her meddling might have cost him all hope of regaining his crown. He had sent for Henry and kept him with him, and it had been the first taste of freedom the lad had ever enjoyed.

Of an evening Charles regaled his mother's household with such exciting and amusing stories of his almost incredible escape after the Battle of Worcester that they forgot the meagreness of the fire or that it was snowing outside. He encouraged Henrietta to play on her harpsichord while he learned from Janton the words of the latest Paris song, and in return taught the delighted girls some rather less respectable ones in English. Especially they loved an odd ditty with which the London 'prentices were forever plaguing every steeple-hatted Puritan. While the apparently innocuous words were all about blackbirds and maytrees, each verse ended with:

> "'Tis hoped before the end of June
> The burds will sing another tune!"

And these two lines, he explained, were always bellowed with added gusto.

"They know it is the Stuarts who will call the next tune!" cried Frances, clapping her hands and letting a holly wreath with which she was decorating the hall fall upon Madame de Motteville's unfortunate cat.

The girls were planning a masque which was supposed to be a secret. "Like the one we saw that one time Queen Dowager Anne invited us to the Louvre," insisted Dorothy Culpeper. Lady Dalkeith had been prevailed upon to write the words, and Janton was to arrange the music. "And Frances must invent the dances," they decided unanimously.

"We could never emulate those graceful French nymphs," sighed Frances.

"You know you have been trying to do so in front of the mirror ever since," laughed Henrietta.

"Well, we can do our best," agreed Frances, nothing loath. "After all, it must be years since poor Charles has had a chance to enjoy a real Christmas."

Living in the sheltered atmosphere of Queen Henrietta-Maria's household, she had little idea of the many disreputable pleasures at which Charles had managed to snatch. And here, at Colombes, he seemed content to forget both passing amours and political anxieties and to rest a while, assured of three meals a day and enjoying the engaging company of his young sister. "*Minette*" he called her—"My little puss"—and swore that as soon as he found himself back at Whitehall he would send for her and make her learn to speak less execrable English. "Shame on you! And you Exeter born!" he teased, when she talked about General Monk sending a sheep to take him home.

But the Christmas they planned so hilariously was not to be. After little more than a week's visit Charles received an urgent message advising him to return to Brussels, partly because he was still not too welcome on French soil, and partly so that he might be nearer at hand if events should move more quickly than was expected in England. The snow had ceased. A thaw had set in. Through squelching mud, with borrowed money and his mother's blessing, he set out on his travels again.

"For the last time, please God!" he prophesied cheerfully, letting Toby fasten a fashionable new cloak across his shoulders but insisting upon adjusting his own saddle girth. "Like I used to do when I was William Jackson, the groom, escaping from Worcester," he reminded Henrietta, hoping to change her tears to smiles.

For days after he had ridden away, rain lashed desolately on the grey waters of the Seine and against the windows of the château. Most of the Christmas festivities were abandoned, and those which were attempted fell remarkably flat. The much-discussed masque was never performed at all. Henrietta-Anne could talk of nothing and no one save her wonderful eldest brother, so that poor Frances, who had to listen to her, grew distinctly tired of him. And as Twelfth Night passed and wilted wreaths were pulled down from tapestried walls, the deferred retreat to the convent at Chaillot loomed ahead.

But Charles did not forget them. Henrietta received an affectionate little note from him while he was still on his unpleasant journey. And later, from Brussels, although he made no mention of his own important affairs, he wrote commiseratingly of the tedious time she must be passing at Chaillot in the rain, and promised to sit specially for a portrait which he had promised to her beloved *femme-de-chambre*, Madame des Bordes. And when he ordered clothes for himself from his French tailor, he did not forget to make purchases for her and for her friends.

A large parcel arrived by pack-horse, and Frances and Madame des Bordes helped her to unwrap its welcome contents.

"And, of course, we do need new clothes now, just as he foretold," said Frances, excitedly spreading out the lovely silks and damasks in the privacy of the Princess's bed-chamber. "Everyone comes to Queen Henrietta-Maria's salon these days. Gifts of game and venison pour in from King Louis and his mother, and we are all invited to the Louvre."

"Where you dance like a nymph indeed, so that Louis himself notices you."

"And where his young brother Philippe cannot take his eyes off *sa belle cousine* Henrietta-Anne. Heaven preserve the poor love-sick young fop if he ever sees you in that flowered damask!"

They sank down laughing on a chest at the foot of the Princess's bed, with all the unaccustomed finery spread about them.

"Truly, it is like a dream to have pretty clothes and enjoyable meals," sighed Frances, happily.

"Because we have never before had them, either of us."

"You know, when all King Louis' dressed-up pages were handing round those luscious sweetmeats at the banquet last week it was all I could do to take one languidly like the other guests and not to snatch."

"*Moi aussi*," confessed the youngest Princess of England.

And then their frivolous laughter died away and they sat looking honestly into each other's eyes. And when Madame des Bordes had gone away on some errand, Frances said quietly: "Tell me, 'Rietta: at the Louvre, surrounded by all that unaccustomed pomp and ceremony and luxury, how do you *really* feel?"

"Frightened," admitted Henrietta, after a moment's thought. "As if most of the people were too grand to be real."

"But you were born to it. By blood, if not by usage. And even in our poor circumstances your mother has never for a moment let any of us forget it."

"All the same, I have been overwhelmed—uncertain— sometimes. When my mother expected Louis to lead me out first in the coronto, and everyone could see he wanted to dance with Cardinal Mazarin's niece, I did not know what I should do. Maman was right about the etiquette, of course, but I found it very humiliating. And when one is not accustomed to being humiliated one goes all proud inside. So I pleaded a strained ankle and danced with no one at all."

Frances jumped up and kissed her.

"My poor 'Rietta! How dull it must have been for you when the rest of us danced till dawn!"

"*You* certainly didn't look overawed," laughed Henrietta, "with all the fashionable French gallants clamouring to partner you."

Scarcely more than a child as she was, Frances stood still, staring ecstatically before her.

"Once I stopped talking too much through sheer nervousness it was like coming into an exciting new world. Finding that men liked me, I mean."

"How could they help it, *petite imbécile*?"

"They like us both. But how could we know? Hidden away here we scarcely ever *see* a man who hasn't a tonsure!"

"You saw my brother a few weeks ago, and he kissed you."

"And then discovered his mistake and never looked at me again." Helping Henrietta to spread out a taffeta gown with tiny pink bows down the front of the skirt, she paused to look up searchingly at her cousin's contented face. "They do say that he should be a good judge of feminine beauty, because if he sees a girl who attracts him . . ."

"Who are 'they'?" enquired his sister, quickly defensive.

"Well, Dorothy and the older ones," mumbled Frances. "With a bachelor king, of course, these bits of gossip always get exaggerated."

She was only repeating sedately what Mistress Stuart had said when she herself had been probing for further information on the interesting subject. But she had learned what she wanted to know. She was sure that even his sheltered little sister was not wholly ignorant of his reputation. That it must have penetrated even to the strictly-run, priest-ridden château.

"As soon as he is really King again I expect he will get married," prophesied Henrietta, as if that would automatically be the end of all such unpleasant rumours.

Frances sank down on a window-seat with hands clasped on her lap.

"And then we shall all go back to Scotland!" she said, as if relating the happy ending of some exciting romance.

"Or England," said Henrietta, with rather less enthusiasm.

"Well, anyway—for all of us—home."

"But you cannot possibly remember your home."

"No. But my father used to tell me about it. And there is a painting of our manor hanging in my mother's room."

"I have seen it. A charming turreted house beside a loch."

Frances scarcely heard her. She was back in her own interpretation of the magic word "home".

"We used to stand before it, my hand in his. And he would tell me about it—what was behind each pictured window and each garden wall. I think he was not only trying to make it real for me, but wanting to keep every detail of it in his own memory."

"It must have been much harder for them—for those

older ones who loved and remembered," said Henrietta softly. "They had so much more to give up—for our cause."

"But at least they have *had* a real home. One could love a house almost as passionately as a person, don't you think? And with a family estate one inherits a love that has always been there. There were deep window-seats, and little stools for the children about the hearth. And a wide, shallow staircase—to welcome guests, he said. And copper warming-pans hanging in the firelit kitchen. And a long cool dairy where my mother superintended the maids making butter. And at one corner of the picture you could just see her herb garden."

It was Henrietta's turn to survey her friend quizzically.

"But I did not know you cared for domestic things like that."

"What chance have I had? When my mother and Sophie and little Walter and I go home . . ."

Henrietta, in real distress, went to her and laid a hand on her arm.

"But, Frances, surely you do not want to leave us? My mother is so fond of yours, especially now that they are both widows. And you and I . . . of course you must stay at Court with us."

Frances dragged herself back by an almost visible effort from the home in which her mind often secretly wandered.

"We are probably not important enough to be asked," she said lightly.

"Are we not cousins? Or is it that you really were so frightened by the formal grandeur of the Louvre?"

"Oh, I expect I should really prefer living at Court. Where there are plenty of men. And probably it would be different at Whitehall. Our monarchs have not the money to be so—ornate. Louis seems to have hundreds of slaves to build his palaces and do his bidding, but my father used to say that in England even the poorest ploughman was master of his own soul. Besides"—even in the midst of such un-wonted gravity Frances had to smile—"can you imagine a

24

Court where Charles the Second reigned being frighteningly formal and inhuman?"

"No, I cannot," said Henrietta.

But she answered almost absently, her cleverer mind being taken by surprise that scatter-brained Frances should have arrived, either by deduction or intuitively, at such a true conclusion.

3

When at last the good news of the Restoration reached Colombes the roses were in bloom and the girls playing bowls in the garden. Princess Henrietta heard the gate-keeper cheering a horseman clattering into the courtyard. She looked up and saw Master Prodgers, who had been her mother's faithful courier even in her father's time. Dropping the poised wood from palm to turf, she picked up her skirts and ran, hoping to intercept him before he entered the château.

"Master Prodgers! Wait and tell us!" she called. "Has the King landed?"

Half dead with fatigue, he slid down from his horse, grinning with joy.

"Landed at Dover and met with an unbelievable reception," he panted, as the rest of the running girls crowded round. "England has gone crazed with joy."

"Tell us! Tell us!" they cried, and the servants came crowding out into the courtyard, and the lame old groom hobbled round from the stables to take their welcome visitor's horse, promising the sweating beast the best feed in the stables.

As soon as Prodgers had regained some breath, he complied right willingly.

"They sent the fleet for him to Scheveling. He and his two brothers went aboard the *Naseby*, only she is now the *Royal Charles*. James, Duke of York, took over command as Admiral. The King and young Henry of Gloucester won the hearts of the crew by insisting upon sharing their victuals. And by the time they dropped anchor off Dover you could not see the beach for people, cheering and waving. All the bells were ringing and the castle guns thundering. When Charles the Second stepped ashore the first thing he did was to kneel and kiss a handful of his native earth, just like that actor fellow Shakespeare makes the second Richard do in his play, and half of us had tears running down our cheeks with the emotion of it all. Even stern little General Monk welcomed him on bended knee. 'God save the King!' the crowds shouted, and when your lively young brother Gloucester could make himself heard he yelled at the top of his voice: 'God save General Monk!' And that seemed to put the final seal on the glad reunion of a long-divided nation."

"Henry has never forgotten how they released him from Carisbrooke, and how some of them showed him a rough kind of pity after our sister died," said Henrietta.

"And did King Charles and all the rest of them go on to London?" asked Frances, agog with excitement.

"Yes. But after such a tumult the royal brothers were thankful to sleep the night at Canterbury, where I parted from them, being charged by His Majesty to sail with all speed and bring you the good news . . . and bring a letter which he wrote Your Highness, himself being half asleep."

The faithful Prodgers fumbled in the pocket of his mud-splashed coat and handed it to her with a respectful bow.

"You mean, in all that tumult and weariness he found time to write to *me*, who am so little worthy of it!" she exclaimed. Hungrily, her sparkling eyes ran over the brief lines. "He says, 'My head is so prodigiously dazed by the acclamation of the people that I know not whether I am writing sense or not'," she read aloud, between laughing and crying.

But Master Prodgers had another letter in his hand, and a firm recollection of his duty.

"It is good to be bringing Her Majesty good news at last, after being the reluctant harbinger of so much that was bad in the past," he said, as the pompous, newly-made Earl of St. Albans appeared to lead him into the château.

"If only we could have gone to Dover with them! If only

we could have seen it all!" exclaimed Frances, executing a *pas seul* around the fountain in the forecourt.

Forgetting her domesticated dreams of home, she pictured the scenes of wild excitement all day, and dreamed that she was taking part in the pageantry and processions all night. Until some more news came, this time from London.

"King Charles rode into London on the twenty-ninth of May," the next messenger told them.

"His thirtieth birthday," said his mother, torn between joy at his restoration and rage that he had had to wait so long.

It was the same story. Across Blackheath thousands followed him. Bells rang out from all the City churches. Salutes were fired from the Tower and from all the shipping in the Thames. Every street and window had been full of cheering people. The conduits ran wine. Lord Mayor and Aldermen and the City Guilds turned out to meet him. Over London Bridge and home to Whitehall, Charles rode bareheaded, returning the greetings of those who now so suddenly found his return propitious and those who had so long and silently prayed for it—wondering ironically why he had not come home before, since everyone seemed to be so anxious for his return.

"Whitehall is to be redecorated," added yet another messenger. "All the gentry are taking possession of their riverside houses again and giving parties. The pleasure-gardens and play-houses will be open again."

"Surely, Henrietta, the King will send for you," said Frances for the hundredth time.

"Of course he will," said Henrietta. "But consider how much business there must be for him to attend to first."

"But will not the Dowager Queen go and live there?"

"I expect so. She will certainly want to go there on a visit, if only to have some settlement made about all her dower lands which Cromwell distributed among the other regicides."

"And then she will take us all with her," concluded Frances, trying to possess her soul in unaccustomed patience.

Henrietta sat very still, hands in lap, regarding her. Much

as she loved her, their relationship was subtly changing. The two years' difference in their ages was, for the first time, accentuated. Henrietta's brief happiness with her brother, and his undoubted affection, had given her a sense of security and importance. And something else was coming into her life which would enhance it. For the first time there was a touch of regality in her reply.

"There may be another pressing affair for my mother to attend to before she leaves. Here, in Paris."

Frances was quick to note the change of manner.

"You mean the matter of a marriage for you?"

"They are all discussing it—Queen Anne, his mother, Cardinal Mazarin and the rest."

"They are not going to give you to the Duke of Orleans?" she asked, springing up almost angrily.

"And why not?"

"Oh, we all know that he wants you. But now that the Stuart fortunes are so different, King Louis will allow it?"

"*Mais naturellement.* The French King's brother and the British King's sister. A very equal arrangement."

Frances went and knelt beside the Princess.

"Oh, 'Rietta, I didn't mean that. There is no king or emperor in the world who is good enough for you. But you—and Philippe of Orleans!"

"At least he wanted me when we were still penniless exiles, and that is more than you can say of any other man," said Henrietta, with some of her elder brother's cynical common sense.

"But can you call this one a man?" Frances spoke hesitantly of something she scarcely understood, but was impelled to do so with sincerity. "You know how we have all laughed at the way he loves dressing up, posing for his portraits more like a woman. And his ridiculous, jealous tantrums. . . ."

"It is time you stopped talking like a romantic schoolgirl," said Henrietta, speaking sharply because she was hurt by the truth of it. "Kings' daughters can scarcely expect love in the political marriages which are arranged for them."

"But no one wants a husband whom other women *laugh* at," thought Frances, too kind to clothe her thought in words. "When I marry it will have to be a real man—a man of action who does things—whom I can respect," she said aloud. "And out of respect I should think some kind of love might grow."

Henrietta looked at her with tears in her eyes. Once again she was amazed that this gay companion of hers could at times so accurately sum up a situation.

"I hope you will get that kind of husband, but I don't suppose that you either will have much say in the matter. So you had better give up your delightful dreams of dairy-maid dalliance."

"I know you are right, 'Rietta. My mother, being a widow with three children on her hands, will probably jump at the first titled man who asks me, and I may come to tolerate him. But I want you to be happy, *ma chère*—you who have had such a wretched childhood. After all, some royal marriages *are* love matches. Your mother and the late King, for instance."

"Oh, of course, there are the lucky ones. But, as good Father Cyprien says, we must make the most of our blessings."

"And what particular blessing is Louis' young brother likely to bring you?" enquired Frances frivolously.

Henrietta rose and walked past her to the window. "He will always live in France," she said.

Frances swung round gracefully as a weather-vane to gaze after her.

"You mean, you don't *want* to come to England?" she said in slow amazement. "Not even to be near your precious brother?"

Her pertness was inexcusable, but Henrietta answered patiently, without turning: "Of course I want to go to England. But not with a kind of fierce longing as you do—as if it were the end of every dream. For, I ask you, how long should I be there? There would be only another marriage arranged. With Spain or Portugal or Italy perhaps. Oh, I have heard my mother and Monsieur Jermyn talking. We princesses are pushed across the board of life like chess pawns. And I would rather stay in the only country that I know. *Je suis française, moi*—just as you are a Scot."

"I see," said Frances, sinking down on the nearest window-seat, and feeling a fool for not having seen further into her friend's mind before.

Like Charles, she had always been able to alleviate her years of exile by light-hearted enjoyment of ordinary, every-day happenings. But now a new thought hovered like a grey cloud at the back of her inconsequent mind. Either she would have to part from beloved Henrietta or stay in France.

But during the exciting days that followed, Frances lived only in the new gaiety of the present. As soon as it was known that the Dowager Queen of France had formally asked for Henrietta's hand for her younger son, all the aristocrats of France flocked to Colombes. If the sweet-meats were not so luscious nor the servants so grand, the whole atmosphere of the place was more informal, and the two hostesses, mother and daughter, more charming. And Frances herself, learning the art of being a lady-in-waiting, added much to the gaiety of the parties, particularly where the men were concerned.

"How lovely she is!" remarked Queen Henrietta-Maria, watching her teach an enamoured young marquis the steps of a new pavanne.

"But not very clever, I fear, for the daughter of a learned doctor," said her mother. "I wish she would concentrate more on her books. Her spelling is atrocious. Why, even small Sophie spells simple words more accurately."

"Perhaps you are too ambitious, Mistress Stuart, to expect both brains *and* beauty," said the Dowager Queen, mellowed by the attention and laughter of which she had been so long deprived.

And certainly, as she grew into very young womanhood, Frances Stuart was so strikingly beautiful that young men could not take their eyes off her. She was tall and slender, and her love of dancing had lent her every movement an unconscious grace. Her skin was flawless and her eyes blue as the sea, and when candlelight or sunlight glowed on her fair hair there were rich auburn lights in it. And, besides men's senses being inflamed by the warm beauty of her body, their hearts were charmed by the radiance of her gaiety.

"She is going to be a terrible responsibility," sighed Mistress Sophia Stuart, wishing more than ever that her husband were alive.

But if the attention lavished on her in the security of the château became a source of anxiety, the days when they were invited to the Louvre rendered poor Mistress Stuart almost demented between pride and fear. While Philippe of Orleans escorted his bride-to-be everywhere, effectively preventing any other flirtations on her part, it was often King Louis himself who contrived to get Frances alone, and, beautiful as she was, Frances was no eligible princess. The frequency with which she was seen with His Majesty at masques and hunts and banquets was becoming the main gossip of the Court, and such flattery was beginning to turn the girl's head.

"I entreat you, talk to her, dear Father Cyprien," said Mistress Stuart. "She is too young to protect herself. His Majesty can have no honourable intentions, particularly with a wedding being planned between him and the Infanta of Spain. Yet I dare not offend His Majesty by contriving to keep her away."

"But our own Queen could. She could take your daughter with her when she goes to England," consoled wise old Father Cyprien. "And in the meantime do not worry overmuch, dear Mistress Stuart, for in spite of all her frivolity, there is much of her father in Frances, and I imagine the sweet child is very well able to take care of herself."

"I fear Her Majesty will not go yet. They say the small-pox is rife in London. Master Prodgers says that Prince Henry had caught the terrible thing, but is now recovered."

And then came news which made the household at Colombes forget all about the newly-tasted splendours of the French Court. After all the May-time celebrations and the wild happiness across the Channel, almost before the leaves were turning russet on the English beech trees, that promising young prince, Henry of Gloucester, died.

"And I saw so little of him when he was here," mourned Henrietta regretfully. "We were so poor that he went out into Paris every day to school like any other boy, or was with his tutor."

But in the last few months this youngest brother had become even more to Charles than their murdered father.

"He shut himself all day and night in his private room and would speak to no one. Only his favourite spaniel was with him," Father Cyprien told them, having heard.

Henrietta scarcely knew how to write to him.

"This cruel misfortune has caused you so much sorrow that one can but share it with you. I think it best to be silent, but what I desire most on earth is the happiness of seeing you again," wrote Henrietta, fearing to write more when her stricken mother said so little.

"Prince Henry left without her blessing," remembered Frances. "Surely she must feel terrible about that. I liked him, but he was always afraid of her." She found herself weeping for the lad who had, for some reason, once opened his lonely heart to her, and perhaps a little for Charles, with all his fine new kingdom about him, shut up alone with his spaniel and his grief.

"I should think this smallpox scare will make Her Majesty put off her visit," said Dorothy Culpeper.

But Janton seemed to know her better.

"I doubt if anything would ever make her change her plans because she was *afraid*," she said. "And now that the Orleans marriage is arranged and King Charles has given his consent, perhaps Her Majesty will put off her visit indefinitely."

"But the Princess wants so much to go."

"So do we all," sighed Janton.

33

"But perhaps Queen Henrietta-Maria herself does not. I wonder if it is true . . ." mused Frances.

"If what is true?" they asked.

"Something I once heard Master Lovell, the Prince's tutor, say," said Frances, caught back over the years by an association of ideas. "That the people in England do not like her."

Loyally, Dorothy kept silent. She had received much kindness from the Queen. But she knew it to be only too true.

"If I were a queen I should not want to go and ride through streets where all the people kept silent."

"I am quite sure, being pretty Frances Stuart, you would not," snapped plain Dorothy. "But there is small need for you to worry, since, however much men may flatter you, at least you are never likely to be a queen."

4

Almost before her household had finished discussing whether the Queen Dowager would go to England or not, she had packed up and gone, taking the Princess with her. It was now or never so far as Henrietta was concerned, because she was to be married so soon. But there were other reasons for her mother's sudden urgency.

"At least they cannot stay long because of the wedding," concluded Frances, who, to her bitter chagrin, had been left behind.

"The château seems dead without them, and especially after all that hustle of packing!" sighed Mistress Stuart, sinking into the nearest chair after the coaches and luggage waggons had finally rumbled away.

She and Frances had run hither and thither until their legs ached, and then stood wearily in the wind-swept courtyard waving goodbye. Now they were alone in a sad, disordered château with familiar gewgaws and garments, discarded at the last moment, lying around them. The servants were at last gone to their long-delayed meal. Tears from parting with a beloved mistress still moistened Sophia Stuart's eyes, but the tears that brimmed in her daughter's were of angry disappointment.

"They are sure to have a bad crossing," she pouted, as though rather hoping they would.

"Her Majesty always does. And she was complaining how damp England is in October," recollected Mistress Stuart anxiously.

"It will seem even damper to poor old Father Cyprien, with his gout," added Frances, feeling bereft of all her

35

friends, and knowing how much the dear old man had dreaded the journey.

It was seldom that Frances spoke so caustically. Roused from her own weariness, Mistress Stuart began to realize the depth of her daughter's dejection.

"I know how you feel about being left behind," she said.

"Did not you too expect them to take me? Am I not a relation?" flared out Frances.

"But Dorothy and Janton are older. Dorothy can really make herself useful. Whereas you are so—so——"

"Frivolous. I know. I heard you say it to Madame de Motteville."

"Besides, the visit was all arranged so hurriedly."

"Because James of York has been making love to Edward Hyde's daughter and she is going to have a baby," said Frances, who was learning too suddenly about life.

"I suppose you heard the servants talking."

"Actually, it was Monsieur Jermyn. Milord St. Albans, I should say. He was whispering about it to Walter's nurse. She is very pretty, you know."

Mistress Stuart, shocked by the sophistication of the young, closed her eyes in a gesture of helplessness.

"Her Majesty would scarcely have undertaken such a journey because of that," she said, unaware that she herself was now seriously shocking youth. "It is because the Duke of York wants to marry the girl."

Forgetting her own grievances, Frances got up and faced her mother.

"Is it not the right thing for him to do?" she asked, her blue eyes wide with ingenuous honesty.

Mistress Stuart shifted uncomfortably in her chair.

"Well, yes, if he were—just anybody. But the King's only brother. Were he to marry her, this Anne Hyde might one day become Queen."

"Why? Surely King Charles himself is sure to marry soon?"

"Of course. That is another reason why his mother left so hurriedly. She wanted to have some say. . . ."

"And then he will have sons and everything will be all right."

"But, my dear child, suppose, for some reason, he could not . . ."

"He has one already," laughed Frances. "'Jemmie', they call him. Milord Crofts pretends to be his father."

"Frances! Frances! Where *do* you gather all this scandal? I will speak to Her Majesty and have some of these servants dismissed. Who told you this?"

"Louis the Fourteenth of France. In an arbour by the tennis court," whispered Frances dramatically, making a gamin gesture of mock elegance.

Poor Mistress Stuart threw up her hands in despair.

"Oh, merciful God, if only your father were alive! He was wise. He would have known what to do. And now our good Queen is no longer here to advise me."

Immediately Frances was all contrition.

"Oh, *ma chère Maman*, everyone talks like that at Court. It is not really as bad as it sounds."

"But to tell such things to a child like you!"

"I am not a child. I am only two years younger than Henrietta. In a year or two you will be looking for a husband for me."

"The sooner the better," murmured Doctor Stuart's distracted widow. "And then there will be Sophie, and some sort of career to find for Walter." But with her daughter's warm young arms comfortingly around her, she soon felt capable of returning to the all-engrossing subject of the Dowager Queen's journey. "As I was saying, Her Majesty is naturally worried—and very angry. If York marries this Hyde girl their child would be in the direct line of succession. And, as you know, the King is always riding his own race-horses, and might break his neck any day. Or suppose he were to die of smallpox like his youngest brother."

"Heaven forbid!" cried out Frances, somehow realizing that England would immediately become a much sadder place.

"So the Queen hopes to reach London in time to prevent

such an unsuitable marriage. Sir Charles Berkley has offered to pretend the infant is his, and even milord Clarendon was loyal enough to tell the King he would sooner his daughter took the consequences of her folly."

"*Her* folly? Or the Duke's?" muttered Frances under her breath.

For a moment or two she stood silent beside her mother's chair, feeling decidedly sorry for this Anne Hyde. She had never in her life set eyes on the girl, but, not unnaturally, pictured her as some ravishing beauty. She could not help knowing that she herself was beautiful, and was beginning to find out how difficult it was to deny flattering royal advances. Now she began to wonder how it must feel to be placed as poor Anne was.

"Never, never will I be such a fool," she vowed, "such a *wicked* little fool," her pious upbringing forced her to add. And if the Hon. Walter Stuart's daughter was making her earnest resolve partly through adolescent fear, it was also largely through genuine reverence for all she had been so carefully taught. "And what did the King himself say?" she asked, pulling herself back to the case in point.

Mistress Stuart rose and began hurriedly collecting up some of the travellers' scattered possessions.

"It seems he told his brother that since he had got the girl with child he had better marry her. If they both wished it, of course," she answered over her shoulder with a kind of embarrassed reluctance, as she led the way upstairs to her own room with an armful of shawls.

Frances gaped after her in surprise. That sounded more human, she thought. And liked Charles better than she had ever done during his brief visit to the château. "They say he didn't want Cromwell's body dug up and hanged," she remarked, once inside her mother's room.

"What has that to do with it?" asked Mistress Stuart. "How you do fly from one subject to another, Frances!"

To Frances the two subjects seemed to be related because both lent assurance of tolerant kindness in a censorious world. But she was soon off on another tack.

"Her Majesty probably wants to make sure Charles chooses a Catholic queen. So she will have a busy time. Two marriages and the money," she summed up disrespectfully. "Why do you look so surprised, madam? Are you wondering how I knew about the money? Henrietta told me about all her poor mother's estates having been given away to the regicides, and that she hopes to get some compensation because they are now so hopelessly dilapidated."

Sophia Stuart laid her mistress's sable-lined cloak, which was also hopelessly dilapidated, across the back of a chair and stood absently stroking it.

"It was not only Queen Henrietta-Maria's houses," she said, speaking slowly and with difficulty. "Did the Princess tell you about ours?"

Frances suddenly stood very still, just inside the door, staring at her. "Ours? No. You mean our home?"

"She probably didn't know. I have only just heard myself. It was given away. And afterwards used by the soldiery. All the best rooms were knocked about—the tapestries and portraits stolen. And after Cromwell's death—perhaps by accident—it was burned down."

Incredulously, Frances lifted her face to look at the painting which had so often sustained her during their exile.

"Then it doesn't exist any more," she said brokenly.

"When General Monk came down from Scotland he told Prodgers that it is just a shell. That is what I meant when I said the other girls had homes to go to."

Stunned as she was, Frances' first thought was for her mother. She ran to her and kissed her, and fell to stroking the sad-looking fur with the same small motion of impartial pity.

"You should have told me," she reproved gently. "Then I could have tried to comfort you instead of talking smartly and adding to your worries."

"I don't think I really cared whether it existed or not—after your father died."

She spoke dully, but gradually warmed to Frances' loving blandishments.

"But it was your married home. It must have meant

everything to you. He used to show me the terrace where you walked together. And where you grew your herbs. He was so proud of the way you ran your household. And I am such a pert, vain, undomesticated hussy. Dear *Maman*, let me stay here quietly until Her Majesty returns and I will help you more with Sophie and Walter. I promise you. I shall try to be less frivolous."

"I would not wish you to be less gay. It would be like caging a bird," smiled Sophia Stuart, happier than she had been for some time because she felt closer to this lovable, exasperating elder daughter of hers.

But after she had gone briskly to put away some of the Dowager Queen's possessions, Frances stood for a long time before the painting, putting away her vicariously acquired memories—and in particular that part of herself which wanted to create a lovely home, just as small Sophie wanted to dress dolls. She had the sense to recognize this as the best part of herself, and she was aware that, like most precious things which must be stored away for a long time, it would need deep and careful packing. "Well wrapped up in a bale of pretence with the light protecting straw of laughter," she thought, with one of those shining gleams of perception which sometimes illuminated her careless thoughts.

Tired out with giving eager help, and lonely for her friends, she cried herself to sleep that night. And in the days to come she was careful never again to turn her lovely head to look at the beloved picture.

Instead, she counted the weeks until the royal party's return, and busied herself with choosing the most becoming clothes she had ever possessed in order to beautify herself as maid-of-honour at the Orleans wedding. She could scarcely wait to hear all about the merry doings at the restored English Court.

But when the prospective bride returned to Colombes, she and all the Dowager Queen's party were in sombre mourning for yet another of the beheaded king's children. Like her youngest brother, twenty-seven-year-old Mary, Princess of Orange, had caught the smallpox and died.

"They bled her and gave her a stiff draught of ale which made her swoon. But I am sure your clever father could have saved her," said Henrietta, while Frances and Madame des Bordes helped to tuck her up in bed so that she might recover from the fatigue of her distressing journey. "She died on Christmas Eve. So we never had that Christmas *en famille* that we had all been looking forward to so much."

"Was your Highness with her when she died?" asked devoted Marie des Bordes, thinking of the infection.

"No, *chère Madame. Maman* sent me away to St. James's Palace, although she did not seem at all afraid for herself."

"First the poor imprisoned Princess Elizabeth, then your youngest brother, and now—this," murmured Frances, lingering to settle the pillows more comfortably. Downstairs, she had been far too overawed to ask questions about anything, in face of Queen Henrietta-Maria's shocked and silent grief, but had been hoping for her cousin's confidences; and Henrietta, weary as she was, was well aware of it.

"You need not think that this was the great personal loss to me that it was to Her Majesty," she said, with an encouraging smile. "I never even saw my poor sister Elizabeth, and Mary I scarcely knew."

"But surely you grew to know her during the weeks you were in England? All this time I have been so glad for you, that you would at last learn what it was like to have a sister, as I have."

"Dear Frances! But, truth to tell, I didn't see very much of her. By the appreciative way Charles always spoke of her hospitality in Holland I had expected her to be lively and gay, like you. I envied her for being the only one of us who could help him. But the fact is . . ." The young Princess, who was learning how impossible privacy is in a royal household, peeped round the bed-curtains to where her dressers were putting away her newly-acquired jewels, and lowered her voice. ". . . she seldom attended any of the fine festivities which Charles and his friends arranged for us."

"Why ever not?" asked Frances. "Nothing on earth would have kept me away from them!"

"I am sure of that, Frances Stuart! But Mary was piqued because he was allowing Anne Hyde, who had been her dresser, to become her sister-in-law."

Frances settled herself more comfortably on the foot of the bed behind the half-drawn side curtains. Evidently she was to enjoy a good gossip after all.

"So the Duke did marry her?"

"Yes. In spite of all our mother's opposition. And in the end Her Majesty even consented to be the babe's god-mother—perhaps because he had called the mite Mary. You know he can be every whit as obstinate as she. Charles is a positive master of compromise—but not James." Henrietta, who had been forced to compromise with life ever since she was born, leaned back against her pillows with a sigh. "Such people make life very difficult sometimes."

"Did you like her?"

"Who? The new Duchess of York? Not particularly. She isn't very interesting."

"Is she very beautiful?"

"*Mon dieu, non!*"

"I took it for granted she must be, else why did your brother the Duke almost disrupt the kingdom to marry her?"

"I really cannot imagine. But men *do* love women who are not beautiful."

"I suppose so," agreed Frances half-heartedly, sliding off the bed and dancing like a piece of thistledown towards the dressing-table.

Henrietta watched her with amusement. How entertained by her Charles would be, she thought involuntarily. "There are plenty of happily married women who are not attractive as you are," she said. "Indeed, many of them might be shocked by you."

The departing dressers had left one inexpensive jade necklace lying on the table. Holding the two ends, Frances tried it against the whiteness of her slender throat. "What is there so shocking about looking beautiful?" she asked, with unabashed assurance. Then, with one of her lightning

42

changes from frivolity to seriousness, she let the necklace trickle through her fingers and stood pensively in the middle of the room. "Her Majesty has had to bear far more than her share of sorrow," she said.

Henrietta, who was soon to be a married woman, caught at the understanding words as she did at all her friend's more adult moments these days.

"Indeed, yes," she sighed. "And it was not only poor Mary's death. Imagine what it must have been like to her, going back to Whitehall. Charles told me afterwards how he had arranged for her to arrive by the back way from the river so that she should not have to pass through the banqueting hall. He hates having to use it himself. So how could she have eaten there, trying to talk gaily to guests, within a few yards of the window through which her husband stepped out onto the scaffold . . . through which they must have brought his . . ."

"Severed head." Quietly, Frances supplied the words which her cousin could not speak, and quickly changed the subject. "And did Her Majesty manage to get some satisfactory settlement about all her dower houses? Were they all destroyed as Master Prodgers said?"

"So badly that Parliament decided it would not be worth while to evict the present owners. So they granted her an annuity of thirty thousand pounds a year instead."

Having had the spending of only a few shillings in all her life, Frances could upon occasion be keenly interested in money. But she knew only too well that there could be other considerations.

"If she had never lived in any of them—if none of them was ever her *home*, but just a source of income—I suppose she must have been very pleased."

"Especially as Charles nearly doubled it."

"But who really paid out all that money?"

"The tax-payers, I suppose. And something Charles calls the Exchequer."

"Yet, by what that nice Master Lovell said, the tax-payers do not particularly like her."

43

But the royal bride-to-be was not even listening. "And to me of their own free will the Members voted forty thousand a year. For my dowry."

"Forty thousand pounds!" gasped Frances, who had never owned as many farthings. She stood looking down at the grateful, shining-eyed girl in the big bed. "Of course you had probably bewitched them all with your Stuart charm. But *forty thousand pounds*! Imagine, after not having enough to *eat*!" Suddenly she leant over the embroidered coverlet to embrace her, and burst out laughing. "Oh, 'Rietta, if only they could have seen you and Dorothy and me dividing that partridge your brother James shot for us! Or how grateful I was to wear Janton's chemises when she had grown too fat for them!"

Both girls dissolved into reminiscent mirth. Painful as such memories were, they would be always precious—and extraordinarily binding.

"I know what we will do tomorrow," exclaimed Frances, still bound by the communal world of unquestioning, sharing, as when they had so hungrily and so meticulously divided the unexpected bird. "Let us persuade milord St. Albans to have the head groom take us to the Neuilly Fair and buy as many of those delicious Provençal sugared almonds as we can eat."

The exhausted Princess sank back sleepily on her pillows, and the tragic gloom which had pervaded everything since Mary's death seemed to melt away.

"Oh, Frances," she yawned, "will you never grow up? But I am so happy to have you with me again."

5

If Frances had not been taken to England, at least a whole world of glittering social excitement now opened before her. Henrietta had asked that she might be one of the ladies of her new household at St. Cloud; and although both their mothers felt Frances to be too young for this appointment, she was allowed to accompany the new *Madame* of France everywhere. She joined in hunting parties, boating expeditions on the Seine, *fêtes champêtres* and formal banquets. But it was at masquerades that she was most in demand, since Philippe loved dressing-up and posturing, and few girls danced as well as his new young wife and Frances Stuart.

Because they had both been so strictly brought up, their new freedom and the intoxication of men's flattery went to their heads like wine. Being so young, and so long starved of fun, they grasped at all the proffered pleasures, and, as if to increase the new Duchess of Orleans' popularity, the new Spanish Queen proved very dull, and her Court all the duller, since she became *enceinte*. Whereas Henrietta, becomingly dressed at last, more than fulfilled her early promise of attractiveness, and charmed the hearts out of the Parisians. King Louis himself spent most of his leisure in her company. Frances, who had always been secretly alarmed by his attentions, was rather relieved. But it was noticeable that Philippe, although always vindictively jealous, already began to neglect his bride.

"How can you seem so gay and happy, married to a man whom you do not love?" Frances could not refrain from asking, wondering how much Henrietta's change from gentle self-depreciation to almost hectic high spirits might be a mask for marital disappointment.

"Because I do not ask the impossible," replied Henrietta with a sigh. "And surely both you and I have had good training in making the most of what we *can* get."

It was so seldom in this sparkling new world that the two of them could talk quietly alone, as they used. And inevitably Henrietta's exalted status made their relationship more formal. But now, after the departure of Madame de Motteville, who had been sent by the Dowager Queen to try to persuade her daughter to a more sober way of life, Henrietta was resting for a few minutes on the terrace, with only her cousin in attendance.

"Now your various guests have gone I expected to be *de trop*," said Frances, looking down into the rose garden where the Duke could be seen strolling arm-in-arm with a remarkably handsome courtier. "But although you have been married only a few weeks, *Monsieur* seldom comes and sits with you now. And when he does there is always that odious Chevalier de Lorraine."

Bleakly the bride's glance followed hers, and, being momentarily without any of her usual animation, she looked much older than seventeen.

"Yes," she said quietly, before turning to dazzle another approaching group of guests, "there will always be the Chevalier de Lorraine."

Frances did not fully understand. She disliked the young man instinctively, not only because he never noticed that she herself was pretty or because he so often provoked the Duke to be rude to Henrietta. She would have liked to ask more about him. But the Chamberlain of the household of *Madame* of France was bowing low and ushering forward some more frivolous visitors who were to help her arrange a ballet. Several of them were Henrietta's personal friends, and because they were of the younger set she hastened to put them at ease, so that they were soon chattering and laughing, and inevitably the conversation soon turned to the exciting prospect of her eldest brother's marriage to the Infanta Catherine of Portugal.

"So it is definitely settled?" said the Comte de Guiche,

manoeuvring his way through the throng as usual until he could drape his elegant figure over the back of Henrietta's chair. "At the Countess d'Arblay's card party last night the betting was on that Princess of Orange. Everyone thought that as he had received so much hospitality in Holland . . ."

"They should know him better," said his sister. "Princess Louise refused him when he was a penniless exile. Is it likely that Charles would marry her now?"

"What is this Infanta of Portugal like?" asked Frances, with her insatiable curiosity about other people.

But nobody seemed to know.

"Small and dark," someone suggested.

"And almost certainly very pious, having been brought up strictly in some Lisbon convent," put in someone else.

"Charles Stuart will soon undo all that," sniggered de Guiche behind his hand. And the other young men laughed knowingly.

"Our mother is pleased by his choice," Henrietta told them reprovingly.

"Because the lady is a Catholic," said Mistress Stuart, who had come to take her elder daughter back to Colombes. "Have you heard, *Madame*, when Princess Catherine of Braganza will be sailing to England for her wedding?"

"In the spring, they say, dear Mistress Stuart."

"And who will be appointed to her household?" clamoured several eager feminine voices.

"She will take her own ladies from Lisbon, of course," Henrietta reminded them.

"For, poor thing, she will not even know our language," murmured Frances, only half listening to the blandishments of Monsieur Baptiste, the clever Florentine, who arranged all the King's classical ballets at Fontainebleu, and saw in her a likely Venus.

"But it is not usual for many of them to stay longer than to see her settled down," Henrietta was explaining. "The Queen of England must have an English household."

"Which should mean many handsome new appointments for the wives and daughters of your brother's ministers,"

47

remarked the Comte de Guiche, offering Henrietta his arm for a promenade.

"And especially for those who have shared his exile, let us hope!" Mistress Stuart told him tartly.

After the good-looking pair had drifted away for a mild flirtation by the water-lily pond, chatter and speculation went on, and Frances found herself listening to it avidly across the amusing ditties with which Monsieur Baptiste was regaling her, and which at any other time she would have been storing up for future use.

"Not only must our new Queen have English ladies—dressers, maids-of-honour and so forth—but since she cannot be very old herself, some of them should be *young*," some aspiring English girl was saying.

"Never a dull moment now, at the new English Court, with King Charles and the amusing Duke of Buckingham," said another yearningly.

"It could be a wonderful appointment . . ."

"If the Queen herself is kind to serve," joined in Frances over her shoulder.

"All we know is that she has been strictly brought up. She could be a vixen."

"The vixen from Lisbon," mimed the Florentine, trying to hold Frances's wandering attention by pretending to scratch at her flawless skin with hands clenched like claws.

But she managed to elude his drolleries, making the excuse that her mother had come for her and that one of the Dowager Queen's coaches was waiting for them in the courtyard.

As she went indoors the sound of chattering voices died away. The suggestion of other girls' vague ambitions faded. Her own began to crystallize. A servant brought her cloak to a quiet anteroom. "Catherine of Braganza," she murmured softly, when the man in the fantastic Orleans livery had bowed himself out. ".What a lovely name! She *should* be kind."

Frances arranged the hood of her cape as becomingly as possible over her bright hair. She loitered, consideringly. The thought of being in a household where she might be curbed from worldly pleasures again, appalled her, but since too she had been strictly brought up—although not in a convent—surely such a mistress need not be wholly incompatible? And, being alone, she could not forebear from striking an attitude or two before the mirror. "And Mistress Frances Theresa Stuart," she added, announcing herself with a flourish to the empty room. "Maid-of-Honour to her Britannic Majesty Queen Catherine."

She and her mother drove homeward in their borrowed coach through the Paris streets in unusual silence. Both, had they but known it, were thinking along the same lines. Frances wanted to be where life was fullest. Deprived of home and husband, Mistress Stuart was growing more astutely ambitious for her children. Neither of them spoke of their hope lest the other should laugh at its sheer impossibility.

But, sooner than lose time, Mistress Stuart almost forced an opportunity to speak of the matter to the Dowager Queen. She approached it circuitously, speaking as tactfully as possible of their mutual anxiety for their daughters' morals in so lax a Court.

"For their good name rather than for their morals," corrected Henrietta-Maria proudly. "The serpent tongue of gossip and scandal are too dangerous to be given any encouragement. That is why I asked Madame de Motteville to speak a judicious word of warning to *Madame*."

"Your Majesty means because of the King? It must be hard indeed, because there is so little you can do. Whereas a while ago I nearly asked your permission to take my children back to Scotland."

"You mean before Louis' marriage, when he was making so much of your Frances?"

"Yes. And when he heard of it, in order to keep her in the country, His Majesty even hinted to me that his intentions were honourable." Mistress Stuart's face was softened by a reminiscent smile. "But I am not quite so gullible as that."

Henrietta-Maria, too, had to smile. "Obviously he was not accustomed to a Scotswoman's habitual common sense.

And I must say your daughter herself acted shrewdly for her tender age."

"She certainly tried to avoid being alone with him. Indeed, Madame, I am sure she was much relieved when His Majesty suddenly became aware of *your* daughter's devastating charm."

"'Suddenly' is the word, dear Sophia. As soon as someone had the heart to see that she had enough to eat and the right kind of clothes! Far from admiring her before, he has said on more than one occasion that he could not understand why his brother wanted to marry the bones of the Holy Innocents."

"He said *that*—about our beloved Princess!"

"Milord St. Albans overheard him. When—so meagre was my relatives' charity—the poor child was well nigh starving. She certainly was thin. And innocent, I hope."

"And now so much material comfort is thrust upon them that we begin to fear it may destroy their carefully instilled spiritual values." With calculated effect Mistress Stuart heaved a prodigious sigh. "I have been wondering if I might be doing the right thing, if I might perhaps ask Your Majesty to spare me to take her to England *now*? If by some miracle a small place might be found for her at the new Queen's Court?"

Beginning to perceive the object of the eagerly solicited interview, the Dowager Queen rose wearily and placed a kindly hand on her faithful friend's shoulder.

"Do not worry, dear Sophia. Much as I shall miss you, I shall not stand in your way," she said. And, crossing the room to her bureau, she picked up a letter. "Had you allowed me more time to read and consider my correspondence from the Lord Chamberlain at Whitehall, I would have told you sooner. I already know that your Frances was one of the first to be chosen to attend my future daughter-in-law."

All protocol forgotten, Sophia Stuart sank down on an oak chest before one of the long windows. "Already chosen. . . . One of the first . . ." she gasped.

"To be one of the four maids-of-honour."

"Because she is a Stuart? Or for her liveliness and beauty, perhaps?"

"*Vraiment, elle est la plus belle fille du monde,*" agreed Henrietta's mother generously.

Mistress Stuart slid to her knees to kiss the ageing Queen's hand. "And Your Majesty will let us go?"

"I will not only let you go, but I will keep your younger daughter in my household and train her to attend me."

Although Sophia Stuart was overwhelmed with gratitude, she was not the woman to let the grass grow under her feet.

"If Your Majesty would write a letter to King Charles, recommending my Frances. . . ."

But Henrietta-Maria was not a Medici for nothing. Her shrewdness in such matters outran even Scottish common sense.

"Do not ask *me*. Ask my daughter," she recommended, rather ruefully. "A letter from his beloved Minette will do your Frances far more good."

So after the Christmas revels were past and the King of England's marriage definitely arranged, Henrietta wrote the letter to him with tears in her eyes.

"I would not miss this opportunity of writing to you by Madame Stuart, who is taking her daughter to be one of the maids of the Queen, your wife. Had it not been for this purpose I assure you I should have been very sorry to let her go from here, for she is the prettiest girl imaginable and the most fitted to adorn a Court. . . ." And then, out of her approaching loneliness, she added: "To see Your Majesty again is the thing I most desire."

"How you will miss her after all these years," sympathized Madame des Bordes, standing beside the writing-table with a little gold tray of sealing-wax in her hand.

"Yet somehow of late the difference in our ages seems more apparent," said Henrietta, sealing her letter and sitting empty-handed before it.

"Surely that is only natural, Madame, now that you are married?"

"Yes, of course, dear Borbor," agreed Henrietta, reverting to the nickname which she had used from babyhood. "But quite apart from that, my cousin is such a strange, incalculable creature. Sometimes she amazes my by the clarity of her insight, but more and more often of late she exasperates me because she will not grow up."

Widowed Marie des Bordes looked down at her young mistress with tender understanding.

"Few of us mature until we are moulded by suffering," she said.

"Frances grieved deeply for her father and her lost home."

"But she has not yet had to meet difficulties in her everyday life, and overcome them," said Madame des Bordes, knowing all too well the difficulties of her beloved charge's marriage.

"You are thinking of the Chevalier de Lorraine, and how facing that problem with apparent equanimity has made me seem older." Henrietta's words came slowly, it being a subject she never spoke of—not even to her mother, who had been so pleased about the worldly importance of her marriage. "Were I a true Medici, I suppose I should poison him," she added, pressing her seal down savagely into the hot wax. "But as my blood is diluted with the gentleness of a Scots saint I endure the humiliation of Lorraine's constant presence, and face the world with a masquerade of gaiety. What hurts me most about Frances," she added, almost inconsequently, "is not that she will be leaving us, but that she wants to go."

Madame des Bordes reached for the handbell to summon her mistress's dressers.

"Your Grace will not miss her so much in a few months' time, when your baby is born," she prophesied.

"Please God it is a boy! Particularly now the Queen has one," exclaimed Henrietta fervently, knowing how her husband, if jealous or frustrated, could darken the whole palace with his vindictive bouts of temper. "If it should be a girl I shall feel like throwing it into the Seine."

Knowing the Princess's lifelong struggle against ill health

and the revulsion she must feel towards physical contact with her husband, was halfway towards forgiving the wicked petulance of such a remark.

"Yet if the same disappointment were to befall your brother," soothed Madame des Bordes, who worshipped him, "much as he needs a son, he would love the sweet mite just the same."

"I believe he would," admitted Henrietta, rising to kiss her with a shame-faced smile. "But let us hope that Catherine of Braganza will give him a whole string of sons. All as tall and strong and tolerant as he."

6

"The Palace here at Hampton Court is old and fasinating," wrote Frances to her mother, who, now that her daughter's position at Court was established, was visiting relations in Scotland near her old home. "The gardens are beautifully set out, and all we mayds-of-honour are well lodged. We are not at all grand here, as the King and Queen seeme to enjoy being simple. The Queen is most gracious and kind to me, and has twice asked me if I am homesicke for France, hopeing that I am not. She and the King seems to be very happy. . . ."

Here Frances, who was never to spell correctly or to be a fluent letter-writer, and who, although bi-lingual, wrote more easily in the French language than in English, dropped her quill and read through her letter from the beginning. Surely it was long enough and descriptive enough to please even her mother, who was avid for details of her new life. How could she be expected to sort out and to put down on paper all the new impressions which were now crowding upon her? It was impossible, Frances decided. Such confidences would have to wait until their next meeting, for Mistress Stuart was to live in London with the younger children when the summer was over. It would be some time before Sophie would be old enough to be of any use to Queen Henrietta-Maria.

Frances hastily scrawled an affectionate message to her sister and the little Walter and signed herself: "Your dutiful and loving daughter, F. T. Stuart."

Gazing dreamily at her name as she had just written it, she fell to wondering how long it would be before that name was altered—a train of thought natural enough, for here at

Hampton Court, with the King and Queen still on their honeymoon, love and marriage seemed to be in the very air.

"He is really fond of her," Frances thought, "and she is madly in love with him. That's not surprising, for he has so much charm, and a kind of ugly attraction; but she is not beautiful at all except for her great eyes and her smile and her dark curls. She is tiny . . . and those little, fragile hands! Do men usually admire small women?"

Her beloved Henrietta was small, and *Monsieur*, odd person though he was, had certainly appeared to adore her when he married her, only—it had not lasted. Which had not been surprising to those at Court who were well acquainted with *Monsieur*. This honeymoon at Hampton Court had already lasted for several weeks, and Charles showed no sign of tiring of his Portuguese bride. When he was obliged to leave for London on business connected with State it was evident that he tore himself away from her with the greatest reluctance.

Sentiment was infectious, and the ladies and gentlemen in attendance at the Palace watched these partings and reunions with sympathetic sighs and smiles.

Frances generously hoped such a state of felicity would continue. Although she was not yet sixteen, now that she was separated from her mother and in an important position as a maid-of-honour, there were intervals in which she felt quite mature, and she told herself that no doubt the King at over thirty was of an age to settle down. The amours which had been so freely credited to him were of the past, and he would be content to devote himself to his wife, who, if not exactly beautiful, was deliciously feminine in her scented silks and laces.

Struck by a passing doubt of her own more robust charms, Frances turned, as so frequently, to her mirror. Her mother had seen to it that she was adequately equipped for her new position, and she was today wearing a pale-yellow silk damask which well became her.

After weeks spent at the French Court, petted and admired, she could have no doubt of her own beauty, but now she

wondered passingly if Catherine of Braganza possessed some
subtle allure that she lacked. Perhaps it was a disadvantage
to be so tall; she had such long legs. The Queen, for all her
low stature, had a swimming grace. . . .

But Catherine was twenty-two to Frances' less than sixteen.
"By the time I am as old as that, I too shall have what they
call presence," she thought—and was suddenly glad that
she was still so young that when she was tempted to frolic
and to initiate childish games such as hide-and-go-seek
and blind-man's-buff, for which games the long, dark,
winding corridors at Hampton Court were ideal, her elders
smiled upon her tolerantly.

Her letter being finished and ready for the courier, it was
a waste of time to stay indoors on such a fine afternoon;
evidently the King had thought so, for of all things he had
taken the Queen out on the river, not in a State barge with a
retinue of attendants, but in a small skiff which he could
row himself.

Less than an hour ago Frances had watched from her
window as they had set off, and she had laughed aloud to
see Charles throw off his coat and hat and wig and roll up
his shirt-sleeves. The Queen had looked startled, almost
aghast, and then she too had laughed as heartily as the
secretly watching Frances.

On this occasion it had been easy for the royal pair to
escape their attendants, for in the heat of the early afternoon
most of them had been drowsing; and to Frances, Charles
had seemed once more the informal, long-legged, shabby
young man who had visited his mother and sister at the
Château de Colombes.

Those days now seemed very far away; the old sheltered
life had a dream-like quality. Strangely enough, Frances
had had a greater sense of protection at the exotic French
Court, for Le Roi Soleil, before he had transferred his
attentions to Henrietta-Anne, had been so open in his
admiration that others had been kept at a distance. Here,
at the English Court, unless she took refuge under the Queen's
wing, there was none to shield her, and the Queen, though

kind, was, in Frances' opinion, dull company--and, in any case, too absorbed in her twin passion for religion and her new husband.

It was not easy to frolic harmlessly with English admirers, as Frances had already discovered. They expected devotion to be rewarded by more than the gay comradeship which was all she had to offer.

None of the other maids-of-honour being particularly congenial, Frances was sometimes lonely for the companionship of one of her own sex, and especially lonely for the Princess Henrietta, who, it was clear, would rarely be allowed to leave France, for the irrational jealousy of an unloving husband was centred more on her two brothers than on anyone else.

Leaving the cool shelter of the Palace, Frances was at first dazzled by the brilliance of the sunshine. But beyond the velvet green lawns there were shady walks and enclosed gardens and immense lime trees casting their shadows in the park.

Frances wandered away from those who were loitering outside the Palace. She had not yet fully explored the grounds which fascinated her—to use a word she had adopted since her arrival in England. By now she knew much of the history of the old Palace, and it was strange to think that Anne Boleyn and Jane Seymour and poor little Kathryn Howard must have walked through the winding paths as she was walking now. It was all so calm and mellow, and the red-brick Palace itself, with its numerous slender turrets, their cupolas surmounted by gilded weather-vanes, had the beauty of a fantastic fairy-tale castle.

Oh, how fortunate Charles was to own this romantic place, as well as so many other desirable homes. Did they mean as much to him as they would have meant to her, his obscure young cousin?

"When I marry," mused Frances, "it must be to a nobleman who has an estate which is as beautiful as this, or one which can be made equally beautiful. Yes, it would be fun to improve and rebuild according to one's own taste, which also of course would be his. He must be handsome and kind and rich—very rich, for, like Cardinal Wolsey who made this Palace, I shall be content only with perfection."

Unconsciously she spoke the last words aloud, and then was startled out of her fantasy by a trill of laughter. Abruptly she came to a standstill—and found herself face to face with a young woman as tall as herself and beautifully gowned, who was approaching her from the opposite direction. An amused, melodious voice said: "Another moment, and you would have walked into me regardless, as though into a ghost, which as yet I am not, though but a short while since I would not have been surprised to find myself one."

Frances, immediately conscious of an exquisite sophistication, apologized in a confused voice. She had been in a dream, she explained.

"And why not? Hampton Court, especially in such weather as this, is a place for dreaming. You are new to Court, are you not? There will be many new faces—to me. I have been ill these last weeks and am only now about again."

Candidly the two took stock of one another; and although Frances did not realise it, the envy was not all on her side. She thought she had never before seen anyone who approached such loveliness. Glorious red-gold hair, perfect features, wide grey eyes shaded with black lashes, a dazzling smile and such grace. . . .

Perhaps the ravishing creature was a shade too thin, but that was to be expected as she had been ill. What a delicious gown of pale-green taffeta with silver bows—a green which seemed to change its hue with every movement; and such pearls roped about the slender neck! How poor in comparison was the string which Frances' mother had given her and which had been her father's wedding gift to his bride.

The older woman, for her part, saw one who was scarce more than a dewily-fresh child. Untroubled blue eyes gazed at her with flattering admiration; fair curls tumbled on a white forehead, soft lips were slightly apart showing pearly teeth.

"Tell me your name," she coaxed. "Are you one of the new Queen's ladies? I had heard they were all dark, stiff creatures like ravens, and clad in the most extraordinary clothes strung on wires."

Frances burst out laughing.

"Farthingales. It is impossible to get within yards of them, but those ladies have nearly all been sent back to Portugal, and now the Queen wears beautiful, flowing gowns of the King's choice. I am Frances Stuart from France, and the Queen Dowager commended me to His Majesty to be one of Queen Catherine's maids-of-honour."

"How rash of her, if this marriage is to be a success. You would, with your looks, turn the head of even an enamoured bridegroom. Luiza of Braganza showed more wisdom when she surrounded her daughter with black crows, unlikely to distract any man's attention."

"The King, though he welcomed me kindly when I first arrived, has not given me another glance," Frances said truthfully. "Everyone says that he is completely captivated by the Queen."

"Do they indeed?" The other's laugh was not altogether pleasant. "It would be a rare thing to see Charles *wholly* captivated by any one woman."

Caught by the underlying venom of this, Frances' eyes widened questioningly, and the silent interrogation was answered.

"I am Barbara Palmer." The information was imparted nonchalantly and yet with pride.

"Bar . . . Lady Castlemaine?" The name broke from Frances' lips in a gasp. She stared with unabashed curiosity.

"No other. So even you, a newcomer, have heard of me?"

"Who has not? Your ladyship's beauty is world-famous."

"A tactful remark. But then if you are a Stuart and the King's kinswoman you would naturally have a turn for a compliment."

"It is no more than a distant cousinship," Frances said modestly.

"The King has many such," Barbara remarked with an

indifference which was more weary than snubbing. "Shall we," she added, "find a seat somewhere near? I still tire easily, I find. It is but two weeks since . . ."

She broke off, but Frances could have ended the sentence for her. There had been much Court gossip over the fact that Lady Castlemaine had but recently given birth to a second son of whom the King was reputed to be the father. Probably the Queen was the only person at Hampton Court who was unaware of it.

Frances' state of mind was chaotic—excitement mingled with apprehension. She had scarcely thought it possible that she would be brought in contact with the notorious Lady Castlemaine, whose name must not be mentioned in the Queen's hearing; yet here she was, with Barbara's hand on her arm, guiding her towards a stone seat set under the shade of a lime tree.

They sat, and Barbara smiled at her.

"What a sober face! You are still young enough to be shocked," she said.

This to Frances was a shaming truth, but she hastily repudiated it.

"I am not—but I had not expected . . . it was a surprise."

"You are more than half inclined to gather up your skirts and to run away from me," Barbara teased.

Frances shook her head, momentarily bereft of speech. Would her mother, had she been present, have insisted that she did just that? Glancing sideways at the exquisite face, it was difficult to believe the stories she had heard about Lady Castlemaine's effrontery and rapaciousness, her tantrums and corruption, which included faithlessness to her royal lover.

"I know full well much of what is said of me," Barbara sighed. "I pray no such calumnies may be attached to you, though, being beautiful as I once was, it is scarcely likely that you will escape them."

"As you once were!" echoed Frances. "But your ladyship is surpassingly lovely. When we—when I saw you, not knowing who you were, I was struck breathless with admiration."

"Generous one!" A slender hand pressed Frances' hand. "But child-birth dims beauty, for a time at least, though it is true I am still young—of much the same age as the Queen. Tell me about her. I have not yet seen her. She is of no great beauty, so I have heard."

Of very little beauty, Frances thought, when compared with Barbara Castlemaine, but she loyally said that the Queen had great sweetness of expression, much grace and glorious eyes.

"She is also virtuous," Barbara commented with another deeper sigh, "and no doubt, in common with all such women, she will have no forgiveness for me, even though I repent to the very depths of my soul, as does Charles himself."

Here Barbara broke off, gazing down at her clasped white hands, gleaming with rings. Frances was for once tongue-tied, and after a moment or two Barbara went on:

"It would be as useless as absurd to deny that we have been lovers, but that is all over—from the time when this royal marriage was arranged. Now if Charles wishes to honour me, it is solely because I am the mother of his children and have sacrificed much for him. Were he to give me a position about the Queen's person, would it not be proof that our loving is of the past? How could he, who honours her and cares for her, insult her by wishing her to receive me, unless I were humble and contrite?"

To one more worldly-wise than Frances this pathos would scarce have rung true, but she was already more than half convinced that Barbara must have been misjudged, at least to a great extent. In loving the King she might have done wrong, but to Frances, young though she was, this particular wrongdoing did not seem heinous. How could it, when for years, even in her sheltered life under Queen Henrietta-Maria's domination, she had heard much of such relationships, and it was discretion not virtue that won praise.

A girl, mused Frances, would have to be possessed of a very strong character to refuse the King, newly restored to his kingdom—that is, if she loved him, and he loved her. Neither Barbara nor the King had wronged the Queen, since all that had passed between them was before the King had even seen her. There was Barbara's husband, however. . . .

Even as the thought of the unknown Roger Palmer crossed Frances' mind, Barbara said sadly: "My husband cares little for me. He is a kindly man, a scholar, but women mean nothing to him. The marriage was arranged between his parents and mine when I was but seventeen. Poor Roger, it is not his fault, but he . . . well, there are some men who *cannot* love, and that, Frances Stuart, is God's truth. It was a relief to Roger when I ceased to try to make myself desirable to him, and fell in love with Charles, who is so utterly different. That left Roger free to follow his own pursuits. He has left me these several weeks and has gone to France, where he purposes to immure himself in a monastery."

"But—but that would be terrible for him," Frances uttered.

"Well—yes, and once it would have sorely grieved me, but before Charles ever entered my life I had given up the effort to understand Roger. And now," concluded the incomparable Lady Castlemaine with an infinitely sweet though wistful smile, "I have told you, Frances, what I have told to nobody else in the world."

Deeply flattered though she was, Frances, with the common sense that rarely wholly failed her and had disconcerted more than one of her admirers, found this incomprehensible. There must be many others more suitable to receive the confidences of the King's *maitresse en titre*.

"Why have you?" she asked bluntly.

If Barbara was taken aback by this artless question, she concealed it.

"I confess I have two reasons," she said. "One is—and the most important—that immediately I saw you I felt immensely drawn to you. The other is that you are so pretty and young that I am sure the Queen is fond of you, and it occurred to me that if you heard my story with truth from my own lips you might speak kindly of me to her."

"Oh, I see!" Barbara's second reason struck Frances as plausible, but she shook her head regretfully. "The Queen is very gracious to me, and I do see much of her, for she often singles me out to talk to her, because I speak Spanish fairly well. I was never any good at my books, but I picked up other languages quite easily. As for the Queen, it is almost her mother tongue, and as yet her English is halting. But that doesn't mean she pays any attention to what I say; she often tells me I am no more than a child, and I doubt she would think anything I said of importance."

"She might," Barbara insisted. "For myself, I would pay attention to a child's opinion of a grown person. Children are clear-sighted, honest, not easily to be deceived."

"As I am nearly sixteen, I have passed that phase of childhood," stated a none-too-pleased maid-of-honour.

Barbara laughed. "Indeed you have, and you must be creating a sensation at Court. How many, I wonder, have already laid their ardent hearts at your feet."

"None that I know of," and irrepressibly Frances giggled. "I vow I wouldn't know what to do with them if they did."

"Kick them away," the other recommended with some venom. "Don't be beguiled by them, deceived into thinking they will suffer. Play with men, Frances, have sport with them, but never, never give them their own selfish way."

It might have been a half-concealed, vicious anger which shook the dulcet voice. It might have been pain, the sense of having given far too much, of having suffered through a husband's neglect and coldness. Frances, by now under the spell of experienced charm, chose to attribute all the best motives for such sudden vehemence, and she said impulsively: "If I have any chance at all, I will say how kind you are as well as beautiful, and how you wish that the past . . . well, that it had been different."

At this Barbara again squeezed her hand and gazed at her gratefully.

"We must be friends—close, dear friends . . . true to one another, for you are immensely understanding though you

63

are still so young. Do not be afraid that I shall sadden you. One's heart may be sore, but one must do one's best to be gay. It would be too selfish otherwise."

"Oh yes, indeed," Frances agreed, finding this sentiment altogether acceptable.

"Although I have taken a house here, it is dull at Hampton Court," Barbara went on, "but it is impossible to return to London while there are still so many cases of the plague. When we do—well, you and I, my dear, will make remarkable foils for one another. Your fair hair and my red; your blue eyes and my dark ones. I adore giving parties, and you will be a wonderful new attraction. I vow you shall be my most admired and honoured guest."

This dazzling conversation might have continued for longer, had not Barbara glanced up to see two gentlemen of the Court approaching, one of whom was the handsome Duke of Buckingham, who had already taken notice of Frances, singling her out for a smile or a compliment; a fact which had caused some heart-fluttering, since Buckingham was not only handsome but gay and brilliant, and as great a favourite with Charles as his father had been with the two monarchs before him.

Little wonder that he was, thought Frances, for he had fought valiantly in the Battle of Worcester and had shared the King's exile as his boon companion.

Now Buckingham raised his fine brows in surprise at seeing these two young women together and in intimate conversation.

"The moon and the sun in company," he exclaimed, "as does occur either at early morn or approaching dusk. And it would be impossible to say which surpasseth in beauty."

He swept a low bow, and then took Barbara's hand and kissed it.

"I had no idea you were already about, coz," he said. "Is it wise?"

That such a query was not concerned solely with Barbara's health Frances did not suspect, and Barbara answered with apparent lightness.

"I have been too long set aside as it is, and enclosed within four walls I am in danger of perishing from boredom. Now, as you see, I have discovered an antidote."

Her warm, lovely smile flashed upon Frances, who, still young enough to be flattered because one who was seven years older treated her as an equal, smiled back at her.

Henry Jermyn, Buckingham's companion, who was Master of the Horse to the Duke of York, fell in by Frances' side, as they all leisurely walked towards the river.

Frances knew him better than most of the young men about the Court, for he was nephew to the Earl of St. Albans, and had visited his uncle during the years of exile in France. Jermyn was a more than ordinarily comely young man, and as he and Frances laughed and talked together, Barbara Castlemaine's softly inviting gaze turned more than once to rest on him.

Across the river, the King's skiff could be seen approaching the bank. A group of courtiers and ladies had already assembled there, and to a chorus of delighted laughter the King replaced his wig and shrugged himself into his coat before he alighted and gave his hand to his bride, who with her glowing, happy face was sufficiently attractive to please any eye. Barbara Castlemaine's eyes were attentive, though as the others crowded round she drew back as if in modesty. The King espied her, however, and seemed not to know whether to frown or smile. The smile won, as it so often did with him, but Catherine, surrounded by her chattering ladies, who were much intrigued by the informality of this water excursion, did not notice it. Nor did she observe the red-haired beauty who promptly sank in a deep and graceful curtsey.

7

Not a few of the more decent-minded of those who witnessed Barbara Castlemaine's genuflexion were anxiously concerned; but although storm clouds threatened, the Queen was to be blissfully unaware of it for a few days. Then that happened which even to thoughtless Frances appeared shocking and inexcusable.

She, with the other maids-of-honour, found herself pushed aside and redundant, while the older ladies and the King's physician ministered to a grossly insulted Queen, who, perhaps fortunately for herself, had at such a crisis been overwhelmed by fainting and a violent nose-bleeding.

"Oh, how could he?" whispered Joan Wells, the maid-of-honour nearest in age to Frances. "So fond of the Queen as he seems, and then to trick her cruelly by himself presenting to her that pushing, shameless creature, knowing that the name of Palmer would be no warning to her?"

"We cannot be certain that the Queen's fit had anything to do with the Presentation; it might have been only a coincidence. The Queen may have agreed to it, for all we know," Frances defended.

The other girl stared at her incredulously.

"You know full well that she would never have agreed. The King made sport of her before all the Court. Everyone is talking of it."

"If they had any real feeling for the Queen they would *not* talk," Frances said hotly. "It could have passed off without remark, but immediately there was the whisper going from one to the other, and that Portuguese crow who is always hovering at her ear, telling her that Lady Barbara

66

Palmer was none other than Lady Castlemaine. Could she not have kept it to herself until the evening was over?"

"Better that she did not," said Joan Wells virtuously, "for at least when the poor Queen fainted and her nose bled the King was put to shame."

"And that made me feel ashamed—for him."

"It will be long," said Joan, "before one so spotlessly good as Catherine of Braganza will pardon such an affront."

The same opinion, though in different words, was expressed by the Duke of Buckingham as he lounged in Barbara's boudoir.

"It was unwisely done, as I told you when you nagged Charles into agreeing," he said. "You should have bided your time. And then acceptance might have stolen upon the Queen by degrees. It is hopeless to expect easy condonation from such a convent-bred saint."

"And am I to be hidden away until the saint becomes less saintly—if ever?" fumed Barbara, in appearance no longer the wistful penitent who had so disarmed Frances Stuart, but rather, with her flashing eyes and bitten lips, an enraged tigress. "Charles told her days ago that we are no longer lovers, and were both penitent. That comedy I would have maintained to oblige her, and it would not have been too difficult. Worth it also if it meant the Court position which is the least Charles can procure for me after all our family have done for him and for his father. How *can* he forget that my father was killed at Edgehill? And there was the ignominy we suffered when Cromwell was Protector. Does it not occur to him that it was a matter of loyalty when I accepted him as a lover . . . ? Don't laugh, George, or I vow I will strangle you."

But Buckingham could not control a paroxysm of mirth at the thought of Barbara's loyalty being carried to this length. He held her off easily as she rushed at him, and the brief struggle ended with a kiss or two more ardent than was called for by their cousinly relationship.

"There is no certainty that you will get your own way," Buckingham said. "Charles is chivalrous and they have been wedded scarce two months. The Queen has only to announce her pregnancy and you, fair coz, may find yourself banished to the Ireland from whence you have derived your title."

"Charles would never do that to me—never!" stormed the *maitresse en titre*. "How can you seem amused, you buffoon? You know well that you detested this marriage and did your best to set Charles against it, suspecting she might convert him and turn the Court into a nunnery, which it seems she has a mind to do. But, for all your vaunted influence, the marriage has come about, and here am I, the mother of his two sons—and God knows I bore them with agony—treated as a mere concubine."

"Concubines have had much power ere now. This marriage may not last, and the more dullness and piety and sulks, the more greedily Charles will turn to you, who still hold him on a chain, though perforce a loosened one. You must be as generous, Barbie, as the Queen is niggardly; provide gaiety and amusement and, above all, novelty."

"I had thought of that myself," Barbara said. "It came to me the first time I saw Frances Stuart—a pretty romp, and with that gift for laughter which appeals to Charles. Once brought out from behind the Queen's petticoats and the child could divert him. Tomorrow, though he is cast over with gloom, I have persuaded him to sup with me, and I shall ask Frances as well."

"And supposing he falls in love with her?"

"Charles has his scruples. She is too young, and she is his mother's protégée. Also she is quite unawakened—the little Stuart—and he would never force himself upon her. But as a pastime she will do well enough, and will not only divert his thoughts from his stubborn wife, but his jealous eye from me."

"Ah-h! Young Jermyn, I assume. 'Pon my soul, Barbie, and the King's babe less than four weeks."

"Harry Jermyn is for me just such a pastime as I design for Charles. As for the babe, while I groaned in labour, *he* was consummating his marriage. I prayed," said my Lady Castlemaine viciously, "that it was proving of small pleasure to him, and even if it was, I vowed that he should pay for it—not only with titles and settlements and every honour I can grasp for my poor whelps, but with doubt and jealousy and a more fevered love, so that in the end it may seem to him a small thing to be King of England if Barbara Palmer tires of him; as I shall do, many a time and oft, before he tires of me."

Buckingham did not doubt it. He would never make the mistake of underrating this gorgeous cousin of his who had the temper of a fiend and no more moral sense than an animal, though at will she could subdue the one and give a convincing exhibition of betrayed virtue. As a lover, though well-born and carefully reared, she was as accomplished as any cocotte. Her beauty was startling, and more surprising than all was her genuine maternal passion for her children, no matter by whom they were conceived. With her infant in her arms, and her little daughter and son at her knees, seeing her tenderness for them and their love for her, it was hard to believe ill of her.

"Poor Charles!" murmured Buckingham, who in his way was fond of his boon companion, though he was not weighed down by loyalty to his King.

He knew his power, and this was rooted in something of the same qualities that Barbara discerned in Frances. He was gay and frivolous and had a sense of the ridiculous. Who without such would, while the Roundhead soldiery were searching for him, have disguised himself as a mountebank and taken part in a public performance on an open-air stage at Charing Cross?

Charles, when Buckingham had escaped to join him in exile in Holland, had doubled up with laughter when this absurd masquerade was retailed to him. And Frances Stuart, hearing some rumour of it, had but a few days since coaxed him to tell her of it, her blue eyes dancing with gamin amusement. Now, to Buckingham's thinking, the Court of England had become mighty dull, and was in sore need of such feckless maidens.

"If the King and the fair Frances are to sup with you

tomorrow, I would beg to make a fourth," he said. "If Charles is put into a good mood, it would be an opportunity to reveal the low state of my exchequer."

"As though he ever turns a deaf ear to you when you are in need of funds," Barbara said. "Nothing—according to Charles—will ever repay the privations you shared during his exile. And for the matter of that, when did I ever disavow the claims of kinship?"

"Never, that I know of," Buckingham admitted, for this was another facet of Barbara's complex character. Immoderately grasping where her royal lover was concerned, she would yet lavishly replenish an empty purse did it belong to one of her own family or a passingly favoured lover.

Now she remarked carelessly that Charles had sent her both gold and jewels after the birth of her second son by him, and that of the former Buckingham was welcome to a share. Tossing the small but heavy leather bag into the air and catching it again, Buckingham remarked that within the next few hours he hoped to double its contents.

"De Gramont is out of luck these days, but my luck is in," he said, "since I am one of the few not to be distracted from play by a fair wench who has a circle of gallants round her while she builds castles of cards, with a dozen aspiring architects eager to assist her."

"Does Frances do that?" Barbara was amused. "Then indeed De Gramont must have a sour face. By my life, a professional gamester is the dullest of all dull company, for that in truth is what the elegant Chevalier is. Now that gaming is the one diversion of the Court, it is little penance to stay away from it. I am tormented with ennui when there are card-parties here."

But such card-parties, as they both knew, were but a smoke-screen for other diversions. Barbara had the sense to provide an ample meal for the gamesters and she would then retire to her bedroom with the favoured one of the moment, planting outside a trusted maid who would be on the look-out to warn that the King was on his way, though as a rule the royal approach was announced by messenger.

Buckingham, remarking that Frances Stuart's knack of monopolizing the attention of all present certainly put the Chevalier de Gramont off his game, took his departure, leaving Barbara to restlessly pace her apartment. Although by a ruse she had been presented to the Queen and it was therefore permissible for her to appear at Court, she had haughtily told the King that she would absent herself until the Queen was prepared to accept her with courtesy.

But this was what Catherine steadfastly refused to do, and gloom pervaded Hampton Court Palace which only a short while before had been the scene of such happiness.

The Queen kept to her apartments, and the few Portuguese ladies she had been allowed to retain hovered round her in sighing commiseration, retiring with black looks when the King visited her. These visits invariably ended in recriminations, and finally Charles sent Clarendon, his Lord Chancellor, to reason with Catherine. But apparently to no avail, for that evening the storm broke in fury, and the King and Queen railed at one another with a gusto which could not have been bettered by a married couple of low degree.

The maids-of-honour, gathered in an anteroom, gazed at one another with appalled eyes when even through the closed door the enraged voices penetrated to them.

The Queen's sobs were heartrending as she accused her husband of tryanny and lack of affection and declared that she would return to Portugal, whereupon he retorted that she would do well to first discover whether she would be welcomed there by her mother, and reminded her that as yet only half her dowry had been received.

"We must not speak of what we have overheard," said Mary Boynton, a sober young woman.

"It is not only we who have heard," Frances retorted. "If you were to look into the corridor you would find at least a dozen loitering there."

"Oh, the poor Queen!" Joan Wells mourned. And then as Frances was silent: "Surely you must pity her."

"I think she could be more sensible," Frances said,

speaking her mind as usual. "After all, she must have known what to expect, and royal wives have to put up with certain disagreeables to offset the pageants and the glory and their high position."

"But the Queen cares so little for those things," objected Lady Anne Herbert, who was even younger than Frances.

"I wonder. Does any woman? But at least she cares for the King and wishes to please him."

"How dreadful for her if he sends her away," Mary said in a shocked whisper.

Frances shrugged her pretty shoulders.

"He will not. He has too good a heart. *Madame*, his sister so often told me that he was incapable of real unkindness, especially to a woman."

"But he is being dreadfully unkind now, Frances."

"And so is she. Why cannot she believe him when he says it is all over between him and Lady Castlemaine?"

"Could you?" Joan enquired sceptically.

Loyalty to her new friendship with Barbara induced Frances to say: "Yes, I could," and then out of an uncomfortable doubt to qualify it: "At least I would try to believe, and I would pretend I did, and think that I was the Queen—which no other woman could ever be. As the Princess Henrietta once said to me, there is no happiness for one of royal birth if they ask the impossible, and such as they must make the most of what they have—which, after all," concluded Frances reasonably, "is a great deal."

When she and Mary Boynton waited on the Queen the next day, Catherine's eyes were swollen with weeping; but although the Palace gossips were still avidly relating all that had been heard to pass, it was evident that a compromise had been reached, for that morning Catherine rode with the King, and amongst those riders who followed in their train was Barbara, Lady Castlemaine, bearing her head high, and with a small smile of triumph curving her lips.

8

At the end of August Charles and his Queen made their
state entry into London. The King had bestirred himself to
give detailed orders, and when the eventful day arrived,
Frances, though accustomed to the pageantry at the Court
of Le Roi Soleil, was impressed. The journey from Hampton
Court Palace was made by water, and the royal barge alone
was a gorgeous sight. Fortunately it was a hot and sunny
day. "Not a cloud in the sky, Your Majesty," Frances had
said delightedly, hovering about the Queen, presenting
jewels on a small velvet cushion for her inspection and
choice, while Catherine was robed in a silver gown, inter-
woven with gold threads and cleverly moulded to show her
pretty figure to the best advantage.

Catherine had smiled upon the bevy of young girls who
fluttered around like brilliant butterflies, too excited to be of
much use to anyone. The Queen, though only a few years
older, had the poise of her royal training and was outwardly
calm, though her heart was soft to her husband because she
knew that he had arranged this pageant to do her honour.

As the splendid, open vessel started on its long journey
up the Thames, it was seen that the banks of the river were
crowded by spectators, who cheered loudly at first sight of
their Sovereigns.

The twenty-four bargemen who rowed the vessel were
dressed in scarlet livery, and the King and Queen sat
beneath a canopy of cloth of gold, supported by flower-
festooned Corinthian pillars.

Frances with the other maids-of-honour stood in a cluster
behind the Queen, and for once it was no temptation to
chatter, so much was there to see and hear.

Other barges sailed alongside in procession, the river being broad enough to accommodate them. Those of the City Companies were disguised as floating islands with realistic trees and shrubs and rocks, and from these professional actors in the classic garb of river-deities declaimed dramatic verse lauding the new Queen.

Catherine, thought Frances, could not have understood much of those finely turned phrases; but when the bargemen rested on their oars to give the orators the chance to be heard, she gave every appearance of listening with pleased attention.

But even those who did understand could hear but indistinctly, for now there were several orchestras playing. The church bells were ringing, the people were cheering themselves hoarse, and the Thames was so crowded with vessels filled with rejoicing spectators that it was scarcely possible to see the water.

It was Catherine's day and she was at her best, darkly pretty and glowing with satisfaction, her hand clasped by that of the splendidly dressed Charles. The admiration of the crowd was unstinted, and did not ignore the handsome courtiers and lovely women in the background.

Barbara Castlemaine and Frances stood near to one another, and the former, conscious of evoking much curiosity, bore herself with such excessive decorum that more than once Buckingham cast an amused side-glance at her.

She had got her own way and was satisfied, at least for the time being. The pampered cat gorged with cream, he thought, shaken momentarily by silent laughter. The Queen, as he had prophesied from the first, would be no more than a figure-head, for all the King's obvious intention that she should be treated with honour.

All the same, Buckingham had a shrewd suspicion that Barbara's hold on him had slackened and that he was sometimes bored by her demands and caprices. Though so beautiful, she was in danger of eclipse and that by the enchanting child whom she had decided to cultivate.

Frances was not yet sixteen; not yet, Buckingham judged,

at the zenith of her beauty, but she was tempting enough even so. It was true that Charles had not paid any particular attention to her, but a woman was a fool to become too confident. Barbara's last thought was that she could ever be out-rivalled by such an inexperienced girl, but yet. . . .

The procession at last arrived at Westminster, where there were more loyal addresses and quantities of rose-petals thrown at the royal pair. Some of these fell upon Catherine's attendants, and Frances gathered them from the folds of her skirts and buried her little nose in their fragrance.

"Somehow these are sweeter-scented than the roses in France," she said.

Her words caught the King's attention, which had wandered from the last long speech delivered by a civic dignitary.

"She herself resembles an English rose, does she not, *ma mie?*" he demanded of Catherine, who smiled upon Frances and said in her broken English:

"But that, is it not, is what she is? Not of the French country, but ours."

Charles was pleased by the "ours". He said: "A daughter of Scotland—a product of Britain. Observe that aristocratic little nose—it is all Stuart."

"La Belle Stuart!" murmured His Grace of Buckingham, and it was a sobriquet which henceforth was to be generally applied to Frances.

The flattered girl laughed joyfully. "Oh, what a marvel of a day!" she exclaimed. "How all these people must have hated the long-faced Puritans who wouldn't allow them any pleasure. Now everyone is so happy. . . ."

Catherine agreed. She certainly was happy, though she knew she would be terribly weary by the time the long day ended. For the time being she had forgotten Barbara Castlemaine and the humiliations to which, through her, she had been subjected. Perhaps she might dare to believe Charles to whom she had so readily given her heart. Perhaps, as he said, as Lord Clarendon had implored her to believe, and as Barbara had avowed, that affair was all in the past, had been over before Charles made her his Queen, and the only link now was the fact that Barbara was the mother of his children.

In that case it would not be so galling to assume friendship. Catherine would feel less false and despicable. She could never, of course, really like the woman, and to remember that Charles had fathered her children was as painful as a throbbing wound. But when she, Catherine, had a child of his . . .

She observed Frances' flirtatious glances with amusement. Over and over again Catherine of Braganza was to be called a prude, but she was sympathetic towards the frivolities of the pretty girls in her entourage, especially towards young Frances Stuart. Catherine knew her circumstances and the history of her loyal family. No doubt it was her mother's hope that she would make a brilliant marriage, and why not? It would be a pleasure, the Queen thought, to take her especially under her wing, to help her with her wardrobe, which was not particularly extensive—to invite her confidences.

But although these benevolent reflections coursed through the Queen's mind, she had little opportunity of befriending Frances in any special way, for it was to Barbara Castlemaine that the girl turned.

Deceived by the amity which apparently existed between the Queen and Barbara, Frances saw no reason to avoid Barbara's flattering advances.

The Court settled for a few days only at Whitehall. Barbara had her own separate apartments, and her attendance on the Queen was only a matter of form. She put in routine appearances, but entertained lavishly on her own account, and both the King and the Duke of Buckingham were frequent guests at her parties, which were amusing in a way that Frances found more satisfying than the brilliant entertainments at the French Court.

Barbara was nothing if not informal; she treated the King as casually as any other man, and this he seemed to enjoy. She invented games and even more elaborate entertainments apparently without forethought. Charles was usually in high spirits and played a ready part in the most romping sports.

The Queen could not have been denied had she expressed a wish to be present, but this she did not do, though in a discreet way she questioned Frances.

"The King stayed but a short while last evening, Madame. Then he said you might be lonely and left before the masque was half over," Frances told her, one autumn afternoon, when she and Catherine were alone in the Queen's apartment and occupied with their embroidery.

Donna Penelva, the one Portuguese lady who still remained with Catherine, the others having returned to their native land, was confined to her room with a heavy cold, and the Queen had dismissed her other attendants in order to have Frances alone with her.

Catherine's small, dark face was impassive. There was nothing in her manner to indicate that if Charles had made an early departure from Barbara's party it had not been to return to her.

"The King," she said, "so soon wearies of the card parties which are the main feature here in the evenings. He is no gambler."

"Only the dull men are," Frances said, positive as usual. "How it bores me even to look on, and everyone frowning if one dares to joke or to say a word. But then I haven't the money to lose at cards, and if I play I nearly always do lose."

"You are wise to abstain," the Queen approved. "The King dislikes to see the ladies of the Court playing and sets a good example by rarely risking more than a pound or two."

"Very unlike the Chevalier de Gramont," Frances remarked. "The gentlemen of King Louis' Court played, of course, but not with his earnestness, and it is only since I've been here that I have seen enormous sums of money staked. The Chevalier wins hundreds sometimes. It is almost as though it is a profession with him."

"You might without loss of charity omit the 'almost'," Catherine observed dryly.

"Your Majesty means that he lives on his winnings?"

asked Frances, and then winced as her embroidery needle stabbed her finger.

"So it is said."

Frances sucked her pierced finger as she remarked: "For my part I find it more amusing to build castles of cards than to risk my allowance by staking on them. The Chevalier is annoyed then because some of the others help me. Sometimes he is left alone at his table shuffling his pack and waiting for the play to start."

Catherine laughed. She had a momentary impulse to stroke the fair head so close to her knee. Frances had an endearing habit of drawing her low chair close to the Queen when they were together, or even of sitting on a cushion at her feet. She was still hardly more than a child, thought Catherine, and wondered how she could warn her to see less of Barbara Castlemaine. She dared not do so openly for fear of offending Charles, who had now satisfied himself that Barbara and Catherine were on reasonably good terms.

"You have skill," the Queen remarked. "I had no idea such complicated castles could be built up with pieces of cardboard."

"One needs to have a light touch," Frances said. "Few men have. Cards fall at a breath almost." She added with a wistfulness to which the Queen had no clue: "They are like one's dreams."

Dreams of a home, a beautiful home of her very own. Her fancy played upon this much more than upon the husband who would presumedly share it.

Although she was no political pawn as was her royal cousin Henrietta to be moved about on the chessboard of life, she was almost equally lacking in romantic expectation. Her mother would say it was her duty to accept the first eligible suitor who offered for her. These months in which she was free of Mistress Stuart's supervision were a respite.

Barbara Castlemaine was teaching her much—amongst other things how to hold her admirers at bay with smiles and jests which promised far more than she had any intention of giving. Frances closed her eyes and ears to much that she did not wish to recognize. She accepted Barbara's affection and Buckingham's half-teasing attentions without analysing the sincerity of either.

The Queen, as Frances once more bent over her embroidery, silently considered the girl's fair face. Although she was fond of Frances, who from the beginning had been companionable to her because they both spoke fluent Spanish, she was often baffled by her. Just how real was her seeming innocence? She must, after all, see much that the Queen, by virtue of her exalted position, did not see. The Castlemaine, thought Catherine, would not trouble to throw dust in Frances' eyes, and surely the girl must know if, at the parties which Barbara gave, Charles made opportunities to be alone with her.

But Catherine's pride was such that she could not bring herself to give or receive confidences. In fact she had coldly checked Frances when striving to further Barbara as she had promised, the girl had haltingly attempted to speak of her friend's penitence for a love affair that was in the past.

Frances sighed as she plodded on with the embroidery which the Queen considered a suitable occupation for her maids-of-honour in their spare time. It was an honour to be singled out as she was for the Queen's companionship, but it could be prodigiously dull. On this wet afternoon the other girls were rehearsing a poetic play to be performed at Hampton Court when they moved there from Whitehall, and somebody would be standing-in for Frances, who had been cast for a leading part.

How much more entertaining that was than to sit here with her stupid needlework, keeping a respectful silence unless the Queen chose to speak.

Then—suddenly—she was galvanized into full attention by an unexpected remark, and she looked up, startled and newly animated.

"The Queen Dowager? Is she really coming on a visit to England? It has been rumoured so many times, but you said—I thought Your Majesty said that she is on her way, already on the high seas."

"I did, and if the elements are clement she should be here next week. The King hopes that this time it will be a long visit, for she has not left Paris since the Princess Henrietta-Anne married. She gave but short notice of her intention, and there will scarce be time to put Greenwich Palace in order. At its best it is not too convenient. Somerset House, the King says, must be converted into a permanent residence for her."

"Will our Princess accompany her?" Frances asked eagerly. "We grew up together, Your Majesty. Shared the little we had to share in those days. After all, we are cousins."

"And almost as close as sisters," the Queen said with quick sympathy.

Frances stopped herself on the verge of saying that she had been far closer to Henrietta-Anne than the poor Princess Mary, who had died so tragically of the smallpox.

"I have seen the letter she wrote to the King," Catherine went on, "when she recommended you to be one of my ladies. It was generous of Henrietta. She was loath to part with you, as I shall be also, if you marry some nobleman whose estate is too far away for you to be often in London."

"I do not suppose I would marry such a one," cried Frances, whose taste for Court brilliance was far from sated. She remembered herself sufficiently to say, "I thank Your Majesty for such graciousness."

There were times when the Queen could dispense with formality, and this was one of them.

"You are well aware, Frances, that I am fond of you," she said, "and as the King's cousin you hold a special position here. The Queen Dowager mentioned you in her last letter, saying she was sure you are a comfort to me."

"Oh dear, I doubt if I am that to anyone, much less to Your Majesty; though the Princess in her letters to me has said much the same. Surely it is time she paid the King, her brother, a visit. They are so fond of each other. And then, too," went on Frances, "she must want to make the acquaintance of Your Majesty in person. It is not the same thing knowing a person by exchanged letters."

As the Queen was already inclined to be jealous of Charles' beloved Minette, with a jealousy more poignant than that which Barbara Castlemaine evoked, she avoided comment on this, but said with seeming regret: "I fear it is impossible for Henrietta-Anne to leave France at the moment. She has her many official duties there. Moreover, her little daughter is so young . . ."

"It is Philippe who will not allow her to leave," Frances cried petulantly. "Your Majesty can have no idea . . . he is the strangest man; outrageously jealous though he so neglects her and makes it plain that he infinitely prefers the Chevalier de Lorraine. Do you not think that very strange, Madame? Such a fop of a man, always talking about the cut and style of his coats, and fluffing out his lace ruffles. But then Philippe, too, is just such another fop. Not really a man at all, we used to say at Colombes, though he seemed to change when he first met our beloved Princess and was in love with her for a short while. But neither he nor Lorraine are really interested in women. Dorothy and Janton teased me because, though I tried, I could not provoke a compliment from Lorraine. He would look at me," related Frances with surprised injury, "as though I were not there at all."

Which must certainly have been a novelty for the confident young beauty, Catherine reflected, yet felt a tenderness for her because she was so obviously unaware of the deep and treacherous undercurrents that imperilled Henrietta's married life.

The convent-bred Queen had herself been ignorant of much a few months ago, but since then her eyes had been opened to many unpleasant truths. It seemed, however, an impossibility to thus enlighten Frances. Was she wilfully obtuse or genuinely dense? The Chevalier de Gramont was convinced of her stupidity. It was hardly possible, he had said contemptuously, for a woman to have less wit and more beauty. Catherine, to whom this remark had been repeated, was not so sure of it.

Although Frances had been awed by the Queen Dowager when she had been one of her household at Colombes, she was fervently anxious to see her and talk with her again, for thus she would be given first-hand news of Henrietta. She was in attendance when Charles and Catherine drove in state to Greenwich to welcome the Queen Dowager, and a few days later, when the Court were at Hampton, Henrietta-Maria paid a return visit to the royal pair.

"This means," said Joan Wells with satisfaction, "that we shall see less of the Castlemaine. Even she will not have the effrontery to show herself at Court while the Dowager Queen is here."

"But why not?" Frances asked. "The Queen has consented to overlook the past. She shows much amiability towards her."

"Oh, Frances, sometimes you are so sensible, and sometimes such a simpleton! Such friendship is nothing but a pretence, and now the Queen speaks better English there is many a barb that passes between them. Were you not present the other day when the Queen was spending much time having her hair dressed in the ringlets which His Majesty has said he admires . . . ?"

"Yes, those ringlets take a long time to dress and arrange," Frances agreed.

"Exactly! And Lady Castlemaine, who was hovering around, and getting in the hairdresser's way, for, although she pushes herself in everywhere, she is nothing but a hindrance and a nuisance, asked her how she could have the patience to sit so long a-dressing, and then ran her fingers through her own red mop, flaunting it because her curls are natural."

"What of it?" Frances asked. "Barbara couldn't have meant to be impertinent. She has a way of saying the first thing that comes into her head."

"You do, too, Frances Stuart! So perhaps it's no wonder you get on so well with her. But the Queen saw her chance and she took it when she replied that she had so much reason to use patience that she could well bear such a trifle. Everyone else realized what she meant, if you did not."

"I was paying little attention. The fringe of the Queen's

shawl was knotted and I was having difficulty in unravelling it."

"Her Majesty may be gentle, but if ever I saw resentment and hatred in anyone's eyes . . ." and Joan made a dramatic gesture. "For my part, I think, and I have heard others say the same, it was a great mistake for the Queen to give way over Barbara Castlemaine. She should have stood by her principles."

"But there was so much at stake," Mary Boynton reasoned. "The dowry, for instance. It has not all been paid, and then, too, our country gives so much political support to Portugal. The Queen was bound to consider such matters. Besides, she loves the King, and cannot bear to be at strife with him."

"Well, I suppose she does love him," Joan conceded. "Poor thing, it is sad for her. But, anyway, it will be easier for a while. It was wonderful to see the way the Dowager Queen behaved, not allowing Queen Catherine to make obeisance, but taking her into her arms and kissing her and showing everyone that she was eager as well as willing to give her precedence. How regal the Queen Dowager is, Frances. But she must have been a much more severe mistress than Queen Catherine, who is always so kind."

"Oh no—she was kind too, though often sad, poor thing. My mother was one of her ladies and thought her perfection. But cruel things happened—even after the Restoration, which we all thought would bring joy into her life. There was Prince Henry's death, and then Princess Mary's . . ."

"Her husband and three children—all lost," Mary Boynton murmured, "and people say that the Duchess of Orleans is excessively delicate. The Queen Dowager must have been very anxious when her baby was born."

"So was I," Frances said, which was true though her manner was absent and her voice unconcerned. She was pulling off the cord from a parcel which only a few minutes before had been brought to her by one of the Queen Dowager's pages.

The two other girls laughed. They could not imagine that

the gay Frances was ever anxious or worried. She was more carefree than any of them, though her mother and her young sister and brother had been in Scotland for months, and it was known that Frances had no real home and but little money. Nothing seemed to cause her concern; and although they were rather shocked by her intimacy with Barbara Castlemaine, they envied her too, because the proud beauty paid no attention to them. Nor did the splendid Buckingham, who flirted so audaciously with Frances and could be beguiled by her into playing any childish game she fancied.

"You will see," Joan said, "for the next few weeks or months, or as long as the Queen Dowager is here, the Castlemaine will retire to her country home where she keeps her children well out of sight."

"That won't suit the King," Mary Boynton opined. "Whatever his mother may say, he will soon have her back again. Frances Stuart, what in the world have you got there? Oh, how exquisite!"

Frances had brought forth a length of pale-green and silver brocade from the parcel. She held it up against her slim figure, dexterous fingers fashioning folds of it into the semblance of a tight bodice.

"A present . . . from my cousin, from *Madame* of France," she said proudly. "It will make a charming gown."

The two other girls, somewhat older and both daughters of rich noblemen, gazed with envy. Frances was constantly receiving costly presents. On her sixteenth birthday there had been shoals of them from France—even a jewelled bangle from King Louis. She might be comparatively poor, yet in some ways she seemed to have more than either of them, they both reflected.

9

". . . and when your dear mother returns from Scotland she will tell you precisely what I have told you," said Henrietta-Maria. "This friendship with Lady Castlemaine is not *comme il faut*. The Queen, my daughter-in-law, has hesitated to speak of it, but she is in complete agreement with me."

It was the end of a long lecture to which Frances had listened with becoming docility. She sat at some little distance on a carved stool which the Queen Dowager had indicated at the beginning of the interview.

"But I thought . . . Barbara is one of the Queen's ladies. It is impossible to be cold and unpleasant to her. Besides, the Queen is not that." Frances, unable to hide her resentment, spoke with more defiance than she would have dared to show while living at Colombes.

"Diplomacy, my child, is sometimes essential. It should not be necessary for me to say more. You are not a child, though my daughter has said time and again that you are taking a long while to grow up. She does not forget you. She writes frequently, does she not?"

"Oh yes, Your Majesty." Frances was eager now. "When you sent for me, I hoped that it was to talk of her—that there might be messages, though she did send a short letter with the lovely brocade."

"Suzanne, who is here with me, and whom you no doubt remember, will make up the gown according to a sketch which Henrietta-Anne herself devised for you. I was entrusted with several messages, and was asked to be sure to show you this."

Evidently, thought Frances with relief, the lecture was

over, and she had not been required to give any definite promise to break off her friendship with Barbara. And why in the world should she? It was absurd! In Paris, after Henrietta-Anne's marriage, she had consorted with fine ladies who were every bit as lax as Barbara, and who were yet *persona grata* at Court. One just ignored that side of their lives, thought Frances grandly. It might or might not be true that Barbara and the King were no longer lovers. If they were, Queen Catherine countenanced it; and if she so disapproved of Frances' intimacy with her rival, she should have had the courage to say so, not left it to her mother-in-law. Of course one understood that Catherine feared to provoke the King, but if she had spoken in confidence it would have been respected. "And I could even have told her that with Barbara it is now Monsieur Jermyn . . . or no . . . perhaps I could not . . ."

"Come now, are you not interested?" the Queen Dowager asked reprovingly.

"Your Majesty! Yes, indeed . . ."

"You are still a dreamer, I see. Your dear mother so often complained of your inability to concentrate on your studies, and on many other things, for that matter . . ."

Henrietta-Maria had drawn a gold, pearl-studded chain from the bosom of her gown. An elaborately chased gold locket, also encrusted with pearls, depended from it. This she snapped open. Within was a delicately tinted miniature of a little face above bare, dimpled shoulders.

"My grandchild," Henrietta-Maria announced with fond pride.

"Oh, but she is an angel," cried Frances, though wondering why a grandchild should seem a novelty to the Queen Dowager. Everyone knew that Jemmie was Charles' son by Lucy Walters. And there were Barbara's children as well, and Princess Mary's son in Holland, let alone the Duke of York's baby daughter.

"Yes. She is a beautiful babe," the Queen Dowager agreed. "But my poor Henrietta—she suffered greatly. For a time we were all in the most agonizing fear. And then, when she revived, she was for a while so disappointed her infant was not a son."

Frances shivered slightly. Her dear 'Rietta! She could not bear to think of it—had indeed frequently thrust the thought away from her.

"I knew the day that she expected. She had told me. She was always delicate and so . . . so tiny. Believe me, Your Majesty, she was never out of my mind."

"Ah well, that is all over now, and the dear child has made a good recovery. We must all pray for a son and hope there will not be the same danger with this next one."

"The next one?"

The Queen Dowager, although not given to laughter, did laugh now at the horror in Frances' voice.

"*Mais certainement!*" she said. "It will be in the late spring. *Madame* is overjoyed."

"Then—then of course I am also joyful," Frances said correctly and with complete insincerity.

"It is the great happiness of marriage, Frances. The birth of such sweet babes atones . . ." But here the Queen Dowager broke off and said: "It is with dear Mistress Stuart that I should be discussing such a matter, though you are now of marriageable age and one hopes you will soon have a good, kind husband, and a sweet expectancy for yourself."

"I hope it won't be just yet." Frances could not refrain from blurting out the words, but hastened to obliterate them by saying: "My mother has written, Your Majesty. She will soon be returning to London, would have been here ere now, only that little Walter has been ill. Besides, all our relations in Scotland are loath to part with her. She will be grieved if she does not see you before you leave England."

"I shall be here for some weeks. I also have heard from your mother. I will reply to her letter." The Queen Dowager made a slight dismissing gesture to signify that the interview was at an end and Frances rose from the stool. "Do not forget what I have said, child. Queen Catherine, as you should realize, is in a most disagreeable and delicate position with regard to Lady Castlemaine. I rely on your tact. No open rupture but a gradual withdrawal from this association. It will be the easier for you, because Lady Castlemaine will be staying at her Richmond home for some time, the Queen having graciously given her leave of absence."

Frances curtseyed in silence and kissed Henrietta-Maria's outstretched hand. She had made no promise and her foremost thought was that it would be very dull without Barbara, especially now that the summer was over. Queen Catherine's "graciously given leave of absence" was, as Frances knew, virtual banishment, though Catherine would not have ventured to impose it without the weighty backing of the Queen Dowager.

Not that Barbara would care overmuch. She was bored when at Hampton Court, and was, Frances suspected, far more interested in young Mr. Jermyn than in the royal father of her children. And Henry Jermyn had also vanished for the nonce from the Court circle. Frances thought it probable that Barbara had enticed him away.

She had hoped it would be livelier when the Court was at Whitehall for the winter. The King might be sad and oppressed when living in the vast building where his martyred father had met his fate, but Barbara's luxurious suite of rooms was near to his own private apartments, and she was adept at dispelling his moodiness. She had original ideas; so had Buckingham, her useful collaborator; and the King's tastes for which they catered were well-known. Wit, charm, originality—he demanded all three in any entertainment devised for him. Spiced with impudence they might be, but brazen vulgarity bored as well as repelled him, and of this his favourite in inventing masques, charades and ballets, to please him, was guiltless. Lasciviousness was presented either with scintillating wit or a polish that could not have been excelled even at the Court of Le Roi Soleil.

Many such forthcoming plans had been discussed, but Frances now wondered if they would be carried out. As the autumn days shortened, she became dismally certain they would not. Truly all had become excessively dull. The

Chevalier de Gramont held his gaming parties evening after evening, not in the least regretful that the King, taking Buckingham and young Jemmie with him was at Newmarket, where it was said that he was actually training and exercising his race-horses, and for once revelling in the camaraderie of his own sex.

Affairs of State were reduced to a minimum. Even for the King living was rough, and fair ladies would have turned up their delicate noses at the sight of their gallants in perpetually stained and muddy clothes and smelling of the stables. Such interludes were occasionally welcomed by the King, who since the arrival of the Queen Dowager had been so lectured and exhorted that he had with difficulty preserved his patience.

Yes, even the winter at Whitehall was likely to be tedious, thought Frances, forgetful of the fact that in the old days at Colombes her present life would have seemed wildly gay. She was as bored by the continual gambling as was the King himself, and no longer had the heart to irritate De Gramont. Henrietta-Maria's piercing eye was upon her, and evening after evening she perforce sat meekly with the two Queens and their ladies, while they listened to ballad concerts and lute players.

There was also the matter of religion. Both Queens being devout Catholics, much time was spent at their devotions in Catherine's private chapel, and Frances, to whom religion meant no more than a conventional exercise, was expected to follow their example. She could only submit, for a letter of petulant complaint to her mother in Scotland brought a swift rebuke. Frances must remember their poverty, which in spite of the King's money-grant to Mistress Stuart at his Restoration, and the help given since by many of their Highland kinsfolk, was still a source of embarrassment. Queen Catherine had it in her power to dismiss Frances, if she chose, which would be a calamity for them all.

"You have forgotten, it seems," wrote Mistress Stuart, "the importance of your Court appointment, and your general flightiness may well bring you to grief. It is time that your thoughts turned upon more serious considerations than frivolous pleasure. I had hoped that ere now they would have been directed towards a desirable alliance. Owing to poor little Walter's recent illness I have been advised that it would be unwise to take him on a long journey which might throw him into a fever, otherwise Sophie and he and myself would have been in London by now. This, I now fear, will be delayed until after Christmas. It will be a great grief to me if my dear mistress, the Queen Dowager, leaves again for France and I have missed the opportunity of seeing her. Commend me to her, I pray you. I have the greatest envy of you that you are able to see her day by day. God grant that all will be different in the spring, when one of our Blantyre cousins has offered to put his London house at my disposal and for as long as I may need it. Then, my child, I trust I shall have the leisure to attend to your affairs. . . ."

There was a great deal more. Frances could not remember when her mother had written her such a long letter. But she was in no mood to read it from the first word to the last. It could wait. Her lovely face was darkened by a petulant scowl as she put the closely written sheets away in her bureau. It was plain that her mother was disappointed with her. She must have hoped for a rapturous letter about some rich nobleman who was paying her serious attention.

Frances guiltily admitted there was no chance of this, since she had frivolously rebutted any and every courtier who had shown a sign of being serious. She had shown more favour to Buckingham than to anyone else, for he had charm and looks and he amused her. But at the same time she was on friendly terms with Buckingham's adoring young wife, who gazed at Frances with trusting and admiring eyes. The possibility of betraying this young wife, who had been Mary Fairfax and wooed for her fortune, did not enter Frances' head. All she wanted was to flirt heedlessly, not to become romantically enamoured of any particular individual.

Dismissing her mother's letter from her mind, Frances put

on a cloak with a warm hood, and, although it was cold and damp, went out into the grounds. She was weary of the company of the three other maids-of-honour whom she had left playing battledore and shuttlecock in the long gallery; she was even more weary of her dutiful attendance on Queen Catherine, who, although she must, Frances supposed, be missing the King, was complacent because Barbara had been banished, and the King was at Newmarket without her or any other lady to divert him.

Nobody was about, and never had the beautiful Hampton Court gardens looked less inviting. The leaves on the trees were falling, the flowers touched by the first frosts were fading.

"A few months ago it all looked so wonderful," mourned Frances, remembering the sunshine and the sparkling river and her first exciting meeting with Barbara. "I've become dull and old already," she thought foolishly. "It's all prayers and duty and goodness. Everyone really interesting has left Hampton, and who can wonder?"

By this time she was so sorry for herself that tears sprang to her eyes, which surprised her, for she rarely wept. Luxuriating in her grief, dramatizing it, she suddenly realized that this was ridiculous and giggled feebly as she caught a large, salt tear on the tip of her tongue.

Dabbing her eyes with her kerchief, she was about to turn back to the palace, when she heard the clatter of horse's hoofs and glanced round to see two horsemen riding up the drive. An instant later she realized that the foremost was the King himself, and he at the same moment recognized her. Swiftly dismounting, he flung the reins of his horse to the groom who followed him, and strode towards her.

Evidently he had ridden hard and for some distance. His wig was disordered and his clothes were dusty; but his warm, brilliant smile flashed out, and perhaps because his eyes were so friendly, Frances' heart warmed to him. It was only at rare moments that she had felt any particular liking for Charles or was affected by the charm of which so many women spoke languishingly, but this was one of them.

The groom rode off to the stables and Charles took Frances' hands in his.

"La Belle Stuart in tears!" he teased. "I would not have thought you were given to them, though, as I know to my cost, women weep easily."

"I am not one who does," Frances instantly retorted and forgetting to curtsey. "But it is a melancholy afternoon— everything seems so . . . one becomes affected."

"Nothing more serious than that? I expected to hear of a love trouble which mayhap I could have put to rights for you."

"I have no love troubles, Your Majesty."

Charles looked at her keenly and then said: "Upon my word, I believe you! It would not surprise me to find that for all those melting blue eyes you have a hard little heart."

"Oh no, Sire!" Frances was indignant, for had she not been shedding tears because of a forbidden friendship. "When I am attached to anyone it means a great deal to me. It is grievous to be told that I must give them up."

"And was that why you were weeping?" Charles still held one of her hands and now he led her towards a rustic seat nearby. "Sit down and tell me about it."

"But the Queen will be awaiting Your Majesty."

"Nothing of the kind. I am not expected for another day or so. But at Newmarket the weather was bad—continual rain this last week—and I decided to return. I outstripped the others on the road. They won't be here for another half-hour at the least. We have time enough."

He was genuinely curious and for the first time felt a flicker of more than casual interest in her. To Charles she had been only one of the many pretty girls he saw at Court, though Barbara had taken a fancy to her and he was aware that Buckingham greatly admired her. His beloved Minette was responsible for her appointment, and that alone, he thought, should have evoked his interest. But of late there had been such pother between his women-folk that he had thankfully taken refuge with his male cronies.

Newmarket had been a respite, but it was too far from

London where many affairs of State needed his attention, and he had dallied there too long. This and not the inclement weather was responsible for his return, and perhaps, too, he had been moved by the Queen's letters which revealed an uncomplaining loneliness. In any case he had decided to spend a day and a night at Hampton Court before he left for Whitehall.

But now Frances had caught his vagrant attention and his wife's loneliness could wait. Suddenly he recalled a scene which had seemed to be entirely forgotten.

A shabby room in a French château. A galaxy of laughing, chattering young girls, one of whom was wrapping another in a shrouding fur cloak, and who had on his entrance turned a surprised face towards him.

"By the lord, I remember now! You were the one that I mistook for my sister, not having seen her since she was a child!" he exclaimed.

Frances laughed and coloured.

"Oh, that was too bad! Poor, darling 'Rietta. I had hidden her in my fur cloak. It was the one respectable-looking garment we possessed between the lot of us. I was persuading her to wear it, but she is smaller than I, and it was far too big for her."

"You were in my arms and I had kissed you before I discovered my mistake. After that you seemed to disappear."

"Your Majesty did not notice that at the time. Why *should* you have noticed it? Your visit was to her, and of course you were soon enchanted with her. We were all so happy for her. She had been longing to see you again. Though I must say," added Frances reflectively, "that as I was very young and silly in those days and eager for attention, I'm surprised I had the wit to put myself in the background."

At this candour Charles burst into delighted laughter. "And are you so wise and old now?" he enquired.

"Well, more so—or at least I should be, Your Majesty."

"No majesties when we are alone, Frances. Are we not cousins? Now tell me why you were alone here and spoiling your pretty eyes with tears. Or shall I make a guess at it? The most obvious one is that you are in trouble with Mam, through neglect of your religious duties or some prank that was brought to her attention."

"No-o! I am not exactly in trouble with the Queen Dowager. She was very kind to me—and it wasn't only what she said, but what my mother wrote from Scotland. They are right, I suppose, but they don't *seem* right to me. When I was a child I was taught that one of the predominant virtues was to be faithful to a friend, and I try to be, I like to be . . . so do you, sire."

"I hope so," Charles agreed, momentarily sobered.

"Everyone says it of you. You remember all who shared the years of exile, who suffered through their devotion to his late Majesty. My mother was only one of the many you recompensed."

Charles brushed this aside with a gesture.

"Who is persuading you, my pretty one, to be other than loyal? And what friendship is it that is so precious to you? Who is the lucky man?"

"Not a man at all, and it's not only the friendship I hate to give up, but all the fun that goes with it. Parties and laughter and dressing-up for charades, and games and meeting amusing people who have been kind to me. There were such years and years of dullness at Colombes. I feel as though it would kill me if I had to live like that again. Well, of course it couldn't be as bad in one way, because there would be always enough to eat and fires to keep one warm. But it would be worse in another, because I am far away from 'Rietta."

"You love my little Minette so much?"

"Oh, dearly, dearly. What wouldn't I give to see her again!"

"Yet you were ready to leave her, to join the Court here?"

"Britain is my home . . . and we were exiles. Besides, everything had changed. Henrietta-Anne was *Madame* of France; she had become so important and she was wrapped up in the thought of the babe she was expecting. It wasn't the same. . . . We still loved one another, but—sometimes I thought I was disappointing to her. She said I was taking a long while to grow up."

Charles, to whom his sister still seemed no more than a dear child who had been cruelly sacrificed to political ends, married to one who was personally detestable to him, and whose perversions could no longer be glossed over or ignored, sighed before he smiled.

"Exactly how old are you, my pretty cousin? Seventeen—eighteen?"

"Sixteen."

"Then I would say there was no hurry to acquire the sedateness of years. Has anyone here been finding fault with you?"

"Not—not exactly; though my mother writes that I ought to be considering marriage. It's only natural. I am the eldest—she would be glad to have me settled—to have one less to worry about. She seems to think it odd there is not anyone especially. But I don't want there to be. It was all such fun until . . . oh, why must everyone always be so serious and thinking of the future?"

"Why indeed?" said Charles, who shared Frances' gift for living in the present.

"Today is important, too. There is so much sorrow. Why shouldn't one be gay and enjoy oneself whilst one can? Is that so wrong? Barbara says it is one's duty."

"Does she? It is not a word I have often heard her use."

"She says glum faces are an offence to everyone, and it's true. Think how the people all hated the Puritans who thought it a sin to laugh. But it isn't only that . . . everyone thinks ill of her because . . . oh, because . . . I don't care what they say. I won't give her up," ended Frances confusedly but with emphasis.

"Who has said that you should give her up? Your mistress, the Queen?"

"No—oh no!" Although Frances had a strong suspicion that Catherine had prompted the Dowager Queen's lecture, Catherine had been too kind to deserve disloyalty.

95

Charles was frowning. His dark face looked older and heavier. Why, Frances wondered, did so many women fall in love with him? He was really ugly. For herself she was unaffected by his famed charm, though she had found it easy to talk to him and had readily turned to him as a friend.

If not Catherine, it was certainly his mother, who could not forbear to meddle, Charles reflected. Although he often wearied of Barbara's demands, of her tantrums and extravagances, he would not brook interference; and if in his absence she had been dismissed, she would be recalled.

"The Queen Dowager thinks it an unsuitable friendship," Frances admitted impulsively. "She hinted that unless I behaved more discreetly I might lose my appointment as maid-of-honour . . . might be sent away."

"Not with my permission, and you could not be banished without it."

"Oh, Charles!"

"Never before has my name sounded so well," Charles said, laughing at her.

Frances also laughed, but she was truly grateful, and in her gratitude she was beautiful in a new way. Womanliness shone through her superficial childishness as she turned her great eyes upon him. Charles' natural taste was for more sophisticated beauties, but now he was moved by her, and he veered. What could be more entrancing than aquamarine eyes still dewy with tears; more enticing than a flawless skin flushed by a fruit-like bloom; more appealing than fair, disordered curls and a mouth which, even in grief, trembled upon a smile?

"Why, my pretty one!" he exclaimed, and his arm was around her, drawing her in her warmth and sweetness towards him. "I would no more allow you to be banished than I would allow Minette to be sent away from me, if by good fortune I could have her here in England."

"Oh, how I wish you could!"

"So do I, but it is useless to pine for the impossible, and I am disposed to content myself with such delights as *are* possible. The Queen Dowager means well, but she is . . . her

96

ways are not always mine. Soon we shall all be leaving here, and then she will have her own Court, and apart from State functions will have little concern for the régime at Whitehall."

"And Barbara will return to London?"

"Assuredly. Nothing but my express decree could keep her away."

Frances sighed with pleasure.

"She had planned so much. There were to be the most exciting frolics."

"I do not doubt it."

Charles looked down on the lovely, innocent face and perhaps felt a moment of remorse. In his heart he knew that his mother was right. This exquisite, heedless child should be preserved from Barbara Castlemaine and her kind; preserved from him. But she was in no danger, he assured himself virtuously. Minette had entrusted her to him. She, at all events, had had confidence in him. He would have a word with Barbara—impress on her that his young cousin was to be respected and guarded.

For the moment, although he had no illusions about himself or his capacity for knightly chivalry, he was sincere. And Frances, with the astonishing intuition of which she was capable, guessed the thoughts that passed through his mind and secretly smiled. She was safe—completely safe with Charles, so long as she did not fall in love with him, and that was unlikely. He was her King and her cousin, and in many ways she admired him, but she also had a real affection for the Queen and had no intention of adding to her troubles.

But Charles could make everything wonderful for her, so why should she not harmlessly charm him? Actually she would be doing the Queen a favour, Frances decided, and her heart should be set at rest. Barbara was now in love with Henry Jermyn, and, according to gossip, there was no other woman who had captured the King's fancy.

Only herself... and she would be no menace to Catherine's happiness, since, whatever Charles might later expect, she

97

had no intention of succumbing to him. Frances might seldom consider the future, but she knew what she wanted from it, and it was not the position of a royal mistress. As for the present which she constantly assured herself was sufficient for many a day, all she craved was excitement and pleasure. And as Charles was of the same mind, why not make the most of his newly aroused interest and affection?

Although she refrained from putting her thought into words, the thought was there. He would never force her to be what she did not want to be, or take her against her will.

Frances, with wonder, saw Charles bestir himself on her behalf. She could not doubt that it was for her when she received the gift of a sapphire and diamond star brooch, accompanied by a brief letter in the King's handwriting. Barbara would be at Whitehall the following week, he wrote, so would all the Court. She must keep up her heart. The brooch was a belated present for her sixteenth birthday, which he should have remembered before, as Minette had mentioned it in a letter.

That brooch was the first of other jewels which Charles bestowed upon Frances during the winter months, but such gifts were customary to ladies of the Court, and nobody apparently remarked on the fact that the pearls given on Twelfth Night and the diamond ring on St. Valentine's Day were more than usually costly.

The Queen Dowager held her Court at Greenwich Palace to which flocked many of the more sober spirits amongst the nobility. Barbara had her own suite as before at Whitehall, and it was impossible to deny that Queen Catherine was neglected. Worse than this, she was surrounded by enemies of whom George Villiers, Duke of Buckingham, was the most dangerous. He had the ear of the King and used every opportunity to underline Catherine's deficiencies—to insinuate that she was a bigot and a prude, who evidently hated her husband's country; that she had no looks and a rigid stiffness which took the place of dignity.

Allowed unmeasured freedom of speech, Buckingham reported to Barbara that the King, though he pretended to ignore or not to listen to the remarks about his wife, was normally glum these days. Barbara, when she was in a good mood and bent on conciliating him, could always make him laugh, and in the closing weeks of 1662 she was seen everywhere with him and the Queen. To those who did not know the circumstances it might have been thought that she was Catherine's bosom friend, for she drove with the royal pair in their coach, was with them at Court functions, and when a great ball was given on the last day of the Old Year Charles singled her out to dance the brantle and the coronto.

Frances appeared to receive no more of the King's favour than many others, for, although Charles was now fully alive to her attractions, he was cautious. Barbara was indulgent and actually appeared to throw Frances in his way. Catherine and the Queen Dowager were unsuspicious, for it was Buckingham who paid Frances open attentions.

"Your Mary and the Queen must have much in common," Barbara told Buckingham with some disdain. "They both endure more from their husbands than I would endure from any man, legally united to me or not."

"Mary knows better than to baulk me. Moreover, she understands me," Buckingham said with complacency.

"Then it is more than I do, George. My idea was that, in order to free me occasionally, Frances might divert Charles and distract his jealous attention, but she seems to prefer you, and you encourage her. You partner her in all her pranks."

"I find La Belle Stuart refreshing," said Buckingham nonchalantly. "And in some respects our tastes are similar. In mimicry, for instance, and music. She has a tuneful voice."

"Better than yours. Nobody can doubt it when you sing duets. As for mimicry, she is an impudent rogue. Imitating me to my face as she did."

"Flatteringly, Barbie. The child has nothing but admiration for you."

"Borrowing my sables and my velvet cloak and a red wig," Barbara said; but she laughed, for Frances had prevailed upon a dozen courtiers to follow her meekly on their hands and knees and had spurned them with an elegantly shod foot. The King had been immoderately amused, for this was how it pleased him to think of Barbara. His, but scorning all others. It has also satisfied Henry Jermyn, her present secret lover, who was every bit as jealous as the King.

Barbara certainly bore Frances no resentment for her spirited impersonation. Men were absurd. Though with no inclination to faithfulness, they were threatened with an apoplexy if they suspected their women folk of a like veniality.

"I wish I could fathom what is at the back of this," Barbara said with an uneasiness new to her.

"Why should there be anything but a pleasant dalliance? Frances Stuart is a butterfly born to amuse and delight, but there is no guile in her."

"I am inclined to believe that."

Buckingham regarded his cousin thoughtfully. Barbara was obviously conscious of undercurrents and aware of Frances' developing personality. Sure of her domination over the King, she had not considered Frances as a rival, but by now a doubt must have struck her. How far, Buckingham wondered, could he expect Barbara to co-operate with him.

"This marriage with Catherine of Braganza is already tottering," he stated.

"Small wonder with such subtle undermining. But your personal dislike of her apart, what could either of us gain by a divorce and another marriage? Catherine, the poor moppet, has come to terms. She is of little obstruction to me; whereas another more attractive Queen, with influence over Charles because he was in love with her, could send us both into permanent exile."

"Not if this more attractive Queen chanced to have a *penchant* for both of us."

The remark was thrown out casually, the while Buckingham gazed from the window upon the street beneath and the people who passed by. But Barbara was too quick-witted to be deceived.

"You can't mean—not Frances Stuart?" she cried; and then as Buckingham did not immediately reply, "You do mean it! You devil! Oh, I see it all now. Every action of yours has a sinister motive. Your foolery with the girl is to inflame Charles. You plan that he shall rid himself of the Queen . . . for her. But I'll have none of it! I warn you I'll have none of it."

"Calm yourself!" Buckingham turned from the window. "This is a fantasy of your own devising. How think you could I bring such a thing about, even if I desired it?"

"It might not be so impossible."

"I'm bound to say," observed Buckingham, "that if La Belle Stuart were Queen, the Court would be livelier, for you and I would be the powers behind the throne."

"That is of no consideration to me. It is well enough as it is. I *have* power. The Queen is amenable and the country is at peace. Who knows what the repercussions in Europe would be were Catherine divorced. . . ."

"My sweet life, you are putting the strangest notions into my head!"

"Can you swear they were not there before?"

"On my honour," Buckingham vowed without hesitation, "I did but dally with the suggestion when you presented it."

"*I* present it?"

"Be realistic, Barbie. Even if this marriage were dissolved, Charles could not marry you, much as he might wish it; but he could make an alliance with a young girl of his own royal blood."

"Much diluted!" Barbara exclaimed scornfully.

"A young girl of untarnished reputation. Strong and healthy, who would give him children," Buckingham continued.

Barbara was furious. She stormed: "Unless you make an end of this I shall tell Charles what you plan."

"Do not—for your own sake. You might find him not unwilling to fall in with it."

They glared at each other. Buckingham had little fear, for, as he knew, Barbara was loyal to her own kin. But she had every fear, for she had long since discovered his devious nature. If it suited him, he would betray her with a smile.

"This," she said, mastering herself, "sees the end of my association with Frances Stuart. I will no longer count her a friend."

"But the girl is entirely innocent. She hasn't a remote idea," Buckingham protested, cursing himself for his lack of caution.

"That may be, but she will do better to dance attendance on the Queen, to work on her embroidery with the other girls, and to pray in the Queen's Oratory. I mean what I say, George."

Buckingham had no doubt of it and he groaned in spirit when at Barbara's next party there was no sign of Frances, with whom Barbara had contrived an adroit quarrel. The girl's impersonation of her served as an excuse, to Frances' bewilderment, for at the time Barbara had seemed much entertained.

"I have no use for false friends," Barbara declared, lashing herself to anger. "In future, Frances Stuart, you will go your way and I will go mine."

"But it was no more than a frolic," Frances protested, seeing her bright dreams for the future fading.

"Possibly, but I prefer to devise my own. Go play your childish games with those other little white mice of maids, and do not think to sharpen your wits on me. The Queen will be only too pleased if you seek shelter again beneath her wing."

At the first of her parties, which Frances did not attend but which Charles did, Barbara made glib excuses. The Queen had a prior claim on the girl. Frances had found it impossible to get away. But such specious explanations could not be spun out indefinitely. Charles sought Frances and demanded an explanation.

"I offended Barbara by my mimicry of her. She seemed to take it in good part, but it was a pretence. I hurt her feelings," Frances said.

"Nonsense. She was as amused as I was."

"She *appeared* to be. I am *miserable* about it," Frances told him. "I am fond of her and I admire her. I meant no harm."

"Of course you did not. That was obvious."

It was also obvious to Charles that someone had been making trouble, though in this case he acquitted both his wife and his mother.

"I expect she will come round," said Frances, who, although she avowed that she was miserable, did not seem to be particularly so. She was touched because Catherine had been so pleased to have her with her.

"You shall read one of the English books aloud to me in the evenings," Catherine said. "It will help me to improve in the language and will be less tedious for you than the embroidery, half of which it has been necessary for Mary to unpick. The King is pleased when I speak better in English, and it is your duty to please him, is it not?"

Frances was conscious of the earnest sweetness of the small, dark face. Surely Charles, for all his casualness, must be fond of her. But as for pleasing him . . .! The way in which Frances could best please him would not commend itself to the Queen, who trusted her and was so kind to her.

"The other girls are contented enough, why can't I be?" Frances wondered, but Mary and Joan were already betrothed and would be married by the end of the year, and even for little Anne there were rumoured plans.

However, the few winter evenings, which she now devoted to her royal mistress, reading aloud William Shakespeare's *As You Like It*, and answering Catherine's questions when she came upon a word or sentence which puzzled her, were not so dull as she had expected.

As usual, gaming tables were set up at the other end of the vast chamber, but in the Queen's far corner the little group around her unexpectedly enjoyed themselves, for Frances not only read but acted some of the parts. The other girls, though they could not match her ability, joined in. The Queen listened with pleasure, throwing back her ringlets as she laughed.

Meanwhile Charles questioned Barbara, who had for so long treated him with impunity that now when challenged she threw aside all caution and stated flatly that Frances had become impudent and treacherous, and that she had had enough of her.

"Nobody, not even you," shrilled Barbara, "can force me to receive that girl in my own apartment or to have any private dealings with her."

Time was when her rages had intimidated the King, but now he was unaffected. Two of his petted spaniels had followed him, and he seemed more engrossed with them than attentive to Barbara as she worked herself into a fury, conscious that these tornadoes but increased her beauty. Up and down the long, luxuriously furnished room flounced the beauty, her seductively exposed bosom heaving tumultuously, her great eyes flashing, her jewelled hands clenched.

No soothing or conciliating words were forthcoming from Charles, who watched her sardonically from beneath hooded lids, the while he pulled caressingly at his spaniel's ears.

"A chit such as that to make game of me!" Barbara raged. "You should be indignant on my behalf, instead of defending her."

"Barbie, you know well that you are using this mimicry as an excuse. There was no malice in it, and it amused you."

"It did not! How could I make a scene in public?"

"It would not be the first."

"I did not choose to let everyone see that I was hurt and offended. Oh, what a fool I was to draw your attention to that uncouth schoolgirl. She is little more."

"Not in years, I grant you, but uncouth . . . she could never have been that. Frances had grace and beauty even when I first saw her at Colombes."

"You are in love with her! You are faithless to me, Charles. Oh, how can you? Do you never give a thought to our sweet babes, now hidden away at Richmond?"

Barbara came to a standstill before him, allowing her

worked-up fury to dwindle, throwing a plaintive appeal and a dulcet softness into her voice.

"What actresses you women are!" said an amused Charles.

"I am *not* acting. I mean every word. I will *not* receive Frances Stuart or have anything more to do with her."

"In that case, my dear, you will also have nothing more to do with me. Continue to give your entertainments as you choose, but I shall not be seen at them."

"Charles!" She wailed his name. "But you know ... you know they are devised for your pleasure and are of your choosing."

"The company should be also of my choosing." Charles rose.

Barbara cast herself upon him, dislodging the one spaniel he still held, who yapped at her indignantly and tore at her skirt. Barbara, with her foot, thrust the little creature away from her.

"Have a care! Trix is due to whelp at any time!" the King said, rescuing his pet.

Barbara angrily examined a shredded frill on her skirt.

"A female! The spiteful little brute! I might have known it!" she cried.

Charles, his good-temper restored, burst out laughing.

"Frances bears you no ill-will," he said. "A word from you will be enough. See that you speak it." He tapped her cheek good-naturedly and left her.

Barbara was incensed to the point of hysteria. Hitherto her rages had invariably brought Charles to heel. That peace-loving man, who hated scenes and was horrified to see the beautiful Barbara with panting bosom and bitten lips, had before now knelt to gather her in his arms, thereby incurring her everlasting contempt. But today it had not been so. He had patted her cheek much as he might have patted the head of the lumbering, pregnant Trix, and then he had left her to work off her rage at leisure. But if he thought for one moment that she could be so intimidated as to recall Frances ...

Barbara had no illusions about Charles. From time to time since she had become his mistress there had been other women, as there had been other men for her; but no other woman had succeeded in holding him. How could she suppose that Frances would—a mere child, beautiful though she might be?

Controlling herself at last, Barbara commanded her maids to pack for her and for themselves. Her coach was to be ready for her in an hour's time. She was leaving Whitehall for Richmond, and she stamped her foot when one and all protested that it would be impossible to be ready in so short a time. *Nothing* was impossible when she wished it. Not yet could Barbara believe that she was on the verge of eclipse. She might no longer love Charles—had she ever loved him? But he was essential to her. King he might be to all else, but not to her. Her beauty and vivacity had made him her slave. He had heaped honours and riches upon her and would heap more. When he realized that she had left Whitehall, not by anyone's orders but by her own will, he would come tearing after her as he had done before.

But it was Frances, not Charles, who was dismayed when she discovered that Barbara had departed without a forgiving word to her. The play-reading group had now attracted an audience. One evening, when the Queen was indisposed and did not appear, it progressed to full acting, with Frances enjoying the rôle of Rosalind and wishing that she could instil some of her histrionic flair into Joan Wells, who was the Orlando.

The Tzar of Muscovy had recently sent an imposing Embassy to England, and on this occasion the Ambassador was present. So was the King, and he laughed immoderately.

"'Alas the day! what shall I do with my doublet and hose?'" cried Frances in a panic, her eyes dilated and both hands pulling at her skirts, thereby exposing an exquisitely shapely leg almost to the satin-gartered knee. She broke off to giggle as she added: "It would be more seemly if I *were* dressed as a boy."

His Grace of Buckingham was listening with courtly

attention to the Ambassador, and then retailed his remark. The Ambassador had thought that only Russian women had such handsome legs.

"I vow you would find none to compare with those of La Belle Stuart," said Charles jocularly.

Fond though Frances was of the Queen, there was no doubt that her absence brought with it a sense of freedom, and, intoxicated by the general admiration, La Belle Stuart lifted her skirts a shade higher and executed a *pas seul*. The youthful bravado was ingenuous rather than provocative, and the laughing girl made a charming picture as she whirled down the long room.

The Duke of York alone was critical.

"Too slender," he pronounced; "the perfect leg should be shorter and thicker and, for perfection, should be encased in green silk stockings."

There was general laughter. Frances' stockings were of shell-pink. Milord Chesterfield uttered an explosive exclamation, and Lady Chesterfield made a hurried withdrawal. She was wearing green stockings of the finest silk, and most of those present knew that the Duke of York had of late been paying her marked attention.

"You will see," prophesied Mary Boynton later, "that milord Chesterfield, who is the most jealous husband in Christendom, will soon whisk her ladyship out of London."

"And he'll take her further than Richmond, where the Castlemaine has gone in the sulks," said somebody else.

Frances was struck to silence. She had been planning ways by which she might conciliate Barbara, and the news that she had left Whitehall was a shock. She was distrait when the King complimented her on her acting and her dancing.

"I should have more dignity," Frances said. "I get too excited."

"Not in the way I would have you excited," Charles said meaningly.

Frances evaded the fixed gaze of those hot brown eyes. She said: "But now I feel sober enough. Why has Barbara left London? Is she in disgrace with you?"

"More likely the jade would say I am in disgrace with her. What matter? She will return when it suits her—and chastened, let us hope. For once Barbie has failed to get her own way. My lovely romp, did you think I would countenance the slight she put upon you?"

"Did you send her away, Charles?" Frances persisted.

"No—but I told her that if she refused to receive you, then I should seek my pleasures elsewhere."

Frances was startled and distressed.

"Oh, but no! It mustn't be that way. I was giving Barbie time to cool, and then by some means or other I would have made my peace with her. I thought . . . well, I thought as you gave me several presents at Christmas, and as Barbie admired that gold belt clasp with the rubies . . . "

"My sweet Frances, I have given Barbara many jewels. All you possess would not fill one shelf of her smallest coffer."

"All the same, she *did* admire the clasp," Frances said stubbornly. "Rubies are her favourite gems, she said. I could not give it to her without your permission, but I hoped if I asked you . . . "

She broke off, and Charles gazed at her with a baffled expression. She acted like a child, yet not a child. She was tenderly yielding when he put an arm around her, though it occurred to him that the opportunities afforded him were strangely few. Her lips were the most promising. . . .

Although there were watching eyes upon him, he stooped and kissed her. An innocuous kiss for the great room was still adorned with the Christmas decorations, and he had only to steer her a few paces towards a sheaf of mistletoe depending from a rafter. That evening, more than one of the Court ladies had been saluted beneath it.

The promising lips promised nothing at all as his touched them. They were cool and uninterested—a child's lips.

"Have it your own way—give it to her, then, as a peace offering," he said.

"But I shall have to take it to her at Richmond. Suppose she has me turned away from her door?"

"I warrant that even Barbie would scarcely go so far, but if you have set your heart on this reconciliation, you must have an escort." And Charles beckoned to young Lord Berkeley, who was a general favourite at Court, and gave him instructions to take Frances to Richmond the following day.

"And bring that foolish jade Barbara Castlemaine back with you," Charles commanded, "since it seems that this equally foolish jade cannot be happy without her."

Although he spoke brusquely he was not ill-pleased. Barbara was still the mistress of revelry, and she had so much life and vitality that she inevitably made herself missed.

Young Lord Berkeley contrived to convey as much when the next day, after an insolent, long delay, Barbara consented to see him and Frances. Hearing that they were there, she had made a careful toilet and received them in state, with two women of her household in attendance. She had noticed, or believed she had noticed, a lack of deference in her servants since her hurried flight from London, almost as though the fools fancied she was no longer in the King's favour. Now they would see that he could not do without her, that he had sent his emissaries to beg her to return. Berkeley, a born diplomat, made it appear as though this was the case, and there was nothing in Frances' manner to contradict it, for she gazed at Barbara with entreating eyes.

Secretly Barbara was much relieved, for when three days had passed and the King had made no move she had been apprehensive, the more so when Buckingham had paid her a visit and, hearing an account of the scene she had inflicted on Charles, had told her she was a fool. He had not, he assured her with brazen insincerity, had any serious intention of using Frances as a bait to induce a royal divorce. It was a passing thought only, and even with Barbara's cooperation would have gone no further. It was no more than a fantasy and she had been wise to set her face against it, but not wise to provoke a quarrel with the King, and to so exasperate him that he would all the more readily be persuaded by his more sober advisers that it was time he reformed and treated the Queen with tenderness and consideration.

At this Barbara had scoffed.

"Charles," she said, "would not know how to reform. If there is anything he detests it is boredom, and who could be more boring than Catherine of Braganza, with her prayers and her pruderies, and her eyes following him as sentimentally as one of his wretched spaniels?"

"Charles is devoted to his spaniels," Buckingham reminded her, "and there is a rumour abroad that the Queen is pregnant. An heir to the throne is what he desires above all things."

Buckingham had left Barbara in a rare state of self-doubt. If the Queen were pregnant it would have a salutary effect on Charles, at least for some months. He might not be so urgent to recall her, and she certainly could not afford to stay away from Court until after the Queen's delivery. By then she would be practically forgotten, and there were others besides Frances eager to step into her shoes.

Frances was not eager. This, Barbara, who was shrewd enough when not giving way to temper, admitted. Frances was not in pursuit of place or power. She was harmless enough and would remain so unless Buckingham involved her in the mesh of his intrigues. Since he had dismissed the wild idea of so inflaming the King that he would be prepared to put her in Catherine's place, Frances might as well be forgiven, Barbara concluded, unaware that Buckingham's original plan would have been carried out without her help had it not been for the rumour of the Queen's pregnancy.

Therefore, when Frances pleaded, Barbara listened to her relentingly, and her eyes glistened covetously when Frances brought forth the case containing the ruby clasp.

"Please do take it," Frances begged, "and forget all this foolishness. It is wretched without you."

"It will certainly be wretched for us if you insist on staying here," Berkeley said. "The King's orders must be carried out on pain of his displeasure, and we were ordered to bring you back with us at all costs."

Barbara smiled at them and accepted the ruby clasp.

"As a peace offering, then," she said, "though indeed I am happy enough to be here, where all is so quiet and restful and I have time to bestow on my babies. In this rustication I had an intention of giving sittings to Mr. Lely—a family portrait with my little ones. If I return with you that must be postponed, for I would not have them exposed to the unwholesome London air."

"Can we not see them?" Frances asked eagerly and Barbara graciously assented. A messenger should be sent to the nurse to bring them down from the nursery.

Joyful to be restored to favour, Frances flitted about the room, admiring Barbara's many beautiful possessions. There were pictures that ravished her, cabinets containing ivories and miniatures. There was a large portrait by Huysman of Charles, which had been commissioned as a gift for Barbara when she had first become his mistress.

Then the three children were brought in, attended by two nurses, and Frances saw another facet of Barbara's character. The little girl and her brother ran to her with love and confidence, and Barbara caressed them and displayed them with pride. The baby boy was taken from the arms of his nurse and Barbara crooned over him. The two younger children bore a marked resemblance to the King and this was pointed out by their mother.

"Catherine of Braganza will never give him such lovely babes," Barbara said. "If she has a family, they may well look like little black savages, he and she both being so swarthy. They will never mean as much to him as my beautiful babes. He dotes on them."

"How could he help it?" Frances said, popping a sugar-plum into each willing mouth.

Barbara's maternal pride touched some hidden chord in her heart, though when she thought of having children it always evoked a shudder of fear and repulsion.

It might be worth it, she supposed, if one loved the father of one's children, and if they were as beautiful as these, though it might be that she could be just as fond of children who were not her own.

11

The rumour of the Queen's pregnancy was well founded, but a few weeks later she suffered a miscarriage; and although the young maids-of-honour were hustled out of the way while doctors came and went, afterwards, when the Queen shed bitter tears, Frances was in the room, and her soft if heedless heart suffered for her.

"Oh, what a miserable business this child-bearing is," she said rebelliously to Mary Boynton. "I hope I shall never have a sign of one."

"Then your marriage is not like to be happy," said Mary in her superior way, "for all men, of whatever degree, desire a son and heir."

"And as often as not quarrel with their heirs and disinherit them, or try to," Frances retorted. "Why should not a man and woman find themselves sufficient if they love? Why should one worry about the generations that come after?"

"It is natural to be proud of one's family and to wish to see it continue. As for the King, it is most important for him to have a legitimate son, otherwise the throne will pass to the Duke of York and his children, and as yet they have only girls."

"What matter? Wasn't Elizabeth a great Queen? It must have been wonderful to be her. Above all others, and refusing to give herself to any man. That would have suited me. All the power and the glory and the balls and the pageants, and men kneeling to kiss my hand, and promising those who courted me, but never being forced to keep the promise."

Mary, who was eager for her own wedding and looked forward to producing a family, eyed the Stuart girl with mingled scorn and wonder. If Frances thought she could plan her life on those terms she was even sillier than she appeared to be. By now there was a good deal of surreptitious gossip about the King's fondness for her, and it was not to be expected that she could hold him off for ever.

"Kissing her hand and being content with promises. Not King Charles," thought Mary sardonically, yet a shade enviously, for it seemed as though with every day careless Frances blossomed into greater beauty.

The King was kind to his wife over her disappointment and cheered her by saying that such mishaps often occurred early in marriage. In no time at all she would be hoping again. Barbara shrugged nonchalantly and cared not at all that for some weeks the King neglected to sup with her. Buckingham was smugly jubilant.

"A mishap that has happened once can happen again," he remarked to Frances. "It is often so with high-strung, jealous women who are in a fret and a fever when their husbands are out of their sight. You will see—this marriage is like to be as unfruitful as that of Katherine of Aragon, and Charles wants an heir as badly as did Henry VIII. Any childless Queen must be haunted by the memory of Anne Boleyn."

Frances retorted flippantly: "It's a memory to haunt any King's favourite. Better to keep one's head on one's body than to be Queen for a few years."

"Henry was a brute, but Charles is a horse of a different colour. He might divorce a woman but he would never have her executed," Buckingham said. "Don't let that worry you."

"Worry *me*?"

Frances, who had been plucking at the strings of a harp while Buckingham, who was no inconsiderable composer, tried out verses by Mr. Dryden, which he had set to music, now turned from the instrument and stared at him.

"If this marriage were broken the chance would be yours, Frances. Myself, I have nothing but admiration for your tactics. All men burn to the point of fever for that which is persistently denied them."

"If you mean the King . . .? I like him, he is kind to me, we are cousins."

"On the Blantyre side," Buckingham supplemented mockingly, having heard both Charles and Frances say the same thing. "It is not a near cousinship, and, even if it were, cousins, and more especially royal cousins, frequently marry."

"I would not have thought that even you could be so fantastical," Frances said, sobered as she was not often sobered. "Even if Charles were free, and I were royal, I could never care for him—romantically."

"A Queen does not need to be royal or romantic either. What of Anne Hyde, who now that she is York's wife is near to the throne? You would make a delicious queen, my pretty one, and what matter if unlike most women you are not enamoured of Charles? Queens can have their lovers. They are not all as prim as the little brown Braganza hen."

"This is an odd kind of humour. I don't understand it," Frances said, and indeed the sea-blue eyes were so blankly expressionless that Buckingham did not find this difficult to believe.

"You do not know your own power," he said, but now his voice seemed to mock her.

"I have none. I want none." She rose from her stool beside the harp and went out of the room without another glance at him.

But there was a turmoil in her heart which did not readily subside, though after a time she was able to tell herself that she had taken the rattle-pated Buckingham with unnecessary gravity. Did he not always say the first thing that came into his head? Had not Barbara been heard to declare that he never meant a word he said? Frances generally found him an engaging companion, for his extravagant exploits could move her to helpless laughter. Save on state occasions he rarely displayed any dignity at all.

Only yesterday a bevy of them had played Buckingham's version of "Animal Farm", and what riotous fun that had been. Frances, decked up as a peacock, racing through the long corridors and from one room to another with shrieks of laughter, had been pursued by a dozen or more ardent young men, who had been promised a kiss for every feather they could tweak from her. And then Buckingham had wrapped himself in fur rugs and had leapt out of a dark corner upon one of the Queen's dressers, who had not known such a game was in progress and had been scared nearly out of her wits. In the end he had sobered and had played on his lute and had commanded his little mouse-like wife to sing for them. And so she had with a surprising sweetness and clarity.

"Live with me and be my love," sang she who had been born Mary Fairfax, and they had all joined in the last verse.

"He did not mean it," decided Frances. "It was all an absurdity. He compared the Queen with Katherine of Aragon though there is no resemblance. Besides, even if there were, Henry's first wife had a daughter, and if the Queen gave him one, Charles would not disinherit her for anything in the world. Men are often proud of their daughters. *Monsieur* of France, peevish toad though he is, is proud they say of the little girl 'Rietta has borne."

It was ridiculous that for the space of a few minutes she had been frightened, Frances told herself.

Nevertheless, for the next day or two she avoided Buckingham and was thankful when, almost without warning, Mistress Stuart, with Sophie and little Walter, arrived in London. There was a letter delayed en route, and within a few hours of its arrival all the excitement of reunion.

The London house which the Blantyre cousin had lent Mistress Stuart was a pleasant one. There were servants who had been with the family for years and who were delighted to have a mistress who was kind and efficient and who promised them that she would be there for months, if not longer. The middle-aged housekeeper, and the not-so-young maids under her, the elderly butler, had been lost and aimless since the death of the last owners, an old couple who had gone within a few weeks of one another. The heir, who lived by choice in Scotland, had kept them in his service, but they had felt insecure, so the housekeeper told Mistress Stuart. There had been nothing said about the future, and their dismissal would not have surprised them. Now it was a joyful thing to welcome one of the Stuart family again, especially as there was the sweet little boy and the pretty Sophie on the threshold of young girlhood. Frances, when she called round on the first day of her family's arrival, found the confusion blissful. It was heaven just to see the trunks and baskets and scattered belongings. Did Sophie still have her dolls? "Why yes, though she was getting too old for them. She would soon be in her teens," said Mistress Stuart. But Frances found the puppets she had dressed while at Colombes out of odds and ends of material, and was as delighted as though they had been living beings.

She need not go back to Whitehall for a few days, she told her mother. The Queen had said she could stay with her family.

"That hardly sounds as though you have made yourself indispensable to Her Majesty," said Mistress Stuart with some misgiving.

"Indispensable? None of us is that. When Joan Wells was ill before Christmas there were a score of important people pressing the services of their daughters upon the Queen, but she has said more than once that she is pleased with me."

Frances was even lovelier, her mother thought, than in the days when as the friend of the young Duchess of Orleans she had been so admired. But she was still flippant and careless and as little disposed to take anything seriously. Questioned, she admitted to friendship with various young men, but nearly always qualified this by saying that they were already betrothed, and had been for years, to girls who even now were too young for marriage.

"There is a lot to be said," observed Mistress Stuart, "for these marriages that are so arranged. Parents know then that the future is settled for their sons and daughters, especially for their daughters, and need no longer worry about them. I only wish this had been possible in your case, but how could an exiled, widowed mother make any such safe provision for you?"

"I am thankful you could not," exclaimed Frances with her light laugh. "How I should have hated to feel that I was tied-up and settled. I don't want to feel that even now. There is time enough. Barbara Castlemaine often says she was far too young at seventeen to be married."

"You are not influenced, I hope, by anything that woman says or does," and Mistress Stuart cast an anxious glance at her daughter. "Naturally, as the Queen countenances her, you are obliged to meet her, but any real friendship would be preposterous."

"Yes, I suppose it would." Frances' too expressive face was averted as she played with her little brother.

She felt guiltily deceitful, but was thankful that in her letters to her mother she had rarely mentioned Barbara. She was also thankful, though Mistress Stuart was grievously disappointed, that the Queen Dowager had left for France to be with Henrietta-Anne, and would stay there until after the birth of her second child.

Although Mistress Stuart would be received by Queen Catherine, it was unlikely she would be seen much at Court. She was too preoccupied with the delicate little Walter, and it would be surprising if the Queen mentioned the friendship to her.

"The Queen, it is said, will be some time picking up her strength," Frances said conversationally.

"Poor soul! Rumours abound even as far away as Scotland, and it is said the marriage is doomed to failure, that the King cares nothing for her, and that, as the conditions of the marriage were not complied with, it will be annulled, and she sent back to Portugal."

Frances, who had been kneeling on the floor, assembling a quantity of small, carved, wood animals that she had brought for Walter as a present, sat back on her heels and stared at her mother in consternation.

"No such rumour has been heard here," she declared. "Nobody would dare . . ." She broke off, and a sense of fear swept over her as she recalled the scene with Buckingham and some of his disturbing remarks. "The King is vastly fond of the Queen," she asserted; "and as for the conditions of the marriage . . ."

"It is said that the dowry is still withheld, and that there was some flaw in the wedding ceremony itself. It could be so, as it was conducted in private at Portsmouth."

"Oh no! I cannot believe it. To be parted from him would break her heart," cried Frances, with her mind in chaos. "People spread these stories only for the love of the sensation they cause."

"That may well be," Mistress Stuart placidly agreed. "And the King has a kind heart—we all know that. He would not treat the Queen ill for the sake of such a woman as my Lady Castlemaine, whose favours have been his for many a day. But men are swayed by their desires; and should the King conceive a passion for a girl as virtuous as she is beautiful, who refused to listen to any but honourable proposals, who can say that he would not use to his advantage any loophole there might be in the marriage settlement or the way in which it was conducted?"

Frances was aghast. Her mother, of course, had no idea that her own daughter might possibly be the virtuous damsel to catch the King's fancy, but her prognostications opened up dangers that had not hitherto occurred to her. The impulse welled up in her heart to confide in her mother, but she swiftly dismissed it, for, after all, what was there to confide? The King was attracted to her; he had made tentative love to her, but it had been in a light-hearted vein, and Frances had had little difficulty in fending him off. Buckingham had uttered some mysterious, even sinister remarks, but with part of her mind, Frances still believed them to be ridiculous.

"I hope the Queen has twin sons as soon as may be," Frances cried, "and that will put an end to all such scandalous talk."

Mistress Stuart regarded her with approval. Frances, she thought, was not so feather-pated as she seemed. It was right that she should be loyal to the Queen. She was even better pleased when her daughter rushed into talk about her latest admirer, George Hamilton.

"You have heard of him perhaps, *Maman*. He is the son of Sir George Hamilton and well liked at Court. We often ride together, and we went hawking at Windsor when we were there for a week before the Queen fell ill. He is the most diverting person. Only imagine . . . he can hold a burning candle in his mouth and keep the lighted end of it there for minutes at a time."

Although Mistress Stuart was not singularly impressed by this feat, she was on the alert, since this was the first admirer that Frances had mentioned positively.

"The family is known to me by name," she allowed, "but this is only the second son, if I remember rightly. No doubt, like most younger sons, he has his way to make in the world."

"Oh yes, I dare say he has," Frances agreed, so evidently unconcerned that her mother was exasperated. What was *wrong* with the girl? She was of an age now to set her heart on a man, but it seemed as though none had the power to interest her seriously.

Frances, for her part, was thankful when at this juncture Sophie came in, proclaiming that she had unpacked all her mother's belongings as well as her own.

"She has become such a useful little thing, Frances," Mistress Stuart said approvingly. "It is arranged, you know, that on her thirteenth birthday Sophie will become one of the dear Queen Dowager's household. I could not wish a better start in life for her, and I am convinced she will do well."

"You will spend as much time in France as here, Sophie," Frances said half enviously. "You will often see my dear 'Rietta. You remember her, don't you?"

"Well, of course I do. I wasn't a baby when we lived at Colombes," Sophie said. "But I never thought much of the Princess Henrietta-Anne. She was very plain and thin and her hair was straight."

"She was only plain and thin because life was so hard in

those days. She changed and became beautiful before she married. Even King Louis said so."

"It is easy for princesses to be beautiful, for they have such clever *coiffeurs* and dressers," stated Sophie, "but you, Frances, were beautiful when you were practically in rags. And now they call you La Belle Stuart. Mamma says I have a strong resemblance to you." And the twelve-year-old Sophie paraded before a looking-glass with such complacency that her mother and sister both laughed at her.

Pleased though Mistress Stuart was to have the company of her elder daughter, she was uneasy over her absence from Court and glad when she returned to Whitehall. They could see each other nearly every day, Frances said blithely, though inclined to reproach herself because after the first excitement of reunion she had found it dull to be alone with her family.

There were several at Whitehall to welcome her with rapture, and the Queen, who was up and about again, was pleased to see her. Even though Frances had been away for such a short time there were a few new faces. The first evening her glance fell on a tall man at the Chevalier de Gramont's card table. He was extremely good-looking, Frances thought, tall and with dark hair and eyes. His finely cut features resembled those of a cameo. Yet he bore a slight likeness to the King.

The card game came to an end, and the stranger had evidently lost heavily. The Chevalier swept a pile of gold coins towards himself, and someone else took the place of the newcomer, who remained standing at the table, at first watching the play, but afterwards more intent on watching Frances as she sat near the Queen laughing at the antics of a company of professional tumblers who had been engaged to amuse the company that evening.

When this entertainment came to an end, the Queen retired, and kept Frances with her, though somebody had suggested an informal dance, and Catherine dismissed the others in order that they might join in it.

Frances did not object. She was pleased to see the Queen

again, pleased also that she looked as well as usual and did not seem to be unduly depressed. Moreover, it amused her to tantalize the King who had not been able to get a word alone with her the whole evening, though his eyes had devoured her. He would, she knew, expect to find her either in Barbara's apartments or joining in the dance which Barbara and her particular friends were unlikely to think worth their while. But he would be disappointed, thought Frances with some malice, for when the Queen dismissed her she would go to bed, carefully bolting her door, as she invariably did, though neither the King nor any of her admirers had as yet had the trepidity to follow her to her room.

"I missed you," Catherine said. "You have a sunny nature, Frances, and can generally cheer me. But I was happy to think you were with your mother again. You must have sorely missed each other."

"We had both become used to the separation," said Frances honestly, "but of course we are glad it is over and that we can now often see each other. I am sorry Your Majesty has needed cheer . . . sorry about what happened. I haven't had the chance to say so. I only saw Your Majesty for a few moments. We were all kept away from you."

"It was a sad disappointment," Catherine said simply, "but I am not brooding over it. The King was so kind and concerned and anxious for me to gather up my strength again. Later, in the spring or the early summer, we plan to spend some weeks at Tunbridge."

"So that Your Majesty can take the waters? I know they are said to be beneficial. At Bath too, especially if . . . when . . ."

"For women who have miscarried and desire to be *enceinte* again as soon as possible," Catherine said. "If the physicians are to be believed these spas are a great inducement to fertility. God grant they may be right, as of all things we desire a family—for our own happiness as well as for the sake of the country. Some women seem to achieve this state easily, but for others . . ." and the Queen sighed.

Frances knew she was thinking of the King's children born out of wedlock, and she said sympathetically: "Your Majesty has been married less than a year. Surely it is too early to be anxious. And at least this mishap proved . . ."

"That I am not barren," Catherine interposed. "Yes, there is that consolation. The King and I have found it so. But tell me about your mother and sister and the little brother. Are they comfortably settled? Is the little brother in better health?"

Answering these questions, it was some time before Frances had the opportunity to put one of her own.

"There are quite a few foreign guests at Court," she said. "I noticed especially the tall man in the dark suit with the silver embroidery."

"The Duke of Lennox and Richmond? I am surprised he was not presented to you. I suppose it was forgotten you had not yet met, since he has been here for a few days. He must be a distant kinsman of yours, for Charles says he is his fourth cousin. There is a resemblance between them, and the same name—Charles Stuart."

"Oh, I've heard of him," Frances cried, interested. "When we first knew we should be coming to England, my mother found out all she could about my father's cousins and even his more distant relations. She had not known them all when she lived with my father in Scotland. *This* Charles Stuart's father was Lord Aubigny, and his grandfather was the Duke of Lennox. Lord Aubigny was killed at Edgehill, poor man, and King Charles I then made this boy the Earl of Lichfield."

Catherine threw up her hands in amused protest.

"Me, I shall never fathom these English titles and the new names which suddenly appear. How is it, then, that he is now Duke of Lennox—and yes, Richmond?"

"He is quite an important person," Frances said reflectively. "I remember my mother said so. And there was one of those genealogical trees amongst my father's papers. I am interested in such things."

"You must be, to have carried it in your mind all this

long while. What an odd girl you are—or odd occasionally.
In Portugal I was naturally instructed in my ancestry, but I
cannot say that I took much interest in my remote connec-
tions."

"It is different with Scots," Frances explained. "We
have the name for being clannish beyond the ordinary.
Not that this Lennox lives in Scotland, nor ever has so far
as I know, though he owns much land there. He lives at
Cobham Hall in Kent. Long ago I saw a picture of it . . . oh,
a most beautiful place. . . ."

"But how is it, then, that he is now Lennox and Richmond
when he was at first Aubigny and then Lichfield?" The
Queen painstakingly pronounced the unfamiliar names.

"He hasn't been for very long. It is rather strange, Your
Majesty—romantic and sad too—but I dare say romantic
things often are sad. It does seem as though Lennox's
fortunes followed the King's fortunes, for it was in the
year of the Restoration that his cousin Esmé, who was
then the Duke, died suddenly, and Lichfield—he must have
been twenty or twenty-one—succeeded to the title and
estates and all the possessions."

"So he is now only twenty-three or four," said the Queen,
whose interest was caught. "He looks older. But I remember
the King spoke of a bereavement and also that he . . . but
it is possible that has been exaggerated."

Frances wondered what the Queen had heard about this
distant kinsman which she had been about to repeat but
had then decided against. She said: "He is married, I
believe."

"Twice, so the King told me, but both his wives died.
The second wife only a few weeks ago. You had not heard
of this?"

Frances shook her head. "I have heard nothing about
him, since I was told how as next-of-kin he had succeeded to
all that had been his cousin's. What I chiefly remembered
was the picture of Cobham Hall. I wondered if I should ever
see it."

"This young man has spent much of the last two years

there, I understand. The King told me he was no lover of Court life, and that he had not the address for a courtier."

The Queen spoke with reserve, as though, while ready to satisfy Frances' curiosity, she were putting a curb upon her tongue.

"Does the King dislike him?" Frances asked impulsively.

"How should I know, child? He spoke of him only in a passing way. It seems as though this young Duke has had already in his life much to happen to him."

"Two marriages! Could he have ill-treated his wives? But he has not the look of a cruel man. Not, of course, that one can tell by appearances, though Anne Boleyn should have guessed."

"Anne Boleyn? Why should you think of her? You do jump so, Frances."

"I know—I know, Madame. As long as I can remember, I have been accused of it," Frances said, though the ill-fated Boleyn had been often in her thoughts of late, and more than once she had wondered how she *could* have entrusted herself to that horrible Henry with his close-set, mean eyes and small, pursed-up mouth. *His* character had shown in his face. She felt a surge of affection for the little, dark Queen Catherine. Thank heaven, Charles was not another Henry. He could never behave so wickedly.

But when she was in her own room, with her maid sent away and her door safely barred, Frances gave herself up to thoughts of the young Duke of Lennox and Richmond, and more especially to his ancestral home in Kent. Nobody, not even Mistress Stuart, had suspected that her envy was directed towards those fortunate people who possessed one or more of the great houses of England. And so many of the owners neglected them—were known as absentee landlords. This Lennox, it seemed, was different, though, as he had possessed Cobham Hall for only three years, it might be no more than the novelty of ownership which kept him there.

Frances had a clear and vivid memory, and she recalled almost as minutely as she recalled the picture of her own ruined home in Scotland, the old engraving her mother had shown her of Cobham Hall. A noble building with four towers, set in spreading grounds.

What it must have meant to have inherited it unexpectedly! What elation, what a sense of triumph, even though, for all Frances knew, the new Duke might have been fond of his cousin Esmé, and deeply grieved at his death.

"I must find out all about him, or as much as anyone can tell me, and if possible before he is presented to me," Frances decided before she slept that night.

12

It was fortunate that Frances had not built up a romantic picture in her mind around the personality of Charles Stuart Lennox, for she would have suffered a disappointment.

Buckingham and Barbara Castlemaine both had slighting things to say about him. Barbara's biography was tinged with such personal spite that Frances guessed Lennox was not one of her admirers. According to her he was a gambler and a spendthrift, and yet he was disgustingly avaricious.

"You should hear Elizabeth Hamilton on him," said Barbara acidly. "He professed to be in love with her before this second marriage of his, but he had the gall to say he would not marry her without a portion. The King thought that if Elizabeth was in love with him it would be too bad she should be unhappy for lack of money, and he would have given her a dowry—though how can he be expected to portion all the poverty-stricken young women whose fathers were loyal to the Royalist cause? Elizabeth wouldn't have Lennox though. She refused to marry a brute and a debauchee even for the sake of becoming a duchess."

Frances scarcely realized the sinking of her heart. This or something similar must have been what the Queen had been about to tell her, and had then refrained from telling her.

"Is he really that?" she asked, and the question was put to Buckingham. Possibly a man would give a fairer version of another man's character.

"The fellow is a fool and a sot," Buckingham said, demolishing her hopes. "He has the manners of an oaf, and there's a Puritanical streak in him which accords ill with the way in which he squanders an enormous revenue and chiefly through betting and racing. Married twice and a suitor for Elizabeth Hamilton, and yet he says he is no lover of women!"

"I asked him to take part in a summer pageant to be given while the Court is at Tunbridge," Barbara said, "but he made his second wife's death an excuse, though that will be well forgotten before the time of the pageant. Everyone knows they lived a cat-and-dog life."

"Don't blame him too much for that," Buckingham said. "The woman was a shrew and enough to send any man to the bottle for consolation. She was Margaret Lewis, a widow," Buckingham added for Frances' benefit. "And how any man could have been fool enough to marry her . . . Lennox must have been thankful when death put an end to it."

"Did he ill-treat her?" Frances asked.

"Not that I know of. You seem to be vastly interested in him."

"He is a kinsman," Frances explained.

"No favourite with Charles," Buckingham declared. "The fellow hasn't an ounce of wit in his entire being. Such a temperament is only suited to an obscure country squire."

"If Charles tolerates him it is only because Lennox shares his passion for racing," Barbara opined. "He is a judge of horses, so one hears."

"There's little that is interesting or profitable to say about him," Buckingham summed up. "He's certainly no acquisition to Court circles."

"There are better things to discuss," Barbara said. "Young Jemmie's wedding for one. The final details were only settled while you were away. The Queen put up an opposition to it because the bride is still but a child."

"The Braganza goes out of her way to spoil sport," Buckingham commented. "The King wants to see Jemmie's future settled, though little Anne Scott is still playing with her dolls."

"Not for the last year or so," Frances contradicted. "She likes to help with the Queen's toilet and is quite deft-handed."

"Charles has planned the programme to suit the Buccleuch family," Buckingham said. "The ceremony and the ball will be fine affairs, but the bedding will be a farce. At the crucial moment the bride will be whisked away, and the next day she will return to the schoolroom."

"The ball is the thing," Barbara declared. "These paltry dances the Queen favours are all we have had since Christmas. My dressmaker is at work on my gown—azure blue tissue, Frances. What will you wear?"

"I haven't had time to think," Frances answered. Her wardrobe was always a problem to her. The yearly sum supplied to her by the Privy Purse was barely sufficient for a seemly Court appearance. She supposed she would wear the gown made up by the Queen Dowager's sewing-maid from the material Henrietta-Anne had sent from France, though this gown had been already seen at the ball given on New Year's Eve.

Barbara, guessing as much, smiled with satisfaction. Nothing would have induced her to wear the same gown for two important occasions.

A few evenings later the King himself presented the Duke of Lennox and Richmond to Frances, and she who was by now prepared to be disappointed in him was agreeably surprised. He danced only passibly, but she found his conversation agreeable, too much so for the King's pleasure, as, hemmed in by Barbara, the Queen, and several courtiers, he watched them from afar. The Marquis of Ruvigny, who had recently come over from France on a special mission, was the guest of honour, and it was impossible for the King to detach himself. He must perforce listen with every appearance of pleasure to a concert, at which, as a compliment to Ruvigny, various French singers were appearing.

Lennox and Frances had little difficulty in stealing away, though whether it was by her contriving or his, Frances was doubtful. They took refuge in an anteroom, and adroitly Frances turned the conversation to Cobham Hall, remarking that her father had had an old engraving of the place amongst his papers. Lennox said at once that he would be interested to see it, and Frances, who knew that Mistress Stuart treasured all the few items that were connected with her husband, promised that she would do her best to find it.

"The estate was in a bad condition when I inherited," Lennox said. "The Parliamentarians seemed to take pleasure in neglecting those that they appropriated, even though they must have believed they were to be theirs for ever."

"I wonder if they did," Frances said thoughtfully. "Perhaps they suspected it was too good to last. They had presentiments."

Lennox was amused. "I should be surprised if a stolid Roundhead had so much imagination. Are you really interested in Cobham Hall?"

"Why yes, because of the picture I remember."

"At the moment you wouldn't see much resemblance to any picture. There is great confusion, with builder's men all over the place. I shall soon have to call them off, for I constantly find myself without money to pay their endless bills, and then I have to amass fresh funds. . . ." He broke off, looked confused and added apologetically: "But this is dull, boorish talk for a fair lady."

"I don't find it so. Tell me more," requested Frances eagerly.

"But how can it interest La Belle Stuart, named for her beauty and gaiety?"

Was there a note of mockery in the last words. Frances half-suspected it, but she said: "I find it a very sensible conversation. If my father's home in Scotland had not been burnt to the ground I should want to be there most of the time, and when I wasn't there I should want to talk about it."

"Either you are an extraordinary girl or I am not hearing aright, being addled by taking too much wine at the banquet this evening."

Frances measured him with her clear glance. "It would have worn off by now," she stated, "and it's a marvel how much gentlemen can drink without getting addled. Me, I am in a daze after a glass or two, but Your Grace, I have heard, has a strong head for liquor."

"In other words, I'm a drunkard. Well, it's near enough to the truth. Last year, when on a mission to Scotland with my step-father, I created a scandal, and the King took me to task for it. Likely enough he told you . . ."

"He did not. I have not heard a word about you from the King, but I noticed you a few evenings since, and I was interested and asked questions of all and sundry, getting a mixed bag of information." And then as Lennox was silent, Frances added coaxingly: "Wasn't it natural I should be interested? You were a stranger and you looked at me so long and fixedly, and then I discovered you were a kinsman. . . ."

"Natural enough," he agreed, "and why should any here speak well of me? I'm a stranger to their ways. Drinking is a solace when life goes awry. You wouldn't know anything about that, would you? About fate giving with one hand and taking away with the other?"

"I might," Frances said cautiously.

She was subjected to a long, penetrating gaze before Lennox observed: "Our Royal Kinsman won't approve of your dalliance here with me. Those seemingly lazy eyes of his miss little. He watched us when we slipped away. I'd better take you back, I suppose. More often than not I'm out of favour with him, which sits lightly upon me. But for you . . ."

To Frances, Lennox no longer looked older than his years. He was frowning crossly as a boy frowns.

"The King has no reason to object. "I am not in official attendance this evening," she said lightly. "Tell me exactly what you are doing to Cobham Hall?"

"Pulling it to pieces with no very clear idea as to how to put it together again," and Lennox laughed. "Inigo Jones prepared some rough drawings in his old age, but then he died and now John Webb and I—Webb was his pupil—are working out a design. We were making some headway when my wife fell ill, and the noise of the workmen disturbed her. All was held up until a few weeks ago, when she died. Did you know that I had been twice a widower?"

This was asked with an entire lack of emotion. But once again he looked older than his years—bleak and remote.

"I knew," Frances said.

"Some might say that I am under a curse. Anyone might well say that a woman is unlucky who shares her life with me."

"I don't suppose it would have made any difference to the length of their lives even if they hadn't married you."

"My first wife died in childbed," he said starkly. "The baby—a girl—died too."

"Oh!" For a moment the glib-tongued Frances was silent. Then she put her hand on his arm and said gently: "I am sorry."

He uttered a sound too harsh for laughter.

"It's a comedy. To be condoling with a man for the death of his first wife when he has recently lost his second. But I was very fond of Betty. She had had an unhappy first marriage. We were comfortable together—understood one another—and then she died through my fault, through the child we both wanted."

Few men in Frances' experience took the blame for such all too common misfortunes. She wanted to say something comforting, but Lennox rushed on.

"I was so accursedly lonely, that's why I married again, and quickly, though nothing could have turned out worse." He made an abrupt movement as though shaking off a weight and demanded: "Why in God's name am I boring you with this? In truth I'm an oaf, as I've been told more than once."

"You don't bore me," Frances said sincerely.

"Well, at least I'm not maudlin with drink and pouring it all out to you while under the influence, as they say in Ireland. I'm making a fool of myself with my eyes unglazed."

"Sometimes I too pour out everything that's in my heart," Frances said. "His Grace of Buckingham accuses me of saying the first thing that comes into my head."

"That black-hearted, treacherous devil!" The words were uttered explosively. "How on earth can you tolerate him?"

"He is very amusing. Nobody else is *half* so amusing, though I dare say he could be . . ."

"Could be what? An exciting lover?"

"No. That didn't occur to me. I agree with what you said. He could be treacherous."

"He *is*," said Lennox positively. "I scarcely know you—not well enough to warn you, but . . ."

"Since the first day I arrived at Court everyone seems to have been warning me of somebody," Frances told him. "I'm now so confused that it is easier to trust everyone, but not to care very much for any particular individual. It seems to be quite successful, for no harm has come to me."

"None?" he asked.

Frances understood well enough. "None," she answered.

They exchanged a long glance and then Lennox said:

"Well, I believe you, though few men would. Now, my fair cousin, I have given you the right to turn on me and say I *am* the uncouth boor you were told I should prove to be."

Frances sighed. He was difficult, though, oddly enough, she was not surprised by the flash of hostility in his eyes. It must be true that fate had given him much with one hand and taken it away with the other. She said patiently: "You are an unusual person, cousin, if only because . . ."

"Because of what?"

"Oh, there are several reasons." She was thinking that, although they had now absented themselves for the best part of an hour, he had not so much as touched her hand, far less attempted to caress her, which was phenomenal. "Will you be here at Court for long?" she asked.

"Not for long, but from time to time. Would you care to see some sketches of Cobham Hall? I have made a few and could show them to you tomorrow."

"Please do. If it is fine there will be a riding-party in the morning, for the first time since the Queen was taken ill. She is now well again and can ride. Will you be there?"

"I can be."

"I have a new riding costume, sent from Paris, and I will wear it."

"How can I wait to see you in it?"

Frances burst out laughing, glad to be able to laugh.

"Now you do speak like a courtier, though you don't care at all?"

"Why not? You have heard nothing but ill of me, yet there's friendliness in your eyes, and surely in mine there must be admiration."

"I dare say you think I'm pretty," Frances said, "but that's not important. Do smile, cousin. You can't always be gloomy. This will be an exciting week, you know, for there will be Jemmie's wedding and the ball afterwards is to be the grandest of all, so it is said. Though I have no new dress to wear for it," she concluded regretfully.

"Who is likely to notice that when they look into your eyes? They are the loveliest eyes I have ever seen."

"Oh, thank you. I felt sure you could be human if you made the effort."

He laughed—for the first time a real laugh, Frances thought. Young, amused, comradely.

When the riding party set out the next morning, the admiring gazes turned upon her, confirmed her confidence. That day a thick-set young man called Samuel Pepys, whom Frances vaguely knew had something to do with the Admiralty, was struck spellbound as his glance fell upon her.

As the cavalcade from the Palace rode forth it was noticed that the King and Queen, riding together, were holding each other by the hand, and this gave great pleasure to the loyal populace with whom the little Queen, so gentle and kind, was growing in popularity. But young Pepys, who greatly admired Barbara, had on this occasion little attention to spare for anyone but Frances, whom he described as wearing "her hat cocked and a red plume". He added that with her sweet eye and little Roman nose she was the greatest beauty he had ever seen in all his life.

The wedding of Jemmie, newly created Duke of Monmouth, was the most talked-of event of the early spring, though Frances, witnessing the traditional "bedding" of the young couple, thought it all rather silly. The twelve-year-old bride was so sleepy she could scarcely keep her eyes open as with much laughter her bridal attendants divested her of her lovely white lace dress and put her into a night-shift that was almost as elaborate. Young Jemmie, in silk night-shirt, took his place beside her in the huge bed, and then at a given signal the candles were snuffed and all was plunged in darkness. When, after a few minutes, servants with lighted tapers appeared on the scene, the child-bride had vanished. She had been spirited away by her mother, and in all probability would scarcely see her bridegroom for the next two years.

"It would have been more exciting had they both been grown-up," the young Duchess of Buckingham was heard to remark, much to everyone's surprise, her husband's included.

His Mary was looking unexpectedly pretty that evening, and he tweaked one of her curls good-naturedly.

"Say you so?"

"Well—yes. Suppose Jemmie and Anne were of an age to love, then he could have altered the plan. It could have been he who carried her off and not Lady Buccleuch when the candles were put out, and nobody would have known where to find them."

Everyone laughed, but a sudden malicious light gleamed in Buckingham's eye. "Of a truth, Mary, there are occasions when you surprise me," he said, and she, of whom as a rule he took but little notice, and was so obsessively in love with him, sparkled with pleasure.

If Frances heard this exchange she paid no attention to it. For some unknown reason she felt happier than ever before, and this gave a new quality to her beauty. Although Barbara wore her gorgeous gown at the ball and glittered with jewels, Frances, whose only ornament was a rope of pearls and who had natural flowers in her hair, eclipsed her.

Barbara was not in her usual high spirits. She believed herself to be once more with child, and never before had this suspicion been so unwelcome to her. The King was still her occasional lover, but should she now be pregnant she much doubted that the child was his. It was far more probable that Henry Jermyn was the father. Would Charles have any suspicion of this? Would he refuse to acknowledge the babe as his? Barbara could not be sure. He had been cool to her of late.

In the grey, unhopeful dawn after the ball had finally ended, Barbara paced her room, sleepless, miserable, and cursing her fruitfulness. She was deathly tired and yet too restless to think of sleep. Her one consolation was that Charles could not be certain of her falsity, could not repudiate her. Not at least until the child was born, though then if it bore a marked resemblance to Harry. . . ! In that case the end of her reign as *maitresse en titre* was in sight.

Frances, too, was sleepless. Poor dancer though Lennox was, she had yet given him several dances. Tomorrow he was leaving for Kent and would not be seen at Court again for some time. But he would not forget her. He had promised to write; and although it was now freely said that the King was her lover, he knew better.

Sketches he had made of Cobham Hall were propped up on the mantel in Frances' room, and she pored over them with a strange heart-yearning. Lennox had no great skill as an artist, but the drawings gave a very fair idea of Cobham Hall in the past, and what he designed it should become.

The old central part of the house had been demolished, and there must now be an ugly, gaping space, but the new block should be impressive and beautiful. Four pilasters with Corinthian bases and capitals would support it, and within, it would contain a large banqueting hall.

"Oh, if only I could help to plan it and watch it being built," thought Frances with a longing sigh. "If it were only my home."

Then indeed the stifled aching for the destroyed family home in Scotland would be fully assuaged.

13

"But to me it seems almost of an impossibility," said the Queen, her face paler than usual and her eyes wide.

Although she had now a good command of the English language, fluency was apt to desert her in moments of agitation, and she was profoundly agitated.

"You are sure, really sure of what you tell me?" she demanded.

"No, Your Majesty, I am not absolutely sure. The plot may be abandoned at the last moment. But I do know it is planned."

The Queen gazed in silence at the young Duchess of Buckingham. She knew the girl's story and pitied her and wondered at her. The daughter of the Puritan General Fairfax, she had been wooed and won by Buckingham whose estates had been appropriated by her father. Nothing had made any difference to Mary once Buckingham had entered her life. She would marry him even though she was betrothed to another man, and, being her father's heiress, she would give back to him all that had been stolen from him. So she had. Her father, weak only where Mary was concerned, had been finally unable to deny her. And now he was dead and she was Buckingham's wife, patronized and despised by his fashionable and profligate friends, and usually neglected by her husband.

Catherine of Braganza looked upon the young creature and pitied her. She was barely twenty, yet she had already undergone so much, and must often be unhappy.

"Worse treated than I, by far worse treated," thought the Queen, her mind for the moment distracted from this latest trouble. Her heart these last few days had been especially soft to her husband, for he had heard of the gossip about the supposed flaw in their marriage and had been infuriated.

Catherine herself did not know if the residue of her dowry had yet been paid, but she did know that Charles had summoned Buckingham and others to a private conference, had rebuked them, and had shown them the royal marriage certificate, coldly informing them that there had been not one but two ceremonies—the private nuptials in accordance with his wife's faith as a Catholic, and the second Anglican ceremony the next day, solemnized by the Bishop of London.

Those who had expected Charles to seize upon the chance of annulling his marriage to the wife he neglected then discovered how little they knew him. There were no possible grounds for a divorce, Charles said emphatically. There never would be such grounds. Catherine's enemies had apologized abjectly.

The Queen had been exalted in her love and pride. He *was* fond of her. In spite of all his misdeeds he must be *very* fond of her. And perhaps such fondness was more desirable than a wild and passionate love. So she had argued, but now if the Duchess' story were true . . .

"I put the thought into my lord's head. The blame is mine," the girl said miserably.

"That is a nonsense. You could not have foreseen what would follow after it. But tell me again as clearly as you can how you came to hear of this plot. I may not have completely understood. The language is still difficult for me, and at once—when you said it was to involve His Majesty, I was agitated. Now, as you see, I am calm."

"His Majesty knows nothing of the matter. Of that I can swear," the Duchess said earnestly. "I chanced to say at the wedding of the Duke of Monmouth that had Lady Anne been older he might, when the candles were snuffed-out, have carried her away himself, not allowed her mother to do so. That seems to have set up a train of thought in my husband's mind. Madame, I doubt not he sees it as a prank, but it is too dangerous . . ."

"A scandalous prank," the Queen commented. "And how did *you* discover it?"

"This morning I was sitting in a window alcove with the curtains half drawn. I was alone and sewing. None knew I was there, and then my lord came in with—with two others. . . . Need I tell you their names, Madame?"

"No," said the Queen, pitying the girl's trembling lips and hands, realizing how much this betrayal distressed her. "They are of no consequence. Continue."

"They spoke of the party to be given this evening by my Lady Castlemaine—but she does not know that the game is to be other than she has seen played many a time before. The idea is to imitate the Duke of Monmouth's bedding, with my Lady Castlemaine wearing such a suit as he wore, and Frances Stuart with the white dress of a bride, and something to make Lady Castlemaine sleepy and stupid put into the wine she drinks, so that when the candles are blown out and there is darkness, she can be carried away unprotesting, and everyone will leave too, except the King—who will enter by a door in the panelling beside the bed, being told a surprise awaits him . . . and only Frances in her nightshift will be there. . . ."

"I see. And it is thought that he—that Frances Stuart and he . . ."

"Oh, Your Majesty," cried the Puritan general's daughter, near to tears, "she is very beautiful, and the King admires her. In the confusion Frances will not understand. To her it is a frolic—there will have been the usual play, unbuckling the garters, throwing the stocking. She will think that Barbara Castlemaine is to join her, and to the King, to any man, the temptation would be great. Irresistible I heard my lord say!"

"Yes," agreed the Queen, softly, sadly. "Yes."

Why was Buckingham so urgent that this infamous thing should come about? Possibly as an act of vengeance against herself, and because as one of Frances Stuart's intimate friends he saw advantages to himself in augmenting her power. If Charles desired the girl he would be grateful to

Buckingham for making this conquest possible, or so the hateful profligate reasoned.

One heartening reflection was that Barbara Castlemaine's attraction for Charles must be on the wane, or Buckingham would not have considered Frances as her supplanter, and at least in this instance no blame attached to Barbara, who would be the last to promote a rival's unhallowed nuptials. She who for years had been hand-in-glove with Buckingham was being as unmercifully betrayed as the giddy, heedless Frances.

"This party?" asked the Queen. "When will it start?"

"Oh, not for an hour or more, Madame, but I dressed early and so was able to slip away, my lord being already at Lady Castlemaine's apartments. All day I have been turning over in my mind what I could do, and at last I thought that it was only your Majesty who could prevent . . . prevent. I had not the courage to approach the King, and, even if I had, he might not . . ."

The young Duchess broke off, biting her trembling under-lip, on the verge of saying that the King might not have interfered.

"You could have told Frances or Lady Castlemaine," the Queen suggested.

"I was unable to get either of them alone; and besides—how could I trust them not to tell my lord that it was I who had betrayed him? If he knew he would never forgive me. He might turn me away—for ever."

Which might be the best thing that could happen to her, thought Catherine compassionately, though as she loved Buckingham it would be impossible to convince her of it. She sat for a few moments in thought and then said: "Join the party. Say nothing, and before long I shall be there myself. Nobody can dispute my right to attend. Do not be afraid," as the girl hesitated. "Neither your husband nor anyone else, not even the King, will ever know that you had any part in this."

Kneeling to kiss the Queen's hand, the girl murmured words of incoherent gratitude, and as soon as she had left, Catherine summoned her dresser.

She reflected that this "bedding", at the best a stupid vulgarity and in this case infamous, would not take place until midnight. There was plenty of time in which to make a leisurely toilet. She must look her best. She must be cool, amused, seemingly unsuspicious.

"I will wear the new cream satin with the point de Venice lace," she decided.

The *coiffeur*, summoned unexpectedly, curled her hair in the soft ringlets that suited her. Her cheeks were touched with the rouge and powder she used but sparingly, and around her neck and on her arms were the diamond necklet and bracelets that the King had given her. Small and slight though she was, there were times when Catherine could look magnificent and this was one of them.

Lady Denham, her favourite dresser, was gazing at her with a perplexed expression. "Your Majesty . . ." she began, and then closed her lips with a snap.

"What is it? What were you about to say?" asked the Queen nervously, fearing some further revelation.

"Nought, Your Majesty, but that it seemed so grand a *toilette* for the private puppet-show."

The recollection of this arranged entertainment was an annoyance, for it had been planned for her by the King. The Welsh puppet-master was said to be something of a wonder, but the King, being for some reason sceptical, had refused to sanction a performance at one of the gala evenings when important foreign guests were present, until the Queen had witnessed a performance and had given an opinion on it.

It was to have taken place that evening, and had Catherine been cynically minded she might have concluded that Charles had gone to some trouble to see that she was occupied at a time when he had planned a very different diversion for himself. But in this instance the Queen's faith did not waver. Whatever his sins, he would never lay a trap for an unsuspecting girl.

She glanced at her little gilded clock. It was still early. She would see this Welshman, and although there would not be time to witness his performance, she might be able to discover if it was of any merit.

A message was sent to command the man's immediate attendance. Catherine questioned him, and he replied in a lilting, sing-song voice. He told Catherine solemnly that in his own home amongst the Welsh mountains he ranked as a magician. But his magic was of a harmless kind, warranted to entertain.

The so-called magician was a small, dark-haired man with a remarkably white skin and burning eyes. He described some of the acts that his clever puppets could do, almost, thought the Queen, as though they were real people, not jointed wooden dolls, fashioned by himself. She gazed at one curiously life-like looking puppet as he held it in the palm of his hand. His fingers jerked and the little creature sat upright, its head turning so naturally that Catherine gasped. It put up a tiny hand and self-consciously patted the plaits of fair hair—real hair, Catherine saw—that were glued to its head.

Suddenly she made up her mind. "I will trust you," she said. "Instead of this private performance in my closet, to determine if you can be engaged to give a performance at the full Court, I will make it of more importance, and the King himself shall see your magic. If you satisfy him, you will be well rewarded. His Majesty is always generous."

Lady Denham was frankly gaping at her. It was not often that the Queen showed such initiative.

"Lady Denham, we will go alone, you and I," Catherine said, "and our entertainer with his assistants and his properties will follow us. For this evening we will leave the Countess of Suffolk behind us. Poor soul, she will be glad of an early night, of which there are few enough."

It was a sensible decision, Lady Denham allowed, for the Countess, who was Lady of the Bed-Chamber, would have strongly objected to so much as crossing the threshold of Barbara Castlemaine's apartment, and would have been scandalized that the Queen planned to do so—while as for her orders that she was to be followed by an itinerant puppet-master and his assistants, bearing with them cumbersome stage properties . . . ! Lady Denham was younger, more enterprising and decidedly curious. She raised no objection. After all, the Queen was the one person in England who could dispense with the formality of an invitation.

Later, Catherine would wonder at herself, but now she knew no uncertainty. The King would be surprised to see her, but he would not allow her to feel unwelcome. This evening she was *en beauté* and a spark of admiration shone in Charles' eyes, as Barbara, for once put out of countenance, came forward to welcome the Queen with a deep curtsey and suitably expressed gratification of the honour conferred on her.

The Queen was gracious, offering her hand to be kissed by those who in her opinion were as poisonous as adders. The supper had already started, but a chair was set for Catherine beside Charles, and she explained with perfect confidence that afterwards, if her hostess was agreeable, there would be an entertainment of an unusual kind.

"You so often play these games of Blind Man and the Nuts and May that I thought a novelty might be welcome," Catherine said pleasantly, and Frances Stuart was the first to clap her hands.

The Queen cast a smiling and indulgent glance at her. How far the beautiful, silly creature was from suspecting! The smile veered to the Duchess of Buckingham, whose gaze was worshipping.

"I will see more of that girl in the future," Catherine decided.

Under cover of the general conversation Charles spoke low in his wife's ear.

"But, my sweet life, how can you be sure that the performance of this puppeteer will be of sufficient polish for a critical assembly? There has been no time for you to judge it."

"I have seen enough," said Catherine, thinking not so much of the puppet-master as of Buckingham's sullen face, and of his eyes, which rarely met hers, but which when they did were dark with hatred.

The supper proceeded and Catherine's gay mood was a surprise to them all. She set them laughing with some of her odd turns of phrase. Buckingham wondered if she could have suspected what was afoot, but it seemed impossible. His skilfully laid plan was to be foiled through a whim!

Meanwhile the puppet-master had been setting up a portable stage in the adjoining room, and the guests, having supped, took their places in chairs arranged in a semi-circle. There were green-velvet curtains concealing the stage.

"Now do your best, magician, for yourself as well as for me," Catherine silently adjured him.

Designedly the candles were but few, but when the stage curtains were drawn aside, there was a bright light on the little stage which showed a diminutive but perfect park with trees and shrubs and grass lawns, borders of flowers and a lake. In the foreground fashionably dressed puppets of both sexes were enjoying an alfresco meal. There was a swing in which a girl puppet was dreamily pushing herself to and fro; there were little figures in boats on the lake. The wires by which all these figures were manipulated were practically invisible. And suddenly there was music, the soft, tripping music of a violin, and the puppets moved aside to make way for a handsome courtier attired in blue and white satin and a curled wig. He sat down beside the girl in the swing and put one arm around her as he stooped his head to kiss her lips, her throat, her swelling bosom. The girl puppet went through the motions of half swooning with pleasure.

The audience murmured approval, and applauded as the curtains closed, to part again with surprisingly short delay on a skating scene. The little figures glided on the frozen lake, weaving in an intricate dance. The puppets, who had been lovers in the previous scene, whirled together in abandon.

The swiftness, lightness and lifelikeness of the little figures as they mimed one part after another were extraordinary. After the first exclamations of delight and surprise, a silence fell upon the audience. None who watched could tear their eyes from the brilliantly lighted stage upon which these realistic dolls disported themselves.

The final scene was a ballet in which the two leading puppets played the parts of Venus and Adonis.

"'Tis almost impossible to believe that they have not the breath of life in them," cried Frances when at last the green-velvet curtains closed to be drawn aside no more.

A few minutes later the puppet-master was bowing low before the King and Queen, with several of his actors and actresses hanging limply over one arm.

"A magician in truth," Catherine murmured.

Although impressed, she was not certain that it had been in a pleasant way, for the realistic love-making had been unashamedly sensual. But Charles was delighted, and the puppets were handed round from one to another and their clever workmanship was admired.

Frances held the leading-lady puppet in her hands and felt something of the Queen's mingled fascination and repulsion. So limp and helpless now, yet during the entertainment so vital and eager. It was uncanny, thought Frances, as she handed the puppet to Buckingham who stood near her. He, who appeared to have recovered his good spirits, made an attempt to manipulate the little figure, jerking at the wires which controlled its arms and legs, but the result was a grotesque acrobatic collapse with fair plaits falling across and hiding the painted face.

The watching puppet-master smiled sardonically and took the puppet to place it with the others. The King complimented him and a purse filled with gold pieces was given to him. The King also took a gold chain from his neck and hung it around the Welshman's neck. There was eagerness on the part of several of the ladies present to engage the puppet-master to give performances at their own homes in the near future, but Frances, who had fallen silent and was watching the man closely, was not surprised that he returned evasive answers. There was something strange about him and she was even more strongly conscious of it when the next day it was discovered that he had disappeared.

"He has gone back to his Welsh hills," the Queen said when she heard. "The money the King gave him enabled him to do that."

For her the puppet-master had served his purpose and possibly she was right. He was never heard of again. Frances had the odd conviction that the audience had seen what the Welshman wanted them to see. The show had perhaps been quite ordinary, but he by some magic power had made them all dream his dream.

It was not long before she was hearing rumours from various sources of the "entertainment" which would have been given that evening, but for the arrival of the Queen, and she was not the only one to be at first incredulous and then furious. Barbara Castlemaine was equally so. Buckingham had been prepared to dupe her and she did not believe that the King had been ignorant of it. Frances was shattered as the abortive plot was pieced together. Had the Queen known what was planned? She dared not question her.

Nobody suspected that the Duchess of Buckingham had betrayed her husband to the Queen. It was said that he had taken too many into his confidence and that one or more of them had babbled.

With the King, Barbara staged a scene of herculean proportions. She could reveal now that she was pregnant and flung the information at him, by her manner daring him to utter a doubt as to the child's parentage. And to think that in such a state he would have duped her! To think that he would have allowed her to be drugged and thus have turned a harmless frolic into an orgy.

In vain the King protested his complete ignorance of the plot designed to bring Frances to his arms. He was at a disadvantage, for Barbara was looking extremely ill and declared that she was unlikely to survive this birth. If she died, the King, who owed her the tenderest care, would be her murderer.

Barbara refused to see or speak to Buckingham and once more departed to Richmond, on this occasion fortified by the King's tacit agreement that he was responsible for her pregnancy and the promise that he would ere long give her a palace worthy of her illustrious position. It was to be several months before she again showed herself at Court.

Frances, meanwhile, received messages from Buckingham beseeching her to give him the chance of self-vindication. Finally she agreed to a meeting, but before he had spoken more than a sentence her hand shot out, and with her clenched right fist she hit him across the mouth.

"I was warned of you as a traitor," she cried, "and it was a true warning." And then, as Buckingham started to bluster, she added with venom: "Were I in power—were the King my lover—I would never rest until I had destroyed you."

Buckingham, tenderly fingering a bruised jaw, recovered himself sufficiently to retort: "For myself all has turned out well. The King would have given me no thanks had I put a violent mad woman into his arms."

Charles met with a better reception. For a few days he watched Frances narrowly, observing her clouded face and the listlessness with which she moved and spoke. Between Catherine and himself there had been no explanation. She thought it politic to ask for none, he was thankful to be spared, but within a short while Frances' attitude had become unbearable to him. He could not endure to see her with her radiance dimmed, her eyes averted from his, her gaiety and comradeship withdrawn from him.

"It was none of my doing," Charles said, when he at last contrived to get her alone, in the Queen's private sitting-room, vacant because she had gone for a drive with the Countess of Suffolk. Frances was silent, held first by his hand on hers, and then encircled by his arm.

"Did you know nothing?" she asked at last.

"Nothing. God's truth! Am I not man enough to do my own wooing without calling upon George Villiers for aid?"

"Why should he have thought that you—that I . . . ?"

"I doubt if the fool ever thinks clearly. He has a twisted mind that revels in subtleties, and a sense of humour as perverted as that of the little monster whom my poor Minette has married."

"I never could understand why she agreed to take Philippe," said Frances, her thoughts momentarily diverted from herself. "Nobody could have forced her."

"She forced herself—for my sake," Charles said sombrely. "The marriage was a valuable link with France. A pity, though, that Louis did not fall in love with her before marriage instead of after. At least he is a man."

"It wasn't worth it, just for politics," Frances said. "You would have worked things out without such a sacrifice."

"As likely as not—but nearly all royal marriages are arranged either for political or financial reasons. Even mine."

"*You* are fond of the Queen," Frances said.

"Fond, yes! But there's a difference between that and . . ." Suddenly he seized her, held her in the hard, strong arms that in their day had performed many a strenuous task, and could still break-in a mettlesome horse, let alone a delicate, slender girl. He kissed her, fondled her, finally shook her. "For pity's sake don't look at me with those accusing eyes, you little fraud. You must have known."

"That Your Majesty had a *tendresse* for me? But that is not an unusual thing—for you," Frances retorted in a voice that contrived to be both prim and impertinent.

His embrace had stirred her no more than the rough hug of a schoolboy, but he must not be allowed to suspect it. She trembled a little and cast down her eyes and murmured: "That was an ill thing to do! How can you expect me to be . . . to even think of it after such a squalid plot?"

"Have I said I expect anything . . . at the moment?"

"No, but you are the King, and evidently Buckingham thought I should consider it an honour to be given to you."

"Forget Buckingham. I have seen him. He knows my opinion of this latest devilry, and by my command he has left London. A few months of rustication may drive sense into his head. Until it has he won't be seen at Court."

"Then, since I should have had no other opportunity, I am glad I attacked him at once. I even think I loosened one of his front teeth—with this," and Frances clenched her

149

right hand and brandished it. Irrepressibly she giggled. Irrepressibly Charles laughed.

"I doubt," he said, "if any other woman would have dared, but it was no more than the rogue deserved. Oh, my sweeting, I would I were ten years younger that you might look more kindly on me, with a more tender heart."

"My heart is tender," Frances protested, "as tender as it dare be. But there are too many obstacles."

"Love can demolish them. Tell me what you most want in life, for whatever it is I vow it shall be yours." And then, as she shook her head, smiling more pensively than was her wont: "I love you, Frances. I adore you. Were it in my power I would marry you. It is not, but anything else . . ."

"Would you have forced me had Buckingham's plot gone according to plan?" Frances asked with curiosity.

"On my honour, I would not, nor ever have with any woman."

Irrelevantly Frances said: "When I looked at that puppet doll, limp in my hand—so helpless—it gave me a . . . a *frisson*. Afterwards when I heard the plot, it seemed as though it could have been me."

"Nonsense!" declared Charles robustly. "If you had not wanted me, you would have put up a fight, and I should have left you alone."

"But in the surprise I—I might not have fought," and Frances looked up at him from beneath the veil of her long lashes. Flirting was easy, to beguile a man was easy— pleasant too. She was not afraid of him, and now that he was but gently caressing her she had no objection.

"Tell me what I can do to please you?" Charles urged.

"Nothing, Sire, except to be patient, kind, considerate, as I am sure you always will be." She murmured the words guilefully, beginning to realize how she could keep him at bay though still hot with longing for her.

"But there must be something you want," he persisted. "Jewels—you shall have those which will put Barbara's to shame. Gowns, they can be sent from France by the cartload. An establishment of which you can be proud and titles so that you take precedence of all others save the Queen."

"How *could* I betray the Queen who has been so good to me?" asked Frances reproachfully.

"I doubt not she would prefer you to Barbara Castlemaine," the King said callously. "You would not so goad her or triumph over her."

"Never—but it would hurt her, Charles." Frances' one idea now was to play for time, to keep him hoping, believing and more or less quiescent. She twined her slender white fingers in his strong brown ones and twisted around the one ring he wore, a splendid emerald.

The King made as though he would take it off. "It will be far too large for you, but it can be altered to fit," he said.

Frances shook her head and moved slightly away from him. "Oh no, I want nothing," she protested.

"God's truth! Then you are different from any other woman."

"Your Majesty is unfortunate if you have known only harpies."

"Tell me the truth," he demanded. "Have you any love for me?"

"But of course. Who does not love the King? But I would not supplant Barbara Castlemaine—my friend."

"Barbara can be compensated."

"*Can* a woman be compensated for humiliation? Besides, I have heard that the reason she has left for Richmond is because she is ill and expecting another child. She has *looked* ill of late, and for what might have happened at her party she would not have been to blame. Oh, Charles, you cannot expect me to come to a decision about . . . us, until she is well again. If she heard of it, and she would be sure to hear, it might go badly with her. And besides—until the babe is born—oh, can't you understand that I feel as though you belong to each other, and if I—if we—I could not share a lover."

"Well, no—perhaps not." Charles made the admission grudgingly, smothering a groan and regardless that his unfortunate Queen had been required to do so. But then, though he had been vastly relieved on Catherine's arrival from Portugal to find her so winsome, he had never been in love with her as he was now in love with this beautiful, maddening girl.

Frances was moving her fingers in his, and had he but known it counting on them the months that must pass before Barbara's delivery. She could not be more than three months on the way, therefore Frances could count on a respite of seven. Charles could not tell Barbara that her day was over until at least a month after the birth of the child. "Pray heaven she doesn't miscarry and recover the sooner," was Frances' unuttered thought.

"You were happy at Hampton Court," Charles said suddenly. "I remember last summer when you first arrived from France. You loved the old place. Say the word, give me your promise, and I will make it over to you. Wolsey's old home shall be yours."

"Oh no!" Staggered by such a stupendous suggestion, she was yet touched. She did not in the least want to own that historic dwelling which belonged to the nation more than to any one being. She wanted a home she could change and improve according to her dreams, and thus thinking she remembered Charles Lennox and Cobham Hall, and was suddenly conscious of self-disgust.

She rose and twirled away from the King, laughing at him as she retreated down the narrow pathway of a long, slanting sun-ray.

"I cannot be bribed," she cried. "What I give, I give for love. Is not that how you would have it be?"

The King watched her fascinated and bemused. He thought he had never seen anything more alluring than that laughing girl with her bright curls and her sea-blue eyes and her lissome body.

"Yes, that is how I would have it be," he agreed.

14

Tunbridge and Bath were both visited that summer, and
amongst the galaxy of charm and beauty Frances shone as a
star. By this time not a soul who moved in the Court
circle was blind to the King's infatuation, and many
supposed she was already his mistress. Not so Catherine,
who accepted the situation with tolerance. She had come
to believe that the King's love affairs were mainly ephemeral
and that Barbara Castlemaine was the one woman who
could hold him permanently. Having resigned herself to
this, she was thankful that Barbara was not flaunting her
new pregnancy beneath her eyes, and she judged Frances
to be harmless and sincerely devoted to herself.

She might have been more alarmed had she guessed that
Charles now cared nothing for Barbara and had strong
doubts that her expected infant was his.

When Frances contemplated the future, which was as
seldom as might be, she was apprehensive. She had promised
the King or had half-promised him that which she had no
intention of surrendering, and much of her present importance was due to his confidence in her. Everyone flattered
her, everyone sought her out. She was constantly told that
she was the most beautiful of living beings, and as the King
was naturally generous he was delighted to see her so happy.
There were times when he became urgent and demanding,
but so far Frances had not found it too difficult to hold her
own.

She discovered several ways of placating him, and it was
easy to touch his heart. She would remind him of her austere
childhood, of her poverty and frustration, and then he would

think himself a brute to grudge her her butterfly thought-lessness. Usually she was so effortlessly gay it was a pleasure to Charles to be with her, and in his moodier moments she would coax him to talk of the long, adventurous years of exile when he had not dared to believe he would regain the throne. Very occasionally, when his restraint threatened to break down, she would become serious and vow that his passion frightened her, and that she sometimes thought it might be a good thing if she gave up the world and entered a convent.

This did not seem an altogether absurd threat, for Charles' two gayest cousins had suddenly made the same decision. It was, he realized, often the most spirited girls, those who seemed most attracted to the world, who could without warning abandon it and turn to the religious life.

But Frances knew in her heart that she would never retire into a convent, convenient threat though it was to hold over the royal head.

Twice, while the Court was at Tunbridge and Bath, Frances received a letter from Lennox; but although she had not forgotten him, he now seemed remote, and he wrote in such a stilted style that his letters were disappointing. She began to distrust her memory of him. It might have been nothing more than her own state of mind on that particular evening that had made him interesting and sympathetic to her. He had seemed unusual, but why she did not know. Certainly it was not because he had said anything brilliant. Probably it was his ownership of Cobham Hall which had invested him with charm and importance.

Now his short, formal letters, which told her nothing at all, seemed to confirm the general verdict that he was dull and oafish. In any case he had gone his way, and while the Court was at Tunbridge, which was not so far from Cobham, he made no effort to see her.

Frances did not answer his letters. She made one or two attempts, but these were even more stilted than his. A brief interest had flared up and expired. The pen was not her medium and never would be, and her spelling was as bad as ever. She envied the King his fluency, for although she saw him nearly every day, she received many a love letter from him, written with charm and tenderness and promising her all that the heart of woman could desire.

"Oh, Frances Stuart, a few years ago, who would ever have believed it?" Thus she addressed her reflection in her mirror, as she sat brushing her bright hair. "Then it seemed too good to be true to be chosen as one of the Queen's Maids, and now the King of England is in love with you and is pushing notes under your door, as might a young spark of no account."

Charles frequently gave her jewels as presents, and Frances would sometimes lay these out before her and gaze at them pensively. She was not particularly fond of jewels, but her collection now represented a small fortune. She possessed not only those that Charles had given her, but such as had been showered upon her by other admirers. This was perfectly allowable, for all the pretty girls at Court took a pride in such valuable gifts which were bestowed at Christmas, Twelfth Night, St. Valentine's Day and on other anniversaries.

Mistress Stuart, viewing the collection when she called at Whitehall one day, remarked that when her daughter came to marry, these jewels would serve as her dowry.

"But shall I ever?" Frances queried. "Often I doubt it."

Her mother looked at her consideringly. If Frances had changed, so had she. There was a calculating hardness in her expression which before now had struck her elder daughter. Sophie was in France, where the Queen Dowager spent most of her time. She was high in favour and gave promise of beauty. Walter was outgrowing his childish delicacy, and Mistress Stuart had time to concentrate on Frances, who was now in her eighteenth year. With deliberation she replaced in its velvet case the emerald pendant she had been admiring, and said: "A few days past Sir Henry Bennet did me the honour to call upon me. He told me he had had some converse with you of late."

"So he did. He is ambitious and seeks to supplant milord

Clarendon in office. But why should he have thought that I could advance him?"

"You have influence."

"With the King? But I never attempt to influence him."

"Then you are wasting your opportunities. Clarendon is old and his day is almost over, but Henry Bennet, as he assured me, is willing to be your ally. Did he not make that plain to you?"

"He started to make a speech, but he looked so ridiculous that I had a fit of laughing. George Buckingham used to imitate him perfectly. His pompous manner and repeating his sentences over and over again. I seldom see Buckingham now, we are not on good terms, but I remembered and I couldn't listen seriously to Bennet. If you feel you must lecture me for that, *Maman*, I don't wonder. I was rude and I am sorry. The poor man looked so angry."

"He is no longer angry. As he said to me, you—most strangely as he considers—seem to be unaware of your importance. Yet you have acted prudently, Frances, in a way which any mother would commend. Sir Henry came to the conclusion that you and the King . . ."

Mistress Stuart broke off in some confusion, but Frances, who had known that such probing was inevitable and had prepared herself for it, was cool.

"Yes, *Maman*?" she said enquiringly.

Mistress Stuart made a gesture which expressed both frustration and appeal.

"Oh, my child, cannot you be candid with me? I, as your mother, should be in your confidence. Sir Henry, before he spoke to you, was in no doubt, but something you said, or perhaps your general manner, convinced him that it was not so."

"The King is not my lover," Frances said shortly.

"Oh, my dear child, how clever you have been with him! What a difficult time you must have had! But Sir Henry is certain that all the cards are in your hands."

"What cards did he mean?" Frances avoided meeting her mother's eyes.

"Do not fence with me, Frances. You understand me. The King is in love with you to the point that no other woman is of any concern to him. This is said not only by Sir Henry, but by all who are personally in touch with the King. If you were to surrender it would be a calamity. His Majesty not only desires you but respects you, and if you continue as you have done, Sir Henry believes that before another year has passed . . ."

Frances picked up a chain of pearls and amethysts and held it against her fair curls. She gazed into the mirror and said: "On the whole I think that fresh flowers in the hair are prettier than jewels."

"Frances, will you listen to me?"

"I am listening, *Maman*, or would if you did not so twist the meaning of what you say."

"It can be said with crudity if necessary. The Queen is unlikely to give the King an heir, and she has little hold on him. Nor has Lady Castlemaine, whose last babe is said not to be his. You alone have his heart. He would marry you if he could."

"Yes, perhaps he would—if he could," Frances agreed.

"All things are possible. You may yet be his Queen."

"Are you out of your senses, *Maman*?" Frances tore the jewelled chain from her hair and flung it aside.

"My child, I am only saying what many others are now saying. Last summer the Queen had a second miscarriage and now it is said that she is again *ence inte*, and . . ."

"She has been so for nearly six months," Frances interrupted. "She wished—it was only natural she should wish there to be no talk about it, after two disappointments."

"But naturally—the poor soul. She looks sadly frail and ill. These unsuccessful pregnancies have undermined her health."

"You are hoping she may die," cried Frances fiercely.

"No—no! But should it be God's will . . ."

"I wonder that any woman has the courage to marry, with the ghastly spectre of death in childbed always hovering," Frances said with passion, and suddenly burst into tears, thus confounding Mistress Stuart who immediately set about comforting her.

"Dear, foolish one," she murmured, "there are many for whom it is safe and easy. It was so for myself. I was always in the best of health, and then only a few hours of pain. So it will be for you, Frances."

"If the Queen died, it would go harder with Charles than you imagine," said Frances through her tears.

"Mayhap. But all men forget. They are so constituted. If the Queen again miscarries but recovers her health she may see the hopelessness of this marriage and choose of her own free will to seek refuge in a convent."

"And then there would be an annulment and the King would marry me? Is that what you think?"

"It is what many think. Do not misunderstand me, Frances. I would never counsel you to surrender your virtue. It is a girl's greatest treasure."

"Because then a bargain can be struck," Frances retorted. "And suppose I say that even if the chance of being Queen were mine, I would not grasp at it."

"Would you expect me to believe that, my child?"

Frances dried her eyes and looked hopelessly at her mother. She said slowly: "I suppose not. Nobody would believe me."

She was not even sure that she believed it herself. She was certain that she would detest the position of the King's mistress, even though he might be faithful to her and shower honours on her, but to be the Queen if Catherine died or voluntarily embraced the religious life was a different matter. Frances was not ambitious, but she had sufficient imagination to be enthralled by the pictures that floated before her mind's eye. To be the first lady in the land, to be crowned, to have great possessions and royal homes. And what could she not do for her family? Sophie would almost certainly make a brilliant marriage. Walter could adopt any career he chose, and Charles, probably, would make her mother a duchess. How that would entrance her. Frances giggled.

"Oh, it's all a fairy-tale," she cried, "though not a pleasant one."

"It has happened before," Mistress Stuart said stubbornly.

"And if it has, is that any reason? Do not speak to me of Anne Boleyn. Do not remind me of her."

"But, dear one, the circumstances then were quite different. Poor Katherine of Aragon, one thinks of her with pity; but if the Queen died, or if she decided that the religious life was God's will for her . . . ?"

"What would count with the Queen, devout though she may be, is the King's will," Frances said. "Please, *Maman*, stop thinking in this way. If the Queen looks wan it is because she is but three months from her delivery. This time all will go well with her."

She waited with scornful eyes for her mother's insincere "God grant it", but Mistress Stuart was silent. When she spoke again, she said in her usual placid manner: "I am glad we have had this talk, child, for tomorrow I start on the journey to Scotland. London in the hot weather is no place for a delicate child such as Walter. Last summer I scarce felt safe even when we lodged by the sea, and the expense was great. In the Highlands the plague is scarcely known."

"How long will you be away?" Frances asked, knowing that she would miss her little brother more than she would miss her mother from whom she had now grown apart.

"Until the autumn, until the cold weather. In Scotland there is always a welcome for us from the Blantyres, and Walter is happy there. The Court will be at Hampton, will it not?"

"Perhaps—though I did hear that the Queen wished to be at Windsor for her lying-in."

Mistress Stuart continued to talk about their Scots kinsfolk, while Frances, giving her only a particle of her attention, made mechanical replies. She was far more worried than her mother supposed.

"And let us hope," said Mistress Stuart, "that when we meet again this war with the Dutch will be over. It is grievous to think of the deaths there have been. But now the end seems in sight and victory will bring greater prosperity to the country."

"But always there will be wars," said Frances. "Men glory in them. Wars and long voyages of exploration and wresting their possessions from one another. The King was transported with joy when our navy took New Amsterdam from the Dutch, and of course the Duke of York is proud that it is to be called New Yorke after him, though as success has come about through his leadership it is no more than he deserves. *Maman*, I forgot to tell you. I am to sit for my portrait."

"But that you have done already, and more than once."

"Oh, this is not just a picture in oils, but an engraving and it is to be used on new coins from the Mint, and from the Guinea gold which is being brought from there by the Royal Adventurers of England, as these swashbucklers call themselves."

"Your portrait on coins?" Mistress Stuart looked perplexed. "How can that be? It is the King's head that must always be seen. How glad I was when the circulation of the Commonwealth money was forbidden."

"Oh well, yes, so was I. Cromwell had such a coarse, ugly face . . . not that the King is handsome, but his features are a great improvement on those of the Protector."

"Then what do you mean by saying that your face will be on the new Mint coins?"

"Not only my face but my figure," Frances said, forgetting tears and misgivings, and amused because her mother was so thoroughly perplexed.

"And yet you say . . ." Mistress Stuart started on a speech which she recognized to be absurd. No Queen Consort's face or figure would be ever engraved on English money. "What *is* this foolishness?" she demanded.

"It is sober truth, *Maman*. Like this—or something like this. . . ."

Frances struck an attitude, sitting upright with head

poised high and left hand outstretched as though she grasped an invisible weapon. "Of course when I am really posing for Roettier, the engraver, I shall wear a helmet and hold a trident and I shall have flowing, Grecian robes. It was altogether the King's idea, but James of York thought it should be called Britannia. To represent the nation's might."

Slowly Mistress Stuart grasped the implication.

"You on one side of the coin and the King on the other," she said, and looked so overwhelmed that Frances hastened to say:

"There is really no great significance to it—I mean that I should be chosen. Any girl would do just as well, except that my nose seems to be particularly suitable."

"Your nose?"

"It's described as a Roman nose," Frances laughed, "and is supposed to make me look very haughty and dignified. Though that is about the hardest thing in the world to be— for me at least."

Mistress Stuart wholeheartedly agreed, though she knew that her daughter's frivolity was largely superficial. A mask, she thought, for a strength of character that few suspected. She did not wholly understand Frances and never would. Henrietta-Anne, who never forgot her fondness for Frances and corresponded with her, still thought of her as one who refused to grow up. The Queen Dowager, when Mistress Stuart had the opportunity of discussing her daughter with her, championed Frances and said she was naturally innocent and good; and the so obviously infatuated King made no attempt to analyse her, though he granted her virtue through her resistance to him. Probably Catherine of Braganza understood her better than anyone else, which accounted for her tolerance. She had nothing to fear from Frances, who kept the King in a state of unwilling chastity.

"Giving sittings to the engraver will at least be a change and something interesting to do while waiting for the Queen to decide whether or not she will retire to Windsor," Frances said.

"It is a great honour, but so many honours are now being given to you, and you take them so lightly," her mother complained.

Frances did not contradict her, though as a fact her imagination had been fired by the King's command. She and she alone was fitted to represent Britannia, he had said, and a few days after Mistress Stuart's departure for Scotland, Frances gave Jan Roettier, the eldest of several brothers who were all engravers, his first sitting.

Although the Roettier family was of Dutch extraction, and the new coins were being struck partly to substantiate England's claim to the "Dominion of the Seas" and the victories over the Dutch navy, Roettier was proud of his commission as the chosen new die-sinker. He had been preferred above Thomas Simon, the English die-sinker, who had competed with him for the honour. An unpopular choice with the people as a whole, who also resented the fact that the mill-and-screw method of coining which now replaced the old hammered coinage, was in the charge of a Frenchman named Blondeau.

But Charles, who took a great personal interest in the new coinage, was unaffected by criticism, and merely remarked that Blondeau and Roettier were finer craftsmen than any England could produce at the moment, and that as work would be given to many English workmen under them, there was no legitimate cause for complaint.

Frances was sufficiently interested to make enquiries about the die-sinking process, and Charles was delighted to take her with the usual trail of attendants to the Tower where the Mint was installed.

Here they were received by Master Slingsby, the Master of the Mint, who with pride explained all that could be explained easily to the beautiful Britannia. He was soon surprised by her intelligence and the questions she put to him, for the ladies and gentlemen of the Court who laughed and chatted amongst themselves were mainly enthralled by the heaps of gold coins which they would have gladly appropriated. Frances, however, was genuinely interested in the complicated process of minting coins from the long flat bars of gold and silver cast out of the melting-pot, and she marvelled when these were drawn through a mill and emerged in different thicknesses.

A cursory inspection would have been enough for most of the party, who were forced to feign an interest and to stifle their yawns while the King and Frances listened attentively to the disquisition of Master Slingsby, who was naturally delighted to have the chance of airing his knowledge, not only to the King, but to the lovely girl who was eager to understand each stage by which the milled money was fabricated. The cutters, the weighing machines and the engines which engraved the lettered edges of the larger coins all fascinated her, as did the revolving cylinders which finally dried the coins after they had been blanched in diluted acid.

"I had no idea—I couldn't have imagined," Frances exclaimed more than once. "How we all take things for granted. Shall I really be on every coin from henceforth?"

"Every single one, for generations," Charles assured her, laughing at her ingenuous wonderment, but as proud as he was amazed by her grasp of the various complications.

"Long, long after we are all dead and gone and forgotten," Frances mused.

"But how can you be forgotten when you can be always seen on every coin?" asked Julia La Garde, who on Mary Boynton's marriage and retirement had replaced her as a maid-of-honour. "As for His Majesty, he will ever be remembered as England's greatest monarch."

Charles smiled at the pretty young woman who fluttered her lashes at him, but he had little attention to spare for anyone but Frances, who was now enquiring as to the exact worth of the new half-broads and double-crowns.

The new guinea gold would be issued in five-guinea and two-guinea pieces, and probably there would be coins of less worth, Slingsby told her. He plunged his hand into a pile of small silver coins and announced that this was Maundy money, and issued by His Majesty's command.

"Royal alms bestowed every Maundy Thursday upon certain worthy poor persons," Slingsby said.

"Would it were in my power to give away thrice the amount," Charles said sincerely, forgetful of the fortunes squandered upon his favourites and of his own manifold extravagances.

"However poor they may be, those who have the great honour of receiving alms from Your Majesty rarely spend it," Master Slingsby observed. "Such coins are treasured heirlooms to pass down to their children and grand-children."

"We must have some portrait models struck of you, Frances," the King said, "that those who are given them can also hand them down to their descendants."

Frances, as the visit to the Mint drew to a close, showed a reluctance to leave, which further endeared her to Master Slingsby. When she said, "I have been so interested. I have so enjoyed myself. There is still so much I want to know, but perhaps I can pay another visit before too long," he bowed as low to her as he would have bowed to the Queen.

And how well she would become that position were it ever hers, was the thought that passed through the mind of more than one of the courtiers who watched her as she smiled at Master Slingsby and gave him her little gloved hand to kiss. Miss La Garde was more critical.

"It's ridiculous for La Belle Stuart to give herself such airs," she observed to a companion when they were out of earshot. "It is no such great thing to have the King for a lover. 'Tis said that he goes often now to Drury Lane for the sake of that low play-actress who is appearing there. Nell Gwyn she calls herself, and she has red hair which resembles the Castlemaine's, and a vulgar wit that makes all the gentlemen laugh."

The royal cavalcade returned to Whitehall on horseback, the King leading the procession with Frances beside him; but on arrival there the laughter and gaiety were abruptly checked, for a waiting servant hurried to the King with urgent news.

During their absence the Queen had been taken suddenly ill. Her physicians had been called, and messengers would have been dispatched at once to the Tower, where it was known the King could be found, only that the Queen had forbidden it.

Forgetful of Frances, Charles, with a stricken expression as he realized that his hopes of an heir were once more doomed, hurried to the Queen's room.

15

If the majority of the King's most intimate companions thought it strange that he should be distraught with anxiety for the Queen now that she was so ill, Frances did not. She had always understood Charles' affection for Catherine, who gave him an adoring fidelity no other woman had ever given him.

It seemed now that if she recovered, it was all she *could* give him, for the doctors who attended her said that she would now never bear a child. In the premature birth of a son she had suffered much damage, and within hours a fever set in which was probably augmented by her desperate disappointment.

Day by day she was reported to be more grievously ill. The physicians shook their heads despondently and could give the King no hope of her recovery. It astonished them that he so urgently desired it, for tossing on her pillows and crying out in delirium was a wife he had blatantly neglected when she was in good health, and who now if she were pulled back from death would be nothing but an encumbrance to him.

Charles did not see the matter in this light. Neither did Frances, who also desired Catherine's recovery, partly out of genuine affection, partly because if she died Frances knew that in the course of time Charles would turn to her, and she would be given the chance of marrying him. That she could refuse it was unthinkable, that she desired it was debatable.

While the Queen's physicians wrestled for her life and the King spent hours by her bedside, in her few lucid moments imploring her to live for his sake, Frances had plenty of time in which to consider the future.

The King's fondness for her being so evident, she had for months been a person of consequence, but now she was given an additional deference. In those days and weeks of suspense, with callous disregard of the Queen's sufferings, bets were laid as to whether or not Frances would succeed her. As time passed, and it was seen how Charles turned to her when he was not with the Queen, there were few prepared to stake their money against her.

None but the Queen's attendants who knew something of nursing were allowed near her, but Frances heard every detail of her illness from the King's lips. He sent for her and she listened to him and tried to comfort him, all her butterfly lightness subdued and her sympathy and concern so genuine that for the time being a grateful affection took the place of passionate desire.

Most of these meetings took place in Barbara's apartments. Every evening the King took supper with her, but he demanded Frances' presence and Barbara was forced to comply. Now she fully realized that, whether the Queen lived or died, she was supplanted. The King, because of his tenderness for the children she had borne him, might never publicly reject her, but her influence with him was nil, and her physical attraction had lost much of its power. Neither sulks nor rages affected him, and Barbara had the sense to discard them, and to pretend a friendship for Frances which was now entirely false.

Frances, in her youthful ignorance and her failure to understand the complexities of human nature, was far from appreciating the wound inflicted upon Barbara's pride. She knew that Henry Jermyn was Barbara's lover, and that, tiring of him, she had started an affair with another young man who had recently put in an appearance at Court and was one of Buckingham's satellites. Therefore, why in the world, argued Frances, should it affront her if the King were now indifferent to her? All that Barbara could expect was that he would honour his obligations to her, and this he would do. He invariably did.

For the time being Frances herself was safe. Charles was

not now thinking of her as a longed-for mistress. He needed her as a friend and that she could be. She had never been more of a woman and less of a minx; never more tender of heart than when he restlessly paced Barbara's salon, his face ravaged with grief and his speech almost incoherent.

Barbara, in repressed rage because her apartments were being used as a convenience, because the elegant supper she had ordered had been barely touched, and Charles gazed at her blankly as though he scarcely realized her presence, retired without apology to her bed-chamber, from whence she sent a message demanding the attendance of her latest lover. There was no necessity for secrecy. The King would neither know nor care that she was not alone.

"Don't, please don't give up hope," Frances entreated, as Charles dropped down into a chair, covering his face with his hands. "The Queen is putting up a fight, and that shows she wants to live. Doesn't that bring comfort? It is you who have given her the strength to fight, by showing her how much you need her."

"God knows I do," Charles said wretchedly, "but I showed her little sign of it before she fell ill."

"Oh, but you did. I know you did. Sometimes she would talk to me, tell me how kind you had been to her. And you would never allow anyone to slight her. She knew that— that—oh, how can I word it? That her position was unassailable. She was your wife. You would never put her away from you."

"Yes, thank God, she knew that," Charles muttered.

"And now, just to realize that you are there, beside her, is of more benefit to her than all the doctors' remedies," Frances insisted.

He uttered a scoffing laugh and looked up with angry, miserable eyes. "Those fools! They do more harm than good. If she fights for her life, poor soul, I fight against them for such poor chance as she has. Given their way and they would bleed her until she fell into a coma from sheer weakness; while as for their absurd remedies . . . ! Pigeons slaughtered by the dozen and their carcases laid against her feet, poor love! The stench of them in that room with the closed windows is appalling, and she gasping for breath. As for the priests, they are little if any better with their so-called miraculous cures. Today I had a battle with them. They would have shaved off all her hair and fitted what they swear is a miraculous cap to her bare scalp."

"It's a mercy you are the King whose orders they dare not disobey," Frances commented. "Oh, Charles, her lovely hair . . . !"

"I was obliged to agree that it should be cut short, otherwise did she die it would be said I had murdered her. Like enough, if the worst happens, such *will* be said. She prayed for air and I threw open the windows. I insisted that the linen on the bed should be changed, though they all swore it would hasten her end. I put her into fresh night-gear with my own hands, after I had sponged her poor, fevered body . . . and had you seen their aghast faces . . ."

He dragged himself up from the chair to pace the room once more, and Frances said: "If ever some such illness befalls me, I pray that I may have as good a nurse."

The King looked at her then. For the first time in days seeing her clearly as the beautiful girl he had desired before this grief had come upon him. He would desire her again, and knew himself well enough to own it—as wife if Catherine died, as mistress if she lived. But just now they were in a sexless no-man's-land, and she could give him comfort that was not to be found elsewhere.

"Women can be angels," he said. "I little thought that you—but mayhap we are both fond of her in much the same way."

"We are, and I know the Queen has always trusted me," Frances said, hoping these words would be remembered if Catherine recovered.

"Could you but hear her raving," Charles cried. "She believes that she has borne our son, poor love, and grieves because she fancies he is an ugly babe. What could I do but humour her, and tell her he is a pretty boy? Yet if she recovers who is to break it to her that the child died before she had carried it long enough for it to live? It will destroy her."

"Oh no. Not if *you* tell her. Not if you make her realize that you love her for herself and will always so love her, even though there can be no children."

"Such love as mine, inconstant wretch that I am, can be of little consolation."

"But it is, Charles. You know it is." And then Frances said hopefully: "And why should you *not* be constant in the future?"

He ceased his restless pacing to regard her closely. He said bitterly: "Because it is not in my profligate nature. God's truth, if you can think otherwise, 'tis proof you are still a child."

Strong hands pulled her up to him. He drew her to his breast and kissed her. But there was no fire in him. Frances held him to her as she would have held any suffering human being, smoothing his hair and noticing with awe that in the last tense days the dark locks had become sprinkled with grey.

"It is at this time in the evenings that she is always calm and able to sleep," Charles said. "Later, she will be restless and then I must be with her."

"How I wish I could do something to help," Frances said sincerely.

"You help *me*. Can you doubt it? God's Peace! What a maze is a man's heart!"

That evening, when the King passed from Barbara's apartments to those of the Queen, Frances went with him, walking with her hand in his through the long corridors and the rooms where members of the Court were assembled, regardless of the curious glances as all present rose to their feet and bowed low. The King mechanically acknowledged the general salutations, and Frances did not try to withdraw her hand, though she gave a slight start as, passing through the last room before they came to the passage which led to the Queen's suite, she recognized the Duke of Lennox and Richmond.

She had not seen him for months, and of late had rarely thought of him, but now she blenched as she met his dark and lowering gaze. The King glanced at her as she made an attempt to pull her hand from his clasp, and then he saw Lennox and came to a standstill.

"It is long since I have seen you, cousin," he said, "and now we meet at an ill moment. But for the Queen's illness I would have summoned you here to commend your enterprise and gallantry. It was a shrewd notion to send out a fleet of privateers."

"All I did, Sire, was to repeat the tactics of the Elizabethans. If the scheme had been unsuccessful, 'twould at least have been no charge on the Admiralty. But as it chanced, the Dutch merchantmen were taken unawares."

"So I am told. 'Twas a bold stroke, and but for this ever-present anxiety 'twould rank of first importance to me. As it is, my mind is in distraction, and I go now to the Queen, who at this hour is always wakeful. I will leave our mutual cousin in your care."

Raising Frances' hand to his lips, arresting with a gesture her low curtsey, the King strode on. Lennox and Frances gazed at each other.

"What did the King mean when he spoke of your enterprise in sending out privateers?" Frances asked curiously.

Lennox shrugged. "It was an obvious action once one's mind turned to the past. Drake and Frobisher set the example. The Admiralty might have chewed for weeks over the cost, so I bought the ships, fitted them out and hired the crew. I was in command, and we've captured more than one of the Dutch merchantmen with a full cargo."

"It must have been exciting," Frances said, and thought that the King and all those who had rated him low would now change their tune. Not that there were no grounds for criticism. Doubtless Lennox was a spendthrift, and had, as she had heard one say who was friendly with him, been born with an unquenchable thirst. "It is long since we met," she said, and sat upon an oak settle with a high, padded back. "You are seldom at Court."

"There is little to bring me to Court. I hardly know why I am here now, except that hearing of Her Majesty's dire illness, and the rumours . . ."

"At one time I thought there was to be friendship between us," Frances said with the frankness she had never lost.

"A make-believe friendship is of little worth."

"Why should it be make-believe? But mayhap you regretted our confidences, for on the few occasions when I have caught a glimpse of you you have ignored me."

"You were so well occupied that it is amazing you were aware of me. Not once have I seen you but that you were the centre of a group of sycophants, and at the King's side."

"Was that so significant when by your own showing you have been here so seldom?"

"In itself it might not have been, but the talk . . ."

"I would have said Your Grace was of too independent a mind to pay attention to the everlasting gossip of the Court."

He looked at her with hot, angry eyes, and said: "You did not answer my letters."

Frances shrugged and retorted with maddening nonchalance: "Did you write? So many people write to me. I only know that last year when we were at Tunbridge you stayed at your Kent fastness for weeks while I was within an easy distance of you."

Suddenly Lennox abandoned reserve and exploded into angry speech.

"For the love of God, what is the use? I have heard and seen enough to recognize that it is useless. What friendship can there be, when at the most, should I be fool enough to care for you, the King and you would but use me as a pawn? One thing he has not yet bought you is a husband who can be safely cuckolded, and that is not a rôle I covet."

This furious speech was uttered in tones that Frances feared were loud enough to be heard by those close by. She was dumbfounded. Although her eyes blazed and her cheeks were hot with anger, she cast an apprehensive glance around, and was thankful that nobody seemed to be paying them any attention.

Julia La Garde was playing at a *chemin-de-fer* table, and was holding the bank. No doubt successfully, as a hillock of gold coins was at her elbow. Even the Queen's illness and the sobriety demanded by etiquette could not abate the prevailing passion for gambling.

Frances said bitingly, though in a discreet undertone: "Had His Majesty been less perturbed he would not have left me in your drunken company, for drunk you are. If you remember aught of this tomorrow, then remember what I now tell you. Between the King and me, all is as it was when I first met you."

"Drunk I am not," cried Lennox with an anger to match her own, and by his standards this was a fact, since he could still stand on his feet.

"Then all the more shame to you!" Frances declared stormily. "What you have said is an enormity, which one day I pray you may repent."

"If the day ever comes when I bow the knee to you as my Queen, no doubt you will so prevail upon His Majesty that I shall be forced to repent in order to avoid my ruin. But that day is not yet, and now that we speak together as equals, I would have you know that even if what you say is true, it is of little credit to you to keep a man, though it may be the King himself, dancing to your tune—promising him that which you have no mind to deliver. It proves you a cheat, my cousin."

"You dare to say so!"

"That and more!"

Frances was trembling, and her voice shook though it was little above a whisper: "'Tis well that the King is not here to listen to you, and were I to repeat what you have said, a score of more gallant men than you would challenge you to a duel."

"I have no doubt of it. Why then should you hold to silence?"

"That is a puzzle to me as well as to you." Frances' lips

quivered. "It can be only because I had a liking for you, and that, deny it though you may, you are bemused and do not understand the cruelties you have thrown at me. It must be so, for what have I ever done to make you hate me?"

The last piteous question was almost inaudible, and it was far from Frances' desire that it should be answered. Lennox rose hastily, but as hastily she left him. Down the long room she went, not trying to conceal her agitation, and to those who glanced up as she passed, the men rising to their feet, this agitation seemed natural. She had spoken with the King but recently, probably she had been told that the Queen's condition was desperate, and even though this might well mean her own glittering triumph, a superficial grief was to be expected from her. There were those who would have approached her, but Frances made a blind gesture of dismissal, and they fell back.

To her it seemed an eternity before she reached her own room, dismissed her maid, and threw herself upon her bed in a passion of tears.

Although she knew she would never utter a word of what had passed, she longed to punish Lennox and was furiously frustrated because she was powerless. How dared he! How dared he! The futile question beat upon her brain. He had suggested—what had he suggested? The vilest of all vile things!

Drunk though Lennox was, what could have put this into his head? Could it also have seemed a possibility to the King? Oh no, she did not believe it, could not believe that he had made any such squalid plan for her. If she had surrendered herself to him, yes—perhaps, but at this stage he was too romantically in love with her. It was chiefly through this strain of romance, because she represented youth and laughter to him, that their relationship was still an innocent one. There was that in Charles, unacknowledged though it might be, that hesitated to tarnish what was almost if not quite an innocuous passion. Frances had allowed him more licence than she had allowed any man—kisses and caresses, a fondling that had given her no pleasure, though she had acted pleasure. Time and again she had drawn away with feigned reluctance, and had put him off with promises that were as vague as she dared to make them.

Various factors had helped her. There had been Barbara's pregnancy which she had pleaded was a barrier between them. That had tided her over months; and then when Barbara's son was born, and Charles had sworn that if Frances would be kind, he for his part would finish with her, she, sore beset, had contemplated a visit to the cousins in Scotland. It had not been necessary, for the Queen had told her in confidence that she, once more, had hope of bearing a child.

Frances had not dared to reproach the King. Not all the love he professed for her was sufficient to prevent him from begetting a legitimate son or daughter were this possible. But it had enabled Frances to say steadfastly that she was far too attached to the Queen to betray her while she was *enceinte*, and surely the King could not desire it, since even the merest suspicion of such perfidy would, if it came to the Queen's ears, be sufficient to cause disaster.

Charles had seen the possibility of this and he had grudgingly acquiesced. Frances had breathed freely again, and she had been happy during the Queen's expectancy, and once more disinclined to look too far into the future. The King's favour and the King's love were both desirable while they remained on their present plane. Everyone smiled upon her and she was free to devote herself to an endless succession of gaieties. There were balls and masques and river picnics. She could go riding with the King and a train of attendant courtiers in Windsor Park. There were archery parties and hawking, and of late the diversion of sitting for Jan Roettier, whose handsome brothers crowded round to admire her.

In spite of Charles' veniality, there was an honesty about him. Frances liked him for this quality as she liked him for many others, though she had known from the first that she would never fall in love with him. But he had certainly fallen in love with her, and should the Queen die it was probable that he would marry her. In that case her connection with the Blantyre Stuarts, who were of the Royal House, would be exaggerated and exploited. But if the Queen lived, the pursuit, the persuasion, and her own efforts to evade the King would start all over again. Outright rejection would mean that she lost his favour for ever, and heaven only knew what would become of her. It would be impossible for her to remain at Court, and as she would then be regarded by many as the King's discarded mistress, her prestige would be low indeed. How endlessly her mother would reproach her.

Against her will, for she hated to dwell on suffering, Frances' thoughts turned to the Queen who must have suffered tortures, both physical and mental, during the last few weeks. Now, she might be actually dying, and if she did die, in one sense Frances' troubles would be over. But not in every sense, for, although the thought of being Queen was so dazzling it set her brain awhirl, the thought of Charles as a husband, and especially of Charles as an adoring, demanding and faithful husband, was far from dazzling.

"Oh, pray God she lives," murmured Frances, and found herself praying with a fervour that was new to her. "She loves him and even without a child she can be happy, for he does care about her in his way."

There came a light tap at the door, and Frances dragged herself up and crossed the room. She opened the door and saw Julia La Garde, who surveyed her tear-marked face with some surprise.

"Are you really so grieved about her?" she asked. "Everyone supposes . . ."

"Of course I am grieved. I love her dearly," Frances cried. "I came from France to be with her—I was with her while she and the King were honeymooning. There has been nothing but kindness. You are new here. You scarcely know her."

"Not so well as you," Miss La Garde agreed, "though I agree the Queen is amiable and that this is a sad end for her."

"An end? Do you mean . . . ?"

"There has been no further news, except that the priests are seen going in and out of her chamber, and someone said just now she was to receive Extreme Unction. That means the end of hope, does it not?" enquired Protestant Julia, to whom all such Catholic practices were mummery.

"No. It does not," cried Frances in a passion she scarcely understood. "It means that God is being implored to save her. And you . . . I . . . all of us, of whatever faith, should join in that entreaty."

"Certainly I shall pray for her to be spared," Julia La Garde said, jealous of Frances, disliking her, but since she might soon be in tremendous power unwilling to offend her. "But it is not on the Queen's account that I am here. When you left the Duke of Lennox and Richmond—though I vow I did not know who he was until he told me—his looks were so despondent I spoke to him and tried to cheer him."

"Another bottle of wine will do that," Frances said callously.

"More like it would send him into a coma. He had taken enough. He told me he had offended you in the most dire way, and of course nobody wishes to offend you, least of all at present."

"At present?" Frances snapped, angry eyes fixed on her.

"I mean because you are already so unhappy," explained the diplomatic Julia. "He wrote me a note and asked me as a favour to see that it reached you."

The girl's eyes were bolting from her head with a curiosity which was to receive no satisfaction. Frances took the folded slip of paper from her, wondering if she had had the impudence to read what was written. "Thank you," she said, "that was kind of you. It could have waited until tomorrow, as it is so late. I was about to retire."

This was sufficiently pointed, especially as Julia had not been invited to seat herself. Evidently there was no hope of a cosy gossip, in which she would be given the chance to make headway with one who before many months passed might be the Queen of England.

She left—regretfully—and Frances stood with the twist of paper in her hand, half minded not to read it but to tear it into fragments. But at last, and reluctantly, she unfolded it. Five words only had been written. "Forgive me. I was mad."

Well, at least, thought Frances as she put the paper to the flame of a candle and watched it as a black cobweb fall to the ground, even if Julia had read the message it could not have enlightened her.

Wearily Frances got into bed and slept the sleep of profound exhaustion. When she awoke hours later it was to hear that the Queen had taken a turn for the better. Her physicians had announced that the crisis was past and that she would live. Frances felt nothing but thanksgiving, and those who eyed her slyly, expecting to see signs of chagrin, were disappointed. Her own anxiety could be shelved, thought Frances optimistically. There was time enough.

To some extent she was right. Catherine made a slow recovery and Charles was kind and attentive. He had been aghast at the possibility of losing her, and her love for him had in her delirium been so pitifully clear that for the first time he felt an acute responsibility for her happiness.

Now it was easy to reassure her and to make her believe in his answering love. For a short while at least Charles, when he considered Frances, did so with embarrassment. He was still in love with her, but during the Queen's illness he had revealed his soul to her, which was something he had never done before, however much involved with a woman. As he was to say later when Barbara Castlemaine dramatically announced her conversion to Catholicism, he was not interested in ladies' souls; nevertheless in his grief and suspense, and in Frances' sympathetic understanding, there had been a communication between souls, and he could not immediately forget it.

It was as though they, who were unacknowledged antagonists in the game of love, had signed a truce.

The Queen, starting upon her lengthy convalescence, wanted to have Frances with her, to read to her, to talk to her. Frances could make her laugh as readily as she could make the King laugh, and they were thus equally concerned in steering the Queen towards normal health.

Beyond his absorption in his women-folk, Charles at this time was precariously involved with Louis XIV, whose unofficial mouthpiece was Henrietta-Anne.

The young Duchess of Orleans wanted nothing more fervently than a close alliance between the two countries, and all her letters to Charles at this period were aimed to forward it. But it is doubtful if she fully understood the devious character of her brother-in-law.

Louis' last wish was to see an alliance brought about between the Dutch and the English, thus strengthening the two maritime powers, but his policy was one of pretended mediation, and this was pressed by the arrival of two additional ambassadors from France, in the persons of Henri de Bourbon and the Duc de Verneuil.

Occupied with these two illustrious personages, with Catherine's still precarious health and with the naval campaign, Charles ignored a worse enemy than the Dutch which was making stealthy inroads upon congested London.

Each year the dreaded plague caused a percentage of deaths, but hitherto it had not become an epidemic. This year there was to be a far more serious outbreak. Soon there was a deepening sense of horror as the weekly death list mounted.

The Court hastily withdrew to Hampton Court, where the more frivolous-minded did their best to forget the frightful conditions prevailing in London. But the Queen was unable to forget, for the King, though he acquiesced in the removal of the Court, and arrangements were made to quarter the French Ambassadors at Kingston, himself stayed on at Whitehall, braving the risk of infection.

"He is too courageous. He never thinks of himself, except inasmuch as he would despise himself if he sought comparative safety while his people are in danger," Catherine lamented.

"He is not alone," Frances sought to comfort. "Many of whom he thinks most highly share the same peril."

"Oh, I know—the chiefs at the Admiralty, and that really admirable young Pepys and John Evelyn and others. Even the Archbishop of Canterbury, who, residing at Lambeth Palace, sets an example to some members of our own priesthood." Catherine, who was always just to those whom she considered heretics, added punctiliously: "They put their faith in God, and so should we, Frances, who are of the true Church. But it is so hard, so hard when one loves. It is your good fortune that as yet you are heartwhole."

Frances dutifully agreed, though her thoughts had flown to an angry, glowering young man who had flayed her with cruel words. She had no information as to Lennox's whereabouts. He might be safe at Cobham Hall, but it was equally likely that he was on the high seas, commanding a fleet of privateers, making sorties on the Dutch merchant ships. Risking his life as surely as though he was living in the midst of the plague-stricken capital.

Throughout the summer the plague raged, and horrifying accounts of it reached those who were in comparative safety at Hampton Court—not from the King when he paid brief and rare visits to this refuge, but from those who had at first been valiantly determined to withstand the appalling danger, but had finally panicked.

The Queen spent hours each day on her knees in her private oratory, and had no heart for the diversions in which the others sought relief. Frances, thankful to be relieved of the King's attentions, was gay enough. It was also a relief that Mistress Stuart was in Scotland. When the Queen was reported to be out of danger she had sent Frances a letter which mingled feigned and diplomatic thanksgiving with lamentations over her daughter's lost chance of a royal marriage, and this was followed by close-written pages of ambiguous advice. Frances could be forgiven for wondering if her mother was secretly advocating her to accede to the King's desire.

The Chevalier de Gramont, who rented a house at Salisbury when the Court moved from Hampton, this being now considered too near London for safety, inaugurated card-parties, which started as early as midday and with intervals for refreshments continued until the small hours of the following morning. John Hamilton, who had recently fled from London and whose sister, once coveted by Lennox, de Gramont had married, gave a vivid description of his sojourn there, to an appalled but morbidly fascinated audience.

"It became beyond my bearing," he said, "and had I not left, I vow I should have thrown myself into the Thames out of wretchedness of spirit. I was doing no good there, and the Admiralty would do better to operate from a safer locality, for there will soon be none left to conduct the naval manœuvres. You cannot conceive of the desolation. Grass is growing in the streets, the shops are closed, nearly every other house has the cross upon it with a prayer for mercy, which denotes that those within are stricken down. At nights there is no sound other than the plague-carts as they go upon their way, and the cries to the people that they must deliver up their dead."

"There cannot be sufficient priests left in London to deliver the Last Rites," Frances said in horror-struck tones.

Hamilton's melancholy expression and shrugged shoulders denoted that she had wholly failed to grasp the extent of the disaster.

"There is little or any attempt at religious rites," he stated. "There may be a few devoted souls who give General Absolution at the pit-heads, but I have heard of none. They die in too great numbers for graves or grave-diggers or even for coffins. The Lord Mayor has said that the death-carts may now go their rounds by day as well as by night, for the hours of dark are not long enough."

"But is nothing being done for the people in the way of medicines and treatment?" Lady Denham asked.

"What can be done," Hamilton countered, "when physicians die off with as great a rapidity as their patients? Oh yes, there are ministering angels, as in all such times of distress. Those who are seemingly fearless and selfless and go from one stricken house to another with nourishing foods for those who can take them, and giving such comfort as they can. Some do recover against all expectation, and it is said that few of these self-constituted nurses have sickened and died. It is as though their courage acts as a talisman."

Catherine sighed when these stories were brought to her ears.

"It would be a terrible disaster for the country if the King were to sacrifice his life," she said wretchedly. "But when I do see him and tell him this, he pays no attention to me. He believes that cleanliness is the answer to the sickness. That scrubbed boards and scrubbed bodies are of equal importance."

"Many people think that the reed-strewn floors are partly responsible," Lady Suffolk said, "but for myself I believe that the infection comes from those wretched Dutch merchant-men. That in peace-time the goods they trade are poisoned, and that now by spreading the disease they hope to conquer us as a nation."

"Nobody will conquer England while the King lives," Catherine said with pride.

"Men think only of wars. To them they are exhilarating," Lady Suffolk lamented. "Now that King Louis has dropped all this pretence of friendship, and is said to be ready to come in on the side of the Dutch, heaven only knows how long there may be hostilities."

"It must be a great grief to the Queen Dowager," Frances said. "When she packed up and left Somerset House for Paris she had no suspicion of it."

"But she will be glad that she is there," the Queen said, "for she is constantly worried about her daughter."

Now that the Court was at Salisbury, the Duke and Duchess of York took the opportunity to make a tour in the north, and Charles himself went off to pay a visit of inspection to the fortifications at Portsmouth and the Isle of Wight. From thence he proceeded to make a tour of Dorset and the neighbouring counties, and was then at Oxford, where, because of the persistence of the plague, it was decided Parliament must meet that autumn.

Louis XIV informed Charles that, unless he would allow him to intervene and to mediate, France, because of treaty obligations, would be forced to support the Dutch. The challenge thus flung at him, Charles, after consultation with Parliament, who had no more mind than he to make peace at the command of the French King when all was going their way, took it up, and within days, Parliament having granted a million and a quarter, the country was at war with France as well as with the Dutch.

Frances' relationship with the King throughout these months had presented few problems. The King was harassed, depressed over the fate of plague-stricken London, worried by letters from his beloved Minette, who was heartbroken at the prospect of their two countries at war, pestered by the Queen Dowager, and with one worry on top of another, was far from well.

Frances had plenty of diversions. There were idle young men by the dozen to flatter her and give her all the attention she required. The Queen now went hunting several days a week and Frances was always with her. She learnt how to play bowls and became proficient at it.

Of Lennox she heard from Julia La Garde, who with a great air of secrecy told Frances that he occasionally wrote to her.

"He must have been struck to the heart by your charm and kindness to him, when you thought he looked so unhappy," Frances said with all outward sweetness.

"He *was* unhappy," Julia said positively.

"You may be right." Frances shrugged. "For myself I judged that he was one of those who became lachrymose in their cups."

"Oh, Frances Stuart, what an unkind girl you are!" cried Julia, who no longer treated Frances with any particular deference. "But perhaps you always behave so to the men who are in love with you."

"In love with me? That's ridiculous. I have," said Frances, "met His Grace of Lennox and Richmond less than half a dozen times."

"One look into your eyes seems to do mischief enough," and Julia giggled. "All the poor creature cares about is to know how you are, how you look, what you are doing."

"It is no concern of his," Frances flared, and then asked with irrepressible curiosity: "What do you tell him?"

"That these days you rarely stir from the Queen's side, and that the King only pays rare visits to see her, being so occupied with these official tours."

It was a meaning gaze that the astute Miss La Garde

fixed upon Frances, and she moved restlessly beneath it. Nobody ever openly alluded to the King's love for her—none save Buckingham, whom now she rarely saw. Even when it had been thought that the Queen would die and bets had been freely laid upon Frances' chance of filling her place, hints and innuendoes had served for plain speaking. Now Julia La Garde was telling her as openly as she dared that she was allaying Lennox' jealousy. But she was probably exaggerating. There was nothing between herself and Lennox, Frances told herself, and if he wrote to the other girl it must be because he was attracted to her. Why shouldn't he be? Julia was pretty enough, and her family were rich. Lennox had already wed two heiresses, and had refused to consider Elizabeth Hamilton because she had no dowry.

Why Julia should attempt to reassure Lennox about the King's attentions Frances could not fathom. The two girls were not really friendly, and Julia had a reputation for slyness.

"Oh well, it is no concern of mine what you tell him," Frances said, and went upon her way.

Julia looked after her reflectively. In some ways the light-hearted Frances was an enigma—and not only to her. If the King was her lover, as many believed, she seemed to profit little by it. Barbara Castlemaine, who was an old story to him, did far better for herself even now. Titles had been conferred on her elder children as well as on herself, and only lately she had been given an estate at Hereford. Frances at the most had acquired no more than a few valuable jewels.

But perhaps she was not the King's mistress, Julia mused. Was it possible that if she were, the Queen would be so fond of her? Or *seem* to be fond, Julia corrected herself. After all, the Queen put up a pretence of cordiality to Barbara Castlemaine. Everyone knew the Queen worshipped the King. She would do everything that was required of her. As for Frances, so many men whom the maids-of-honour described as irresistible had made advances to her and had been rejected that it had become the habit to refer to "her cold little heart".

How delightful it would be if the dazzling butterfly were to marry and disappear from the Court circle! Julia was secretly most romantically disposed towards the King, and once or twice he had smiled at her in an especial kind of way, and she was sure his eyes had followed her. But he would never be seriously attracted to her while Frances was around, though if she were once married off he would be bound to forget her in time, and that would give some other girl at Court a chance.

The King was so amazingly attractive, thought Miss La Garde with a yearning sigh, and such stories were spread abroad of his prowess as a lover. How *could* Frances Stuart resist him? At the Court of Charles II virtue was held to be of little account; it was another name for dullness.

Julia La Garde glanced at herself in a mirror, finding no fault with her bright-brown hair and eyes and piquant countenance. Were there no Frances, she would stand a very good chance.

In London the plague slowly abated, and early in the New Year the Court ventured to return to Whitehall. But they were scarcely settled there than they were all plunged into mourning through the death of the Queen's mother, the Queen Regent of Portugal.

Poor Catherine, who had not seen her mother since her marriage, sorrowed deeply, but to her ladies the command to wear black was a grievance. Barbara was infuriated, but Frances was unconcerned because black suited her. Pepys noted in his diary that she was now fairer in looks than Lady Castlemaine.

Fair or not, Frances' inward turmoil was distracting. Her radiance and vivacity were almost wholly assumed. She was too proud to let anyone suspect her secret desperation. She now was forced to face the fact that her relationship with Charles was nearing a climax. Past eighteen, and at the zenith of her beauty, the King was no longer inclined to treat her as an innocent child, unconscious of her allure, and at last was spurred to action as much by anger as by desire.

At Whitehall the original small apartment allotted to Frances as a maid-of-honour had recently been enlarged. She now had a large salon, delightfully furnished by the King's orders, and looking out upon the teeming river. Here she could entertain her chosen friends, and was so doing when he made an unheralded arrival. Charles was too courteous to break up the party deliberately and accounted for his unexpected visit by showing Frances an advance specimen of the gold coins from the Mint. Everyone present was eager to examine it and admire. The King's head on the obverse side of the coin was considered a striking likeness, and the Britannia most splendidly dignified.

"Not a bit like me," Frances said blithely, "except for the nose, but then I don't think these bas-relief pictures do much resemble the sitters. The King looks years and years younger than he does on the coin."

"You think so?" Charles was not a vain man, but as this came from his peerless Frances he was gratified.

Immediately there was a supporting murmur. "Oh yes, in reality His Majesty looks ten or even fifteen years younger."

"But I don't suppose anyone could improve on it," Frances said, not wishing to criticize Jan Roettier.

Lord Berkeley ventured to disagree with Frances. He considered that both likenesses were excellent, and remarked daringly that La Belle Stuart could scarcely have been given greater importance had she been a queen.

This remark met with a cold reception; and as it was clear that the King, though he had paid an informal call, had no intention of making it a brief one, the guests severally curtsied or bowed to him and were given permission to depart.

As soon as Charles was alone with Frances, he said without preamble: "Berkeley was right, if tactless. I have given you all the importance you would accept, and in the future I hope to give you more. That rests with yourself."

187

Never in all the years she had known him had he so spoken to her, not with the tenderness of a lover or the light-hearted raillery of a good companion, but with the authority of kingship.

"I have never wanted more than I have now," she said, wondering if it would be possible still to preserve the light touch which hitherto had served her so well. "I cannot tell you what a pleasure this enlarged apartment is to me. It has given me the chance to offer hospitality instead of always receiving it."

Charles examined the gold coin which lay in his palm. He tossed it into the air and lightly caught it.

"As a hostess, m'dear, you will need a multitude of these," he observed. "Your Privy Purse allowance will scarce be sufficient even for wines and sweetmeats. But you have only to ask, and right well you know it."

"People are always asking the King for money, but I have no mind to be one of them," Frances said. "I can manage. I am not extravagant."

"That I grant you. It is one way in which you and the Queen resemble each other. You are both astonishingly thrifty."

"The Queen has set me a good example in that way as in all others," Frances said meaningly, and then spoilt this most correct rejoinder by adding: "Besides, one has to consider the Scots heritage. It always seems to assert itself on the distaff side. I believe I should be quite successful as a wife—in house management, I mean."

"Successful in every sense, no doubt, but I cannot spare you yet—not for many years—not mayhap for all my life-time. Not, that is to say, unless I marry you off to some titled dodderer who will ask no more than that you bear his name and superintend his household. Such a spouse could be found for you without much difficulty or delay."

So here it was at last, thought Frances with bitterness and resentment. The direct proposition. It was with difficulty that she essayed a laugh.

"A titled dodderer! It is not such an attractive prospect.

Most girls of my age when they marry expect some gaiety and pleasure and companionship. Children too."

"Such a marriage would debar you from none of them."

"But it would be hateful. Living beneath the same roof as one I despised—and with good reason."

"As for that, one could find a plausible pretext for arranging frequent separations."

"That's not what I want from life," said Frances defiantly.

"Then tell me what it is, for I have not yet discovered it."

"Only happiness, only content."

"You can have both at a word. Am I not anxious to give you both? Sometimes I think I love you as no other woman was ever loved, and more than once you have sworn you care for me. Was that a lie?"

"How would I dare to lie to the King?" Frances countered.

"You have dared much, m'dear. You are treating me ill and you know it, but even my patience with a woman has its limits. I have never yet forced one to my will, but . . ."

"Charles, if you threaten me, all will be spoilt."

"What is there to spoil? You have given me nothing."

"How can you say that? Nobody else has been allowed so—so much, and is my affection nothing?" Frances crossed the room to his side. With a silken swish of her skirts she knelt beside him, her hand on his knee. After a moment, gazing down into her eyes, lovely indeed, but clouded with anxiety, Charles said:

"Frances, have you ever known what it is to long for something so yearningly, so constantly, that for lack of it all else is worthless?"

There was a pause before she answered, but when she did it was, so Charles divined, an honest answer.

"Not as intensely as that, but I have longed . . . I do . . ."

"Then, my sweet life, if it is mutual why deny yourself as well as me?"

Down came Frances' long, shielding lashes. It was natural he should misinterpret her words. She had intended that he should, but now she was in worse case than before. She said childishly and frivolously: "At least if I were married off at your will, I would wish it to be to someone who would not look a figure of fun when we were obliged to be seen together. Even a husband in name—well, it would be unpleasant to know one's friends laughed at him. I remember saying so to 'Rietta when she first told me she was to marry that Orleans popinjay."

"I will find you someone more personable," Charles promised. "Zounds! It should be something to any man, young or old, to have you act as hostess for him and to bear his name."

Not any man of spirit and honour, Frances thought, but she did not say so.

"A Duke's title—a Duke's estate," Charles went on. "I will scrape the royal coffer for you if needs be!"

"Your Majesty requires every guinea that can be mustered for this new war with France," she submitted. "Could you not put the thought of me aside until we have won it?"

Stooping, Charles put his hands on her shoulders and gazed steadfastly into her eyes. "How many times," he asked, "have I been induced on one excuse or another to put aside the possessing of you? There was Barbara's pregnancy and my wife's illness. There was your religion. There was the devastation of the plague which kept us apart."

"But was any of that my fault?" Frances asked.

"Sometimes I fancy that your only fault is your virtue, which does but make me love you the more."

"Then Your Majesty is old-fashioned, for virtue nowadays *is* unfashionable," she retorted pertly. "It is expected only of Queens, and sometimes not even of them."

"I should expect you to be faithful to me, none the less."

"Well, and so I would be, if it came to that between us . . ."

"*If!* At other times you have said *when.*"

"When then—but, Charles, you must know how difficult it is for me. It means giving up—practically giving up my religion. I am not a *religieuse* such as the Queen, but nobody, nobody can throw it away with lightness—not even I."

"Where would be the necessity? What are confession, absolution and penance for, if not for fair sinners?"

"Fair sinners who after a few days of chastity settle down to commit the same sins all over again? You know better than that, Charles!"

"Well, yes, I do," admitted he, who but for his kingship of a Protestant country would have been of the same persuasion.

"I thought while thousands were dying of the plague, and with no priest to comfort them, how dreadful it would be to die unshriven," Frances said.

"My sweet love, you are not like to die for many years, and if I am then alive, I promise you that half a dozen priests shall be there to shrive you."

"Oh, for the love of heaven, no! I should die the quicker for terror. One of those black crows would be sufficient, calling upon me to repent . . ."

The repudiation was so swift, the miming which accompanied it so vivid that Charles burst out laughing. So did she. It seemed, mercifully, as though his sombre mood had passed, and there might be no more talk of marriage to one whose complacence would be bought with a title and estate . . . just as Lennox had said, she remembered.

"What am I to do with you?" Charles demanded half-comically.

"I don't know. I cannot endure to be rushed."

"Rushed! God's truth! When I consider the many months . . . I'm no saint, whatever you may be."

"I don't think I am. Probably I'm no more than rather stupid."

"If you loved me . . ."

"I'm fonder of you than anyone else," she protested. "There *is* nobody else. Oh, Charles, it's true. I really am *immensely* fond of you."

He lifted her up and set her on his knees. He smothered her face with kisses until she turned it into his shoulder. He fondled her and heard her giggle and knew the cause. The fashion had changed of late, and she was wearing a dress shaped and stiffened to her slender figure, and high in the neck with a pointed lace collar. There was little to reward his exploring hands other than pleats of silk and whalebone. Charles shook her then and put her away from him. But he was not angry. Blessedly he was never angry for very long.

"Why won't you have me?" he asked bluntly.

"I haven't said I wouldn't—one day. Why won't you understand? I was very young when all this started, and I was flattered and foolish and fond of you. But there's so much to make it hateful—to be the King's mistress, I mean."

"And so much you will miss if you are not the favourite who becomes the King's mistress," he retorted. "This, my lovely Frances, is not a state that can continue for ever. The strain is a killing one for me, and bad enough even for you. You're not the merry, thoughtless girl of a year ago."

"No," she agreed.

"What will it be like, think you, if I send you away for ever, because of the fool you are making me? You have no money and I dare swear your mother, good woman though she is, would rather see you under my protection than adrift without it. Oh, she'd weep and wring her hands and swear that it was by no wish of hers, but she'd soon reconcile herself, and be concerned to know if I'd made a sufficient settlement on you. 'Twould be different if you were a great heiress, but . . ."

"There is always the religious life—a convent that would receive me," Frances said.

"It's not the first time you have made that threat. What reality is there in it?"

"Very little," Frances admitted truthfully. "It would be a last resort."

"And more acceptable than to belong to me, with every honour that could be given to you, and the love of all my heart?"

"Not *all* your love. There is the Queen . . ."

Charles sighed heavily. He said: "Not even for you will I

sacrifice her, poor, devoted soul. And even if I were sufficiently base, you, Frances, would oppose it. The fondness I have for her is different in kind. God help me, am I the only man who finds it possible to love two women?"

"No, you are not, but . . . if only I were not also so attached to her."

"Over and over again I have told you that it will not harm her. It will be the end of Barbara's reign. If I have not broken with her entirely it is because of you who tantalize and deny me. If I seek her from time to time it is to forget, and that, La Belle Stuart, is something any man would understand though you may not. See now, I will strike a last bargain with you. I will possess myself in patience for yet a few months, until you are nineteen and past this year of indecision."

"But that is so near," Frances exclaimed. "It is only three months."

"And an eternity to me. Make up your mind. Either you come to me then, without love if it must be so, or I will see no more of you. You have three months in which to consider."

"You are cruel to me!" Frances flamed.

"On the contrary, I am kind." Charles rose, with his complacency restored. Long-limbed girl though she was, he looked down upon her from a greater height, and although there was tenderness in his expression, there was also resolution.

Because she was pale and shaken, his dignity was restored to him. He should, he reflected, have taken this stand long ago, but it was against his nature to show harshness to a woman, much less to one he loved.

When he had gone, the newly-minted gold coin that he had idly tossed in his hand lay on the ground. Frances picked it up and gazed at herself in the robes of Britannia; majestic with her trident and her palm. Ruler of the sea, but unable longer to rule a royal lover.

17

Mary Boynton said in a shocked voice: "Not even Frances Stuart, reckless as she always was, would be capable of doing such a thing."

"But she did," Joan Wells insisted. "It was the night before last and Lady Castlemaine was giving a party."

"Were you there? It wasn't her habit to ask any of us to her parties—only Frances."

Married for the best part of a year, Mary was on a visit to London with her husband, and had called upon her old friends at Whitehall, smugly pleased to air herself as a young wife, imposing in a sable cape and with her wedding ring conspicuously displayed. Joan Wells had expected to be married ere now, but her wedding had been postponed through a family bereavement and would not take place before the New Year. It was amusing, she thought, to override Mary's complacency. She had paid this visit in such a patronizing spirit—the young matron condescending to those who were not yet as securely placed. But so much had happened at Court that she was quite overwhelmed by the flood of news poured out to her.

"Oh, she does now," Joan said airily. "All is changed. Frances is so much in the ascendant that dear Barbara has become much less haughty and is quite gracious at times. Anyway, there we all were, Julia La Garde and Cecily Angels, who are both new since you left."

Joan's gesture included the two other girls. Although Mary would be received later by the Queen to whom she would pay her dutiful respects as a past maid-of-honour, they were at present all spread around Joan's room, which did duty as both bedroom and sitting-room, with a smaller adjoining apartment for her maid.

Mary glanced towards this door now with an instinctive question in her raised brows.

"It's locked," Joan reassured her, "and Patty is out. There's a ribbon which I need to have matched, and she'll be gone for a while, as it's an unusual colour."

"As the mistress of a household I have found that one cannot be too careful with servants. The best of them are ready to pry and listen," Mary told her importantly.

"Here at Whitehall they often seem to know more of what is going on than we do," said Julia La Garde.

"Buckingham's wife was there as well," Joan continued, "though *he* was away. But there were others. A Mr. Roper, who sings so well as to woo the heart from one's breast, or so others say, for mine is already wooed. And milord Audley, who lost his wife some months ago, and Richard Granger."

"And Frances really said openly that she would marry *anyone*?" Mary enquired in her shocked voice.

"She did, did she not, Julia?"

"She had had too much wine," Cecily Angels interposed before Julia La Garde could reply. "Frances rarely drinks, or at least only a glass at the most and often with water diluting it. But she was in a strange mood that evening. Very gay but in a wild sort of fashion—laughing at nothing, or almost nothing."

"She told us all," said Julia, "that it would soon be her nineteenth birthday and that she intended to give a big party and that we were all invited and many others as well, of course."

"And then something was said about marriage. I forget exactly what." Joan again dominated the conversation. "I believe it was some remark of Barbara's. Yes, I remember now. She said she had been two years married by the time she was nineteen, and Frances laughed and drank off a full glass of wine and then said she would be willing to wed any gentleman who had an income of over fifteen hundred a year and would have her with honour. As you can imagine, everyone was stunned. There was such silence you could have heard a pin drop, but Frances just leant back in her chair, and when nobody spoke she laughed and laughed until the tears were in her eyes."

"But what in the world made her say such a thing?" Mary wondered. "Why, when I was here she had only to lift her finger and she could have had the choice of half a dozen. Besides which, the King . . ."

"Well, *he* can't marry her with honour," said Joan, "much though he might like to."

"I'm sure she had little idea what she was saying," insisted Cecily, whose sweet face was matched by a charitable nature.

"I had the exactly opposite impression. She struck me as being deliberate—throwing down the gauntlet," Joan declared.

"I agree," said Julia. "It was a kind of challenge."

"In very bad taste then," Mary pronounced.

"Bad taste or not, I dare swear she had offers from all the unmarried gentlemen there before another day was out," Joan said.

Mary shook her head. "I'm not so sure. Most look for the King's favour, but many would doubt the wisdom of marrying one whom he does favour. We do not know for certain what the situation is between the King and Frances. The man who marries her may be required only as a front, a shield."

"Frances said a gentleman who would marry her with honour," Cecily reminded them, "and Her Grace of Buckingham said afterwards to me that she was sure Frances meant it. She thought she was in a mood of wanting to get away from Court."

"The Queen as well as the King would make it hard for her to leave," Joan opined. "It's strange that, isn't it? The Queen is not blind. She must have seen for ages how it was with the King. He can't take his eyes off Frances."

"Perhaps the Queen doesn't care much by now," Mary

said. "As long as the King is kind to her and refuses to divorce her, that contents her. It's very sad. To have a faithful, loving husband means more than anything else in the world, as I should know," and Mary twisted her wedding ring on her finger and gazed down at it with a secret smile warranted to irritate any girl who was still unmarried.

"Queens have more than ordinary women and less than ordinary women," Julia observed, "and mayhap it's not so bad for the Queen if the King has one mistress only for whom she has a liking. Frances has more or less routed Barbara Castlemaine who so often affronts the Queen."

"How did the Castlemaine take it when Frances announced . . . well, practically announced that she was up for sale?" Mary enquired, and Joan replied:

"Oh, she laughed it off. She told her she was crazy. But it would suit her if some gentleman as poor as that, I mean with only a bare fifteen hundred, offered for Frances, and she took him, just to be as good as her word. Then she'd disappear from Court and live in the wilds of the country, in some tumbledown manor as like as not. What an end that would be for La Belle Stuart, while Castlemaine would again reign supreme."

"I wonder." Julia La Garde looked sceptical. "Everyone says the King is tired of her. It's more likely that his eye would fall on someone else. Frances Stuart is a flashy beauty, and mayhap obscures more subtle types."

As none of the other girls would have applied the word 'subtle' to Julia, though she was sometimes accounted sly, they did not guess that she was already seeing herself in Frances' place. Twice lately the King had danced with Julia, which was nothing out of the way, as he did sometimes single out a maid-of-honour, but Julia thought she had made some impression upon him, for he had told her that her pink dress was vastly becoming and had asked her teasingly if her lashes were more than an inch long. They *were* quite as long and even darker than Frances', Julia reflected with satisfaction.

Frances, meanwhile, unconscious that her reckless

challenge had caused such a sensation amongst her female friends, had been paying a visit to her mother who had lately returned to London, and was living at Somerset House, the official residence of Queen Henrietta-Maria on the occasions when she was in England.

The Queen Dowager had allotted a large suite there to her old and faithful friend. It was to be her home for her life, Mistress Stuart told Frances, remarking that it was far larger and grander than any ordinary house—really too large just for herself and Walter. A growing family could be lodged in the several enormous rooms. She had thought of having some of them partitioned. The Queen Dowager had given her *carte blanche* to make such alterations as she wished.

Frances was interested and made several pertinent suggestions, glad to be able to divert the conversation from her personal affairs. She knew that her mother was secretly disappointed in her, though she could not blame her because the Queen had made a complete recovery, and because all talk about a divorce had died down.

Nor would Mistress Stuart's conscience permit her to advocate a surrender to the King. She would have no actual part in that, though he was probably right, Frances reflected, in his estimate of her mother. If this did come about, Mistress Stuart would sigh and moan and pour all her perplexity into the ear of a sympathetic priest, and then she would resign herself to the situation.

Frances did not suppose that her mother would hear of the scene at Barbara Castlemaine's. Frances was now ashamed of this, though she had but an imperfect recollection of it, for it was true that she rarely drank much wine. But on that particular evening she had been so low-spirited that she had taken three or four glasses.

Zero hour was approaching and she was desperate in a way that nobody imagined, especially as Joan Wells' expectation that she would have offers from all present had not come about. Only Hugo Roper whose distinguished family and melodious tenor voice made him acceptable at Court, though he was known to be very poor, had written her a poem—a love poem—lamenting his poverty and his frustrated adoration.

She was poor too, Frances reflected, and apart from her looks she had little to recommend her as a wife.

Today she had driven to Somerset House in a palace coach, but, not knowing how long her visit would last, had told the coachman to return to Whitehall with the maid who had attended her. Mistress Stuart, who had no coach of her own, but had authority to make use of those belonging to the Queen Dowager, descended to the main entrance with her daughter, intending to escort her to Whitehall. But there, waiting, was an ornate coach with gilded panels and gold and silver fringe and harnessed to four splendid bays. Frances immediately recognized the coat of arms emblazoned on it. It was no surprise to her when the occupant of the coach leisurely descended, swept off his plumed hat and bowed low to her mother and then to herself. None the less, she gazed at him speechlessly.

"Mistress Stuart?" he queried. "But it must be so—for the likeness is unmistakeable."

And there were those who called him an oaf, thought Frances indignantly. Nothing could have been more courtly. "His Grace the Duke of Lennox and Richmond," she said hurriedly as her mother turned to her for elucidation. "And I think, *Maman*, that he is here to take me back to Whitehall."

"If I may be allowed to spare your mother the fatigue," Lennox said. "I was told at the Palace that you were visiting here, and then by chance I sighted the coach as it returned, and discovered, cousin, you had made no arrangement to be called for again."

"Cousin?" said Mistress Stuart, and then with pleased understanding: "But of course! Your Grace is a Stuart, and my dear husband knew your father milord Aubigny. But are you in such haste to be on your way? Will you not come within if only for a short while to take some refreshments?"

"Her Majesty may be requiring me, *Maman*. I have been

gone overlong," Frances said hastily, having no mind to conduct this unexpected meeting beneath her mother's speculative gaze.

"I was forgetting. Certainly you must not delay," Mistress Stuart agreed, accepting it as natural that this splendid-looking young man in the impressive family coach should escort Frances.

Lennox murmured that he hoped to have the pleasure of calling upon her formally before long. Frances bade her mother farewell, and was handed into the coach. The footman closed the door and took his place beside the coachman, the horses were whipped up and off they went.

"But not immediately to Whitehall," said Lennox, who had evidently given contrary instructions, for the coach bore them along towards Piccadilly and St. James's. "The Queen, so I heard, did not expect your attendance this evening?"

"No. She gives me permission to stay as long as I choose with my mother," Frances owned. "It wasn't true what I told her, but I was surprised to see you, and I thought she might ask awkward questions. How did you discover where I was?"

"I saw Miss La Garde, who told me. Late yesterday I received a letter from her, sent by special courier. I shall be ever in her debt for her good offices."

"Will you? It puzzles me why Julia concerns herself with my affairs."

"Out of pure good nature, I assure you. She discovered how it was with me and she has taken compassion on me."

"Really?" Frances' smile pitied his simplicity. "I would not have said that Julia was particularly kind-hearted. But perhaps I wrong her."

"You do, cousin, you do! She wrote to tell me of how you stated two evenings since that you would marry anyone whose fortune was of a moderate figure, so that they would have you with honour."

In the dimming light of the late afternoon Lennox could

see that Frances had coloured furiously. She turned aside her head, for her gay little feathered hat afforded her no protection from his penetrating gaze. But her hands in their cream-coloured, pearl-sewn gauntlet gloves clenched nervously, and his own right hand closed upon them.

"Am I too late?" he asked.

"Too late for what?"

"Have you not been overwhelmed by eager suitors? Fairness might prompt you to accept the first offer."

"Nobody has offered. I did not expect it. It was a madness. I am sure nobody took it seriously. I drank too much wine, and I am less able than Your Grace to conceal it when I am half tipsy."

"I am not half-tipsy now," said Lennox. "I have abstained for the entire day."

"But 'tis sultry for the time of year, and your thirst must have been excessive."

"Not so consuming as my hopes, which were not too promising, I grant you, and could have been nil. I was far from expecting a clear field, but since 'tis so, there is but one thing to ask. Will you have me?"

"Have you?" repeated Frances stupidly.

"Surely 'tis plain enough. You offered yourself to any who would take you in honour. That at least I can promise, though I'm in debt and shall only clear myself to fall into it again. But I'm worth more than a couple of thousand a year."

Frances turned her head to look at him closely. She said: "Are you in your right senses, or is it just your pretence that you are sober?"

"How can I be anything else, when I have not so much as set my lips to a tankard of ale? I drank water and a great pity it roused in me for the beasts of the field who have no alternative."

"One can only pray it won't give you a chill on your stomach, though with use you may grow accustomed to it," and Frances barely suppressed a giggle.

"Heaven forbid! 'Twas a very special occasion."

"If you married me, there would be many such occasions. Not that I take you seriously, cousin."

"But you *must* take me seriously. Can you suppose that I have driven all the way from Cobham to make foolish jests? I persuaded myself it would be best not to see you again."

"Then why did you?"

"Because when I heard there might be a chance for me I could not help myself. God knows you're a cruel jade, Frances Stuart, and I'm a fool to have set my heart on you. But there it is. Take it or leave it."

"But of course I shall leave it," she retorted disdainfully.

"Then you'll be a fool as well as a jade. Julia La Garde is certain that you are scared half out of your wits. Our Royal Cousin has put his foot down, I suspect. Has said he'll be played with no longer, and that you'll either come to terms or . . ."

"Or?" Frances queried haughtily.

"'Pon my soul, I haven't a notion what threats he used. Don't think I'm not in sympathy with Charles. He deserves it mayhap, but he's met his match in you. Small blame to him if at last his patience is at an end, and he takes you by force as a lesser man would have taken you months ago."

"Don't!" Frances exclaimed in a stifled murmur, and beneath his grasp her hands trembled.

Lennox, however, was now remorseless. "I'd think the better of you if you played fair with him," he said.

"But I can't, I can't. I would rather die. Oh, don't you understand that I can't."

"Yes . . . I understand," Lennox said quietly.

"And it's not because I'm a tease and a cheat. I never wanted to be, or I don't think I did. At first it seemed fun, exciting and—not any harm. I dare say if I had ever loved him I might have forgotten all else—but—oh, I'll be honest with you, though it's more than you deserve for your brutality. Sometimes I think I can never love as women do love. I am fond of the King. Were he my brother I would be—be devoted to him; but to give myself to him . . . no, I cannot. It would have been dreadful had the Queen died,

202

for I could not have refused marriage. All it meant would have been too much for me. The fact is, people are right when they say I have a cold heart, and often I've grieved for it."

There was silence. The horses were now carrying them farther afield towards the villages of Chelsea and Kensington.

"He is too old for you," Lennox said with calm confidence, "and he has had too many women. It has made him repugnant to you. As for the others who have flocked about you, are they any better?"

"Are you?" she retorted with spirit. "You have been twice wed."

"Certainly I am no tyro," Lennox admitted with a self-content that so annoyed Frances the tears ceased to well in her eyes. "But I married my women, and a sorry bargain my last wife was to me, though that she died was no fault of mine, for when I discovered her sickliness I had the best physicians to her. They told me it was a disease of long standing, and when I heard such I gave way to her and told her I wouldn't touch a penny of what she brought to our marriage and grudged seeing spent on Cobham. So she died happily, poor Maggie, not knowing that she was dying. As for Betty—I told you of her when we first met."

The self-satisfaction had vanished from his voice. It had become sombre and regretful. But Frances was now determined to satisfy her curiosity and she said: "There was the matter of Elizabeth Hamilton, which does not favour you, cousin. The Chevalier de Gramont has spread the story of how, while professing to love her, you said you would not marry her without a portion."

"Which was at her instigation. She insisted that the King owed her a dowry for the services her father had rendered to the Royalist cause. When the dowry was promised, she laughed in my face, and told me her heart was given to De Gramont, and that he, who is penniless and an exile, dependent on his gambler's skill, could not marry her without such surety. She has married him, has she not?"

"Yes—but . . ."

"Having treated me scurvily, the pair of them detest me, which is only natural. It was more comfortable for them to present me as a scheming villain."

Frances said importantly: "It may be a pleasant surprise to you to hear that I am not penniless. I have jewels which are worth ten thousand or more."

"And not one of them will you keep. Or at least none that the King has given you."

The sudden violence of his voice was to Frances not only startling but reassuring. She said gently: "Mayhap we have both of us been misjudged. I swear that I have been more foolish than ill-intentioned, but it might be the better for us both if I—if I asked the King's leave to retire into a convent."

"Never! Do so, and I should abduct you."

His arm went round her, he pulled her close to him, he sought her lips, and she shrank from him as she had never dared to shrink from the King. But when his mouth found hers, suddenly and to her astonishment there was no inclination to shrink, for he was infinitely tender, and in her surprised relief she found it easy and even agreeable to respond. He did not fondle her with experienced and urgent hands, in the fashion to which the King had accustomed her and which she had forced herself to endure, but held her with a quiet strength. His cheek was smooth against hers. The little hat perched precariously on her curls was tipped sideways as he pressed her face to his shoulder. She stammered out words that were sincere and humble.

"I am not always silly and flighty."

"Have I not seen that for myself?"

"When have you?"

"Did you not grieve for the Queen rather than rejoice for yourself when she was thought to be dying? Did you not have pity for me when I told you of my sorrow at Betty's death? Did you not show me that the making of a home can be as important to you as it is to me? You may well have more doubt of me than I have of you, of my debauchery, as it is called, and my extravagance. But in truth I am no womaniser, though for the rest it is true—drink and thrift-lessness are my besetting sins."

"Habits," Frances firmly corrected. "Would you drink to excess if you were happy?"

"To that there is no sure answer, though my chief joy is Cobham, and I can be sober there—at least when I am occupied."

"From what you have told me there will be plenty to occupy us for years. As for extravagance . . . it is no mean kind, since you equipped your privateers at your own expense. And then there is Cobham—if it were mine I would not buy a new gown for a year. I would spend my all on it."

"'Tis as I suspected. Cobham will weigh down the scales in my favour."

Lennox was half-pleased, half-hurt, and the hurt, as Frances divined, might be the greater. Instinctively her fingers curled round his.

"There is much else that favours you," she murmured. "I have been angry with you, but I have thought of you. More than a year ago I had dreams, but then you seemed not to care. . . ."

"How could I show that I cared for one who might become my Queen? If I dare show it now it is because Julia was so sure you were in secret trouble."

"I am—oh, I am. The King has given me until my birthday—until I shall be nineteen next month. Then I must either give myself with willingness, or he . . . ! Marriage was my only way out, and I thought his wrath might not fall upon a poor gentleman who would take me far away to some quiet spot where we could be forgotten in our obscurity. But how can that be with you who are of the Royal House and have great possessions? Angry as Charles will be, he could ruin you. . . ."

"Yes," Lennox agreed. "He could."

"The Queen might help us," Frances said hopefully. "But even if she does not, Charles could not hold us apart for ever."

The sense of strain had lifted from her heart and spirit. She lay contentedly in the circle of his arm and thought of much that he had said to her. He had been angry with her and kind to her. He had been honest with her. He might have grave faults, as he owned, but who was there without fault? She could not doubt that he loved her, though in marrying her he would be taking a risk, for how could he be sure that she was capable of giving him a worthwhile love in return?

"I may be bringing great trouble upon you," she said, but he laughed.

"You brought that upon me from my first sight of you. I knew I could never be at peace without you. If you will take me, I swear I will be faithful to you and will love you to the last day of my life. And in time," he concluded, "my love will kindle yours."

"Yes," Frances murmured. "Yes, I believe it will."

It was only when Lennox had ordered the coachman to drive back to Whitehall and they were nearing the river again that the weight of fear and anxiety once more descended upon her, and she said urgently: "Promise me this. In any trouble there should be, let me deal with Charles. He does have an affection for me, and, however angry, he would not punish me for ever, or break my heart through his cruel treatment of you."

At this Lennox put the question which no lover could have forborne to put. "Would it break your heart?"

"To know that I was responsible for your disgrace and downfall? Indeed it would." Aware that this was not precisely what he would have had her say, there was a tinge of mischief in her voice.

Inwardly Lennox groaned. She was a minx and she would always get her own way with him. He said: "Have it as you will, then. It is true that Charles has never revenged himself upon a woman, though Barbara Castlemaine has given him sufficient cause. So did Lucy Walters, if all one hears of her is true. In any case, Charles is no Henry VIII to send me to the Tower and have my head struck off."

In spite of all her natural courage, when the dark bulk of Whitehall loomed up before them Frances' heart took a downward plunge, and she wished she need never again enter that great hive of intrigue, splendid though it was, and privileged though her position had always been.

She and Lennox walked through the long corridors together, provoking nothing but a casual, incurious glance, for Lennox, though no familiar sight there, had long had lodgings in the Bowling Green at Whitehall, and stayed there whenever he was in London. Moreover, as it chanced, there were comparatively few people about, and none at all as they turned an abrupt corner, save the two most important people in England, with whom at this crisis they both wanted and dreaded to come in contact.

Sauntering towards them, and for once unattended, came the King and Queen, both of them evidently in a happy mood, for Charles held Catherine by the hand and bent his head towards her as she looked up at him, and laughed that soft laugh which even her detractors owned was delicious.

Lennox uttered a stifled exclamation, but Frances, with every nerve in her body quivering, knew that this was her chance and that she might never have a better one. Down she dropped in a curtsey of exquisite grace, her gaze turning beseechingly from the Queen to the King.

"Your Gracious Majesties," she faltered.

Both regarded her indulgently.

"Why, Frances!" murmured the Queen and put out her hand.

The King, who had at first smiled at her, now frowned as his gaze travelled to Lennox.

"Madame," cried Frances in a trembling voice, "I crave your approval and your blessing. I implore you to commend us both, my cousin of Lennox and Richmond and myself, to His Majesty. He has asked me . . . Oh, Madame" and now the words came in a rush, though Frances dared not look at Charles but only into Catherine's kind, brown eyes. "We care for each other, and would wed each other."

In the space of a few seconds a dozen conflicting considerations rushed through the Queen's mind. She was immediately aware that the King would be far from pleased. At the same time she was convinced that Frances was not his mistress, and she did not suppose that his fondness for her was much greater than he had already given to many. It would be the best thing possible for Frances to marry one who was so eligible, and it would be wise for Catherine to assume that Charles would share her pleasure.

"Why, my dear child," she said kindly, "this is splendid news. Do not kneel there shaking as though you have confessed to some dreadful crime. With all my heart I wish you joy, and so I doubt not does the King."

The small, jewelled hands helped Frances to rise. Frances kissed them fervently. Charles, subjected as he was to the Queen's radiant and apparently innocent gaze, put forth a grudging hand to Lennox, who speechlessly touched it with his lips.

"Is it not splendid news, my lord?" Catherine persisted. "Splendid and unexpected. I thought they scarce knew each other. They have, as you say in England, stolen a march upon us, but that from time immem . . . immemorial," she stumbled on the long and difficult word, "has been the way of lovers, has it not?"

"It has indeed," Charles agreed grimly.

As Lennox turned to the Queen to kiss, in his turn, her outstretched hand, Charles' lips brushed Frances' cheek in the customary, congratulatory salute. His eyes were hot with anger, but behind the anger she seemed to discern a glint of amusement, and she was sure of it, as he, contriving to draw her slightly aside, said in a low voice that was for her ears alone:

"You minx, Frances! You clever, heartless jade!"

"Your Majesty—please!" Frances gazed at him beseechingly.

"The first round," said Charles, "that you have won, but God's truth, you shall not win the last!"

18

Even had the King sought to conceal the betrothal, the Queen and Frances between them would have been too much for him, and before the evening was over there was nobody at Court who had not heard of it.

Lennox was lost in admiration of Frances' tactics, which, since they had met with such initial success, he now believed would make all smooth for them. Not so Frances herself, though the Queen was honestly delighted and kept her at her side for a long while that evening, discussing her future plans. Catherine did not know a great deal about Lennox's character, but she was sure he was deeply in love with her favourite maid-of-honour, which was more important than anything else, thought Catherine. She had a strong suspicion that in the frivolous, popular, light-hearted Frances there was much latent strength of will, a force which would help her to make a success of marriage.

The King, conscious that many covert glances were directed at him, played up. He was cordial to Lennox, playfully charming with Frances, apparently unperturbed. Nobody quite knew what to make of this new situation, but, as might have been expected, several cynically supposed that it suited the King for Frances to marry.

But even during that first evening Lennox made it abundantly clear that this was to be no marriage of convenience. It was not only the Queen who realized that he was in love. This he did not try to conceal. As for Frances, beautiful though she had always been, there was a new radiance in her smile and a most alluring softness in her eyes.

"Relief," thought Barbara Castlemaine, who had been

taken by surprise when she heard of the betrothal. "She has never wanted Charles, and now she believes she has freed herself while still retaining all her privileges, but he is not likely to give way so easily."

Characteristically, Barbara turned over in her mind how this new development might be used to her advantage. There was now only the semblance of friendship between herself and Frances. Jealousy had soon put an end to it, and unjustly enough she blamed Frances for the unhealed breach with Buckingham. Since the affair of the abortive mock marriage they had ceased to be allies, though Buckingham had cajoled Barbara into patching up their quarrel, and on the surface all was smooth.

Months ago Barbara had faced up to the fact that her influence with the King had waned, although from time to time he came to her as a lover. She was aware that she appealed only to his baser instincts, and with some dread had realized that even this link would be broken if Frances surrendered and satisfied him. Therefore it was satisfactory to her that Frances should not only marry Lennox but also fall in love with him, and thus so wound the King's vanity that his romantic tenderness for her would be destroyed. Thus might Barbara regain her former supremacy.

Let Frances pay then, thought Barbara with savage malice, and the more humiliatingly the better.

Tonight, for pride's sake, the King was acting a part which apparently deceived the lovers and the Queen. Not Barbara, however, for where Charles was concerned she had an acute insight, and she was sure he would put up a fight, though it might be a secret and subtle one. Even Frances could offend beyond forgiveness. There was more than one way in which this could happen, and that evening, when the Court retired, Barbara paced her bedroom for an hour and more, planning, scheming.

At the same time the King and Queen were deep in discussion. Although they had their separate suites, Catherine too often slept alone in the vast double bed which dominated the sleeping apartment. Charles, when in the mood, would spend an hour or more with her before retiring, talking over the events of the day. However tired she might be, Catherine welcomed these interludes, and tonight she sat brushing her hair which after her illness had become dull and without lustre, but which now was growing long again, and to her pleasure had recovered its gloss and springiness.

She made an attractive figure in her silk wrapper, but the King had no appreciation of this, though as always he was comforted and soothed by the sympathetic devotion which never failed him. That she could be less than candid with him was his last suspicion, and indeed Catherine had rarely had any reason for deceit. The King knew that she abhorred Barbara Castlemaine, though she was obliged to endure her. He knew too that she was distrustful of many, but concluded that she was blind to his infatuation for Frances Stuart. It did not occur to him that Catherine understood Frances as one woman does sometimes understand another; that she had long ago penetrated below the froth to the core of sanity and decent feeling. Frances was not designed by nature to be a royal mistress.

"I cannot see," Catherine now said, "that these snags, as you call them, are of such great importance. Frances is an ornament to the Court, and of course she will be missed if she lives chiefly in the country. But it is time she married. She is nearly nineteen and this is an excellent match for her. She will make a most stately Duchess."

"It is not so ideal as you imagine, m'dear," Charles said. "When she marries it should be to one far more stable than Lennox. To some extent I am responsible for Frances. Minette would say so were it possible to communicate with her. This cursed war!"

"Oh, Charles, I know." Catherine was swift in sympathy. "It was not of your seeking, and only brought about by Louis' duplicity. His obligations to the Netherlands forsooth! When all his concern is that England should not become a too powerful maritime nation! In deciding to support the Dutch and breaking with us, it must have caused your sister much grief, since it severed her connection with you."

"Well, it won't last for ever," Charles said with forced cheerfulness. "Poor Minette, poor sweet . . . for her it is only one deprivation amongst many. I am thankful Mam happened to be in Paris at the crucial moment and was obliged to stay there, otherwise she would be distraught with anxiety for Minette. She has no such fears with regard to me, knowing that you, my dear, are the custodian of my happiness."

Catherine's face crinkled into a smile that was not devoid of irony. She said, deliberately drawing back the conversation to Frances, anxious to gain insight into his attitude: "So you feel responsible for her because of her friendship with your sister and because she is your mother's *protégée*. But need that worry you when Frances' own mother is now resident in London? If she approves the match, as doubtless she will . . ."

"Mistress Stuart knows very little, if anything, about Charles Lennox. Unfortunately I know rather more."

"What, for instance? He is very rich, is he not—as well as titled? He is a handsome young man and of a suitable age for Frances—twenty-six or seven. He has estates here and in Scotland, and holds important offices there, as well as being Lord Lieutenant of Dorset. You must have thought highly of him when you conferred the Order of the Garter upon him."

Charles made an impatient gesture. "That was four years ago. It was an honour due to him by reason of his rank and the services rendered by his family. Certainly he seemed to have promise—but he has developed ill since then. He drinks like a fish. He is extravagant and up to his eyes in debt. He is a gambler. He has already had two wives."

"Can he be blamed because they died—I mean if they were natural deaths? Of course, Charles, if you have reason to suspect they were not . . . ?"

"God's peace!" exploded Charles, irritated now by Catherine's unusual obtuseness. "I'm not accusing the man of murder—the deaths were a mischance. Margaret

Lewis was ailing when he married her, and young Elizabeth Cavendish died in childbed. He's a mercenary fellow though. Both those young women had large fortunes, and you may have heard the story of Elizabeth Hamilton, whom De Gramont subsequently married."

The Queen had not, and she listened attentively as Charles briefly retailed it to her, and then she said thoughtfully: "That is De Gramont's story, but it may not be true in every particular. I do not like the man. He has a malicious tongue. Did the Duke himself mention this matter of a dowry?"

"No. I heard of his demands through Elizabeth Hamilton herself."

"And then she got her dowry and married De Gramont. It seems to me that this may have been her object all along, since they are reputed to dote upon each other."

Charles was struck by this, and Catherine added tellingly: "Frances is poor and can have nothing beyond her personal possessions, yet he has evidently not allowed that to influence him!"

Unable to establish the unpleasant quality of avarice, Charles said no more of it.

"He will have to prove his worthiness before I allow this marriage," he pronounced. "I have heard from divers sources that his affairs are in the greatest disorder, and I am convinced that if Mam were here she would insist on having a complete statement from him, and that a suitable settlement is made on Frances. Mam would never allow her to throw herself away on a dissolute young fool facing ruin."

Catherine shook her head in perplexity. "How can that be when he has such great possessions, though for the time they may be, as you say ... ah, what is the word I seek ... ?"

"Involved," Charles supplied.

"Which they will not be, or need not be for ever," the Queen pointed out. "It has happened, has it not, with others who are the owners of big estates? They outrun discretion, and must learn to retrench. Frances is well qualified to help her husband in this way. You will see,

Charles, she will reform the young man who is so extravagant and reckless, though his generosity is a redeeming feature, for you told me of how he helped our Navy."

Reluctant justice forced Charles to admit it, though he listened to Catherine with an unusual discontent. He did not believe she was anxious to be rid of Frances. Whatever others might think, he was convinced that Catherine knew that she was not his mistress. It was possible, however, that she divined his ultimate purpose, in which case she would be shocked as well as grieved, since Frances was young and an innocent. Catherine still had illusions about him, one of which was that in all his affairs it was the woman who was chiefly to blame, and had taken advantage of his weakness not only because he was irresistible—though Catherine was firmly convinced that he was—but because surrender to him meant power, prominence at Court, jewels, titles and general glory.

Nobody in their senses could accuse Frances of such grasping ambition. She desired nothing beyond the ephemeral pleasures of the moment, and the one signal honour he had conferred on her, that of sitting as the model for Britannia, had not turned her pretty head. She had said laughingly, yet had meant it, that her little Roman nose was why she was singled out for this distinction.

Finding no comfort in the Queen's society, the King soon left her for his own apartments. He was not beaten, had no intention of giving up the chase. Procrastination, he decided, might do more for him than sterner means. It was in his power to banish Lennox, but if he did that would but strengthen Frances' love for him. That she was in love, or near to it, Charles could not doubt, though what she could see in the young wastrel was beyond his comprehension. True he had looks and a certain reckless daring, but so had dozens who from time to time had cast languishing glances at her. Lennox had little wit or polish, nor had he the gift of winning friends. He could be downright to the point of boorishness, and his chief interest so far as the King could judge was in his Kent estate—pulling a perfectly satisfactory mansion to pieces and building it up again in some fantastic style at enormous and unnecessary expense.

Never could Charles have supposed that Cobham Hall and Lennox's plans with regard to it were intensely attractive to Frances. He did now suspect, however, that he was far from understanding her. There were unplumbed depths in her character which only made her the more desirable to him. A stubborn virtue beneath her surface charm and frivolity, a lack of greed and a womanly tenderness which had been in evidence during the Queen's serious illness. If Catherine were to be believed, there was also financial acumen. "A pest upon all women!" muttered Charles irately. But he knew that he wanted Frances more than ever.

The strength of this desire was exemplified the following day when Lennox was commanded to attend upon the King. In a suave battle of wits he was no match for his royal adversary, for even one as downright as Lennox dared not level accusations against him. He was forced to accept the King's assurance that he wished him well and had only Frances' interests at heart. She was still very young and must be protected. The King had heard disturbing rumours about Lennox's debts and general standing, for which his passion for gambling was mainly responsible. His liabilities must be plainly set forth, and naturally he would be expected to make a reasonable settlement upon his bride.

"Were the Queen Dowager in England, she as Frances' patroness would be, I warrant, more difficult than myself to satisfy," Charles said benevolently, subjecting the harassed young man to his famous charm. "Your betrothed is still so young that there can be no reason to speed this marriage, and indeed, cousin, it would offend propriety, for your second wife has but recently died."

"Fifteen months ago, Your Majesty," Lennox said.

"Even so, it is scarce seemly."

Lennox yearned to say that this was nonsense as the King well knew. In any case his second marriage had been a miserable fiasco. The Duke chafed because it was impossible to speak openly. Would Charles, had Catherine died, have waited more than a few months before marrying Frances?

Charles went on to say that not only he, but his wife, his mother and his sister were all devoted to Frances, and that her future must be assured. However illustrious Lennox's lineage, this was of small account if he was indeed tottering on the verge of financial ruin. Lennox denied it. Then it would be the easiest matter in the world to prove it, Charles said, and mentioned tentatively the sum that should be secured to Frances as her marriage settlement.

"Two hundred thousand pounds would be reasonable," Charles said nonchalantly, and indicated that the interview was at an end.

Lennox's brain reeled. He was speechless. But for the fact that Frances was impatiently awaiting him, he would have shut himself in his own room, there in an extremity of anger and desperation to drink himself into a state of oblivion. As it was, he was coldly, dismally sober when Frances received him in her salon, and it was she who poured out wine and pressed it upon him. She did not even remonstrate when Lennox finished the bottle. There would be time enough for that when they were actually married.

"God knows all I have is yours," Lennox said, "but without crippling not only Cobham but the lands in Scotland, it is beyond my power to find such a sum. Even so, it would mean inflicting hardship on tenants by indiscriminate rent raising, as well as allowing property to fall into disrepair. In addition to this, the work on Cobham would have to be abandoned and some of the ancestral treasures would need to be sold. Even then the sum raised might fall short of what he describes as a reasonable settlement."

"But I could give it all back to you," Frances said. "Could you not promise to settle such an amount on me, for you well know I would never ask it of you? You would trust me, surely?"

"Oh, my Heart, of course I trust you," Lennox groaned. "But do you imagine for one moment that that will satisfy Charles? Far from it. Betrothal is one thing, marriage another, and he will not permit a date to be fixed for our wedding until the money is produced in hard cash. Even that will not content him. I must first show him that every debt is cleared, and I have many debts."

"Most men in your position have," Frances said comfortingly.

"No," Lennox denied with an effort. "They have not, for they are not such reckless fools. It is true the estates were encumbered when they came to me, but I should have been able to disentangle myself by now. I have been wantonly spendthrift, and have made things worse by gambling, horse-racing, a dozen other madnesses—not only the restoration of Cobham, and the privateer venture . . ."

Frances was undismayed. She said: "Once we are married we can live much more simply, though I promise you I will not let it press too hardly on you."

"Nothing will be hard then," Lennox said; "but the King, for all his smooth ways and his vaunted kindliness, has the cunning of a fox. He will put up one obstacle after another."

Frances surprised him by laughing. In spite of her concern for her distracted lover, she was unwillingly amused and felt something of the lurking admiration for Charles' adroitness that he on occasion had felt for hers.

"It reminds me of the old Greek legends," she said.

"*What* old legends?"

"You must remember—stories in which the hero was commanded to perform the most impossible tasks before he was permitted to marry the girl he wanted, who was usually in danger of being sacrificed to some unspeakable monster."

"Charles does not fall far short of one," Lennox said angrily.

"But I have no intention of being sacrificed. Take heart! The Queen at least is our friend."

"Unless he influences her against us."

"Much though she loves him, I don't think he could. She will stand by us."

"Frances, have you the strength and courage to go through so much for me?" Lennox gazed earnestly at her, and the sea-blue eyes, serious as few people had seen them, gazed back at him.

"Yes," she said, "but it is for myself as well."

"But I am no paragon, my sweet. I love you to distraction, but much that Charles pointed out to me is true. I swear I will reform, if only because married to you it would be an agony to see you miserable and regretting it. Yet I know it won't be easy."

"Well, I know it too," Frances said, "but that makes no difference. It's a challenge to us, and I vow I will never fail you. We will make a beautiful home for ourselves and for those who will come after us. Though we may sometimes be separated, for I do not forget that you hold high appointments in Scotland and elsewhere, you will never be lonely, for even if I am left behind at Cobham my love will go with you."

"Why should you be left behind? I will take you everywhere with me," he protested.

Frances shook her head and said: "That may not be possible. Good wives are often compelled to stay at home to guard their lord's interests. Besides . . . there may be children. I hope there will be, though I am a coward. The thought of childbirth has often made me dread marriage."

"Then you shall have none. I do not forget my poor Betty, and . . .'

She interrupted him. "I shall fight my fear, for I shall want children. We shall both be battling against our weaknesses. We must learn to trust each other."

"It is easy to trust where one loves," Lennox said. "Yesterday it was enough to know you would marry me, that you cared enough to promise me. Now I am grasping at more. Your love, my sweet."

"But I do love you," she said as though surprised. "Once we had met I could never put you wholly out of my mind, and that evening when you were so angry with me . . . oh, I thought I hated you, but it was not hatred which kept you in my mind through all those dreadful months of the plague, when I knew not where you were. I prayed constantly for your safety. People say I have a cold heart, but it lifted when I saw you yesterday. I do not suppose I am a passionate person, but I can be a tender one."

"Oh, my sweeting," Lennox said, "how can I bear to be separated from you? Yet that is one of the conditions the King made. I am to leave for Cobham and there give all my attention to settling my affairs."

"But surely you can be in London from time to time? We are betrothed, and how can he forbid you to see me?"

"He will. Justifying it by saying he has a care for your welfare."

"What absurdity that is," Frances remarked scornfully, "when all he sought was my downfall. But I do truly believe that as time passes he will become more reasonable. Nobody can deny his careless good nature, and mercifully he has so many more important matters to consider that he will not concentrate on us. We must be discreet, but we can yet meet—here in these rooms, which when you are in London will be barred to all others. Who is to know if you ride up from Cobham, not in that great coach, but on horseback? It is not necessary to stay in your Bowling Green apartment. There are inns where you would not be noticed above any other traveller."

This sensible scheme delighted Lennox. They sat together on the window-seat and made their plans. On these stealthy visits he must, Frances instructed, wear sober clothes. He must stay at quiet, unfashionable inns where it was unlikely he would meet any of his friends, and when he visited her it must be under cover of darkness.

As they talked, Lennox had his arm about her, and her head was on his shoulder. When he kissed her she experienced a delicious pleasure and responded to him as she had never been able to respond to the King. It was an exquisite satisfaction to her.

"Don't look too far ahead," she urged, pressing upon him the creed which had always been hers. "It is wonderful the way things turn out, if one does not worry too much. Though I *have* been worried, terribly worried lately."

"Not any longer," Lennox said masterfully. "We are not the King's chattels."

They parted that day with mingled hope and love and grief. Lennox promised that he would ride up to London the following week. It would be wise, they agreed, if he now left London without delay, since to linger would be to arouse the King's anger. But she would wear his ring, Frances promised, for he had already told her of a diamond-surrounded sapphire which had belonged to his mother, and which, as it had fitted her slender finger, should also fit Frances'. Lennox promised either to send the ring by trusted messenger or to bring it with him on his next visit.

So with lingering embraces they took leave of each other, having no reason to suspect that before their next meeting yet another disaster was to fall upon London.

That week at Court was even gayer than usual, and Frances danced at a great ball given in honour of the Queen's birthday, as though the meaning of care was unknown to her. And indeed, having taken a decisive step, knowing that her betrothal was openly acknowledged, she did feel a thousand times happier.

Lennox, as good as his word, had despatched a messenger from Cobham with a small, heavily-sealed package, and when Frances opened it there was the beautiful sapphire accompanied by Lennox's first love letter, in which he told her that she was his treasure, the heart of his heart.

Frances wore her ring openly and triumphantly. The Queen admired it. The King looked glum but made no comment. Frances' fellow maids-of-honour all congratulated her. Kind Lady Denham, whose tapestry-work was famous, promised her that she should have a beautiful screen as a wedding-present. Lady Suffolk supposed that her wedding would be the big event of the following spring.

Brilliant though the ball was, the Queen, who was in mourning for her mother, could not take part in the dancing, but sat on a daïs with the King, who out of respect was also unable to dance. Frances wore a black and silver lace gown which she and her maid had fashioned, and looked more beautiful than anyone else. A few evenings later the Court attended a play at Drury Lane, and Frances wore her hair in a new style. "Very fine," as Pepys recorded, "done up with puffs as my wife calls it." It was a style which did not commend itself to him, though it gave the effect of golden butterfly wings. Frances still acted her butterfly part, though her mind was preoccupied with her dreams.

That night she was restlessly unable to sleep, and, gazing out of her window, she saw to her astonishment that there was a deep red light above the buildings which seemed to be spreading over the City. Two years before there had been a strange light in the sky, but that had been caused by a comet, which according to the astrologers foretold many ills—war, fire, pestilence and disaster. War there still was, and pestilence there had been. Surely, thought Frances fearfully, this could not be yet a second warning from heaven?

But then she remembered hearing some talk of a fire which had started in a baker's shop in Pudding Lane, a district unknown to Frances. The flames, it was said, were proving difficult to quench. But that in the case of a London fire was always a problem, since the streets were so narrow and the wooden eaves of the houses almost met across the thoroughfares. It looked as though this wide-spreading fire must be causing much havoc.

Thereafter, all Londoners took part in a fantastic nightmare. The stench of burning buildings was almost intolerable as the fire spread onwards to Cheapside devouring all before it, whole streets and many charming gardens as well as the houses of rich and poor alike.

The Thames was congested with boats of every description, loaded with the unfortunate people who had been helpless to save their homes, and now crouched amongst the odd pieces of furniture they had been able to rescue.

The Lord Mayor, who was in ostensible control, was half-demented and issued orders that nobody obeyed. Swarms of distracted citizens streamed past Whitehall towards Charing and Piccadilly. Frances heard with horror that the fire had attacked London Bridge and that houses and warehouses built upon it had all been destroyed, though the bridge itself, being built of stone, was inviolate. There was talk of moving the Court to St. James's, as Whitehall itself was said to be threatened, and she saw some of the most valuable royal treasures loaded upon carts, which drove off to Hampton Court. She also saw the King at his best, and the thought came to her that if she could have ever loved him she must have loved him now.

Even as it was she shared something of the Queen's pride and anxiety as he rode out on a white horse towards the burning City, followed by the Duke of York and others ready to risk their lives in their determination to save the rest of London from destruction.

Great resistance had been put up by the property-owners _____ turn_ _ned districts to the only means by which the fire could be arrested. But at last, regardless of their protests, the King gave orders that buildings which the flames had not yet reached should be blown up by gunpowder, thus creating a stretch of waste land over which the flames could not leap. Success was not immediate and St. Paul's was attacked with a fury that the ancient building could not withstand.

Impervious to the danger from burning and falling houses, Charles took control. Grimy and almost unrecognizable in his shirt-sleeves, he held his place in the chain of men bringing water from the Thames, brushed off sparks which threatened to set his clothes alight, had a comforting word for all. At last, after days and nights of toil, after fear and anxiety, the flames died down, though most of the City was reduced to smouldering rubble. Even then the King had little thought for himself, only for his homeless people, and he was out at Moorfields giving directions that tents should be put up for temporary homes, arranging for food to be provided, promising that the first charge upon the revenue should be the building of new and better houses. In London he ordered that churches, and warehouses belonging to the Crown should be left open for those who had no other refuge.

The Queen broke down and wept. "The people will love him now as they never did before," she said through her tears. "So many heard him say that the burning of St. Paul's was as nothing compared to their poor homes, which were all some of them had, and that the rebuilding of these with many improvements to them would take precedence."

"After all," spoke up Frances, "St. Paul's, as everyone knows, was in constant need of repair and an endless expense. So perhaps it is not such a bad thing that there will be an entirely new building."

The Queen laughed weakly. She said: "Oh, Frances, how singularly, oddly practical you can be at times, and how the very thought of building seems to fascinate you. Such a light came into your eyes when you spoke of it."

In her rooms that evening Frances received a begrimed, exhausted but exultant Lennox, who told her that on hearing of the ravages the fire was causing he had come up to London on horseback and had joined the King's party.

"Charles saw me of course," Lennox said, "but he had no time to spare for lashing out at me because I was there. He was glad of me and of anyone who was prepared to help. God's truth, one could not but glory in him, for the dangers he braved and the cheer he gave! I tell you, Frances, I saw him with his arms round an old, weeping woman, a widow she said she was, who had lost her chandler's shop and her furniture and every stitch of clothing, save that which she was wearing. He consoled her as he might have consoled his own mother, and gave her his word to set her up again in business. And she wasn't the only one, though she was so old and more helpless than most. He sent her off with one of the Palace footmen to be lodged here at Whitehall, until he could make other arrangements for her."

Certain that now she was the last thought in the King's mind, Frances ordered a meal for her exhausted lover and insisted on his snatching a few hours' sleep on her own bed before setting off once more for Cobham. She watched beside him as he slept, with her hand clasped in his.

19

Soon Barbara Castlemaine heard that Frances was receiving Lennox in her apartments and never less often than once a week. It had not occurred to the lovers that they would be spied upon by Barbara, who ordered one of her servants to watch for Lennox and to report to her.

The two favourites were on sufficiently friendly terms, and Frances supposed that Barbara, if anything, was pleased by her betrothal, since to her it must seem the end of their rivalry. And pleased Barbara would have been had the King resigned himself to the loss of Frances. Instead, as it was useless to expect sympathy from the Queen, Charles, obsessed by his grievance and grateful for Barbara's commiseration, poured out his resentment and chagrin to her.

"I have cared for that girl as I might have cared for a cherished ward," Charles complained, "only to be rewarded by the most shameless ingratitude."

"Of a truth you have been wonderfully good to her," Barbara agreed, "but I could have told you long ago that Frances Stuart was incapable of gratitude. At one time I did much for her, but I met with a distressing lack of appreciation."

Neither of them deceived each other in the slightest degree and both were aware of it, but all Charles needed was an assenting listener, and all Barbara wanted was to recover her lost supremacy.

"With my consent she will never marry that fellow," Charles said. "Mam and Minette will both uphold me. It would mean misery for Frances. God knows what she sees in him, dissolute wastrel that he is."

"And such a dullard," Barbara murmured.

"Well—er—in some ways he has initiative," Charles, thinking of Lennox's privateering enterprise, was forced to admit.

"No wit, no repartee. His sole interest is in that Kent place of his and all he is doing to it."

"Nothing pleases me better than that he should stay there, and I have told him that the less I see of him the better until he has put his affairs in order, and has made such retrenchments as will enable him to secure a settlement on Frances."

"Such solicitude for her!" Barbara, who had for some time been listening to Charles on the same subject, suppressed a yawn. He who was so rarely boring was certainly a bore on the subject of Frances Stuart.

"She stands in need of protection, Barbie."

"Lennox was in London while the fire raged," Barbara said. "But you knew of that, did you not?"

"Certainly. In a time of such emergency disregard of my orders was forgiveable, and so I told him. But any further trespass on my good nature will be punished as it deserves. How understanding you are, *ma mie*."

Barbara felt comfortably that this long talk re-established her in the royal favour. She pondered, wondering how she might best turn to her own advantage her knowledge of the secret meetings.

"Why did you allow this betrothal in the first place?" she asked, but did not receive a candid answer since Charles was chagrined when he reflected on the way in which Frances had taken him by surprise.

"The Queen was pleased," he said lamely, "and I did not then know the full extent of Lennox's debts. I had thought for some time it might be well to arrange a marriage for Frances . . ."

"But not with such as Lennox," Barbara supplied as he paused.

"No. The fellow has always been difficult. With someone older whom I could trust and advance for her sake."

"I see." Their eyes met. They understood one another perfectly. Although unspoken, it was a moment of truth.

"My dear Barbara, you have never been a jealous woman," Charles said clumsily.

"And I am not jealous now, but Frances Stuart is a problem. A strange girl in some ways. How can this marriage be prevented?"

"If it hangs fire for too long they will tire of each other. I set little value on his constancy, and it will not be an easy thing for him to raise the sum I insisted upon as a settlement."

Barbara, on hearing the sum that Charles had proposed, found it hard to conceal her astonishment and he said with a covert smile: "If Lennox wants her he must be prepared to make sacrifices, even to the extent of selling half or more than half that he has. As well, there are his debts. Until all is satisfactorily cleared up I have forbidden him to see Frances. Prize she may be, but within weeks I warrant he will conclude that her price is too high. His two former wives brought him money, but with Frances it will be the reverse."

"What a fool the girl is," Barbara said involuntarily. "Suppose there is disobedience—what will you do about it?"

"Banish him," Charles said promptly, "and to the other end of the world if needs be. I shall see that Frances is well taken care of by her mother, who already knows that this match is not to my liking. She could take Frances to Scotland for a while. Ornament though she is to our Court and much though she would be missed, that would be a better thing than that she should marry disastrously."

"Oh, Charles, I am sure it would!" Barbara now saw her way clearly and she was elated. "How really arduous for you this guardianship is, for I fear . . . I greatly fear . . . Have you seen Frances this evening?"

"She is not well and abed. The Queen told me she was suffering from fatigue and headaches and that she had thought it best she should rest. It is true she has looked overcast of late."

226

Barbara sighed and gave a convincing play of indecision. "I hardly know if I should tell you," she murmured.

"Tell me what?" And then, as she was silent, biting her lip: "Zounds, Barbara! Have I not shown how deeply this goes with me? If you know anything that is kept secret, why have you concealed it?"

"Because I did not know until now that the Duke had been forbidden to see Frances."

"And you think he has? But no . . . he's not been near his lodgings since I sent him off to Cobham. I assured myself of that."

"He could stay elsewhere," Barbara suggested. "He could even stay with Frances over-night. I put little faith in her fatigue and her headaches, and I fear that were you to call upon her now . . ."

Charles frowned and stared. "Bold as the rascal is, he'd not venture! God's truth, were I such as my Tudor ancestors he'd be lodged in the Tower by now. Think you that Henry or even Elizabeth would have had such clemency?"

"They would not," Barbara said truthfully.

"But what makes you suppose?"

"I have heard rumours. It is said that these pretences made to the Queen are but to give Frances the opportunity for receiving him." Barbara was maliciously amused as Charles, with unusual energy, sprang to his feet. "It might be as well for you to discover for yourself," she suggested.

Without the formality of leave-taking he had gone, and Barbara reflected that this might well mean the end of the favour shown to Frances Stuart. Earlier in the evening Lennox had been seen to enter her rooms, and Barbara assumed that he would spend the night with her. What happened to Lennox was of no importance to her, but the long visit to Scotland planned for a disobedient Frances was eminently desirable. Charles might suppose that after a few months a chastened La Belle Stuart would return to London, ready after such dullness and covert disgrace to submit herself. Barbara thought it more likely she would marry some admiring Scot and make her home in the Highlands.

In the anteroom to Frances' apartments her maid was on duty. She assured the King that her mistress had retired for the night. To this Charles paid no attention. Sure now that he was being duped, he put the girl aside, and without further ado opened the door which led into Frances' salon.

She had not retired. She was there as he had expected, but alone, and not in her nightgear. As Charles entered, she rose swiftly from the cushioned window-seat and gazed at him with astonishment.

"Where is he?" Charles demanded. "Don't lie to me, Frances. I know Lennox is hidden here." His glance roamed around the room and fell upon tell-tale evidence.

Frances, recovering from momentary shock, faced him with valour. She said calmly: "Your Majesty is mistaken."

"Well, we shall see!"

He pushed aside the heavy velvet window curtains which might have offered concealment, and Frances watched him with scorn. She crossed the salon and opened the door which led to her bedroom. With swift movements she threw back the lids of chests and cupboard doors. She flung aside the silken coverlet of the bed.

"You see!" she challenged, "and there's no secret panelling as at my Lady Castlemaine's. My maid's closet has but little in it, but should you wish to search it . . ."

Whatever Charles might wish, that small chamber was now presented to his gaze. It certainly offered no concealment.

"Only Alice sleeps in the Palace," Frances said. "My other maid Harriet returns before dark to her family who lodge nearby. Alice's coffer, as you see, is not large enough to give refuge to a child, but should you wish her to unlock it, I will summon her."

The King, though made to feel a fool, was still furious.

"He has been here," he said.

On the table in the salon there were the remains of a meal, which had been set with glass and china and silver for two. There were covered dishes and an empty wine bottle.

"Am I not permitted to entertain a friend if I so desire?" Frances asked.

"You were said to be ill," Charles retorted. "On this pretext, the Queen has excused you from your duties."

"I was tired, not so ill that I could not eat my supper in company."

"Don't fence with me, Frances. 'Twould be less enraging if you lied outright. Would you have me question your maid, who would not dare but to tell the truth?"

"Poor Alice, she would be terrified, though she adores you. She *is* terrified already, though that is not your usual effect on women. As it seems that evidence has been lodged against me it would be fruitless to lie. Lennox *was* here, but, as you see, he is here no longer."

"Because you were warned of my approach and he escaped in time."

"I was *not* warned. Had that been so, he would not have left me to brave your anger. He stayed but a short while. He saw I was tired, and in any case he has a care for my reputation, not thinking as others do that because of Your Majesty's attentions it is already lost."

"How *dare* you, Frances!"

"But is it not true, Sire? Have you ever cared what was thought of me? Has it ever concerned you that I am young and defenceless? Did I ever show any desire to become your mistress? You, with your experience of women, knew well enough that that was what I least desired, though as Your Majesty's subject I strove not to offend you."

"You promised me," Charles said with bitter reproach.

"Because you pressed me. Because I was weak and foolish. You knew my mind, but that was of no importance to you. Have I not heard you say a dozen times that 'maids' nays are nothing; they are shy but to desire what they deny.' So you persuaded yourself. My religion, my duty to the Queen, my disinclination were all set at nought."

Imperceptibly the King was softening. As she moved away from him, he followed her.

"You know full well that it is no light thing with me—

that I love you," he protested. "I have told you so often enough."

"And as often I have told you I want nothing of such love; only a love with honour which Lennox can give me."

"He can also give you much sorrow, bring you to ruin by his excesses, disgust you with his sottish habits."

"He will not. I know him better. He has my heart."

"You are a fool, Frances. You are a child living in a fairy-tale and hanging on pretty words. If it is a husband and his name that you want, I have told you I will procure such for you."

"I choose for myself, Sire, and not a husband who will deliver me up to you on demand. Have I no right to an honourable love?" Anger gave way to the feminine weakness against which Charles could never harden his heart. Tears welled in Frances' eyes and her voice shook.

Moved and chastened, the King said: "You know that, were I free, the crown would not be too much to give you."

"I wonder if you would dare!" Foolishly, Frances failed to take advantage of Charles' softened manner. "You have my Lady Castlemaine to consider; others as well who have more claim on you. I dare swear that it is she—Barbara—who has betrayed me. Alice told me that one of her maids had been making a great show of friendship, and that she had found it hard to rid herself of the girl. Lest there is to be fresh trouble from Barbara, would it not be politic for Your Majesty to leave? Doubtless she is impatiently awaiting your return."

The King's rage flared up anew.

"Is it for *you* to give *me* orders?" he demanded.

"No—though I dare say Barbara has given you plenty in the past, and may still do so in the future."

This was matchless effrontery, even for Frances. The King said: "For that I could . . . but it is Lennox who shall answer to me."

At this Frances burst into tears and the King turned on his heel and left her, though not to return to Barbara. He had had enough of women for one night and did not go near the Queen, preferring his own quarters and the rapturous greeting of his spaniels.

Frances spent a sleepless night, miserably reflecting that she had but made matters worse. She should have done her utmost to conciliate the King with gentleness and entreaty. Instead she had further incensed him.

The next day she heard through a messenger sent privately by Lennox that he had been threatened with perpetual exile from England if he dared to be seen again at Whitehall. Such exile, as Frances realized, could mean the confiscation of his estates on some fabricated charge of treason, and a wandering life as poverty-stricken as Charles' own life had been for many years. Although she could scarcely believe that the King would go to such lengths, the fear was there, and she was in a distraught state when she sought the Queen and, throwing herself at her feet, besought her aid.

Catherine listened with a consternation which gave way to pity. Her own pain, as she realized that this affair was much more serious than she had supposed, was set aside as she strove to comfort the distracted girl.

"I swear to Your Majesty that I thought of you as much as of myself," Frances cried. "It was long before I realized that my foolish flirting could have such an effect on the King. I never meant it to go so far. I knew Your Majesty was indulgent to me and understood, and it was better, I thought, that the King should divert himself with me who asked nothing of him, rather than affront you with Barbara Castlemaine. But then I found that I—I could no longer play at love with him, and when Lennox asked me, and I knew I could care for him enough to marry him, it seemed so much the best for all of us."

The Queen's hand rested for an instant on Frances' bright hair. She had no reproaches for her, or at least none other than the inevitable: "If only you had told me!"

"Oh, I wish I had. I wish I had."

"And now," pondered Catherine, "what can be done to help you and your unfortunate lover?"

"If you would but intercede for me, Madame, that I may marry him and leave the Court; or if that is too much to ask, that I may be allowed to retire into a convent. Then, perhaps, the King will pardon Lennox."

The Queen shook her head doubtingly. "It would be better for you to marry the Duke," she said.

"But how can I? The King has forbidden it until Lennox can find this vast sum of money to settle on me, and that will be a matter of years."

"To advise marriage, and a hasty marriage, is a great responsibility," the Queen said, gazing searchingly at Frances. "Are you certain that you truly care for this young man? You must not marry him as a means of escape. You must love him, Frances."

"I do, oh I do!" Frances vowed.

"It is not easy for me to help you. Not easy for any wife, royal or otherwise, to defy her husband, and yet how can I stand aside and see your life ruined? I am very fond of you. I trust you and I believe you to be chaste."

"There has never been anyone," Frances said simply.

"That is as I supposed, and I *will* intercede for you, though I do not promise immediate results. You must both have patience." And then the Queen added meaningly: "There would be more hope of success were you already wed."

Still kneeling on the floor with her head against the Queen's knee, Frances was deep in thought. She realized that she could not expect more explicit advice. Already the Queen must feel that her loyalty as a wife had been strained to the utmost.

"Will the King ever forgive me?" Frances wondered, and the Queen replied:

"There are few who have gainsaid him that he has not forgiven—eventually. His is not a revengeful nature."

"Oh, Madame, I know it," Frances agreed eagerly. "He can be the very soul of kindness, and this fancy he has for me will soon be forgotten when I am not constantly in his sight."

"We can but hope so. Do not think I wholly blame him. Whatever your motive or past motive, you have tempted him with your promising ways, and there are few men who could resist such temptation. If you marry the Duke I do beg of you to give him no cause for jealousy by your kindness to others."

"There will be no such trouble," Frances avowed confidently. "Men are well enough as companions, to talk to, as dancing partners, but I have never wanted more from them, or wished to give more. In marriage, of course, it is different. Then it is a wife's duty to give all."

The Queen smiled and sighed. She, herself, was a passionate woman, and the full force of her passion was given to her husband. Frances, she suspected, was of a very different nature. She was warm-hearted, she would make a good wife, but it was unlikely that physical union would stir her to the depths. Would it be on her children that she concentrated the full force of her love? Catherine did not suspect that Frances' great yearning was set upon something inanimate— a home such as she had lost before seeing it.

"Keep to your own rooms for the next few days," Catherine said. "His Majesty will not seek you there, that I promise you, for he will believe me when I tell him that you are greatly upset. That you have confided in me will act as a check—and a shock. I shall also assure him that even if the Duke were sufficiently foolhardy to risk visiting you, you would not permit it."

How forgiving she was, Frances thought, pitying the sadness of the Queen's lustrous eyes. She had learnt to accept the King's infidelities, feeling perhaps that her childlessness was a contributory cause for them.

As Frances rose to her feet the Queen embraced her, and to Frances it was as though she was not only blessed but bidden farewell. It was only after much thought that she sat down at her desk to write Lennox an ill-spelt but eloquent letter in which she told him almost word for word what the Queen had said.

"She did impres upon me," Frances wrote, "that the

King wuld be the reddier to pardon, if I were allreddy your wife."

The letter despatched, she waited eagerly for a reply, the suspense hard to endure. Within a few days the messenger from Cobham delivered a long letter from Lennox, containing detailed instructions over which Frances pored. She read them several times and memorized them.

The scheme as outlined by Lennox was simple, but there were one or two suggestions she dismissed as impossible. They would involve others and perhaps to their lasting disgrace. After more thought she called her maid Alice to her and told her she planned to give her a short holiday.

"A day and a night, Alice," she said. "'Twas only last week you told me you had a new little brother and would fain journey to Islington to see him."

"But how can you do without me, Mistress?" Alice asked. "You are not yet well."

"Oh, but I feel much better today," said Frances, having feigned an illness which was largely imaginary. "And Harriet will be here to wait upon me. It will be a good opportunity for you as I shall not be leaving my rooms, and can manage without you. I will give you extra money for a seat on the post-chaise and to buy a present for the baby."

Alice could not resist this enticing suggestion and she was profuse in her gratitude. When she had gone Frances sighed with relief, though the long hours of the day stretched before her and seemed as if they would never pass.

The girl Harriet who waited on her was dismissed before dark set in, and Frances then, in the space of a few hours, had much to accomplish. During the day she had been shaken by occasional fear, but now there was no time for fear. She judged, and rightly, that Barbara Castlemaine was no longer bidding her maid spy upon her. Although her non-attendance at Court was explained by ill-health and the need for rest and quiet, Barbara probably supposed she was in disgrace and was no longer acutely interested in her. With ordinary good fortune, therefore, she should be able to leave the Palace unobserved.

Her preparations were swift and practical. She could take nothing with her beyond a small parcel to be hidden beneath her cloak. She could not be sure of guarding this, or even of guarding herself, for the danger of the next hour was far from negligible. Had anyone suspected that she was about to embark upon such an adventure there would have been consternation. "But please God," thought Frances, "nobody will know until I am in safety."

Lennox, in his letter, had instructed her to confide in her mother and to borrow one of the Queen Dowager's coaches, but Mistress Stuart was at Winchester visiting friends there and knew nothing of the latest events in her daughter's life. After all, those that were most vital had occurred within the space of a week. Mistress Stuart had approved of the betrothal, but had left London at the time of the Great Fire and had not returned to Somerset House. Frances was glad of it, though she would not have called upon her mother for aid even had she been near at hand. She was not even certain that it would have been forthcoming. Mistress Stuart might well have hesitated before incurring the King's wrath.

Nor would Frances take Alice with her. The girl, being innocent of all knowledge, could not be blamed and would easily find other employment in the Palace.

It might be possible, Frances supposed, to pick up a hackney coach, but many of these were plied by rogues who could not be trusted to carry an unprotected girl to her destination. On the whole, she judged she would be safer by herself, trusting to the darkness of the night and her own speedy feet.

The possessions she collected were few enough. A nightrobe and a few toilet articles were wrapped in a silk scarf. Then she pondered over the contents of her jewel casket. Some jewels she could take with her, for they had been anniversary presents from admirers, of whom Lennox would feel no jealousy. There were also a few trinkets given by the Queen. But those that were the King's gifts must be left behind.

"And more than ever angry that will make him," Frances mused, "but there is no help for it with Lennox to consider. Besides, I never want to see them again."

So the pearl necklace and the diamond star, a bracelet studded with emeralds and a jewelled locket containing a miniature of Charles were left in the casket with a scribbled note to say it was to be delivered to the King, the contents being his property. The other jewels Frances distributed about her person, concealing them beneath the dark dress she had selected to wear. Over all she wore a shrouding black cloak, with a hood that covered her hair and could be drawn about her face.

Thus clad she was ready to start. The night was stormy and this favoured her, though having succeeded in leaving the Palace by a side-door and unobserved, she gasped as the cold air struck upon her.

Fortunately she knew the way and in a coach had once or twice passed "The Beare at the Bridgefoot", a well-known tavern on the Southwark side. Dark though the night was, there were lights from many windows, and in the shadow of the houses Frances sped on her way, fearing that at any moment she might be set upon by one of the many thugs armed with knives and daggers who infested the streets.

Although restorations in the ravaged city were now under way, and the rubble had been cleared, the devastation was appalling, and in the additional disorder there had been many brutal attacks from thieves. Respectable citizens would not venture from their homes, and the coaches of the wealthy were protected by outriders and postilions armed with pistols. In addition, bunches of brawling apprentices were usually abroad, brandishing staves and prepared to use them indiscriminately.

Frances had unusual courage, but she had heard so many gruesome stories that the chill of fear was upon her. No woman, young or old, of her status had ever been abroad at this hour without protection. Down the Strand she went and towards Ludgate. It seemed to her to be by an especial dispensation from Heaven that the streets were comparatively empty, though for this the weather was responsible. The rain was lashing down and a strong wind tugged at the folds of her cloak, which she clutched around her. At last she was at Ludgate; and although a few who passed had brushed against her, nobody had molested her, intent as they were on battling with the wind and the rain.

London Bridge was a sorry sight, with all the houses and buildings that had once fringed it now in ashes. The river was high here, and as Frances crossed the bridge a watery-looking moon came forth from behind banked-up clouds and she saw the darkness of the water. A man, burly and roughly clad, came level with her, and tried to peer into her face, he clutched at her cloak, but he was very drunk, and as Frances desperately pushed him away he slid on the wet stone and gave her the chance to run.

She was still running and was drawing her breath in painful gasps as she arrived at "The Beare at the Bridgefoot". There she saw Lennox's coach, and, wild though the night was, he was pacing up and down outside in his impatience.

At first when Frances breathlessly uttered his name she did not attract his attention, but then she touched his arm and he stared at her incredulously, realizing that she had come on foot and was drenched beneath the shrouding cloak. Her hood fell back and he saw her pale face and wide eyes and wet strands of bright hair.

"What happened? For the love of God what happened?" he demanded.

"Nothing. I am here. I am safe." The dangerous journey accomplished, Frances was only overjoyed to see him again.

"But alone—and you walked! The danger . . ."

"Such as it was, it is over. Should we delay, my lord?"

"Not for one minute!" He handed her into the coach, and the coachman whipped up the horses. Lennox tenderly removed Frances' drenched cloak, replacing it with his own.

"I made no doubt but that your mother would send her servants with you. You should not have ventured. God's truth! When I think of what could have happened to you!

Why did you leave your maid? I deserve to be hanged, drawn and quartered for the peril you were in. . . ."

Anger at himself and concern for her found expression in a flood of stammering words. Frances, laughing now, put her hand across his mouth.

"Hush! You could not know. My mother still tarries at Winchester, and perhaps 'tis for the best, as no blame can rest on her. Alice would have been nought but a responsibility. I had no choice but to take the risk."

Their lips met and Frances put her arms around his neck. She had no regrets. For the first time in her life she was really free.

"At Cobham all is in readiness," Lennox told her, "and the priest will be waiting. The Queen was right. By the time Charles hears that you have gone we shall be man and wife."

20

Frances never forgot her first sight of Cobham Hall, beautiful even in the cold light of a pitiless March morning. It was still very early. They had driven throughout the night along the old Kent and Dover roads, and although six horses were harnessed to the coach they had made slower progress than Lennox had allowed for in his calculations. The coachman was drenched, for all his protective leather livery devised for such weather, so were the postilions, and the horses were exhausted by the time they arrived.

Frances was comparatively fresh, for she had slept the greater part of the journey, cradled in her lover's arms. As she descended from the coach, she stood for a few moments as though spellbound, and not even Lennox shared the most wonderful moment of her life. Here it was at last, the home of which she had so often dreamed, though in her imagination it had been a composite picture of her parents' house in Scotland and the old engraving and sketches of Cobham Hall. Neither these pictures nor her imagination had done justice to its beauty.

With utter satisfaction her gaze dwelt on the mellowed red brick of which the great house was built; on the octagonal turrets, the uneven clusters of Tudor chimneys, the many windows. It was more entrancing than she had dared to expect, and if so on this miserable, rainy morning, how exquisite it would be when the sun shone; when the trees were in leaf and the flowers blooming in the acres of gardens which spread further than her eyes could see.

Lennox, who had given up a few minutes to concern for the weary horses and praise to the coachman, turned to see Frances standing as though in a happy trance.

"It is—oh, it is rapturous!" she cried, as he took her hand in his. "There are no words . . . oh, how happy I shall be to live here with you."

She was steeped in a sense of blissful unreality as she stepped over the threshold of her new home. The servants were lined up to receive her, and smiling at them Frances stood there in her plain gown with Lennox's cloak still around her shoulders, her head bare, and her shoes soiled with the mud of the London streets. When the wedding ceremony was performed in the private chapel a few hours later, it could not have been more simple, with only the head servants at Cobham Hall to witness it. Frances remembered how Lady Suffolk had said that her wedding would be the great fashionable event of the spring, and, thinking of this, she laughed as she gazed at her very new husband, who was now urging her to partake of the elaborate feast which for the whole of the preceding day the servants had been preparing.

"Not fashionable," Lennox admitted, "but nevertheless an event which will be talked of for many a long day."

By tacit consent they spoke little of the wrath which was certain to fall upon them. Neither was really dismayed when they considered this. There had been no choice for her, Frances considered, as between honour and dishonour.

"I pin my faith to the Queen," she said. "She cannot turn the King into a faithful husband, but in other ways she has much influence upon him."

What more wonderful place for a honeymoon than Cobham in the spring-time? Love had come to Frances with a great sweetness, and at times it had a fairy-tale quality.

Together she and her husband studied architectural plans, and the work, which during the last year had come to a standstill, was now started again with a new enthusiasm. Lennox had no secrets from her, for he soon discovered that he had married not only an extremely beautiful girl, but one who possessed a latent flair for household management, and a talent for stretching money rather than a readiness to allow it to slip through her fingers. Within weeks Frances had thought of many economies, and not such as to unduly restrict Lennox. It would, of course, be years before they were out of debt, she acknowledged, for they were committed to the extensive alteration and redecoration of Cobham, but this in the end would be justified as it would double if not treble the worth of the property, as well as giving them both pride and joy. Frances could see now, if she could not see before, how impossible it would have been for Lennox to raise the money for the fantastic settlement upon which the King had insisted.

But there were many ways in which the ordinary mechanics of living could be simplified. The house was over-staffed, and even Mrs. Harvest, the head housekeeper, admitted that if some of the rooms in the wings not at present in use were shut up it would be an advantage.

"Not the beautiful rooms," Frances said earnestly, "but there are clutters of smaller ones which in time, though it will take years, we shall rebuild and enlarge. Mrs. Harvest has two under-housekeepers, but she is fretted by the younger woman and thinks her not honest. She will be glad to be rid of her. There are so many servants that there is not enough for them to do, and it is the same with the gardeners. The grounds are large, but much is parkland, and I have already seen under-gardeners spending half their time in the stables, where they do but hinder the grooms."

"The wages are not large," Lennox said, touched and amused by her serious expression, but inclined to think that little more than a few pounds would be saved by the clean sweep that she proposed.

"My love, it is not what they are paid, but the cost of all their liveries and their maintenance. You have no idea! Mrs. Harvest altogether agrees with me. It is enormous. The mountains of food and the extra cooks needed to prepare it."

In the end Lennox gave her full authority to order the domestic side of their home as she thought best. When he recalled her as he had seen her at Whitehall, the lovely Court butterfly, to whom one would have thought the value of a guinea was no more than that of a groat, he was amazed by her.

"Better to be able to pay the workmen whom we do need than lazy gardeners and servants whom we don't," Frances pointed out.

Although she recommended the temporary closing of suites of rooms in the unused wings, she was at one with Lennox in wishing to make their own rooms perfect. There was also the central block, demolished but only partially re-built and intended to form a connecting link between the two Tudor wings. With the eyes of one who was partly a visionary and partly practical, Frances viewed the proposed banqueting hall, which had a breath-takingly beautiful ceiling designed by Inigo Jones in his last years. It should combine a music-room, Frances decided, and to make extension possible there were various badly constructed, small rooms and domestic offices which could be done away with.

Occupied with these plans which they could now discuss together, wandering hand in hand with Lennox in the first warm days of spring through the lovely grounds, Frances was blissful. The gardens provided a succession of surprises, for the owners in Tudor days had planted shrubs and trees which had been brought from far-distant countries, and these were now in their maturity. There were a succession of gardens designed as pleasaunces, a terrace walk which ran the length of the north wing of the house, and four avenues of lime trees radiating out like the spokes of a wheel from the west front of the house.

These avenues, so Lennox told Frances, had been planted under the direction of his uncle James, who had died during the years of the Protectorate.

It was perhaps the vast deer park which Frances most loved. In years to come she was to wander in it for hours, happy beyond expression, though sadness was to be later associated with her yearning for peace and silence. Nobody knew just how old that vast park was. The villagers genuinely believed that it had existed since the world's beginning.

There were trees of every description. One enormous chestnut was known as the Four Sisters. The deer were tame and gentle and most beautiful. As the park completely surrounded the house, the deer could stray into the formal gardens and sometimes did. One of the first orders that Frances gave was for protective palings to be erected.

Busy with such innumerable occupations, happy in her companionship with Lennox, loving him dearly, Frances was for some weeks forgetful of the outer world. News reached her from London, in letters from Mistress Stuart, who was now at Somerset House. There was room and to spare there for Frances and her husband, she wrote, and she hoped they would soon be coming to her on a visit. There was nothing to prevent them staying there, even though the King was bitterly angry over their elopement.

Mistress Stuart had begged for an interview, and this, after some delay, had been granted. The Queen had been kind enough, but the King had been very cold and had told her that her daughter had behaved disgracefully and would no longer be received at Court. The Duke had been given orders to this effect before the elopement. It was said, Mistress Stuart wrote as an afterthought, that Lord Chancellor Clarendon owed his fall to Frances' action. The King believed he had helped her and encouraged her, and now, having fallen into disgrace thereby, he had left England for exile in France.

"But that is terrible," Frances cried when she read the last paragraph. "Poor old Clarendon and I scarcely knew one another—or at least only in the most formal way. He had no idea of my plan. Were you better acquainted with him?"

"Even less well acquainted," Lennox said. "But it is only an excuse. Clarendon is old, tactless, disliked by many. Buckingham and the Castlemaine detest him, and have been plotting his downfall for years. Charles is weary of the friction probably, and knows that Clarendon is no longer competent."

"Then he should have dealt honourably with him."

Frances was shocked and angry. "He was one of his most faithful supporters in the days when Charles most needed support. Why does not the Duke of York defend his own father-in-law?"

"York's position is precarious being a Catholic, and he is an embarrassment to Charles though he is fond of him. The old man was unpopular with the people, you know. They blame him for the sale of Dunkirk to the French. The Catholics detest him for his fervent allegiance to the Protestant Church, and it's well known that Charles has borne with him patiently for years, though Clarendon has lectured him day in, day out, on what he calls his immorality. It's possible, Frances, that he also lectured him about his infatuation for you."

"He does seem to have been tiresome," Frances owned, but she was still troubled, feeling that Charles had been uncharacteristically harsh and unjust, and grieved by the fear that her own action might have brought disgrace upon the old man. "It is not like Charles to be so unforgiving," she said.

But that when profoundly hurt the King could be unrelenting she had soon good reason to realize, for when Lennox and Frances visited Mistress Stuart, they were implored by her to preserve a strict privacy, not to flaunt themselves driving around London in Lennox's ornate coach, until it could be ascertained if the King were willing to pardon them.

"He would," said Frances confidently, "if I could have only a few words with him."

Her mother shook her head doubtfully. To her the King had been cold and unbending, but she did not deny that Frances could coax most people to do as she wished, and in these first weeks of her marriage she was more beautiful than she had ever been, for love and wifehood had already given her greater poise, to which was added a luminous tenderness of glance and smile.

"If Frances Stuart imagines that she can now carry all before her, she is much mistaken," the King wrathfully told the Queen. "I know you are fond of the girl and I would not prevent you from seeing her. But let it be at Somerset House and not here. As for the disloyal oaf she has married, when she has seen him drink to the point of insensibility day after day, it is scarcely to be supposed she will continue in a state of bliss."

But this was something Frances was never to see, for although Lennox did still drink more than was good for him, this was only when he was away from her. He could be abstemious when they were together, for, as he had truthfully said, the one intolerable thing would have been to know that she regretted her marriage.

"The Duke is young enough to mend his ways," the Queen said, as she had said more than once. "As for Frances, you cannot expect me to be otherwise than happy that she has married. I am fond of her, and how could I have continued to be fond of her had she become a second Castlemaine, or even one of your less obtrusive mistresses? Although I so foolishly love you whatever grief you bring upon me, it would have been hard to forgive had Frances become your paramour."

Charles regarded her with remorse and affection.

"You are an angel to have put up with so much," he said. "But try to understand, *ma mie*. It is not only the losing of Frances, but the way I lost her. 'Twas not only lechery. I was fond of her. If she had told me she was determined to marry Lennox, would elope rather than discard him . . ."

"How could she, Charles?" Catherine was mildly derisive. "You would have stopped her at any cost, even though you had to lock her in her rooms."

"Need she have left every jewel I ever gave her?" Charles demanded. "Even the pearls which were my present to her soon after she came to Court, and before there was any thought of love?"

"Her bridegroom may have insisted on it," Catherine pointed out, and then added dryly: "But I understand the shock it is to you. She must have been the first woman you have desired who has refused to profit by it."

"Except yourself."

"But *did* you ever desire me?"

"You know I did—you know I do. When you were like to die, what was Frances to me save a kind girl who shared my anxiety and tried to comfort me?"

"Then, because of that alone, could she not be forgiven?" the Queen suggested.

But Charles was not to be pacified, and Catherine did not visit the bride and groom at Somerset House, though she wrote to Frances explaining that for the time being, as the King was adamant, she thought it better to stay away.

There were many Frances did see, however, during the short stay in London. Some of those who had admired her and had been friendly with her came to Somerset House to wish her happiness, amongst others John Evelyn, who had always liked her. Frances could now confide in him, and she told him that even if she had not fallen in love with her husband, she would have had to leave Court unless she was prepared to become the King's mistress. She could no longer have held him off, and he had reached the point when his desire had become greater than his scruples over forcing her to submit.

"But I have been lucky," Frances said, "for at last I met one I could truly love and who honoured me and believed in me."

Those who had known Lennox in the days when he had been more unhappy than anyone suspected now marvelled at him. He had grieved for his first wife, had been wretched with his second wife, and now in his felicity it was not too difficult for him to reform. His gambling days were over. He had never been lucky at cards or betting, and had the sense to forgo these altogether. Because Frances so loved Cobham Hall it was twice as important to him, and he would not risk all their plans for it by staking and losing large sums. There was also much that he wanted to give her, though Frances told him that if necessary she could manage for years without a new gown. All her possessions had been sent to her from Whitehall, and a wardrobe which had barely sufficed for life at Court was resplendent for one living in the country.

There, though they were entertained and returned hospitality, their friends had a very different outlook. The women who now made friendly approaches were occupied with bringing up their children and managing their households, the men in administering their estates and in outdoor pursuits. Frances did not actively discourage any of Lennox's once boon companions, but the less reputable now drifted away of their own accord, and he was too contented to miss them.

Returning to Cobham, the days passed rapidly as they concentrated on re-decorating the wing of the house they intended to occupy.

The Dutch war had simmered down during the early months of the year. Louis XIV was now making a sincere effort to negotiate peace. His object had been gained, for both England and Holland had been much weakened in the inconclusive struggle, and peace talks had started at Breda. But although at this conference all the major points were settled, the English commissioners held so rigidly to various minor issues that antagonism flared up once more, and the exasperated Dutch elected to steal a march on their now unsuspecting foe.

The news that the Dutch fleet was at sea again and had been sighted off the Dorset coast came as a stunning blow. Lennox, as Lord Lieutenant of Dorsetshire, received orders to be at his post there and to resist attack. With only time for a hurried leave-taking he was gone, and Frances was left behind, in some danger as it proved, for the Dutch plans had been incorrectly assessed. It was not their intention to strike in the open sea, but with far more devastating effect in the Thames and Medway estuaries, where some of the finest ships in the Navy were lying unmanned and unprepared, it being optimistically believed that the war was virtually at an end.

From the high ground in the park, Frances, with straining, disbelieving eyes, saw the superb Dutch fleet come sailing up the estuary, to meet with only the slightest possible resistance from the great English ships they proceeded to systematically destroy.

Frances and the domestic and outdoor staff at Cobham now had a ringside view of one of the most disastrous events in the naval history of the country. Frances was not the only one to weep with rage and frustration as the old house shook to the booming of cannon, and stories, both true and false, of England's losses reached her ears.

She had no idea how her husband was faring at Dorset, and her anxiety was intense until she received a visit from a Captain Johnson, one of Lennox's privateer skippers in command of the *Frances*, the ship which had been named after her, who brought her a letter and reassuring news o him.

Frances sat in the great hall at Cobham, where Captain Johnson hungrily devoured a substantial meal hastily prepared for him.

"Keep up your heart, Your Grace," he advised with rough solicitude. "The Duke is well and hearty and in command of as pretty a squadron as ever you saw. Those devils got the better of us, taking us by surprise as they did—a right scurvy trick seeing as we had believed in a truce—but they'll soon be sent to the right-abouts, though at the cost of some of our best ships and men, which is a sore blow to be sure."

"Ships can be built again," Frances said. "It's the men— all those who were taken unawares. Oh, Captain Johnson, are you sure my lord is uninjured? If you have come here to break it to me that he is—he is . . . please don't try, for you couldn't. There would be no way of softening such news."

The rough, seafaring Johnson looked at her with astonished admiration. He had never seen a lady so beautiful and so unconcerned for herself. There she sat, facing him at the oak table, her elbows propped on it, and her chin resting on her clenched knuckles.

"In truth the boot is on the other foot," he said. "The Duke has been forced to stay at his post, and so far the Dutch ships having by-passed us, none on the Dorset coast has suffered harm. It is for Your Grace he has been in a sore fret. Cobham is not out of the reach of shelling, and should the enemy have made a landing God only knows what might have happened. Most women," the captain said bluntly, "would have been scared out of their wits."

"Would they? Well, I wasn't," Frances stated flatly, "though it is true the cannons made a great noise and I was in much concern for that part of the house which is only half built and might be brought down by the shaking it has had. But it stood up to it, and so you will be pleased to tell the Duke. It was a dreadful sight though, to see them start firing in the Medway, and none of our cannon to answer them."

"You should have taken cover. Had it been my wife, though she's no coward, she'd have been hiding in the cellar."

"That didn't occur to any of us," Frances told him with truth and simplicity. "There we all were on the high ground watching, and the men cursing. I have never," and she giggled irrepressibly, "heard such language in all my life as I did from the builder's men and Waring, our head gardener. It was—it was inspiring. The pity is that I have forgot all of it."

Captain Johnson joined in her laughter. "It will be my honour," he said, "to tell His Grace that he has the bravest of all brave ladies."

"I mightn't have been brave if I had thought of it," Frances owned, "but the worst is over now, for the bombardment has died down, and Prince Rupert with his forces has arrived at Sheppey to fortify it."

"And those land-lubbers in London have at last bestirred themselves and raised ten thousand pounds," Johnson told her.

"At Sheppey they cannot be too well off for provisions," Frances worried, "for the Prince sent a message to me, asking for a buck to be shot for venison. I have had this done and despatched to him, as well as a load of provisions we could supply from our own stores. I sent the same by road to Dorset. Powder too, of which my lord had an amount. All should have arrived by now."

Before Captain Johnson left to rejoin Lennox there was time for Frances to write him a letter, which the Captain took with him.

"Oh, my dearest, if you love me have a care of yourselfe," Frances entreated. "I am still the hapyest woman that ever was borne in haveing the heart of my Dearest Lord, and the only Joy of my life, which I will rather chuse to die than lose."

Within a few days of Captain Johnson's departure the crisis was over. The English envoys at Breda, due to the shock of the Medway attack, were prepared to come to reasonable terms, and Coventry, the English ambassador, arrived from Holland with a draft of the peace treaty.

Even so Lennox was unable to leave Dorset immediately, though the King had ordered the peace medals to be struck. Although Frances had fallen from favour—badly though she was missed at Court, nobody dared to speak of her in the King's presence—the design for the medals had not been changed, and there she was, a regal Britannia, serenely gazing upon her ships as they sailed on the ocean.

Calmly, in Lennox's prolonged absence, Frances occupied herself with the re-building of Cobham, revealing a capability which would have surprised any of her friends and not least the King.

She wrote to Lennox that their bed-chamber was being painted, she having hired the painter he had mentioned. It was almost done, Frances told him, though in these times it was difficult to get workmen. She was also occupied with the garden, planning a special enclosure for herself, fenced with palings over which she intended climbing roses should be trained. Busy from morning to night, and sometimes in her impatience doing more than give directions, but demonstrating how she wished some particular piece of work to be carried out, Frances was watched with consternation by Mrs. Harvest, the housekeeper, who was constantly begging her to rest and to have a care of herself—not unnecessary advice since it was known by now that Frances was in the early stages of pregnancy.

But rest with so much that she longed to see accomplished was beyond Frances' power, and the housekeeper's gloomy prognostications were fulfilled when one day her young mistress stumbled over a pile of stones for coping, which had been dumped in her path. She fell full-length, bruised an elbow and her knees and was carried into the house in a fainting condition.

An hour or so later, a groom was sent off on horseback for the doctor, and before evening Frances had lost her hope of maternity. Since she had given the matter of her pregnancy little thought, it was surprising how deeply she grieved, turning her face into her pillow and sobbing heartbrokenly.

"There, there! Your Grace is so young there will be others. Several maybe," comforted kind Mrs. Harvest, but Frances shook her head speechlessly. She did not believe that she would be given a second chance of bearing a child. The presentiment was so strong that it amounted to certainty.

The good old family doctor, more sensible than many of his kind, took the housekeeper aside.

"Her Grace is not as strong as she seems," he said. "She has a buoyant spirit which deceives herself as well as others, but of a truth she is fragile. Send as quickly as may be to His Grace, the Duke, and belike he will, the war being over, be able to return to her. And if she has a mother or any older female relation it might be a solace to her were they with her at this time."

Mrs. Harvest knew that Frances' mother lived in London, and had even heard that it was at Somerset House. While a servant on horseback was sent off to Dorset to acquaint the Duke of the ill-tidings, the family coach was sent on its way to London.

Within a day or two Mistress Stuart was at her daughter's bedside, and whatever previous complaint Frances may have had of her, she had none now, for her mother's sympathy was deep, and she tended her with loving care. Soon after-

251

wards, Lennox arrived, having spurred from Dorset with few intervals for rest. When he took his young wife in his arms, he murmured the words she had already heard from her mother and the housekeeper.

"Such mishaps are frequent, my sweet. You must forget it and grow strong again. Never doubt but that we shall have sons and daughters in plenty, for this is but a small misfortune."

It seemed so indeed to Frances, now that he had returned unhurt and with such love for her. How *could* she grieve when their separation was over, and to him she could not bring herself to say what, in spite of the doctor's reassurances, she still believed, that for them there would be no sons or daughters. They must find all their happiness in each other.

Now that the war was over with France as well as with Holland, Charles and Henrietta-Anne could resume the correspondence which had been impossible for nearly two years. The Queen Dowager returned to England, though she told her daughter she would be in France again before the winter set in, and it was from her, not from Frances, that Henrietta heard of Frances' marriage and the King's anger with her.

The Queen Dowager had already interceded with her son on Frances' account, but she had met with no success. Knowing that Henrietta could nearly always get her own way with him, she suggested that she might write herself to Charles, reminding him of her affection for Frances. This Henrietta did, but she received an uncompromising reply.

"I do assure you," Charles wrote, "that I am very much troubled that I cannot in everything give you that satisfaction I could wish, especially in the business of the Duchess of Lennox and Richmond, wherein you may think me ill-natured."

Frances, the King continued, had given him great provocation and had injured him sorely. She was one for whom he had had great tenderness, and it was a hard thing to swallow such an injury.

Charles was one who usually found it easy to forgive, and the Queen sometimes gazed at him thoughtfully. In reflective moments he so often looked melancholy. Frances, more than anyone else, had amused and enlivened him. Although more flippant than witty, she had nearly always been able to make him laugh. They shared a sense of the ludicrous, the Queen thought, and he missed her sorely as a companion.

Was that in reality what he had most needed from her? A gay, irresponsible companionship, a friendship shot with a romantic affection? It seemed unlikely when one considered the promiscuous Charles, and yet, as Frances had not been his mistress, it was not thus carnally that he now missed her. No—it was her gaiety that had entranced him. There was a magnetism in such vitality and high spirits and laughter, powerful enough to banish Charles' dark moods. It came to Catherine that if Frances returned to Court as a happily married young woman, Charles, though setting aside all hope of possessing her, could still find happiness in her.

If only one could persuade him of this. But Catherine knew the time was not yet ripe.

Meanwhile, Henrietta and Frances wrote to each other, and presently the young Duchess of Orleans made a suggestion. Since Charles was obdurate and, even with Cobham Hall to engross her, it was unthinkable that Frances and her husband should be in perpetual rustication, why not spend the winter months at least in France?

In addition to his other titles, Lennox was the hereditary Duke of Aubigny, an estate in Berri, which had been bestowed on an ancestor of his in the fifteenth century by Charles VII, then the reigning King of France. Henrietta was sure that if she raised this matter with Louis, he would put Lennox in possession of the estate of Aubigny. Then, suggested Henrietta, Frances could become one of the Queen Dowager's ladies, or one of her own.

Lennox and Frances talked over the matter, though with no great enthusiasm.

"It is true," Lennox said, "that neither of us would be happy in perpetual exile, dear though Cobham is to us. You would find the winter here dull enough."

"It is not so much the dullness, but being forbidden to show our faces in the King's sight," Frances returned. "What have either of us done to him? And you, if war broke out again, would be immediately torn from me to serve him. Fond though I am of 'Rietta, and dearly though I would like to see her again, I would not wish to exile ourselves in France, as though we had committed some unspeakable crime. Besides, what an undertaking it would be to journey there and back to Cobham. To get to London is easy enough."

"I had thought of Scotland as a change for you," Lennox said. "Your Blantyre cousins would give you a great welcome, but my sister is living on my estate there, and I could hardly make a different arrangement for her; while as for being their guests for any considerable time—well, she is a cantankerous piece, some years older than I, and I doubt if you would get on with her or her husband O'Brien. I have found it hard enough to keep on good terms with them."

"Then it would be even harder for me," Frances said promptly. "When I look back, though I wasn't then conscious of it, it does seem as though few women had much liking for me. It was always their husbands."

Lennox laughed. "You didn't trouble to make big eyes at the wives. But even you would find O'Brien a hard nut to crack, for he's woman-proof if ever a man was. In good truth, he and Kate are a sour-looking pair."

"Then don't let's go near them!"

"If I thought there was a chance that you could win them over to liking it might be good policy," Lennox said. "It is like this, my Heart. If we by ill-chance have no son of our own, I can but leave you a life-interest in both Cobham and the lands in Scotland."

"Don't!" Frances said, and it was as though the flowering gardens through which they walked were suddenly darkened. "If you died, nothing would have any value to me in my loneliness. But why speak of it? You are young and strong—we shall live to be old together." She laughed, and the sun once more steeped all around in a brilliant light. "I shall be a *formidable* old woman. I can see myself—so tall and thin and my nose will look hooked then—a witch's nose!"

He teased her, pretending to see signs already of such a nose, and then he said: "We shall do better in London once the summer is over. Your mother will be pleased to have us at Somerset House, and now that the Queen Dowager is there, you will see your sister Sophie."

"So I shall." Frances' eyes glinted mischievously. "It won't worry the Queen Dowager if the King is annoyed, because she countenances us. It *never* worried her to be at odds with him. We shall be able to hold our own Court there."

So they did, much to the King's annoyance when it came to his ears. Frances, he said angrily, had no sense of what was fitting.

The Queen retorted blandly: "No girl ever made less of ceremony or treated you more as your own sister would have done had she been in England."

"Not precisely as a sister," Charles objected, unwilling to think that he had failed to stir Frances emotionally. But then he caught Catherine's somewhat sardonic smile and laughed sheepishly. "Men are vain fools. I strive to convince myself against all evidence that the minx would have lost her heart to me had I been unmarried."

"I can't think how it was that she didn't, even though you *were* married," Catherine said with perfect honesty, and Charles was as much touched as amused.

"I am not an Adonis," he pointed out.

"Adonis was nothing but a foolish boy."

Charles laughed and patted her shoulder. There was nobody who understood him better and for whom he had more affection. It was a cruelty she was unable to bear children, which might well have reformed him, or so he told himself. With a legitimate son or two there would have been security, not all this dissatisfaction about the succession because his brother James was a Papist. The heir to the throne would have been reared as a Protestant, though that would have been a grief to his Catherine and a torment to her conscience, so perhaps it was as well, thought Charles, who could generally see the redeeming side of any misfortune.

He couldn't, however, be philosophical about Frances, whom he missed as he had never missed any woman. Her laugh echoed in his ears and her face haunted him. She had had the gift of making him feel young and carefree, and nobody else could do that, not even Nell Gwyn, the witty, saucy, Drury Lane actress. Nell's quips amused him, and he believed she had a genuine fondness for him, but she had none of Frances' bright innocence, her breeding and fastidiousness. This had appealed to him more than he realized. Nell's chief asset was a boundless though entertaining vulgarity.

It had been easier to put Frances out of his mind and to harden his heart against her while she was at Cobham, but now he was conscious of her nearness. Julia La Garde prattled of her to Catherine and sometimes Charles was within earshot. The La Garde girl had attempted to emulate Frances in many of her insouciant ways, and there were those who admired her and thought her as charming, but Charles was unmoved by the languishing glances she cast at him, and Barbara Castlemaine, who divined the girl's aspirations, mimicked her as cruelly as Nell Gwyn sometimes mimicked Barbara.

Frances, though forbidden to show herself at Court, was not neglected. At Somerset House, as Charles knew, she gave frequent receptions. His mother had returned to France after a brief visit, and Frances' sister Sophie, who had grown into an exceedingly pretty girl, had gone with her. Courtiers, who had missed Frances when she was banished, now flocked to see her, and Charles could not bring himself to forbid it. He heard of Lennox's obvious content, and of the new moderation in his drinking and gambling habits with secret rancour. Nothing would ever make him like Lennox. Though forced to admit that he had good qualities, he would always think of him as a dull fellow and wonder at Frances' partiality.

Aware as Charles was of the frequent absences from Court of those he most favoured, he was astonished when these truants were again seen there regularly, and he then put the direct question, enquiring sarcastically if La Belle Stuart had left for Cobham. The reply that Frances was ill with the small-pox threw him into consternation. Her life was in no danger, Charles was told, but the disfiguring rash was severe.

Little else could be learnt, for, afraid of the infection, everyone was shunning Somerset House, but it was said that Lennox was distraught with anxiety and hardly left her side. It was thought that her sight might be affected and that she would be badly scarred.

Charles was aghast, so was the Queen when he told her of Frances' illness, and without any prompting from her, Charles wrote to both Lennox and Frances, telling them they were forgiven.

Frances, who had borne her illness with fortitude, broke down and cried when she received the King's letter. "He has a good heart after all," she said, "and even if I am to look hideous, perhaps it is worth it, my dearest, if it restores you to favour."

"I would rather be out of favour for ever," Lennox retorted, "than that you should be pitted with the smallest scar. We should have stayed at Cobham where the disease is a rarity. Should your sweet face be marred . . ."

"Do not scare her," interposed Mistress Stuart irately. "As you know, Frances has shown wondrous self-control and has not torn at her spots."

"Which was chiefly due to my lord, *Maman*, for he went from one apothecary to another in search of a particular eye water and skin lotion which few stocked, but which he had heard averted blemishes. They were most soothing. If when the rash fades I am found to be not badly marked, it will be thanks to him."

Mistress Stuart could not deny it, though her temper through long days and nights of nursing Frances had sharpened. Lennox had become so despondent that she had little patience with him, and now that the doctors said that Frances' state was no longer infectious, the two, who had devotedly tended her, rasped one another. Frances in the early stages of convalescence was in no condition to act as peacemaker, and upheld her mother when she said: "Frances is now more in need of rest than anything else. As the King has lifted his ban, why not show yourself at Court, and reassure those who no doubt have been anxious about your wife? Do not on any account let them suppose that in future she will look unsightly."

Lennox at last allowed himself to be persuaded, and Frances then entreated Mistress Stuart to go to her own room and rest. She got her own way, and was no sooner alone than she searched for and found the mirror that had been hidden from her. Hitherto she had not asked for it, for she had dreaded to look at herself, but she was strong enough now, she decided, though as she returned to her bed with the mirror clutched to her breast she was praying fervently that she might not appear too hideous.

Tears at first blurred her sight, but she dashed them away and then gazed earnestly at her reflection. She was not such a terrible fright as she had feared. Her skin was still blotched and her face looked swollen, her eyes were sunken and dimmed, but the horrible spots had disappeared, leaving no mark. Her once healthful cream-and-peaches complexion might return, she supposed, and her eyes would not always ache so incessantly.

At this moment the door-handle turned and the door was pushed open. Frances turned, prepared to remonstrate with her mother, whom she had hoped was asleep by now. Instead, she gave a startled cry, for it was the King who stood on the threshold.

"My poor Frances! My poor, sweet child," he said.

"Sire!"

The mirror was cast aside. Frances made as though to dive beneath the bed-clothes, but the King's arms were round her. He kissed her forehead and held her tenderly.

"You should not—you should not!" exclaimed Frances.

"Why not? The doctors say there is no further fear of infection and I have longed to see you. I was told your husband had been seen on his way to Whitehall, and I wished first to talk to you alone. I took a boat and sculled myself down the river, but when I landed I found the garden-door was locked, so I climbed over the wall."

"Your Majesty did that!"

"Why not? Once I was within, my troubles were over. I knew your room. I have passed and looked up at the window, with the light burning in it at nights, more than once these last weeks."

"You—you cared enough for that?" Frances said in wonder, and then the mirth which was so much a part of her and which he had so sorely missed bubbled up and she shook with laughter. "But to climb that high wall with the spikes on top. You—the King of England! Oh, Charles, did you tear your clothes?"

"I am not yet so old that I cannot vault over the top of a wall—since there were footholds between the bricks."

"But suppose you had been seen, and by one not recognizing you, who would have taken you for a robber?"

"I had a care of that. There were none about."

Frances' thoughts veered to herself. She faltered. "If I had known, if you had sent a message warning me, I would have put up a better appearance."

Instinctively she had pulled over her face the gauze scarf which she had used of late as a shield for her eyes when the light was strong, and she was thankful that her mother had tended her with such care, changing the bed-linen daily, keeping the window ajar and freshening the room frequently with a lilac-scented water. Her night-shift was of silk and the curtains of the four-poster were of rose-coloured damask. If only he would not look at her face.

But now Charles was gently turning it towards him, and her lips trembled.

"Come now, there is no great difference," he said tenderly. "And these are early days. You will see, within a few weeks the last mark will have disappeared."

"They do say that even at the best my left eyelid will droop somewhat," Frances said.

"Do not believe it. You will be as beautiful as ever. But

it is not only beauty you have, Frances, it is your gay spirit and your happy heart. How I have pined for them, there is no telling. Though having taken stock of myself these last days, I am fain to own that I deserved to lose you."

"No. It was as much my fault as yours," Frances insisted. "I was vain and foolish and I promised you that which I had no right to promise, which in my heart I meant to give only to one who wedded me. I don't deserve that you should be here now, and so—so kind to me."

Her voice shook on the last words and Charles said: "I wish I could have been with you when you were at your worst. Do you remember telling me when the Queen was so ill, that if you were ever in like case you hoped you might have as good a nurse as I had proved myself?"

Frances did remember, but at the thought of the King tending her, of her mother's incredulous dismay and of Lennox's furious anger, she once again shook with laughter.

"Oh, the scandal that would have caused! It would have been retailed in history from one generation to another. Still, if you had, the very madness of it would have gone far to cure me. What heaven it is to laugh again! My poor husband and my poor mother have so grieved over me, and so rated one another."

"Then *you* have missed me a little?" Charles asked eagerly.

"More than a little, and I have sorrowed to be under the ban of your displeasure and to know that I had brought such on my husband."

"You are happy with him?" For the first time there was a note of constraint in the King's voice.

"Very happy. Do not be angry with me for confessing it."

"How could that make me angry? Since you are married to him I should be a churl indeed not to wish you happiness. The madness of love when it is starved and ungratified passes at last, but friendship remains. I know of nobody with whom I could have a happier friendship. However, husbands are apt to be jealous of me, and allowances must be made for them."

Frances replied thoughtfully: "I don't think Lennox will be jealous, or not *too* jealous. He has great faith in me, and I in him. We would not betray each other. It is true that he is of a serious nature, but I, too, can be serious sometimes. It does not annoy him that at other times I am given to laughter."

"If it did, he would be an even greater fool than I take him to be," said Charles tersely.

"Oh, Sire, I wish you could be friends for my sake," Frances pleaded. And then, struck by another thought, she asked: "Does the Queen know of this visit?"

"Zounds! No! She would be beside herself fearing that all infection had not passed. I shall not tell her for a few days, not wishing to alarm her. But she has talked much of you and has wished these many weeks that we could be reconciled, and you once more about her person."

"I wish that too," Frances owned. "Her Majesty was endlessly kind to me."

"Well, we shall see." The King caressed her hand as he said: "We cannot do without you at Court, and you must not be allowed to bury yourself at Cobham, delightful though it may be."

This started Frances on a description of her country home, and the King listened with indulgence thinking that she was like a child with a new toy. But when he heard how she had stood on high ground in the park to watch the Dutch ships sail up the Medway, and afterwards had done what she could to supply Prince Rupert with venison and provisions, and had sent ammunition to Dorset, he applauded her spirit.

They were thus talking, the King sitting on the side of the big bed with Frances' hand in his, when Mistress Stuart came in and exclaimed at the sight of him. Then Frances had to tell her how he had rowed down the river and had climbed over the wall. Mistress Stuart scarcely knew whether to be more scandalized or flattered that the King should have undertaken such an exploit. She was glad indeed that her daughter and son-in-law were no longer in disgrace, but somewhat apprehensive as to Lennox's reactions to this unconventional visit.

But Lennox took it calmly enough when Frances told him, which was not until the next day, for the King left before he returned, and Lennox was somewhat flushed with now more unaccustomed wine-drinking and was ashamed of himself. Frances, however, had expected this after the several days in which he had only left her in order to search the apothecaries' shops for lotions to relieve the dreadful irritation of the rash.

Soon she was out and about again and very delighted the Queen was to see her. Her beauty was only slightly dimmed and a clever use of cosmetics disguised blemishes which gradually became fainter.

Catherine was charming to Lennox and laughed so heartily over Charles' unconventional visit to Somerset House, and spoke of it so openly, that nobody could possibly think it was a secret assignation. She watched Frances and Lennox with more attention than they guessed and satisfied herself that they were truly happy and deeply attached to each other. As for the King, it was as the Queen had thought. He was no longer tempestuously in love with Frances, but he did delight in her company, and there was no doubt of his very real fondness for her.

In the early autumn, after she returned from a stay of some weeks at Cobham, Frances gave a grand supper-party for the King and Queen at Somerset House, and it was then announced that the Queen had been pleased to appoint the Duchess of Lennox and Richmond one of her Ladies of the Bed-Chamber. At the same time, the King bestowed a gift upon her. One of the gold medals struck to celebrate peace with Holland, which bore Charles' head upon it and Frances in her robes as Britannia. The medal had been set by the King's goldsmith in a circle of diamonds, and it hung from a long gold chain, also set with diamonds.

Tactfully, Catherine then presented Lennox with a miniature of herself.

The Bed-Chamber appointment carried with it the

tenancy of a house—a charming Pavilion—in the Bowling Green at Whitehall. Samuel Pepys, calling to see Lennox there by appointment, on business connected with his yacht, described it as a little building with fine rooms. Lennox struck him as "a mighty good-natured man", but Pepys was disappointed not to see Frances, who was once more at Cobham.

Indeed, she spent at least half her time there, which might have caused difficulties had her appointment at Court been much more than a sinecure, and had the King been less engrossed with the sparkling Nell Gwyn.

Barbara Castlemaine had fallen into the background, though the King was never to discard her altogether. In fact, in order to atone for his neglect of her, she was soon given a new title, that of the Duchess of Cleveland, which was no doubt some satisfaction to her, as she could now claim a rank equal to Frances'. Together with the title was the gift of the fabulous Palace of Nonsuch in Surrey.

The Queen had no protest to make, for she recognized that title and estate were both payments considered due to the status of a past mistress who had borne the King's children.

The wording of the bequest and the new titles bestowed upon Barbara and her children stated that these were due because of the great services rendered to the Crown by Barbara's father and other members of her family. Naturally it deceived nobody.

22

The golden years, as Frances herself called them, swept past with speed. She was conscious of this speed and wished foolishly that she could bid Time stay to loiter for a while. It seemed to her that she had barely seen the tight buds of the daffodils and tulips unfold, and walked beneath the lilac and laburnum trees, than it was summer with the roses in full bloom. And then with scarcely a pause the golden leaves from the trees would be scattering on the grass and swirling in clouds as the strong autumn winds stirred them.

Happy though her marriage was, there were drawbacks, for, although Lennox no longer drank to excess or risked large sums on gambling, there were occasional backslidings for which Frances was prepared and of which she made light. For a girl in her early twenties she was a remarkably sagacious wife, and in his letters when they were apart Lennox gave her every praise. The partings, alas, were far too frequent, and were brought about by Lennox's various official appointments, and also because he was desperately striving to improve his financial position. Of this he said little to Frances, for she was all too conscious that she had brought him nothing on their marriage, when he was already heavily in debt.

Several of those debts she had since cleared by her determined economies, but it was impossible to keep up their almost regal position and also to continue with the improvements to Cobham Hall without heavy expenditure.

Lennox left her to superintend these for a few months when he received word from the Earl of St. Albans, who was in France, that if he would present himself in person at the

French Court he would be put in possession of the fief of Aubigny.

As this would mean a substantial addition to his revenue, Lennox set forth with the least possible delay. Frances might have gone with him but for her Court appointment and her preoccupation with Cobham. His visit was to have been a short one, but various matters combined to lengthen it, and many letters were exchanged while Lennox was a guest of the Queen Dowager. Mistress Stuart was also on a visit there, and Frances might have felt the more disconsolate to be left behind, but that the King had told her he was negotiating for his dear Minette to pay a visit to England.

"Will that horrid husband of hers allow her to visit England without him?" asked Frances, knowing that but for the Duke of Orleans' jealousy Henrietta would have paid more than one visit ere now.

"That of course is the obstacle," Charles allowed, "but Louis, who seldom interferes and who usually backs his brother even when he is at fault, assures me he will be adamant about this. Minette will come alone, and the fact that it will be as an ambassador will force Monsieur to agree."

"An ambassador?" Frances was puzzled.

"One who proclaims the goodwill now existing between our two countries," Charles said glibly.

Too glibly, for neither Frances nor the Queen, who was present, believed him. But Frances had never been interested in politics and had avoided being used as a pawn in any such complicated game, and the Queen from the first had been scrupulously careful not to ask questions. Hearing much of the way in which the Queen Dowager had interfered in State affairs with the result that many said she was responsible for the downfall and execution of Charles I, Catherine had decided that she would hold aloof unless her husband confided in her from choice, in which case she would show him by her discretion that she was worthy of confidence.

After much procrastination, Lennox was awarded his

hereditary dues. Even then he delayed his return, for news reached him through his friends Lord Ashley and Lord Bath that a new embassy was being sent to Poland, and that an application to be appointed Ambassador might be favourably received by the King, more especially if this were made by letter, for there was no denying that, although Charles was not now sensually in love with Frances, he continued to resent her husband.

When Lennox's application was refused, he returned to England and to Cobham, where Frances was eagerly awaiting him.

There was much for him to see, for the work on the central building had made good progress during his absence, and on that first day of his arrival there was also much to talk about. Frances, naturally, wanted to hear all that Lennox could tell her about the Duchess of Orleans, about Mistress Stuart and her sister and brother. Sophie's betrothal to Sir Henry Bulkeley, a younger son of Viscount Bulkeley, had recently been announced. It was not a particularly brilliant marriage, though his father was Master of the King's Household, but Sophie was in love and very happy, and Frances was delighted because on her marriage she would be living in England.

"Though I have no doubt the Queen Dowager will miss her," she said. "She is so fond of Sophie, and she does so hate changes in her household."

"The Queen Dowager is looking very frail," Lennox observed. "She has aged much recently. She is an amazingly good friend, and so is *Madame*, who wrote herself to the King with the wish to forward my Polish application. But, as you have heard from Bath, I have been refused."

"I feel certain that was not out of enmity," Frances said.

"For what other reason then? I have had sufficient administrative and diplomatic experience in Dorset and Scotland."

"Dearest, I think the King is sincere when he says that such appointments are unworthy of your rank. You are, after all, his cousin, and a lesser man could well fill this post.

Besides—oh, there are other reasons. We are like to be separated as it is when you are in Scotland on business there, and the King knows this will be a grief to me. How could I be with you in Poland? We knew when the Queen appointed me as one of her Bed-Chamber ladies that it would keep me in England."

Lennox smiled sardonically. "Not even at your word can I believe that Charles would be moved to sympathetic dolour were we separated. I grant that his love of you has become more rational, but he takes great pleasure in your company, of which he would have more were I away."

"But he would dislike to seem responsible," Frances argued. "Usually I know when the King is sincere, and so does the Queen. She and I have talked of this. If you are given a European appointment it will be as an Ambassador Extraordinary. Even then the King might hesitate before sending you so far away."

"Because he has so much fondness for me that he would fain keep me about his person? My sweet, why try to disguise the truth? We both know that in his eyes I am a dull dog. Time after time I have seen him look from you to me with genuine puzzlement as to how you can prefer me to him as a lover."

"I cannot imagine why that should perplex him," cried Frances indignantly. "You are much younger, you are much better looking and you love me and me alone. How can he think that a woman prefers to *share* a lover?"

"But such a lover!" Lennox mocked. "Charles' worst enemies do not suggest that he is ill-versed in the sexual arts. Even my Lady Castlemaine, with her extensive experience, has been heard to say that no man is a match for the King in bed."

Frances, the fastidious, made a gesture of disgust.

"How could I *ever* have admired that woman?" she wondered. "For I did, you know, when I first came to Court. All I can say is that I never coveted the King as a lover, and if he had become mine I could not have endured

it. Whereas you, my dear lord, are vastly agreeable to me."
She added with deepening colour: "I hope much that it is
so with you."

"I find it wretched to be away from you," he told her.
"But you well know the necessity of some such appointment—that is to say, unless Cobham is to go to ruin. My
only regret is when I think of the great marriage you could
have made."

It was the old flirtatious Frances who smiled demurely
and cast down her lashes. "But indeed I always had an
ambition to be a Duchess, and to be called 'Your Grace',"
she confessed. "Do not worry too much about the debts.
We shall straighten ourselves out in time. We are young
and have years ahead of us. All that daunts me is this
necessity for partings, and I do understand the King's
reluctance—not because he particularly *wants* you here, but
he would not have it said that he has taken as a model the
King in the old Bible story of Uriah the Hittite. He might
have been unscrupulous had he still wanted me as much,
but praise be to heaven he doesn't. The small-pox may have
been a blessing to me!"

"Absurd! You are as beautiful as ever."

"I wonder—I look at my face in the mirror and I wonder.
Perhaps I am still fair only in your eyes, my dearest."

"What! With Mulgrave making a perfect ass of himself
over you, and openly avowing that I treat you brutally?
But for the absurdity of that elegy of his, I'd a mind to call
him out for it."

"How could you when you were in France? And I dealt
with milord Mulgrave. I sent for him and went over those
precious verses of his line for line, reading them to him with
great expression, so that he was well out of countenance.
"Wife to a tyrant you by fate are ty'd," quoted Frances with
scorn. "So that he might have no excuse for spreading
abroad this calumny, I showed him some of the gifts you
had sent me from Paris with the messages attached. By the
end I had him on his knees praying for forgiveness. And that
was not the end of it, for the Queen also rebuked him. All

at Court know the contempt I have for milord Mulgrave and have made a mock of him."

"It seems then as though he has been sufficiently punished," Lennox said, laughing. "He is fortunate, none the less, that I have never greatly concerned myself as to what men say of me. It would be different if calumnies were attached to you."

"They were in the past, but not now," Frances said. "The new story is that my chastity is like to make me dull. The Queen, the Duchess of Buckingham and myself are linked together as three prudes. Yet we are all in love with our husbands, though how poor Mary can be with that heartless Buckingham . . ."

The last words brought Frances into her husband's arms and she clung to him. "It would break my heart were I to be a disappointment to you," she murmured.

"My lovely wife, how could you be?"

Lennox caressed her and the shadow of doubt was dispelled; a not infrequent doubt which was caused solely by her self-knowledge. She did love him dearly and exclusively, but her nature was not a passionate one; and while she willingly surrendered to his desire, she felt no urge to provoke it. His tenderness and his companionship, their tastes which were so much in accord, meant far more to her. But for his innate gentleness in his dealings with her, she would, she knew, have recoiled from the act of love, but this never-failing gentleness had set up an adoring gratitude which made all his faults seem trivial. There could never be anyone else for her, that Frances knew, but sometimes she wondered if he were equally well-satisfied. It was true that he told her he was, but she knew that Mary Buckingham's love for her graceless husband was so consuming that he could ignite a fever in her, and she suspected that Catherine's passion for Charles was much the same.

Because Frances was conscious of the lack in herself, she was the more determined to be of value to Lennox in other ways.

The fact that they were as yet childless was rarely

mentioned. Lennox, she was sure, wished for a son, if only because Cobham and the Scottish estates would then descend to a direct heir. But at the same time a family entailed additional expenses and he was not loth to postpone them.

"I might be jealous if I saw you with a babe in your arms and showering your love on it," he said on that first night of reunion, as in the curtained four-poster bed he clasped her in his arms.

"But you are not of a really jealous nature, and how could I ever love a child better than I love you?" Frances asked.

"It happens sometimes with women," Lennox stated, caressing the beautiful, slender body. He might have added that with such sweetly passive women motherhood could give a more intense joy than wifehood, and Frances had grieved desperately, though to her own surprise, when she had suffered a miscarriage. "We can wait. I am well content as it is," he assured her, and Frances also was content to fall asleep in his arms, for in that great bed designed for marital love she had been often lonely for him.

A few weeks later the Queen Dowager died in France, and poor Henrietta-Anne, who had depended so much on her, and had been rarely separated from her for long, was heart-broken. Charles also grieved, though he and his mother had been at odds often enough. Henrietta had sustained a double loss, for her little son had died recently at the age of three years old, carried off by one of the rapid childish illnesses for which there seemed to be no cause and no cure. The English and the French Court were both in mourning, and it was not until the next year that her visit came about. Even so, it was a visit grudged by her husband and restricted in every way.

"But it is quite ridiculous," the Queen said, speaking freely as she felt she could, since she and the King were supping quietly with Lennox and Frances in the Bowling Green Pavilion. "How can he possibly limit her visit to three days at Dover, after a sea voyage which may well be rough and fatiguing? It will but scarce give her the chance to recover from it. Why should he make such difficulties? You have told me more than once that he is not in love with her."

"Which does not prevent the little monster from being jealous of her," Charles explained. "If Minette were plain, or did not provoke love and admiration, he would care nothing. However, once she is here, I have little doubt but that her visit will be prolonged. Philippe can chafe on the other side of the Channel. Louis will not wish her to leave until she has accomplished his purpose. This visit will serve to link us together as united countries."

The Queen divined that the last words were for Lennox's edification. If there was some secret and devious business which brought Minette to England with Louis' approval, Charles was resolved that nobody should know of it—not even the wife he trusted, and certainly not the cousin he disliked.

"Between us and the French there cannot be more than surface amity," Lennox opined. "As nations we are hostile, not to each other's faults but to our virtues."

"Think you so?" Charles glanced at his cousin with some surprise. This could be a sapient observation.

"The French are light-hearted and witty and shrewd, and over here are deemed flippant and treacherous. We are tenacious and more serious—prone to admire others better than we admire ourselves. For this the French rate us as fools. 'Tis a blend that curdles. We are more akin to the Dutch with whom by cursèd fate we are for ever warring."

"There's truth in it," Charles agreed, "but mayhap that is half the trouble. We are too alike."

"With the same sturdy ambition," Lennox mused.

Charles, also musing, allowed that his despised cousin was not devoid of perception. These supper parties à quatre were boring to Charles, though when Frances and her husband were in residence at the Pavilion they occurred from time to time. He was sufficiently agreeable to oblige Catherine, who enjoyed their quiet informality. Frances, herself, was as amusing as ever; almost as beautiful as ever, but it was far from flattering to Charles, who had once so intensely desired her, to see the tenderness in her eyes as they rested on her husband. He had bedevilled her, thought Charles discontentedly, and had he, like Bottom in Will Shakespeare's play, worn the head of an ass upon his shoulders, she would have thought it becoming to him.

"Although," said Charles, "in order to satisfy the egregious *Monsieur*, Minette has to be entertained at Dover instead of London, there will be no lack of brilliance. We shall make a capital city of it while she is there."

And so they did—or so Charles did, sparing neither thought nor money to dazzle and delight the little sister he had not seen for years, and who from an appealing young girl had blossomed into a chic young woman.

For her visit, which, as Charles had expected, was prolonged for nearly two weeks, Dover was *en fête*. The King, the Duke of York and Prince Rupert went out in a rowing-boat to board the *Royal Charles*, which had been sent with a splendid retinue to bring the King's only living sister to England. Charles had barely set foot on deck before Henrietta was in his arms, and then the Duke of York was also embracing her. She had not changed—not in herself, thought Charles, and knew that she was the being dearest to him in all the world. How had he endured the long separation from her? But it should not happen again, he vowed. Henceforth he would see her several times a year, even if he had to leave England, which would be hazardous, as, with his hand removed from the helm, there would be so many plotting against him.

The Queen and the Duchess of York were waiting at Dover to greet *Madame* of France. The town was decorated with flags and banners and flowering arches. Music from many violins floated on the air, and a bevy of pretty girls dressed in white threw roses in the path of the illustrious guest. And there also was Frances, for whom Henrietta had often pined and whom she had done her best to lure back to France.

The young Duchess of Lennox and Richmond had

travelled to Dover in state, in a coach drawn by six horses. She had had time to change her travelling garments and was now attired in one of her most ravishing gowns.

"The girl who refused to grow up," Henrietta laughed as they embraced each other.

"But I have at last managed to do so, dearest 'Rietta," Frances assured her.

They exchanged a long, searching gaze and Henrietta made a gesture of assent. "So you have—and happily. Oh, how long, long ago it seems since we were young together. *Chère* Frances, do you still enjoy sugared almonds?"

"Just as much. I remembered, and brought a large box with me," Frances told her.

It was the start of an idyllically happy visit. All manner of festivities had been arranged, though Henrietta would have been happy enough just to be with her brothers, and especially with Charles. She made a friend of Catherine with surprising ease and no longer wondered that her brother would not hear of divorcing a childless wife. Any moment she had to spare was given to Frances, who was bubbling over with the old irrepressible gaiety, and who was so proud of her handsome husband. It was strange, Henrietta thought, that Charles still resented Lennox, since he was no longer in love with Frances.

"He is fond of you now," Henrietta said, "as Louis is fond of me. We are the best of friends, but nothing more, though when I first married Philippe he fell in love with me, and regretted he had not married me himself. It is good, is it not, that this can happen with men, that they can be fond and kind when their passion has waned?"

"Charles' latest love is Nell Gwyn, the actress," Frances told her. "And although she is dreadfully vulgar, it is impossible not to like her. I believe even the Queen has a secret weakness for her."

"Dear, graceless Charles, his infidelities must be a matter of course to her by now, and you, Frances, must be one of the very few who have ever resisted him."

"I was waiting to meet Lennox—unconsciously waiting.

I must have known, I think, that he was somewhere in the world, and that he was for me."

Henrietta looked at her speculatively. "And of course there was Cobham Hall, this wonderful home," she mused. "It was a home you grieved for years ago at Colombes, when you heard that yours had been destroyed."

During that interlude at Dover, Frances was the brightest of all those collected there. Lennox smiled to see her on the day they all drove over to Canterbury which chanced to be the King's fortieth birthday, as also the anniversary of his Restoration to the Throne. There a giant maypole had been set up, and Frances, her bright hair dislodged from its pins and streaming on her shoulders, danced around it with all the younger members of the Court. A play was acted by the London players, who had been summoned to Canterbury by the King. There were bonfires and a great feast.

Yet that night, when they all drove back to Dover, so weary they could scarce keep their eyes open, Charles and Henrietta were alone together in his closet at Dover Castle and it was there that he signed the secret treaty which was to link England with France, and in time to come was to set Protestant England against the Catholic Stuarts. Henrietta believed that she was doing a service to both countries, and Charles, in an hour of weakness, could refuse her nothing.

"This visit," Frances confided to her husband, "for all the joy of it, was not brought about solely to give pleasure, nor merely to emphasise that an English Princess is also *Madame* of France. There was something beneath it which we may never know. One day 'Rietta hinted at it. She and Charles have spent hours together behind locked doors."

"Louis has a tortuous mind," Lennox said. "It would be in keeping for him to use the Duchess as his secret agent for some political device, but Charles, with all his vagaries, is sagacious where diplomacy is concerned, and has steered his way past many a pitfall."

"The visit has been partly spoilt for the Queen," Frances regretted. "If only the King had not shown so plainly that he is captivated by that Breton girl—Louise de Kéroualle

—who came over in attendance on 'Rietta. She says—'Rietta I mean—that Charles' infidelities must by now be a matter of course to the Queen, but they never will be. Every fresh fancy is a fresh affront to her."

"Surely she need not disturb herself over this Breton beauty. She won't be staying here."

"No—though the King wishes it could be otherwise. But 'Rietta told him she was responsible to Louise's mother, and must take her back to France."

It was sad indeed when the visit drew to a close. By that time everyone, it seemed, was in love with *Madame*. The Duke of Buckingham publicly avowed that he adored her and would be ready to kidnap her, and his poor, ignored wife had a hard task to conceal her humiliation. Prince Rupert, in a much more sober fashion, wished that it were in his power to prevent her leaving England. Before the sorrowful leave-taking he made Henrietta promise that if ever she had reason to be frightened or troubled she would send for him.

"He was always against my marriage," Henrietta told Frances on their last evening together, when for a brief while they were alone. "And now of course he knows I am wretchedly unhappy, and says that at a word from me he will carry me off in a ship to this New England of which he thinks so much—to this wonderful New Yorke which is named for James. Frances, it is as though he has a presentiment, as though he has some strange fear for me."

"Oh no! That's too fanciful," Frances declared. "It is only because we all hate to part from you, and because *Monsieur* is, as Charles says, such a little monster. But you do say, 'Rietta, that Louis is in favour of a separation, and then you can return to England with your two little girls and be happy here."

"How wonderful that would be," Henrietta said wistfully. "I love France. I wanted to live there—but now I think I could have been even happier in England."

"Come back to us," Frances begged. "Come and live with me for a while at Cobham. "Oh, 'Rietta, you would love it there—so simple and peaceful, and you would soon be so much stronger."

For they were all secretly worried by Henrietta's persistent, short cough, by the bright spots of colour in her cheeks and her excessive thinness.

When the King with his brother and Buckingham and Prince Rupert had taken Minette back to the waiting ship, the Court returned to London. Charles was sunk in gloom and the Queen on the verge of tears, so swiftly had the beloved Minette become part of her life.

"But she will never again stay away for so long," Catherine told Frances. "For if necessary James or Rupert would cross to France to fetch her."

Frances had never been more thankful for her own happiness, for a husband who adored her and understood her. It was Lennox who comforted her in her shocked grief when, within a week of returning to Paris, Henrietta was seized with a mysterious illness and in twenty-four hours was dead. Then it did indeed seem as though Prince Rupert, so loth to see her leave England, had foreseen some such tragedy.

The King's grief was agonizing, and, hating Philippe as he did, knowing of his many cruelties and perversions and the threats he had hurled at Henrietta before she left France, he declared that she had been the victim of some subtle poison. But there was no proof of this, no real doubt but that his Minette, as the doctors insisted, had died of a chill and a sudden colic.

Frances was ill through much weeping, and when Lennox took her down to Cobham it seemed as though the old house received her with love and pity. Here at least she could be at peace, wandering in the great park, remembering Henrietta as she had been only a few weeks ago—so happy and so in love with life.

"Nobody will be able to comfort the King," Frances said pityingly. "They will all try, but nobody will mean anything to him, not even the Queen, for from the moment they met at Colombes years ago, 'Rietta was more precious to him than all the world. Other women could come and go, but she was always with him. Separation makes no difference when there is such love as that."

"Even death cannot separate two who love," Lennox said.

Frances looked at him with wonder. In their different ways they were both hedonists and these were strange words for him to speak.

"Do you really believe that?"

"Yes, if it is a great love—of the soul as much as the body. It would be so if I died . . . we should be together still."

Frances shook her head in bewilderment. "I don't know," she faltered. "I cannot think of love as—as anything unearthly. Only as you and I feel for each other, as though life was only complete when we met and loved."

23

The sense of partnership deepened with the months and years. Those who had thought they knew Frances well, and at the time of her elopement and marriage had opined that the foolhardy pair would soon separate, since Frances was too volatile for stability and Lennox too self-indulgent and lacking in charm to hold her, were constrained to admit that they had been wrongly judged.

Frances was as entertaining and vital as ever. She still adored dancing, masquerades, ballets and the play. But when not required by the Queen, she could, it was observed, abandon all such pursuits at a moment's notice in order to travel down to Cobham. The grounds as well as the house were a constant preoccupation to Lennox as well as to herself, and his interests were not confined to flower growing and the planning of individual gardens which were Frances' delight.

With Roger Payne, his steward, Lennox decided which fields should be set aside for pastorage and crop sowing. He bought cattle for breeding purposes and at one time contemplated bringing over from the Near East a particular species of small horse which he thought might be bred in England and become so popular that the enterprise might make him a fortune.

Frances was enthusiastic until it was discovered that, however well cared for, the horses seemed unable to adapt themselves to the English climate and died within a few months.

This was not the only failure, for Lennox was enterprising, but failures only served to cement the link which bound

Frances to him. They were shared failures, since neither took any important step without consulting the other.

Two or three times a year Lennox's duties as Lord High Admiral took him to Scotland, and then Frances had her mother to stay with her, and sometimes her brother Walter, who was destined for the Navy, when he left school. To Frances' pleasure there was an especial affection between Lennox and Walter. Sophie, now married, was also fond of her brother-in-law, and it was a great pity, Frances thought, that there should be no affection between herself and Lennox's sister.

"You might get on well enough if you met each other," Mistress Stuart said. "Why not make the effort and accompany Lennox to Scotland the next time he makes the journey?"

"You know what a bad traveller I am," Frances reminded her. "The roads between here and London are rough enough, and on the coach journey to Dover it was terrible. By the time I got there I was quite dazed by the pain in my head. It worries my lord when he sees me prostrate."

"You were subject to grievous headaches even when you were a child," Mistress Stuart allowed. "Being full of spirit, it surprises one that you are not more robust."

"Since the smallpox my headaches have been worse, *Maman*. The doctor thinks the trouble I sometimes have with my eyes intensifies them. Oh, it's nothing to worry about. I am not like to lose my sight, but it would make that long journey to Scotland a torture, and Lennox will not hear of it, more especially as at the end of it I should have but a cold welcome from her ladyship. It may be natural that she should resent me, for if we have a son hers will be dispossessed. At present he is the heir apparent both to Cobham and to the Scottish estate."

"How I wish that you had prospect of a family," Mistress Stuart said, "for you would be dispossessed were you to be left a widow. One has to consider these possibilities, Frances," she insisted as her daughter made a gesture of repudiation. "Life at the best is uncertain, as we have had good cause to realise of late. When I consider my dear mistress, and *Madame* whom she so adored, gone within a few months of one another. . . ."

"When *I* think of the future, I pray—yes, really pray, *Maman*—on my knees in the chapel here—that I may be the first to go. But if it should be my fate to outlive my dearest lord, and without even a child of his for comfort, then I should not be dispossessed. However much Lady O'Brien might resent it, I should have the right to live at Cobham for the rest of my days."

Mistress Stuart sighed with relief. "I am glad to hear it. It is but sense even in the case of a young husband to make early provision for his wife. Yours, fortunately, knows his duty."

"He would be more like to exceed than to ignore it," Frances said proudly.

"Well, I am sure that if God willed you to be left, you would be far happier here than anywhere else, for you absent yourself from Court on every excuse."

"The Queen reproaches me for it," Frances owned, "but I plan to be there again in a few days. My lord will join me when he returns from Scotland. But, oh dear, I am out of the humour for Court life. It is bad enough to see the King thrown into such melancholy for dearest 'Rietta, but 'tis even worse to see him consoled by this Breton girl. How *could* Louis have sent her over. Men are truly wicked. Had he no thought for the Queen?"

Mistress Stuart shrugged. "You cannot expect men to feel as we do, and if it were not Louise de Kéroualle, it would be somebody else. Neither grief for *Madame* nor consideration for the Queen will prevent the King from seeking new mistresses."

"The more I think of the Queen, the more grateful I am for my own happiness," Frances said. "I deserve it far less than she does."

"As though happiness is bestowed upon the deserving. It is more generally the reverse."

Frances was fain to agree that this was true. The decrees

of fate were bewildering. She was the more bewildered, not knowing whether to rate it as good or ill fortune when the King at length decided to send Lennox on an important mission. He was appointed Ambassador Extraordinary to Denmark with the object of forming an alliance with the English and the French against Holland.

Lennox was jubilant. This was better than Poland, or than Italy, which he had coveted later. Now he could forgive Charles for refusing him these appointments, and even believe in the stated reasons for such refusals, since this embassy to Denmark was to be distinguished by a lavish magnificence consistent with sending as its Ambassador one of exalted rank, who was by birth one of the Royal House of Stuart.

"But it's so far away," lamented Frances, for the first time wishing she could hold him back.

"Not so far as Poland, sweet, or no farther."

"It seems farther because it is all by sea—a dreadful passage so 'tis said. How long will you be away?"

"It's impossible to be sure—some months, perhaps a year."

"If it is as long as a year I shall come out to you. I care not how terrible or dangerous the voyage may be."

Her face was strained and her eyes glistened with tears as Lennox said soothingly: "It is scarce likely to be so long— not unless the Danes prove so obdurate against this alliance that no living soul can prevail with them. But I have no doubt of myself, for the longing I shall be in to return to you will give me such eloquence and such application that there will be no holding out against me. How *could* I have a better spur than to regain all my lost happiness here?"

"I wish I did not care for you so much, depend on you so much," Frances sighed, and pulled his arms tighter around her.

"But what a misery I should be in if you did not. How could I leave you if I thought another could take my place with you?"

"Oh, as for that you can go with an unclouded mind. No

one individual ever did interest me to a consuming extent, and since we married it has been only play-acting when I showed anyone even a slight interest. As the country people here say, all my eggs are in one basket."

"Try to be glad," he urged, "that I am at last being given the chance to show that I can be of real value. Then there will be future appointments which won't take me so far away from you."

"How can you tell? It might be Siberia next time, and even Denmark will be sufficiently comfortless. Something assures me that you won't like it there. I expect Will Shakespeare drew a very true picture of the Danes when he wrote *Hamlet*. All gloom and vengeance."

Lennox smiled at her inconsequence and then became serious. "It's the old story, sweet: apart from the distinction which I own I covet, there is the money which will go far to clear our debts and set us up in ease. But this I shall leave in your hands, for you are as prone to save as I am to spend."

"I shan't have any temptation to spend," Frances mourned. "What pleasure would it be for me to entertain without you, and what inducement to buy new, fine clothes when you are not here to see me wear them?"

She did, however, try to show some enthusiasm as the days passed, for much though he hated to part from her, Lennox was elated. At last Charles had shown some recognition of his ambition and diligence, which Lennox since his marriage had endeavoured to impress upon him. Frances knew that had he been content with herself and Cobham and his responsibilities in Scotland she would have admired him less. She could not expect or genuinely wish him to be so engrossed with her that all ambition was stifled. Men, according to her creed, *had* to be ambitious in order to fulfil themselves, and it was as necessary for her to be proud of him as to love him. Therefore, thrusting her grief aside, she did her utmost to help him in his preparations for this glittering venture, and was glad that for once extravagance was justified by his grant from the State, to enable him to make a magnificent impression when he arrived in Denmark.

His tailor was making him new clothes in the latest fashion, many of them luxuriously fur-trimmed, which was a necessity for the climate. His equipage was breathtakingly splendid. A large staff was to accompany him, including a new associate, one George Henshaw, who was selected as adviser, secretary and general manager.

Henshaw, who had formerly held similar appointments, was at first somewhat sceptical of this magnificent aristocrat, and was prepared to treat him as a figure-head. But even before they sailed he had changed his mind about Lennox, appreciating his enthusiasm, though he was inclined to think that the ostentatious display was inordinate and would be wasted on the Danish Court. However, the King considered this a necessity, since Lennox was "an Ambassador of the greatest quality that England had ever sent to Denmark".

Frances, who had never had tremendous sums of money to spend, and through necessity had become clever at stretching a moderate allowance, was wide-eyed at the expensive liveries provided for the servants, and at the new coaches, each with sets of harness for six horses. The family coach had impressed her with its luxury, but this was as nothing compared to the great velvet one of gold and silver, adorned with fringes, and the secondary coach lined with crimson velvet.

People came and went at Cobham to whom Frances acted as hostess. There were high officials from the Admiralty and many from the Court, who were impressed by Lennox's new diplomatic importance. Lord Essex, who had been his friend for years and who was a former ambassador to Denmark, was frequently at Cobham to give Lennox information about the people with whom it was now his mission to establish cordial relations.

Unknown to Frances, Lennox left her in Essex's care. He had made a new will of which Essex and Sir Charles Bickerstaffe, another close friend, were joint executors. He arranged that by power of attorney Frances was to receive all moneys accruing to him during his sojourn abroad, and by request the weekly payments by the Exchequer for his ambassadorial expenses were to be paid direct to her.

Much of this was only fully known to Frances after his departure. By mutual desire they were left alone at Cobham for the last two days. It was April, and the weather was mild and sunny. Hand in hand they roamed the grounds where primroses were massed on the banks and grouped around the trunks of the immense trees. In a great grove daffodils and jonquils, planted the year before, were now breaking their sheaths. Soon the laburnum trees would be falling gracefully in a shower of golden rain.

Lennox's heart was wrenched by so much beauty, and by the even greater beauty of the girl who walked by his side. He would have given much now to have been taking her with him, and once again assured her that their parting could not be for longer than a year and possibly for less.

"Are the Danish women very beautiful, I wonder," Frances said. "I did ask milord Essex, and he says they are not to be compared with those in England, but it could be that he only wishes to please me."

"Beautiful or not, you well know that it would matter nothing to me," Lennox retorted, "unless there should be some face that faintly recalls yours and sets me yearning the more keenly for you."

For the last time they went over the great house, and Lennox spoke to the workmen who would have little more to do at Cobham until he returned. The music-room that Frances had desired as an extension of the banqueting hall was now complete. Frances, whom this beautiful room never failed to entrance, gazed at the golden Inigo Jones ceiling and the walls which had been exquisitely marbled by the order and design of Lennox's uncle. The somewhat inadequate minstrels gallery alone discontented her.

"To be truly magnificent and in keeping with the ceiling it should be gilded—but gold leaf is so expensive," she said.

"Nothing will be too expensive if this appointment is the first of several. Wouldn't it divert you to have such work started while I am away?"

"No." She shook her head emphatically. "I have loved carrying out our plans together these last years, but it is something we share. I want it to be that way. Not my ideas, but ours. I shall be here from time to time, but I expect I shall live mostly at the Pavilion. The Queen will need me, or she says she will."

"The King might be saying the same but for his Breton mistress. I should be grateful to her. Do not try to outshine her, my sweet. You could so easily succeed and turn his thoughts back to you."

"I doubt it. Poor, dear Charles is really very lazy, and when he looks back I fancy he wonders at the disproportionate amount of time he spent on me. Of course he likes a little opposition—I believe Louise put up quite a show of modesty and resistance, but Charles knew it was an act and that he would win. With me there was always the doubt, and he must think now that, even had he succeeded, such patience and energy were scarcely worth while."

"No," said Lennox, doing his royal cousin reluctant justice, "you are wrong. He genuinely loved you."

"Well then, if he did, it is, as poor 'Rietta said, fortunate that he can be kind—a good friend—when passion has passed."

"I wish I were as positive that it *had* passed. Promise me you will tell me in your letters if he makes any attempt . . ."

"I promise you. And you must give me yours, my dearest—not as regards other women, but for your health's sake. . . ."

He put his hand across her lips. "Don't say it. I swear to you. Never more than two bottles, however depressed I may be. I've stayed by that for over a year."

"I know you have. It sounds formidable to me, but I suppose not to you."

"Barely sufficient to moisten a dry throat."

"Then don't, for pity's sake, allow those Danes to provoke you into making long speeches, or your throat will be too dry for endurance."

The jokes were feeble that last day, and that night when they made love Frances was angry with herself because his passion meant comparatively little to her and his tenderness everything.

24

Throughout that summer, spent mainly with the Court at Windsor, Frances strove to be reasonably happy. This seemed an obligation since her husband in his letters urged cheerfulness upon her. They were both young, Lennox wrote, and they had all their lives before them. Soon this separation would be over and in time to come would seem no more than a bad dream.

Frances believed him.

"Oh, why did I believe him?" she cried heartbrokenly, less than a year later.

Why hadn't some instinct warned her that the long life-time together was a myth, and that his days were numbered? Then, whatever the claims of her Court appointment, she would have travelled to him, braving the long journey, making nothing of the headaches, the sickness that when she travelled was inevitable.

With no such prescience, patience had seemed a merit, and she counted each day that passed as one that lessened the time of separation. From her point of view nothing could be better than that Lennox should dislike Denmark, and yet be making such good progress with the diplomatic negotiations. Not unsure of him, she yet knew that to men, especially to men such as Lennox, women were not essential, whereas to her life without him was a shadow-show. But she wanted the King to be proud of him.

And so he was, and astonished, too, when reports of the progress Lennox made came through in the despatches sent from Copenhagen.

When Lennox did make friends they were true to him. Henshaw had speedily become his devoted adherent, and had written of him glowingly, assuring Lord Arlington, the Secretary of State, that the Duke was so competent there was scarce anything left for him to do. It was Lennox in person who had treated with the Danish statesmen and who had impressed them with his capacity.

Charles, reluctantly generous, made Frances happy by his belated appreciation of her husband. The Queen, sympathizing fully with her, had taken care to repeat every word of praise that the King uttered.

"He knows now that he was mistaken," Catherine said, "and that you made a wise choice. When Lennox returns there will be real friendship between them and his gifts as an ambassador will not be neglected."

Frances had her own part to do and was assiduous in her application to her husband's concerns, accounting to him for all the money which came into her hands. Roger Payne, who was devoted to Lennox, wrote of Frances to him with unstinted admiration. The Duchess, he stated, was "the only instrumental cause of clearing all difficulties in your business, and the serving of Your Grace's interests here."

Frances divided her time between Court life and life at Cobham. Every letter from Lennox was an illustration of his love for her—his "dearest Heart".

Jarvis Maplesden was instructed to hand over to her Lennox's own coach horses, as Frances' set of greys, he thought, must be jaded, while his had now been sufficiently rested. Maplesden assured Lennox, when he answered his letter, that on leaving Cobham after her latest stay there Frances had gone off in the coach driven by the six rested horses.

Later, hearing that she was occupying herself with re-decoration to the Whitehall Pavilion, Lennox sent instruction for five hundred pounds to be used for this purpose. Frances knew that she could effect all the improvements necessary for less than half this sum.

And so the months passed, so purposelessly, so trivially when seen in retrospect. There were the hunting parties at Windsor, the balls, the masquerades. Frances had felt remorseful sometimes because her life was so much more pleasurable than her husband's, who found the climate and the Danes thoroughly uncongenial. "Never was a man so weary of a place as I am of this," he wrote to Lord Essex. Henshaw was equally emphatic. "This," he complained, "is one of the dullest places that ever mortals laid out their precious minutes in." But all was going well, and both men hoped that their mission would be completed by the spring.

It was a spring that Lennox was never to see, for on the 12th of December at Elsinore, whither he had gone on a visit to the English fleet which was then in those waters, he was taken with a sudden seizure and died.

The news was broken to Frances, who was then at White-hall, and for days she was too stunned, too ill to ask for further details.

All she knew was that the light of her life had gone out, never to be re-kindled.

When it was possible for her to endure the journey to Cobham, she was taken there, with her mother and Mrs. Harvest to care for her, though both were sadly conscious that there was little they could do, since Frances' sole desire was for solitude.

But presently she roused herself to ask questions of Lennox's personal servant Flexney, who had returned from Denmark, and of Lord Essex, who had been in correspondence with Sir John Paul, the English Consul. Paul, it seemed, was with Lennox at the time of his fatal seizure.

"He had not been drinking heavily, though such is the story that has been put abroad to account for the convulsive fit that killed him," Lord Essex said.

At this Frances showed her first sign of spirit. The lethargy of grief passed from her as she retorted.

"It is needless to tell me that, my lord. He gave me his word. No more ever than his usual two bottles of wine, which were a small matter to him."

"Paul confirms that he was but a little merry," Essex agreed. "Many of those who were at the Fleet banquet drank far more. It was the climate that killed him. He made light of it in his letters home, for had it been known how much the cold endangered him, he would have been recalled, leaving his mission unfinished. Yet it seems from the report of his doctor that more than once there was anxiety felt for him."

"My lord could not have known, or he would have thrown all over and returned, rather than have left me alone and broken-hearted." Frances was in tears, though she had shed few for weeks.

"What man in his thirties can believe that he is doomed?" Essex said. "Though he did undermine his health before ever he met Your Grace."

"But since then—once we were married—he was splendid. Often in the saddle for hours on end, and nobody could match him on the tennis-court."

"It was the climate," Essex repeated. "At Elsinore, as John Paul says, it was freezing and with thick snow. Orders had been given for the Fleet to sail out of the Sound. There was the risk of being frozen in. We in this far milder isle have little conception of the Scandinavian severity. To such as are not accustomed to it the cold can be a killer."

"My lord wrote that without furs it was impossible to live," Frances said brokenly, "and although I did not think he meant that literally, I at once sent out extra blankets and a sable muff, and a heavy coat lined with squirrel. Oh, if only I had taken them myself—gone to him. I could have cared for him better than doctors or anyone else and he . . . he would have been happy."

Essex, gazing at the beautiful, forlorn young woman, slender as a wand, her eyes enormous in her grief-ravaged face, shook his head. "It might as easily have been death for you," he said.

"Oh, what matter! We should then have been together. What have I to live for now? He *was* my life."

Essex, a little in love with Frances, as were most men who came in contact with her, and greatly pitying her, said compassionately: "He was fortunate. For five years you were his greatest joy."

But the five years had gone so swiftly, thought Frances. If she had known, how she would have grudged every day as it passed. And she had not given enough, she told herself, as often before. All she had—but such a meagre all. She had honoured and loved him, but in a fashion which only another woman of similar temperament would have understood.

Essex reflected that she was not yet twenty-six and would recover with time. There would be no lack of suitors ready to console her. Only Frances knew that she would never wholly recover, and would never put another in Lennox's place. Falteringly she asked the hardest questions of all.

"They told me—my mother said she had heard it was certain my lord would be brought home to England. But when? Weeks have already passed."

Essex evaded telling her the actual details. Lennox's body had been embalmed, and a special leaden coffin had been obtained with difficulty. This had been put into another, covered with velvet, and now waited in Sir John Paul's house at Elsinore until it could be shipped to England.

"The King of Denmark," said Essex, "has offered a Danish ship to bring His Grace's body back to England, though at first there was talk of sending the *Royal Charles*. The final arrangements are not yet known, and the voyage itself usually takes several weeks."

"Full six weeks when he left England," Frances remembered.

Delays there were in plenty, and incredibly the Danish ship of mourning did not reach England until the following September. Early in August, Henshaw wrote announcing that it was on the verge of departure, and when Frances heard that the ship was expected to put in at Gravesend she nerved herself to be there.

Courage she had in plenty, even after months of grief and seclusion—and courage was needed. Surrounded by her friends and by high officials sent by the Secretary of State and by Charles himself to represent him, Frances stood there in her widow's mourning to look with anguish upon the black-painted, black-sailed ship which brought back the body of His Britannic Majesty's Ambassador Extraordinary to his own country.

In spite of her grief, Frances could not but realize that Lennox with his love of pageantry would have been gratified by the pomp of his long-delayed funeral, and afterwards she discovered that Charles had given orders that his cousin's body was to be interred in a manner reserved for royalty. Imaginatively, he must have surmised that this was something Lennox would have appreciated, and that such honours might relieve Frances' long and stony grief.

They did, since this was the King's acknowledgment that his cousin was a profound loss to the country he had served.

Nothing could have given Frances more pride than Charles' edict that Lennox was to be buried at Westminster Abbey. There, on an autumn evening, with the lights from hundreds of candles piercing the dimness of the old building, the ceremony took place. There was scarcely one of the nobility that did not attend it, and the Knights of the Garter, wearing the Collars of their Order, were present to pay their last respects.

Curious eyes rested upon Frances, and she was not unaware of it. Buckingham, with his outwardly reverential aspect, must, she knew, be pleased that this was the end of Lennox, since he had never forgiven her. But what should Frances care? Garter Principal King of Arms was now proclaiming the dead man's style and titles. But words other than these passed through Frances' mind.

> "Fear no more the heat of the sun,
> Nor the furious winter's rages;
> Thou thy worldly task hast done,
> Home art gone and ta'en thy wages.
> Golden lads and girls all must,
> As chimney-sweepers, come to dust."

It was over at last, and the Duchess of Buckingham, who loved Frances if her spouse did not, was one of those who took her home to the Whitehall Pavilion, and spent the night watching over her.

From thenceforth Charles was all considerate kindness to Frances. He had given instructions that the greatest care was to be taken to see that Lennox's personal property in Denmark was restored to her. Added to which, the valuable gold plate that had been taken from the Jewel House for use during the embassy was given to her as a present.

It was the first of many such presents, bestowed after consultation with the Queen.

The King of Denmark sent Frances his own miniature set with diamonds, this being the gift he had intended for Lennox on the termination of his embassy.

Charles personally received the captain of the Danish mourning ship and presented him with a gold chain and medal, and, on behalf of Frances who was pitifully ill again, he was sent a handsome belt and a gold sword.

Now she was besought by all those who cared for her to pick up the threads of her life once more; to remember that she was young, beautiful, naturally joyous.

"Would not this," asked the Queen on their first meeting after the Abbey funeral, "be his dearest wish?"

"Oh, Madame, how can I know? He never thought of dying," Frances replied.

"Dear Frances, I think he may have done, for he took such care to make all the provision he could for you. Cobham Hall is still your home, though had not Lennox made a will securing you the life interest, it would have reverted to his sister."

"And great resentment she bears me because of it," Frances retorted. "She had the impertinence to write to milord Essex that she was in great fear lest the beauty of the house and park would be utterly defaced by the alterations already made and which I may continue to make. Not that I shall. It must stay now as it is. There are too many debts to be paid, and the hard task to settle all left to Sir Charles Bickerstaffe."

"I am so anxious about you," Catherine said. "But there

will be enough for you to live in comfort, dearest Frances. The King has busied himself about this. He feels, and rightly, that he owes you a life, as much as though the Duke had died for him in battle."

"He has told me so," Frances said. "It may not be quite true . . . but I do know that Lennox, in spite of their different temperaments, was never so proud and happy as when he was given the chance to serve the King in this Denmark appointment."

"Do not hide yourself altogether at Cobham," the Queen entreated. "You are needed here as much as you are needed there. You are too young for solitude."

"I doubt if I *could* bear much more of it and live," Frances owned, adding with the first flicker of humour for many a day: "I am not by nature a bemoaning turtle."

"A turtle?" echoed the perplexed Queen, and then to her delight and astonishment she heard the once familiar gurgle of spontaneous laughter.

"It was a poem that was written at the time of my lord's funeral," Frances explained. "Who wrote it I have no idea, but it was sold in the London streets and one of my maids bought a copy and thought it immeasurably touching. Hoping it might please me, she gave it to me after a while. It is little more than doggerel and I cannot remember the whole of it, but the last verse went like this:

> 'Let none into her presence dare t'intrude
> Once to disturb her graceful solitude.
> She needs none of your help, let her alone,
> The turtle by herself loves to bemoan.'

There was a good deal more absurdity about my sighs like perfumed incense and my panting breasts like little mournful birds drooping in their nests. It would make the King laugh."

"I must tell him about it," Catherine smiled. "It is good to be able to laugh as well as to sigh over the past. Charles can, even when he recalls his beloved Minette, because of some of the amusing things she said. One should try to remember the happy times."

"Our time together was nearly all happiness," Frances said. "I am thankful that I *knew* I was happy. But it was so short. I cannot bear to think it has gone like a dream, and that when I die there will be nobody to remember him. It is not as though I bore a son."

"None can understand that regret better than I," the Queen said.

But to Frances, as the months passed, this longing to leave some memorial of Lennox which would survive through the generations became a secret obsession.

Thanks largely to the King's generosity her means were more than adequate, but they consisted of Crown annuities and life interests from Lennox's estates. If the plan that slowly matured in her mind was to come to fruition, she would need to be thrifty. Not so difficult for Frances, who had never squandered money, and whose remarkable dress-sense depended more on her taste and skill than on extravagance.

The greater part of her life was spent at Court, where she was rightly considered an ornament, but when she was alone at Cobham, then her dreams took possession of her. Lennox had said that even death could not separate those who greatly loved, with the soul as much as with the body, and sometimes Frances could believe it. Certainly it had been with her soul that she had loved him, and there was this constant yearning to commemorate it, to show the world that love could be stronger than death.

Strange sentiments these would have been thought to fill the mind of the beautiful Duchess, who to all outward appearances had recovered her zest and gaiety, and whom many men loved without hope of reward.

She, herself, was immortalized, Frances sometimes thought for there on the coins of the realm was her portrait, with which generations yet to come would be familiar. But who would remember Lennox?

Cobham Hall no longer meant what it had once meant

to her. Catherine O'Brien's jealousy succeeded in making her feel that she was a usurper, and finally she half reluctantly decided to sell her life interest in the estate to Lord O'Brien, and thus end the constantly recurring animosity.

It was at this time that Frances took her cousin Lord Blantyre, whom she saw from time to time, into her confidence. Due to various bequests she was comparatively rich, and was now saving industriously. When she died, she told Lord Blantyre, she wished the bulk of her fortune to pass to his son and heir, Walter Stuart, Master of Blantyre, and thence to his male heirs. But this fortune was to be used for a special purpose. It was to be invested in a purchase of lands in Scotland, and was to be named Lennoxlove. Thereafter it was to be preserved in perpetual memory of her husband and herself, enshrining their portraits and many of the ancestral treasures.

Assured by her legal advisers that such instructions could be carried out, satisfied that she would thus inaugurate another ancestral home where the Stuart clan would live, always conscious of the ancestor it immortalized, Frances was satisfied. She might have several years yet on earth, but she had found an absorbing, fascinating objective.

She was like a little girl with a wonderful secret, for only those most intimately concerned knew anything about this dream project, which as the years passed became more and more real to her. Cobham had been a splendid toy which had lost half its allure when Lennox was not there to share it, but now she firmly believed that he shared all her visions of Lennoxlove. Whether or not a new and stately mansion would be built, or some already historic estate bought and improved, scarcely mattered to Frances. All she saw was her beloved husband's memorial, and the resurrection of the old family home that had been destroyed by the Cromwellians. The fact that her dream was a fluid one, almost allegorical, only made it the more fascinating to this inveterate dreamer, whose life was paradoxically so orderly and practical.

Sometimes the Queen, who was fond of her beyond all

other women, vaguely realized that the Frances so gay, so amusing, so kind and attentive was not the whole Frances; and had her life been less open and immaculate, Catherine might have wondered if the expression she occasionally surprised was that of one who brooded upon a secret lover.

"Do you not notice it too?" Catherine asked the King. "Oh, I cannot describe it. It is a kind of remote expression as though her real being is in another world. It could be," Catherine suggested, though doubtfully, "that she has given her true self to religion."

The King shrugged. "It may be so. Certainly no man seems capable of making an impression on her."

That evening a pageant of classical beauties was being shown in *tableaux*, and at the end those who had taken part in it paraded before the King and Queen who smiled upon Frances as she passed by, a statuesque Pallas Athene in which rôle Gascar had painted her.

How different she was, Charles thought, from the girl he had once madly desired. In this stately woman he was not particularly interested, though he would always have a kindness for her.

"Sometimes she is more beautiful than ever," the Queen said.

And the King smiled down upon his little dark wife who could so whole-heartedly admire another woman.

The Historical Novels of
MARGARET CAMPBELL BARNES

THE PASSIONATE BROOD

A tale of the Plantagenets and Robin Hood, first published as Like Us They Lived

"The characters live in this book. I have thoroughly enjoyed it."—EDWARD SHANKS (*Daily Dispatch*)

"A story of fierce fighting, exciting escapades, intrigues and full-blooded loving, told with tremendous gusto and, so far as I can judge, complete historical accuracy."—S. P. B. MAIS (*Oxford Mail*)

"She has made a glittering tapestry of her story. Her men and women live and win our regard or our dislike."—BRENDA E. SPENDER (*Homes and Gardens*)

MY LADY OF CLEVES

The story of Henry the Eighth's fourth wife

"In Mrs. Barnes' skilful hands Anne herself becomes a real woman who will make many friends."—*Sunday Times*

"The tale is so convincingly told, the characters and background so well drawn, that the picture will remain in your memory, to crop up again whenever you hear the name of Anne of Cleves. And that is the sort of testimonial at which books like this should aim."—*Good Housekeeping*

"The important and the chief thing is that these historical characters of hers do come alive in a succession of memorable scenes; not only Anne, but Henry and Holbein and Cranmer and Culpepper and Thomas Seymour and the rest. This is a real achievement."—*Saturday Review*

CANADIAN BOOK OF THE MONTH CLUB CHOICE

WITHIN THE HOLLOW CROWN

The story of Richard the Second

"Logically constructed and finely written, and the chapter in which the young king loses Anne of Bohemia, a victim of the plague, is memorable for its depth of pathos."—*Scotsman*

"A superb delineation of the poignant, passionate, dramatic figure that is Richard of Bordeaux."—CLAUDE RAINS

"One of the most charming books I have ever read. Well worth reading and keeping to read again."
—*South African Broadcasting Company*

"Full of the pageantry and pride of medieval days."
—*Sunday Express*

LITERARY GUILD RECOMMENDATION

BRIEF GAUDY HOUR

The story of Anne Boleyn

"This book has glitter and grace and human feeling. I enjoyed every word of it."—PAMELA HANSFORD JOHNSON (B.B.C.)

"Immensely entertaining and absorbing."—*Chicago Tribune*

"Mrs. Barnes has resurrected a real flesh-and-blood figure from the past and in her portrayal of this temperamental but unhappy woman has achieved something substantial and immensely attractive."—*Birmingham Mail*

"A plausible as well as a lively picture."—*Punch*

LITERARY GUILD RECOMMENDATION
DOLLAR BOOK CLUB CHOICE

WITH ALL MY HEART

The love story of Charles the Second and Catherine of Braganza

"What is it that makes Margaret Campbell Barnes' historical novels so fresh, so convincing, so easy to read? She has a gift for narrative and does not overload her canvas with detail. The scholarship is there, but it is not obtrusive. Above all, she has a directness and sincerity that carry her tale out of the artificial atmosphere of the historical romance into the brighter air of reality."—DR. KATHLEEN FREEMAN (*Western Mail*)

"The story of a little-known royal romance, told with a woman's keen understanding of another's happiness and sorrow."

—Irish Press

"Combining sound history and a well-told story."

—Glasgow Herald

SELECTION OF THE LITERARY GUILD

THE TUDOR ROSE

The story of Elizabeth of York—the mother of Henry the Eighth

"This admirably written story."—*Truth*

"Was Richard the Third responsible for the death of the young Princes in the Tower? Did one of them escape? Throughout the vivid narrative the question keeps on recurring, heightens the dramatic events of the historical background and adds depth to the characterisation."—*Daily Telegraph*

"An historical novel of considerable merit."—*Church Times*

"An exceptionally readable reconstruction of history. I do recommend it to your notice."—VERNON FANE (*Sphere*)

"A sure, sensitive understanding of the period . . . In this affectionate study of the mother of Henry VIII she brings out all the trials and ambitions of the early Tudor world."

—Eastern Daily Press

POPULAR BOOK CLUB CHOICE

MARY OF CARISBROOKE

A tale of Charles the First's captivity in the Isle of Wight

"She applies to this fine story her gifts of historical scholarship as well as the rich imagination of an author."—*Cork Examiner*

"Margaret Campbell Barnes succeeds admirably in this wholly charming story of a young girl suddenly plunged into intrigue by the coming of Charles I to Carisbrooke Castle."

—Montreal Gazette

"Writes with a warmth and a detail which free her book from the cardboard quality of the standard historical romance."

—New York Herald Tribune

"Fact and fiction, history and romance, weave a colourful pattern in Margaret Campbell Barnes' latest novel."

—Catholic Herald

LITERARY GUILD RECOMMENDATION

ISABEL THE FAIR

The story of Edward the Second's Queen—the she-wolf of France

"This portrayal of Isabel Capet is drawn in rich detail and forms an historical novel of exceptional interest . . . a glittering tapestry of medieval life."—MARY ANNE BERRY (*Sunday Times*)

"An outstandingly good historical novel."—*Western Mail*

"A full-blooded historical romance rich in pageantry and excitement."—*Daily Telegraph*

"For the connoisseur of historical novels."—*British Weekly*

"She infuses life, vitality and understandable reactions into her medieval characters."—*Bulletin*

"Mrs. Campbell Barnes' method of sticking closely to historical fact while filling the gaps with realistic conjecture is seen at its best in this finely dramatic novel."

*—*WILLIAM KEAN SEYMOUR (*St. Martin's Review*)

KING'S FOOL

A novel of Will Somers and the Court of Henry the Eighth

"Exactly right, both in real historical knowledge, in the construction of plot and in English prose . . . Mrs. Barnes is the only writer who refuses to blink the King's vast catalogue of faults and crimes, and yet shows him to be fundamentally lovable and human."—E. D. O'BRIEN (*Illustrated London News*)

"A thoroughly satisfying piece of work."
—*Church of England Newspaper*

"Seen from the viewpoint of Will Somers, the court jester. Place and period are faithfully conjured up."—*Daily Telegraph*

"Mrs. Margaret Campbell Barnes' vivid portrayal of Tudor life seen through the kindly eyes of this most remarkable of courtiers."—VERNON FANE (*Sphere*)
SELECTION OF FAMILY READING CLUB

THE KING'S BED

A tale of Richard the Third's natural son, Dickon

"A spirited and lively novel . . . The life of the time, both in the London streets and in provincial Leicester, is vividly conveyed, and the action moves briskly . . . an excellent, crisp narrative, true in colour and character."—*Vanity Fair*

"Fact and fiction convincingly blended."—*Daily Telegraph*

"A brilliant sense of period."—*Reynolds News*

"Lively and kaleidoscopic."—*John O'London's*

"A fine story marked by skilful characterisation and by a convincing and authentic historical setting."—*British Book News*

"A colourful tale."—E. D. O'BRIEN (*Illustrated London News*)

"Scholarly picture of everyday life in this period."
—*Rochdale Observer*

"A splendid historical novel."—*Newcastle Evening Chronicle*